chemistry

NAr

Library and Archives Canada Cataloguing in Publication

Lynch, C. L., author
Chemistry / C.L. Lynch. -- First edition.

Issued in print and electronic formats.
ISBN 978-0-9953070-0-1 (paperback).--ISBN 978-0-9953070-1-8
(ebook)

I. Title.

PS8623.Y63C44 2016   C813'.6   C2016-906297-X
                                             C2016-906298-8

onetalltreepress.com

DEDICATION

To my mother, who always believed that I would publish a book... but never dreamed it would contain so many swear words.

PREFACE

I used to fear the imaginary: monsters, ghosts, mummies, things that go bump in the night. These days I focused on more realistic threats, like car accidents, social humiliation, or conservative world leaders. But here I was, facing attack from the kind of horror that I long ago relegated to childish nightmares. Except I was awake, and this was real, and I was probably going to be killed in a painful and gory way.

Maybe I should've gained some comfort from the fact that I was loved. When you're in love, you're supposed to hold hands and face death with serene acceptance. We could share a dramatic kiss as we died in the tradition of star-crossed lovers everywhere.

"Fuck that shit," I said as my chainsaw sputtered to life and began to roar. "Let's slice off some heads."

1

The world was ending.

At least, that's how it felt at the time.

"I'm not moving to a whole new school! I'll be eaten alive!"

"They're human beings, not ravening wolves, Stella," said Dad. "You will adjust."

"Adjust! It took me over a decade to 'adjust' here! Do you remember my first day at kindergarten? They said I looked like a Weeble! They kept trying to push me over in the playground to see if I'd fall down!"

"But now you know kung fu," Dad pointed out.

"Besides, we aren't sending you back to kindergarten," my mother said. "Although you're certainly *acting* like a five-year-old."

"I have a right to be ANGRY when you pluck me out of school in the middle of the school year with VIRTUALLY NO WARNING."

"This could end up being a good thing, Stella. When you move to a new place, you get to start out fresh! You can start with a whole new look, a whole new attitude!" said Mom.

"What's wrong with my FUCKING ATTITUDE?"

"Do you want the short list or the unexpurgated version?" snapped Dad.

"Listen," I said with folded arms, "I don't care if they offered you a golden Cadillac and a mansion on a hill. I'm NOT going. I'm not starting over. I'm not going through ALL OF THAT AGAIN. You were there! Don't pretend I had it easy! And now, when I'm FINALLY starting to fit in…"

My mother started to cry and my father pointed up the stairs. I stomped up to my room and slammed my door. Feeling unsatisfied, I slammed it several more times. For some reason, that didn't make my parents reverse their carefully-thought-out decision.

I sat on my bed and hyperventilated with anger and fear. School had been a nightmare for so many years, but lately, I felt like I finally had it under control. I took martial arts classes and no one pushed me around anymore. People started to tolerate me in class projects because I actually understood the material. They started wanting me on their team in gym because I could blast a volleyball across the room.

Most kids still didn't like me, and I didn't like them, but they left me alone. I even had friends now. Only two, but how many does a person really need, anyway?

Now my parents wanted me to start all over. Friendless again, fresh fodder for bullies, back to having to be paired up with the teacher because no one wanted to partner with me, back to being the only person not invited to so-and-so's birthday. I couldn't do it all over again. I just couldn't.

I had to talk to my friends right now. I sat at my laptop and started a video call with both of them.

"Oh my God, they will eat you alive," said Liz when I filled them in.

"You can't go!" said Jeremy, panicking. "Who will I complain to about Liz? And who will she complain to about me? It doesn't work with just two!"

"No, seriously," said Liz. "Jeremy, she is doomed!"

"What am I going to do, guys?" I covered my face. "Can I come live with one of you?"

Liz rolled her eyes. "You're kidding, right? You don't want to live with my parents, *or* with Jeremy's. You're the one with the cool parents. Tell them to adopt us and take us with you!"

"Oh yeah, they're *so* cool," I said. "My mother thinks it is totally possible that I could just remake my image and attitude and everything'd be just fine." I sat scowling while I waited for them to stop laughing.

"Seriously, though," said Liz when she calmed down. "You are going to have to try and change a bit if you want to have the slightest hope of making people like you."

"Like her?" said Jeremy, "How about just *not hate*?"

"You two are so good for my self-esteem."

"We love you, Stella, but you're about as friendly as a hungry cobra. Do us a favour and try not to beat anyone up on your first day, okay?" Jeremy folded his hands together pleadingly.

"I don't start fights. I finish them. Besides this is all moot because I AM NOT GOING."

There was a knock at my door.

"Go away! I'm busy trying to figure out how to become an emancipated minor!"

"Let me in, Stella." Dad's voice had an uncharacteristically ominous tone.

"Call us again later," said Jeremy hastily, and my friends ended the call.

I dragged my feet to the door and yanked it open. "I don't want to talk about it anymore, Dad."

"Good," he said in a sharp tone, "Maybe that means that you'll listen." He sat on my bed and studied me for a moment. His lean face was creased with smile lines, but he wasn't smiling now. "Your mother getting this job... it's a really big deal."

"I know," I said, staring at my quilt.

"It's her dream job, and it's a big raise from what she's making now."

"I know."

"You can go to high school anywhere. I can be an accountant anywhere. But your mother has a lot of talent which is going to waste where she is. It's a near-miracle that she got chosen over the competition in Vancouver, but she did because she is *that* good."

I took a deep breath and let it out slowly. "I know."

"So, we are picking up our lives and dragging them over the Rocky Mountains, because if we didn't, your mother would regret it forever. You may have trouble settling in, but the world *will not end*. Even if it's terrible, you'll be graduating and going to university in a couple of years anyway." Dad clapped his hands together. "So. You have two options. You can stomp and swear and make our lives miserable, and still end up in Vancouver. Or you can put on your big girl pants and spare your mother's feelings a little."

"Dad. I'm a size eighteen. *All* my pants are big girl pants."

"I am speaking figuratively and *you know it*. Look. We can drag you there kicking and screaming, or you can feign a little bit of grace and keep your mouth shut. It's your choice. But either way, we're going."

We were quiet for a long time while I picked at my fingernails. Then I nodded.

"I know."

"That's my girl. Now, go and apologize to your mother. For some reason, she's crying on *my* pillow, and if you don't stop her, it's going to be a damp night for me."

My parents tackled our move to Vancouver with the indecent enthusiasm that they brought to all of their endeavours. They researched the hell out of the city and planned everything in excruciating detail. But I couldn't share in their excitement. All I could do was suppress my hatred of the whole affair and keep my mouth shut.

I kept my mouth shut when they put our home up for sale. I kept my mouth shut when they told me to cull half of my possessions and sell them on Kijiji or donate them to the Diabetes Association. I even kept my mouth shut when they assured me that I'd do fine in a new school, which was optimistic to the point of sheer idiocy.

Usually, our house was full of playful banter and lively debate, but during the move, our family dynamic took on the solemn atmosphere of a viewing at a funeral parlour. It really started to bug my parents.

Dad spent the interminably long plane ride to Vancouver trying to get me to talk.

"Stella, where do you think the white goes when the snow melts?"

I shrugged.

"I'm thinking of boycotting shampoo. I think we should demand the real poo."

I nodded.

"I've decided that I want to become a professional male escort with my own reality show, but I'll need you both to change your names to Darlene."

Nothing he said could make me rise out of my sullen misery.

During the layover at Edmonton Airport, Dad smacked his thighs irritably. "Stella, I appreciate that you're trying not to make our lives miserable, and I love you for it, I do, but this sullen silence is not actually any better. Can't you find some middle ground?"

"Nope." I turned the page of my book.

"Something. Anything. You're freaking us out."

"Look," I said. "You say 'move' and I move. I can try not to piss and moan out loud, but if you want me to smile and act thrilled to be moving to the yoga pants capital of Canada, you're asking too much. There's a fine line between accepting your fate with dignity and being a freaking Pollyanna, and that line is a fake smile."

"Then piss and moan," said my mother suddenly.

"What?"

"I mean that I'd rather you gripe at us than sit there all mute and sulky. It feels weird. We're just not used to it. We're used to you complaining."

"Thanks, Mom… That makes me feel so beloved."

"Look, we're not asking you to be someone you're not. We're just asking that you try not to be mean in your misery. And this stubborn muteness is not actually any less mean. It makes us feel guilty. So go ahead and complain so that we can argue with you a bit and feel a little more righteous and a little less like murderers."

"Fine. I'll try to complain. As a favour to you."

"That's my girl."

"But my life is still over," I said.

"I'm sure it is, honey, I'm sure it is," Dad said cheerfully, reopening his book. "As long as you complain about it."

I made a point of complaining as we boarded the plane for the last leg of our flight.

"Do you notice that all airplane seats seem to have been designed to fit juvenile anorexics?"

"Money," Dad said, trying to find somewhere to put his legs. "They squeeze us on like cattle so they can make more money per flight."

"Hell, why not just stack us like cordwood and get it over with."

"We should be able to lift the armrests up and... oh, I guess these ones don't," said my mother as her fleshy arms pressed against mine. "Oh, well."

I dutifully whined about the plane food, the weight of our luggage, the wait at the rental car place, and even the totem poles in the airport, which looked very unwelcoming to me at that moment. My parents cheerfully bantered back with me, and Dad gave me a grateful arm squeeze.

"Thank you," he said.

I just nodded. We both knew that what I really wanted to do was tie myself to the afore-mentioned totem poles and refuse to leave the airport until they promised I could be home-schooled. Instead, I moaned about the weather. Like an adult.

"It's raining. In *February*."

"Get used to it, Stella, they don't get much snow out here."

"Oh, good. I didn't like snow anyway. It's so pretty and sometimes they cancel school because of it. Who wants that? Rain is so much better. Wetter. Muddier. No chance of school cancellation. Love it."

"If only we could tell when you're being sarcastic," Dad said.

"Besides," said my mother, "the sun is coming out!"

"That was not the sun coming out," I said. "That was the sun making a desperate attempt to escape from the clouds before being caught and dragged back inside."

Once we were on the road I got some relief from having to pretend to be only moderately grumpy, because my parents were busy navigating Vancouver's highways and saying things like, "Look at the mountains, aren't they beautiful?" and "Watch out for that asshole in the SUV!" and "I think that sign back there was our exit," and "shit."

That left me free to wallow in silent dread. I had left anger and denial behind me and I was well into the bargaining stage. I don't know who I was bargaining with, since I'm not religious or anything, but I prayed constantly, just in case.

Please let them not hate me. Or, at least, make them not notice me, okay? Just let me be invisible. I promise I won't beat any of them up if they just leave me alone.

Our new place was a narrow townhouse with a postage stamp for a backyard.

"This place cost twice as much as our old house with the porch swing and the willow tree?" My voice echoed in the barren living room.

"I'm afraid so. Vancouver prices are steep," Dad admitted, dropping his suitcase on the floor.

"It was nice of the realtor to let the movers and the furniture delivery men in for us," said my mother.

"For a fee," Dad added.

"Where's the furniture?" I turned around in a circle, looking at boxes.

"It... uh... it's going to have to be assembled."

"I can't believe I have to start work tomorrow!" my mother moaned.

"Don't worry, I'll get through a lot of this while you're gone. By the time you two come home, this place will be way better," said Dad.

"Why don't I stay home and help?" I suggested immediately.

"No, you are starting school tomorrow."

"Can I point out how awful it is to send me to my first day of school while jet-lagged, in wrinkled clothes?"

My father sighed. "Stella, tomorrow is a Thursday. It's better to go, and do just a couple of days knowing you're about to go into a weekend. Otherwise, you have to start on a Monday and have a five-day marathon. I don't think four days of stewing about it will help, either. Besides, your mother starts her new job tomorrow, and as a gesture of solidarity, I think you should both sail off into the brave new world together."

"Yeah, okay. I'm going to go look at my new room."

It was a room, all right. Square, with a window. My new Ikea bed was in a box and the mattress was propped up against the wall, along with another box that contained a dresser. My possessions were still hidden in the boxes piled in the living room. I spent some time finding them and lugging them up to my room. I pulled out some clothes and hung them up in the closet. Then I sighed and trudged back downstairs.

"Hey, you're back," said Dad. "I thought you'd brood dramatically all evening."

"Misery loves company," I said. "There's no one to irritate up there. Did I mention that I hate the stucco ceiling?"

"I assumed you would."

I reached down and examined the instructions for assembling the kitchen table. "You've got this all backward."

"I assumed I would." He looked up at me, smile lines crinkling. "Thanks for the help."

"Yeah," I grumbled. "I'm the bigger person here. Metaphorically as well as literally."

"What have I told you about making fat jokes about yourself? Also, where do you think this little knobby thing goes?"

"I'd guess that it goes here, Dad, because that's what the instructions say."

"What would I do without you?"

"I don't know, adopt some other kid to torment?"

My father sat back on his heels and looked at me for a moment. "Stella, can I ask you a favour?"

"I'm kind of in the middle of the whole moving-to-Vancouver favour."

"Just... try. Will you? Will you try?"

"Dad, this *is* me trying. That's different from succeeding. Kind of like the way you were trying, but not succeeding, to put this table together."

"I mean, try at school. I know you can control yourself. Your Sifu told me that you never once caused a problem in kung fu. No swearing. No yelling. Can you do that at school tomorrow?"

"That was different. No one *there* ever pissed me off."

"Don't assume that they all hate you, okay? You push people away. Just... try to be friendly. Smile or something tomorrow, okay?"

I grunted as I finished another table leg. "Fine. But I'm not smiling until then."

"Deal."

I woke early, because I was still on East Coast time, and right away I started quaking with dread. I spent an hour in front of the mirror, running a brush through my thick brown hair again and again. I put on my favourite shirt, which had a flattering V neck, and then straightened it repeatedly. I brushed my teeth for so long that I'm surprised I didn't wear the enamel off. I triple-applied my deodorant. I plucked imaginary lint off my jeans. All of this had no effect on my parents, who were still stubbornly hopeful that I'd somehow be met at the doors of the school by a smiling committee of friendly Vancouver teens.

I will give them this – they didn't make me figure out the transit system on my first day in a new city in the pouring rain. Dad said he'd drive me in and help me get my paperwork sorted at the office.

Mom, on the other hand, insisted on taking the Skytrain downtown. "It'll be much faster than trying to drive," she said. "You can drop me off at the station first, then take Stella in."

At the Skytrain station, after we had kissed Mom goodbye and wished her luck and all of that mushy stuff, I tried to fill the silence in the car.

"Well, the Skytrain is a misnomer."

"Oh?" said Dad, pulling back into traffic.

"Something called a 'Skytrain' should be a gleaming futuristic monorail that goes whoosh way up in the air. Not a clunky subway train on cement blocks one story up."

Dad gave me a look. "You'll do fine at school, Stella."

"Really? Do you *really* believe that?"

"I... yes. I believe you'll do fine at *school*. Just try not to decapitate anyone who speaks to you, okay?"

"No promises."

The high school looked big and bleak, although no more so than my old school. Dad found parking and dragged me inside, and we roamed around until we found the office. He got all my paperwork sorted out, gave me a loving shoulder-squeeze and left me alone and terrified.

"Okay, so, you're enrolled in four classes this semester," said the office lady. "Chemistry, English, Physics, and Social Studies. Their order will reverse halfway through the semester. Here's your schedule, your locker number, and here's an agenda. It has a map of the school in it."

And that was it. Welcome to Vancouver, here's a crappy paper agenda that you'll never use.

The bell rang, and I didn't even know where I was on the map, let alone where I had to be. I studied it for a minute then dove out of the office into a sea of humanity. The hall was packed, I mean packed, with students. I mean, to the point where you start wondering how they are all supposed to fit because clearly, they *don't*.

Luckily, I know how to get through a crowd.

Now, tiny people don't know this trick, maybe because they don't need it. They can dodge between people and probably slide through cracks in the floorboards when they're trying to get to class. But I'm not dainty. I'm not petite. I don't dodge well. Besides, people notice me.

I don't think it's my weight – I'm tall and heavy, but they aren't going to make any documentaries about me or anything. Somehow, I just stand out. I think everyone has a little mental beacon that announces their presence to the world. Some people are so self-effacing you barely notice them. Others walk into the room and everyone turns their head. That's me, for some reason.

I don't enjoy being noticed by all the bullying cock-roaches who love to make people like me miserable. The only time my visibility is actually a good thing is when I need to get through a crowd. All I have to do is convince myself that everyone is going to get out of my way, and they do. It takes some concentration, but it works. They see my determination in my body language or something. People make way. They do it almost unconsciously like they don't even realize that they have a choice.

But even if they don't notice that they're making way for me, they still tend to notice *me*. So I blasted my way through the crowd of strangers, and they all saw me come barreling through.

"Watch where you're going, fatty!" someone said to me as they jumped out of my way.

And so it begins, I thought.

The Chemistry classroom was a standard lab, with sinks and Bunsen burners at each table. All of these tables were fully occupied, except for one; the table closest to the teacher's desk had a solitary occupant. A skinny boy was sitting bolt-upright, staring mindlessly at the door as if hypnotized.

It's funny how you can recognize a true loser from twenty paces. There was nothing blatant about him. His blue tee shirt didn't say "World's Best Dungeon Master" and his light blond hair didn't have that greasy three-days-unwashed look. He was wearing plain khaki slacks, not grey sweatpants, and he didn't even have acne.

Maybe it was the glasses. Maybe it was his sallow, unhealthy complexion. Maybe it was the fact that he was sitting alone in an otherwise crowded classroom. Maybe it was just an internal beacon, like my "make way" vibe, except his said, "Will never be elected student body president".

The boy's head turned when I walked in and he looked directly at me. His eyes were a strange, cloudy kind of blue. Maybe he had cataracts or something. That might explain the glasses. I nodded to him and sat down cautiously at the other end of the table. He seemed to be mouthing something to himself, which just made him look even farther down the road to Nutsville.

In social situations like this, like when you find yourself in an elevator with someone who keeps humming "Happy Birthday" to his socks, you pretend the weird person isn't there. So I studied my map of the school and my day's itinerary to try and figure out where the hell I was supposed to go next. I listened to the announcements on the school's PA system. I opened a binder with some fresh note paper in it. I checked to make sure my pen worked.

After a while, I started to get the creeps because I realized that the boy was still looking in my direction. I turned my head and glanced at him, expecting him to look away. That'd be the normal reaction, right?

Yeah, not this guy. He just held my gaze in his foggy blue stare. His look wasn't intense or hostile. He seemed to be daydreaming with his head turned at a 90-degree angle, and when I turned to look at him, he held eye contact with me as if he could just happily look into my eyes forever.

It felt horribly invasive.

"Can I *help* you?" I asked, a little more sharply than I meant. I just wanted to startle him into at least blinking. It felt like we were in a staring contest, now, and my eyes were starting to water.

My voice seemed to break the spell. He broke eye contact and looked down at the table with an embarrassed kind of hunch of his shoulders. So, of course, I looked away from his embarrassment, because that's what normal people do.

A few seconds later, he mumbled something, but the words were eaten up by the hubbub of all the other chattering teenagers. Then the teacher stood up, so I couldn't have reacted even if I had been sure about what he had said, which I wasn't. I must have misheard.

It had sounded like, "You're amazing."

2

That class was the most uncomfortable hour and a half that I have ever spent.

The staring guy didn't seem to take any notes or even pay the slightest attention to the teacher. This would've seemed normal if he had been sneaking texts on his cell phone under his desk or picking zits or something, but he wasn't. He was gazing at me. Like, chin on one hand, content to sit like this forever, might as well be gazing out the window kind of staring.

So there I was, trying to focus on chemistry, with those glazed eyes boring into my brain. And the thing that sucks about coming into a new school mid-semester is that the teacher was talking about stuff they learned yesterday and *I wasn't there yesterday*.

This class was learning organic chemistry, and my class back home had been learning molarity. So instead of talking about things that would've made sense to me, he spoke gobbledygook about cis and trans bonds. Then the teacher drew a picture of a molecule on the board and ask us to name it. Someone volunteered that it was *obviously* named

2-methylpropan-1-ol, and I was like, *how the actual fuck*, and it was hard to try and figure any of it out with Stare Boy giving me the heaving heebie-jeebies.

Of course, the teacher called on this guy since he was blatantly not paying attention.

"So how many lines would we draw to indicate this bond? Anyone? Howard? Howard? HOWARD?"

Apparently Stare Boy's name was Howard, which meant that he had problems on multiple levels of his life. A good-looking guy behind Stare Boy – I mean, Howard – kicked his seat.

"Hey, wake up, genius," said the chair kicker, and the class tittered like a laugh track. The kick seemed to wake Howard.

"Hmm?" he said, tearing his eyes away from my face and turning toward the teacher.

"Howard, I realize the presence of a new student among us is a novel event in an otherwise lackluster week, but could I trouble you to try and pay attention to me? It would make me feel so useful," said the teacher, whose name I didn't know, because teachers don't walk into classes that they've been teaching for a month and say, "Hello, class, my name is still Mr. Repetitive."

Stare Boy smiled awkwardly. A minute later he had lapsed back into his bizarre reverie, and now, thanks to the teacher's intervention, the whole class was noticing it and consequently noticing me.

"HOWARD," said the teacher, "EYES TO THE FRONT, PLEASE, OR I WILL ASK YOU TO EXCUSE YOURSELF. Can you tell me what change I'd need to make if I wanted to turn this into an ester?"

Howard looked blank. Or, I should say, continued to do so. Then he slowly shook his head.

"Well, I suggest you figure out where you have stashed your brain and dust it off, because it appears to be growing cobwebs," said the teacher dryly. "And please face forward. You're making the young lady self-conscious."

There were some hoots, and the attractive chair kicker said, "Howard's a chubby chaser."

"You got bad taste, man," said another voice in the class. There was more laughter.

Have you ever felt like you were going to spontaneously combust through sheer shame? I was having violent fantasies about everyone in the room, especially Howard.

I leaned in close to him and whispered in his ear. "If you don't quit staring at me and leave me alone, I swear to God, I will *end you*."

He glanced down at his shoes, but he didn't speak. When the bell rang, the teacher came up to me and asked me what I had been learning in my old class, and said he'd put together some notes for me so I could catch up.

Stare Boy didn't file out with the rest of the students. He just stood there, holding his stuff. At least he was staring at his sneakers now, instead of my face. I cast him a dirty look and got the hell out of there. For a minute, I thought he had followed me, but I blasted through the crowd and when I took a second to glance back, there was no one I recognized behind me.

My next class was English. I was desperately late by the time I finally found the damn place, which was about as far away from the chemistry lab as physically possible. The second bell had already rung by the time I arrived, and I was bursting with anxiety over it. I cracked open the door and attempted to sidle in unobtrusively, which was about as successful as you might expect.

The classroom was jam-packed, making the population of my Chemistry class look sparse by comparison. I could see absolutely nowhere to sit, and everyone was staring at me.

No one offered to make room.

The teacher greeted me, introduced himself as Mr. Barrett, and then asked me to introduce myself.

"We're doing public speaking as part of the curriculum, so you might as well start now," he said jovially.

I already disliked him.

"I'm Stella Blunt, and I'm from Nova Scotia," I said. There was no response from my audience, all of whom looked like they deeply resented being forced into literacy, and didn't give a damn about getting to know the big new chick. I folded my arms and raised my eyebrows at the teacher. That was all I was willing to do. He nodded.

"Welcome, Stella. Now, let's find you a seat and a copy of *The Chrysalids*."

"It's okay, I have it at home."

"Oh, you do? Have you already covered it in school?"

"No, my parents just own a lot of John Wyndham."

"Have you read any of them?"

"Yeah. I like *Day of the Triffids* better."

"Oh? More thrilling, maybe, but not as politically astute."

"I just like Josella a lot more than I like Rosalind."

"What's wrong with Rosalind?"

"You mean, besides having the hots for her cousin and being useless except to function as a love interest to keep David from getting it on with Sophie?"

He raised his eyebrows. "She does kill a man, you know."

"I still say Josella is more fun."

"Well. Welcome to Vancouver. I think it will be interesting to have you in my class."

We got forty minutes for lunch. This was the part which I had been dreading the most, because eating alone sucks balls. Since no one had magically jumped out from behind a door and said, "Welcome, fair stranger! Allow me to befriend you instantly and usher you to a table filled with kind and smiling faces," I'd have to eat alone - If I could even find a seat in the crowded cafeteria.

The food selection was weird, with things that no normal East Coast kid'd ever eat, like sushi. People were buying it, too. I got in line for some pizza, which, being Vancouver pizza, was covered with vegetables instead of being a simple slab of cheese and garlic like I'd be able to get back home.

With lunch acquired, I wandered around looking hopelessly for a place to sit, feeling like a complete loser. That's when I spotted Stare Boy.

What surprised me is that he actually seemed to have friends. He was sitting with another boy and a girl and they were all drinking out of thermoses. The boy and the girl were talking to him. He didn't seem to be answering much. Probably he couldn't manage real words.

I don't know how he saw me, but all three of them turned to look right at me at the same time. Howard's face relaxed in a shy grin as we made brief eye contact.

What do you do in a situation like that? I wasn't sure if I should smile back or glare. Then he stood up and started to move in my direction. He had a jolting, uncoordinated way of walking. God. Was he coming to stare some more? Or to invite me to sit?

For a moment, I considered finding out. Then I bolted out of there and ended up eating on the floor under a stairwell.

After lunch, I made my way to Physics and looked for a seat. I even found one, only to have this tiny Asian chick with purple eyelids turn up and say, "*Excuse* me, I think you're in the wrong seat," in that completely bitchy way that popular girls have. And, since seat-stealing is a blatant violation of high school etiquette everywhere, I muttered an apology and got up again.

I ended up right under the baleful eye of the Physics teacher, who looked like she had stopped finding joy in life eons ago. The woman didn't crack a smile through the whole hour and a half that we were there.

At least I recognized the stuff we were learning. This class seemed to be about where my class back home had been, except that she referred to "Hooke's Law" a couple of times, and I didn't know what that was.

After class, I went up to her and introduced myself and asked her if she had any notes on Hooke's Law that I could borrow.

"You'll just have to look it up in your text and figure it out for yourself," she said dismissively. "That may not have been the only thing you missed, and it's your job to figure out where you are behind and catch up."

Right then, thanks, Mistress Bitch.

"Sorry, I thought you were the teacher," I said before I could stop myself. "My mistake. I'll go home and teach myself, then."

I stormed off before she had time to respond. Way to score one with the person who has power over your grade, Stella. Well done.

I made my way to the last class fuming over that Physics teacher. I felt like kicking away all the people pressed up against me in the hall, so my "make way" vibe was definitely on full-blast. That made me feel very visible, which is not what you want to be on your first day of school in a new place. Teens are natural predators, seeking for weakness in their prey – and being a new girl who takes up more than her fair share of room in the halls, well, I might as well hang a big sign around my neck that said "Stumbling Wildebeest."

I got some nudges, and one guy said, "Out of my way, tubby," and pushed me deliberately as he went by. The joke was on him though, because he was originally directly in front of me. He drifted right and then shoved me as he went by. You know, after *he* got out of *my* way.

I actually got to Social Studies a little early, because I'd been booking it through the halls fueled by rage-ahol. I grabbed an empty seat near the front and hoped like hell that I wasn't stealing someone's seat again.

And then guess who drifted in? Stare Boy, of course.

He stood in the doorway, staring at me for a minute, while people barged past him, giving him little shoves as they went. I tried to look elsewhere and hoped like hell that the seats next to me would fill up.

But everyone was filing to the back and eventually Stare Boy seemed to remember that he had legs and moved jerkily towards me, dropping himself into the seat next to mine and giving me an entranced and thoroughly unnerving smile.

I would *not* spend another hour and a half getting drooled on by this mouth-breathing troglodyte. It was too much. I had to find somewhere else to sit.

With my mind made up, I bounced to my feet.

"Whoa, down in front!" shouted a boy from several rows back.

"Thar she blows!" hollered someone else, and everyone started to laugh. I felt a surge of rage and whirled around.

"Listen up, you small-dicked cock-hitlers," I started, stepping forward, but I heard a throat being cleared extremely loudly behind me. I turned and saw a teacher standing in the doorway. She raised her eyebrows at me and pointed at my chair.

I glared at the douchebags in the back and threw myself back down in my seat. I tried to ignore Stare Boy.

"Luckily for three of you, my old age has rendered me selectively deaf, and I didn't hear any of that," said the teacher, who looked like a near-retirement age Susan Sarandon with hair in a bun. "But I suggest that some of the class try to be more welcoming of new classmates, and others try to make more polite first impressions with their teachers. Now, I believe that yesterday we were discussing the political atmosphere in Canada at the start of the second World War..."

I lasted for over an hour, suffering creepy-crawlies while Stare Boy sat quietly, looking at me.

His eyes really were very blue, in a kind of milky way, if that makes any sense, which it probably doesn't. Anyway, they certainly didn't blink much. He watched me dreamily, cupping his chin in one hand - just drinking me in while I seethed and tried to take notes.

It wasn't as bad as that morning, but that's not saying much. The flu isn't as bad as Ebola but that doesn't mean you want to catch it. His stare was less vacant, more like a normal human. But it was just as unwavering. It was highly uncomfortable.

So, I kicked Stare Boy in the shin. Just to get his attention, you understand.

He didn't really react. Okay, that's not true, he did look a bit more alert and he raised his chin from his hand, but he didn't jump, or scream, or bend over moaning with pain the way he was supposed to.

I raised my eyebrows and glanced at the teacher, who was getting some handouts from her desk. "Listen," I whispered, "You really need to quit it. Like, seriously. Stop."

He nodded and then he spoke in a weirdly monotonous, husky drone. "I'm sorry, I... I really thought I'd do better this time."

"Better at... not being creepy as fuck?"

He smiled briefly, and I saw a dimple appear on his cheek. "You could say that," he mumbled.

"It's not working."

He nodded again and looked down at the desk. He totally ignored the pile of handouts that got passed to him. I reached out, grabbed them, put a sheet in front of him, a sheet in front of me, and passed them on. I looked over at Stare Boy. He was back to staring at me.

So I kicked the asshole again. In the shin, not the asshole. Obviously.

He blinked. Then he stood up, gathered his things, and walked out, and he didn't come back before the bell rang.

That night, my parents and I ate KFC at our slightly-wobbly kitchen table while I ranted about my disastrous day. Highlights included the Physics teacher who didn't want to teach, Mr. "Thar-She-Blows", and of course, Stare Boy. They were appropriately appalled by most of it, but my impression of Stare Boy had them in stitches. I did leave out the part where I physically assaulted a fellow student on my first day of class. That would've stopped the laughter quickly.

"What a shame his name doesn't lend well to a rhyming nickname," my father mused. "Like Howard the Coward, only with staring."

"Or at least alliterative," said my mother, "like... Steve the Starer."

"Leering Larry."

"Gazing Gregory?"

"His parents should really have thought about this," I agreed. "At least they should have thought twice about naming him HOWARD, period. It makes him sound about eighty years old."

"It could have been worse," my father pointed out. "It could have been Alfred."

"Or Ezekiel," said my mother.

"Or Herbert," I added.

"Feel flattered," said my mother. "The poor boy may have an unfortunate name and may be lacking some social graces, but he must be absolutely besotted with you."

"Sure, because that happens to me all the... oh, wait, never in the history of ever. Besides," I said, wagging a chicken bone at her, "isn't it anti-feminist to tell your daughter that every guy who acts like a creep must have a crush on her? That's promoting rape culture, Mom. You should be ashamed."

"I'm not saying it's okay," protested my mother. "But can you think of any other reason why he'd just stare at you like that?"

"Maybe he does that to anyone who sits next to him. Maybe that's why no one *does* sit next to him."

"Should I threaten him with a rifle?" Dad asked eagerly, "If we're sticking with gender stereotypes, I'm pretty sure that as your father I am obligated to threaten him with a rifle."

"You don't have a gun, Dad," I reached for another drumstick.

"I could get a Nerf gun. There's a really cool Nerf rifle I've always wanted to have," he said. "And they can't arrest me for shooting a teenage boy with a Nerf gun, right? I mean, who *doesn't* want to shoot a Nerf gun at teenage boys?"

"Anyway, I seriously doubt that he was overwhelmed by my beauty. He probably thinks I'm hideous and was staring in horrified fascination. You know, for the same reason Mom watches shows about mummies."

"I doubt that somehow," said Mom, "and while I completely acknowledge and recognize that you are not responsible for men's reactions to you, teenage boys' brains do tend to shut down when they see a pretty girl."

"It's all about boobs," said my father. "He was staring at your boobs, right?"

Okay, all conversation should come to a halt when your father mentions your breasts.

"Gross, Dad, no, my *face*," I said, making one. "I don't think he looked at my boobs at all."

".... Really?"

They both looked surprised, which pissed me off.

Okay, yes, I wear E cups, but that's just proportional to my general largeness. And yes, I did go to school in a V-neck top, because any other shape of neck makes me look so much rounder, and it did show off a certain amount of cleavage, because my chest is *all* cleavage, but still.

"Yes, really. He stared at my face. Into my eyes. Unblinkingly."

"That's *really* weird," said my Dad.

"What's wrong with my face?" I asked. "I have a nice face. It's my best feature. People are always saying I have a pretty face. Mind you, it's usually with a compensatory note in their voice, as if to say, 'It's a shame the rest of your body is so ideally suited to a life in the Arctic,' but still."

"You have a beautiful face," my mother soothed. "It's just that teenage boys tend to get distracted by other... er... parts..."

"He was staring at my face," I repeated through clenched teeth. I may have been starting to blush.

"Oh, we believe you. We just think it's weird," said my Dad. "Guys stare at boobs. I'm sure I stared at your mother's boobs when I met her."

"Dad!"

"What? Your mom had nice boobs."

"HAD?" said my mother.

"Now you have great boobs," said my father hastily. "I think that giving birth to Stella unlocked hidden potential in them. But they've always been and continue to be very nice. I'm sure Stella inherited them from you. I mean, along with your pretty face."

"Well, when you're finished discussing whether my boobs are more stare-worthy than my face, I'll be in my room," I snapped, and I got the hell out of there.

I thought I heard my parents laughing as I went up the stairs.

I didn't sleep well that night. I mean, nothing about that first day of school had been good. I tried to get a hold of my friends, but Nova Scotia is four hours ahead, so they were in bed before I was even done dinner. We still didn't have the internet and my phone was roaming. So, basically I had no one to talk to about this, other than my parents, and they wouldn't react supportively if they knew that I'd smiled at nobody and had threatened, and then *committed*, physical assault.

If possible, I dreaded school even more the next day. I was distinctly anxious about Stare Boy. I mean, a drooling creepazoid is better than, say, a bully, but not by much. I could kick a bully's ass, but I didn't know how to deal with Howard. The shin-kicking incident had left me feeling vaguely guilty, even though I still thought he totally deserved it.

I dithered outside the chemistry lab.

Maybe he wouldn't be there. Maybe his eyeballs dried out from all the staring. Maybe he was in the hospital getting an eyeball-ectomy. Jesus, was that a normal thought to have? Anyway, I glanced in and didn't see him. Good. He wasn't there yet. I had to find a seat somewhere else before he came in. I approached one of the less crowded tables and took a deep breath.

"Excuse me," I asked, "do you think I could take a seat at the edge here? I can bring up a chair."

Two girls looked at a third girl, who must be the leader of their little clique. "Um, I'm sorry," she said with a fake smile, "I don't think there's room for someone of your... uh... proportions." The other two girls giggled. My face grew hot.

"Yeah, well, I can lose weight but you'll always be ugly," I snapped without thinking.

Way to make friends, Stella. Charming. Easygoing. That's you.

I looked around but every other table was even more crowded than theirs. The only option was that totally-empty table where Stare Boy and I had sat yesterday. I sighed and sat down and waited for him to come in. Should I apologize for kicking him? Should I threaten to do it again if he so much as glanced in my direction?

But he never came in. The bell rang and class started and I was blissfully, blessedly alone at my little lab table for one. At first, I was just really relieved. Then as class wore on and I struggled to concentrate on the material which I still understood virtually nothing about, I began to worry.

Maybe it was my fault that he wasn't here. Maybe I had, like, splintered his shin. The second kick was pretty hard. I mean, not, like, brutal, but a definite tap. A strong, sharp tap. Probably bruise-worthy.

Or maybe I had just shattered him, personally. I mean, the guy clearly had social problems. Maybe I was, like, the only girl he had been near in years and I kicked him and now he was going to need therapy. Hell, maybe he walked out and killed himself. No. That was nuts. I didn't have that much power over some random kid with a star-ing/mumbling problem.

Did I?

I was starting to feel like a terrible person. I mean, the guy spoke weirdly, walked weirdly, and behaved weirdly. Maybe he was brain damaged or something. Maybe I was just another bully in a string of people who had made his life miserable because of factors beyond his control.

Maybe I had just become what I had always hated most.

Crap.

3

At the end of class, the Chemistry teacher handed me a bunch of supplemental papers and worksheets to help me catch up. This was a nice contrast to the appalling Physics teacher from yesterday and I counted it as the official first good thing that had happened to me since I started school.

"Thanks for thinking it's your job to help me learn," I said.

The teacher looked at me sideways. "It… is…" he said.

"Yeah, well, I appreciate it."

Then, on my way to English, a girl with dark, pink-streaked shoulder length hair caught up to me and introduced herself.

"Hi, I'm Kelly. You're new here, right?"

"Yeah…" I said.

"I'm in your English class, and your Social Studies class, too. What's your name again?"

"Stella."

"I like that name. It's my dog's name."

"That should make it easy for you to remember."

Was someone actually trying to make friends? This was a totally foreign script for me. I made friends with Liz and Jeremy by default – we were all rejects, so eventually, we stopped sniping at each other and started laughing with each other instead.

Be nice, be nice, be nice, be nice…

"Well," said Kelly, "you can sit next to me and my friends in English if you want. It's so boring to be in a class where you don't know anybody."

"…Thanks, I'd like that."

"Do you like English?"

"Yeah, I guess so," I said warily. In the past, my interest in education had made me less likely to make friends, not more likely.

"I find it really boring," she said, leading me to the back of the class. "This is where we sit," she waved at a blonde girl and plunked down next to her. "Why don't you pull up a chair here? We'll squish over."

Kelly's friend sent her a dirty look as if to say, "Why have you dragged that in here?" but Kelly ignored it and I tried to do the same. I grabbed a chair from another row and squeezed myself in at the edge of the table.

Things were looking up.

After English, I trailed behind Kelly to the lunch line. She got a plate of sushi from the cafeteria and looked with distaste at my pizza slice. She led me to a table full of people who were obviously popular. You could tell by the way they sat in a prominent location and interacted with other people openly like they weren't afraid of being publicly humiliated at every turn.

Why was a popular girl letting me hang out with her? I mean, I kicked people and made them want to skip class rather than sit next to me, the girl who kicks.

"Uh, what's that?" said a faux-redhead to Kelly when I pulled up to the table.

There. That was the kind of treatment I was used to.

"Are you sure you should eat that pizza?" asked a girl with sparkles on her mascara, looking me over. I opened my mouth to say something nasty, but Kelly broke in.

"This is Stella. She's new," she said, giving me a beaming smile. I smiled back. Maybe she was that rarest of rare things – the popular girl who deserved her own popularity.

"Are you the one that Howard Mullins was leering at yesterday?" asked the blonde chick from English.

"YES. Were you in my Chemistry class?" Maybe I could sit with her.

"No, Social Studies. Everyone was talking about it."

Oh, great, that was going to be my reputation. The one who gets stared at by freaks.

"Oh my God," giggled the redhead, "I would barf. He is such a loser."

I wondered how big a freak Howard was considered to be. Maybe he was known as That Weirdo Who Masturbates Openly in Class or something.

"What's his issue?" I asked.

"Ugh, who knows," said Kelly. "His brother and sister are just as weird. They talk like robots and are totally awkward. They all have some kind of medical problem and they don't eat regular food. No one talks to them."

"What kind of special problem? Are they, like, special needs?"

"Nah, they don't go to any supplemental classes or have aides or anything."

"So, does he normally stare at people?"

"I dunno, I don't look at him, like, ever," said the blonde chick.

The conversation drifted and I just ate my lunch quietly, trying to be unobtrusive and to fit in, which was more challenging for me than for the average person. From what I could gather, Redhead had boyfriend problems, Mascara Sparkles was going to a concert, Blonde Chick was pissed off that her father wouldn't buy her a car, and Kelly was in danger of losing access to her parents' car if her grades didn't pick up.

Sometimes attractive guys would stop by and flirt, and I'd just try to disappear, and not kick anyone.

I didn't feel like I had anything in common with any of these girls, but they were being nice to me at least, accepting me as Kelly's new pet or something. I felt a little lonely for my old friends. But after all, it took years to get close to Liz and Jeremy. I couldn't expect too much too fast from total strangers.

"I can't believe you talked on the phone while driving. That's so illegal! Just text," admonished Blonde Chick to Redhead.

And I really, really couldn't kick anyone.

Physics went better than last time, mostly because I knew what Hooke's Law was now. The teacher still would have won awards for "Best Impression of Someone Who Has Just Swallowed Something Both Sour and Toxic", but whatever.

When I got to Social Studies, I scanned the room for Kelly. Once again she was at the back of the room with a gaggle of friends and some boys, one of whom was the guy who yelled "thar she blows" yesterday. When I walked over to her she shifted to make room for me.

I felt so out of place. I did not belong with these girls. I had never been the type to run with the popular crowd. Liz and Jeremy and I had always hated the popular crowd, but it went without saying that they hated us back. Actually, that's not true. It went with saying. They said it a lot.

How long would this really last? And should I even accept Kelly's friendship? No, that was cynical and snobbish. They were so far the only people to be remotely welcoming and here I was thinking of rejecting them? Because my other options were so palatable?

So, I tried to be nice.

I smiled at their whispered jokes while trying to keep proper notes. Kelly was watching my note-taking in awe. Her own paper was covered with flowery doodles. When the bell rang she pointed at my notes.

"Can I borrow those?" she whispered. "How do you do that?"

"I just write down what the teacher says," I whispered.

"But it's so organized."

I wasn't sure what to say to that. "Sure, you can borrow them."

"That'd be awesome. Can I borrow your English ones, too?"

I nodded. She looked at me expectantly.

"Oh, now? I figured you'd want them, like, before a test or something. Sure." I opened my binder and handed her my Social Studies notes for the past couple of days and my English notes from yesterday and today.

"Thanks!" she said with a bright smile. I smiled back. Niceness was niceness, and while I suspected that her friends were only tolerating me for her sake, Kelly had been genuinely nice from the start. Shame on me for judging her.

My parents were deeply disappointed not to get an update on the Stare Boy Saga that evening.

"Not there? Lame," said Dad, shoveling spaghetti into his mouth.

"Fine by me," I said. "It was actually a good day. The Physics teacher didn't bitch me out for being an ignoramus, I didn't eat lunch alone, and I may have actually made a friend."

"Really?" my mother sat up straighter.

"Try not to sound so surprised, Mom, okay? For me."

"It's... I'm... it's just good news, honey!"

I looked at her with sudden sympathy. Had she been losing sleep over my complete inability to be likable?

So I told them about Kelly. They pooh-poohed my complaints about Kelly's gaggle of hangers-on (of which I was now one).

"Oh, I bet you didn't like Liz and Jeremy when you first met them, either."

True. "I'll give them a chance. I mean, it's not like I have other options, anyway."

"I'm sorry, are you moping because the FOUR girls you sat with at lunch today aren't enough friends for you?"

Maybe. "No."

"So all in all, a good day - no Stare Boy, and nice new friends," said Dad.

"Oh yeah, but Stare Boy's reputation fills in for him when he himself is absent. Get this - one of Kelly's friends totally recognized me as "that girl that Howard Mullins stared at"! Apparently people are TALKING about it."

"Huh. Well, they say there's no such thing as bad publicity."

"Yeah, that's not necessarily true," said my mother, the viral marketing guru.

"Well, soon they'll know you as Stella, The New Popular Girl."

"Hah. Somehow, Dad, I doubt that."

I would never be popular. Not even if I sat with the popular girls for every day of the rest of my life. And that only pissed me off a tiny bit. Popular girls were bitches. Except for Kelly, apparently.

Okay, so I was a bitch, too. I must be careful not to be a bitch to Kelly, the only non-weird person who seemed to like me.

I spent the weekend unpacking the house, studying Chemistry and Physics, doing what homework I understood, and trailing after my parents. We got new cell phones with local numbers, although my parents refused to spring for a data package for mine. Dad had returned the rental car and bought a "new" previously enjoyed car. Then he took Mom and me on long, exploratory drives of the city.

I encouraged my parents to stop at coffee shops and restaurants often for the free Wi-Fi so I could get in touch with my friends. They weren't online, but they had left me messages reminding me to be nice to people. I messaged them back and told them that I had kicked a guy on my first day and he skipped class the next day. I didn't give any other details. It'd be funnier to let them freak out.

There didn't seem to be any hope of getting internet in the house that weekend. Something about the router being delayed in the mail? Anyway, it didn't happen. But that was probably for the best because otherwise I'd have lost hours on Facebook instead of unpacking and studying.

By Sunday evening, our house was looking way better. Dad had assembled most of the furniture, and Mom and I had fixed most of what he had assembled. The boxes were starting to blend into the natural scenery of the place and we weren't noticing them so much. Our clothes were folded and put away, our toiletries were stocked in the bathroom, and our dishes, pots, and pans were all in the kitchen, although not organized in any logical way.

Sometimes we'd realize that we needed something and then have to rummage for it. Most of the boxes contained the stuff that they were supposed to, but every now and then something wouldn't be where it should be. It took us half an hour, for example, to discover that the potato masher was in with the photo albums, and the remote control for the TV was in with some old baby clothes of mine that my mother was holding on to for unknown reasons.

"While you two are gone tomorrow, I'll alphabetize the book collection," said my unemployed father, determined to be useful.

"You sure you don't want me to stay and help? I could be sorting books instead of dealing with staring boys and Physics teachers who think it isn't their job to help me learn."

"I know you didn't have a good day on Thursday, kiddo, but Friday was better, so tomorrow should be better still. You feel more caught up in your classes, right?"

"Sort of. I spent most of my time on Physics because I feel like that teacher has already pegged me as a moron. I'm still behind in Chemistry."

"But the Chemistry teacher actually planned to help you, right?"

"It seemed that way."

"You'll be fine. And if Stare Boy ogles you…"

"…. kick him in the face?"

"I was going to say 'just enjoy it,' but I realize that that sounds really dismissive of possible sexual harassment."

"Yeah, not cool, Dad. Not cool."

"Then kick him a little lower, if you know what I mean."

"Oh, I probably will," I said.

"I mean a lot lower. I mean kick him in the…"

"I'M PERFECTLY CLEAR ON WHAT YOU MEAN, DAD."

I dawdled on the way to Chemistry that Monday morning, and when I arrived, I peered into the lab.

Frig. Howard was back and looking at me with those hazy blue eyes again. I felt relieved that I didn't have his suicide on my conscience, but also horrified because now I felt obligated to apologize for the shin-kicking incident.

I sat down next to him reluctantly and opened my mouth.

"I'm sorry," he said.

I closed my mouth.

"I'm really sorry I bothered you," he elaborated. "I made you uncomfortable, even after you asked me to stop, and that was wrong." His face looked earnest, but his soft voice was calm. "Let's start over. Hi, I'm Howie. It's nice to meet you." He held out his hand and smiled shyly. That smile changed his whole look. Dimples appeared in his cheeks, and he looked almost cute, in an adorable kind of way.

"Stella." I shook his hand cautiously. It was dry and cool to the touch, not all sweaty the way I would've imagined it to be. "I shouldn't have kicked you."

"I deserved it. Where are you from?" he asked in his strange monotone, leaning forward in his chair slightly as if he expected a fascinating answer, like "Khartoum" or "Rio" or "Candyland".

"Nova Scotia..."

"I've never been there. Did you like it there?" It was like being interviewed by a robot. A somewhat cute robot.

"I guess. It was home."

"What brings you out to Vancouver?"

"...My mom got offered her dream job, so we moved."

"I'm sorry you got uprooted. But that's neat about your mother getting a new job. What is it?"

"She does viral marketing, and she made this video that got millions of hits, maybe you've seen it..."

Just then the teacher stood up. Howie winked, put his finger to his lips, and turned around smartly in his seat. It was like a totally different guy. Instead of being sluggish and dozy, he was alert and responsive.

"We'll be doing an experiment today. Howard, it looks like you have a partner... if you can manage to keep your eyes on the experiment."

Howie nodded, and his eyes dropped down to look at his desk as he smiled in an embarrassed way. Actually, he was really cute. You just didn't see it until he smiled.

The teacher faced the class. "Today we will be performing two esterifications on the same substance: salicylic acid, a toxic irritant. One of these esterifications will result in oil of wintergreen. The other results in something completely different: aspirin. This experiment is excellent at demonstrating how a simple change in chemical reactions can create two entirely different results. Before we begin, I have a pre-lab assignment. I want you to look at the two equations involved, and draw the resulting esters, and then calculate how many moles of each substance we will be using, and calculate the theoretical yield."

I groaned when I looked at the sheet. Judging by Howard's inability to answer the teacher's questions last week, we were going to be Dumb and Dumber.

"What's wrong?" asked Howie, looking seriously concerned.

"We hadn't started organic chemistry back home yet," I said. "I did some reading on the weekend, but I have no idea what esterification is. I didn't get that far."

He brightened up. "I can help you. You're smart, you'll catch on in no time."

On what was he basing his confidence in my intelligence, exactly? Not that he was wrong, but he didn't know me in the slightest.

Then he took out his pencil and gave me the clearest chemistry lesson I have ever received. Within five minutes I felt like I could have written a test on this, no problem. It was more like dealing with a teacher than a fellow student.

"I see you're back, Howard," said the teacher dryly, glancing at our paper. "Carry on."

"You're good at this," I said.

Howie glanced at the ground, looking embarrassed. "It's one of my best subjects," he said in his bland, husky way. "My dad is a scientist."

"What kind of scientist?"

"He's a virologist at Simon Fraser University. Look, I know I acted strangely on Thursday. I get kind of stupid when I'm hungry."

"You were... hungry? Like, low blood sugar?"

"Like that. It's... a kind of medical condition. I'd rather not talk about it."

"And that's why you were staring off into space?" I tried to say it tactfully, but he looked right at me and I knew that he knew what I really meant.

"I wasn't staring off into space," he said quietly. "I was staring at you. I'm sorry I made you uncomfortable. I just think you're completely beautiful, and you took me by surprise."

I felt my cheeks begin to burn and I became obtrusively aware of my own heartbeat. I mean, what do you say when someone says something like that right to your face?

Random people don't pay me compliments. I am tall and heavy set, and in a society where tiny girls with thigh gaps prance around complaining about being fat, that puts me well outside the accepted standard of beauty.

It used to bother me a lot. When my parents put me in kung fu, they were hoping I'd learn to control my temper, but I hoped it'd help me get rid of the bullies and lose weight. It helped a bit with the anger, a lot with the bullies, and not at all with the weight. I came to terms with that a while ago. I looked at a lot of Renoir and Rubens paintings, read some fat acceptance blogs, and realized that I could still be pretty without conforming to the anorexics in mainstream advertising. Now I was fairly happy with what I saw in the mirror. I had good hair, nice skin, big eyes, and full lips – If I wore the right clothes, I even had an hourglass figure.

So why did this come as such a shock? Why shouldn't he think I'm beautiful?

Because no one outside of your immediate friends and family ever has.

He was still looking at me.

"I... don't know how to respond to that."

"I'm making you uncomfortable again." He was so monotone that I couldn't tell if he was asking a question or stating an accepted fact.

"Yes."

He looked away. "I don't want to make you uncomfortable. Let's do some science."

4

I left Chemistry feeling bemused. Howie had been courteous and competent throughout the class. We made aspirin and minty smells and occasionally I'd catch him looking at me, but when I raised an eyebrow he'd look right back at the beaker again.

Once I passed him a flask, and when our fingers brushed he held his hand there a little longer than normal. I pulled away and we both acted like it hadn't happened.

When the bell rang, Howie picked up my bag and handed it to me. The smell of wintergreen still lingered on him.

"It was a pleasure to have you as a lab partner," he said. He sounded as if he were reading something off a cue card, but he looked like he really meant it. It was very confusing.

"Um... thanks," I said. "Well... see you."

He was gathering his own stuff and looked like he wanted to walk out with me, but I had to speed if I wanted to get to English on time, so I just blasted out of there, leaving him standing at our desk, watching me go.

I had trouble focusing on my way to English because I kept hearing his voice in my head. Completely beautiful. He called me *completely beautiful*.

I bumped into at least three people.

I joined Kelly and the blonde chick (who I had never been properly introduced to, but I thought might be named Danielle) in English class. They were whispering to each other but when they saw me, Kelly made room for me next to her.

"Welcome to Boredom Hell," she said to me.

"You find the teacher really boring?"

"It's just English that's really boring," said Kelly "Mr. Barrett is kind of cute."

"I like English," I said.

"I don't," said the blonde, rolling her eyes. "What's the point of reading Shakespeare and all these boring books? And then talking about them for hours?"

I shrugged. "Literacy?"

Shut up, Stella, said my brain. *These people are being nice to you, and you're being a bitch.*

Shut up, Brain. I'm not sure if I even like them that much.

Snob.

"Don't listen to her, she's just in a bad mood," said Kelly with another smile. I'm not sure if she was talking *to* me, or *about* me, but I decided that it didn't matter. She was trying to make peace. I felt bad for snarking at them. A kind friend is more important than a smart friend.

The teacher stood up and shuffled some papers together.

"Okay, no more talking, I'm going to start passing around the test," he said.

"There's a test?" I whispered in surprise to Kelly.

"Oh, I forgot all about it," she said, eyes wide.

"Stella, I know you're new so you can sit this one out if you like, and write it in a couple of days," said Mr. Barrett.

Kelly shot me an envious glance.

"That's okay," I said, "I've already read the book. I can write the test now if you want."

Kelly looked pleased with my show of solidarity.

"Sure, you can give it a go if you like," said the teacher, and he laid one in front of me.

I finished in about half an hour. It was long but fairly easy. I wasn't sure whether I was supposed to hand it in right away or wait until the teacher came to collect it, so I spent the next twenty minutes idly re-reading my answers and making small corrections and trying not to think about how Howie called me beautiful, and how smart and cute he looked when he was teaching me science.

Eventually, someone else got up and took their test to the teacher's desk, and then they left. Okay, so that was the procedure. I stood up, laid my test on my desk, and I was free, half an hour early.

For the first time, I was able to navigate the hall without feeling like I should be decked out in riot gear. It was nice. I took a trip to the bathroom. When I came out of the stall, Kelly walked in.

"Hi," I said, as I washed my hands. She smiled.

"What did you think of the test?" she asked, pulling out a lipstick and applying it carefully.

"Not too bad," I said cautiously. I learned a long time ago that people don't appreciate hearing, "Boy was that easy!" when they have just spent the last hour failing that same test. "How about you?"

Without acknowledging my response, she went into a bathroom stall and closed the door, which I thought was a bit abrupt. I could hear her peeing. I waited around to see if she'd make conversation from the stall, but she didn't. She came out as the bell rang and went back to studying herself in the bathroom mirror. I hung around uncomfortably for a few minutes, and then Kelly said, "I have some stuff to do. I'll see you later," and she left.

At lunch, I found Kelly and her friends at their usual table and asked if I could sit with them. God, I hated this crap. I missed the ease and comfort of friends who you knew would welcome you, albeit with a loving insult or two.

Kelly nodded and moved over for me, but I didn't get the beaming smile of yesterday. A couple of the girls whispered things into each other's ears when I sat down too. Lovely. Just what I needed. A good dose of paranoia.

Lunch conversation was filled with the same chatter as yesterday. I swigged my Diet Pepsi and tried to contribute pertinent remarks, but no one really seemed to respond to or even notice the things I said. My mind kept drifting to Chemistry class, Howie's cool hands, and his shy smile.

Completely beautiful, he had called me.

Completely beautiful.

Physics was ridiculous.

During lab, a girl with short hair went up to the teacher and asked her a question. The teacher not only didn't answer but actually turned her back, like a little kid who isn't speaking to someone. The girl just rolled her eyes and went back to her desk behind me. For some reason, maybe because she reminded me a little of Liz, I leaned back in my chair and whispered to her.

"Did the teacher just totally blow you off?"

She grinned. "Oh yeah, Ms. Bond hasn't spoken to me since I summarized Newton's third law as 'shit hits back.'"

I laughed.

"Whatever, she's got problems," said the girl. "Hey, are you the one that weirdo was staring at?"

"Yeah." Apparently, that was my thing now: The One the Weirdo Stared At. I wished more people had eavesdropped on our conversation in class this morning. I wouldn't mind being The One the Weirdo Called Completely Beautiful.

Then again, maybe I would.

The girl shook her head sympathetically and we went back to our work.

In Social Studies, there was an awkward moment where I had to walk past Howie. He didn't know that I had changed seats, so when he saw me he lit up and pulled out the chair. I just shook my head and pointed to the back and gave him a polite smile. A look of crushing disappointment swept over his face and I felt like a steaming pile of dog vomit.

Kelly shifted over to make room for me but barely glanced in my direction. Had she lost interest in me already? Maybe it was just novelty or a wave of altruism that had led to her original friendliness. Or maybe my snap about literacy this morning had pissed her off.

She did ask to borrow my notes again at the end of class. I handed them to her, wondering if she was just being friendly to me for my notes. Then I remembered a time when Liz went off on me because she'd asked to borrow my notes and I had accused her of using me.

"Why do you find it so hard to believe that anyone likes you just for you?" she had fumed. "I fucking like you,

you're my fucking friend, and you know what friends do? HELP EACH OTHER WITH SCHOOL. I'm not using you, I am asking you, as a friend, for a little fucking help. You fuck."

Liz was right. Here I had someone who had been nothing but nice to me – if occasionally a little distant – and I was trying to judge her ulterior motives. I resolved to be a better person.

That night, over dinner, my parents tried making fun of Howie again, but I wasn't into it.

"No, he didn't stare as much today. He was almost normal. He was talking and stuff."

"Oh ho! What did he say?" Dad rubbed his hands.

"He explained organic chemistry to me. He was nice but weird. Did you seriously just say 'Oh ho'?"

"I might have. Nice but weird?"

"Yeah. His voice is weird, but he was nice. Look, I'm kind of tired. Can we talk about things that are not awkward Chemistry partners?"

"I have an awkward coworker," said my mother helpfully. "She's technically equal to me but keeps sending me emails about how I need to report to her to discuss my projects. Then I go to her and ask her why I need to talk to her about my projects, and she tells me she needs to coordinate this and that and I'm like, 'Isn't that my job?'"

"That doesn't seem awkward so much as overbearing and bossy," I pointed out.

"Well, I was trying to segue from Howard. I thought you'd be grateful."

"I am. Have you mentioned her to your boss?"

"Sort of. You don't really want to spend your earliest days at works complaining about your coworkers. I just showed her what I was doing and asked if I should be doing anything differently and she said no."

"So just ignore bossy lady," said Dad.

"I'm trying but it's hard. I don't want to be the office bitch."

"I'm so glad social interaction gets easier after high school. You're really making me feel optimistic, Mom."

"What about Kelly?"

"Well, she was mostly nice to me, but then after English, she peed abruptly."

There was a delicate silence. "Explain further," said Dad.

"Oh, we were sort of having a conversation in the washroom and then she just walked into the stall and shut the door. It's kind of a conversation-ender when someone shuts a door in your face. Doesn't make you feel like this person is loving your company."

"So it's a mixed message situation?"

"I guess. I dunno. I mean, I'm out scouting for a new best friend but she's just being nice to the new girl. I don't even know if we have much in common."

"We'll try to find you a martial arts club that does your style of kung fu. You might meet a friend there. You should join some after-school groups, too. Maybe join the band?"

"I do seem like the band kid type. Why have I never been in band?"

"You said you'd rather die than turn your face red blowing on a trumpet all night."

"Oh yeah. Well, it's a little late to start now."

"You'll make friends, dear. It's already started. These things take time."

"Well, if I don't, it's only a year and a half 'til university, right?"

"You'll have friends!"

"Hi," said a voice behind my shoulder as I walked through the school halls the next morning. I spun around and resisted the urge to do a foot sweep. Behind me stood Howard.

"You scared the crap out of me! What the hell's wrong with you?" I snapped. He ducked his head.

"I'm sorry," he said.

"Tap a girl on the shoulder or something first. Don't just... sneak up behind me. Okay?"

He nodded.

"Anyway. Hi, Howard," I said.

"Howie."

"Hi, Howie."

He tried to keep pace with me, but people kept crashing into him, so I pulled way ahead. When we got to class he hurried past me and pulled out my seat like a waiter in a snooty restaurant. I raised my eyebrow at him but he just looked back innocently.

To hell with it. I sat down and he perched on the chair next to me, leaning toward me slightly.

"How are you this morning?"

"I'm... fine, thanks. You?"

"Fine," he said slightly breathlessly. He continued to watch me as if I was about to do a magic trick or something.

"You're being weird again."

"Sorry," he said, flashing his dimple and glancing down. "I will be wholly absorbed in our Chemistry lecture, I promise."

"…Good."

And he was. He went through the whole class only looking at the teacher and occasionally making a note. I felt slightly miffed, for no justifiable reason.

Then English happened.

I smiled at Kelly when I sat next to her and asked her how she was, but she just gave me a tight smile back and didn't answer me. At the end of class, as I was standing up, Mr. Barrett said, "Miss Blunt and Miss Svancara, would you please stop by my desk for a minute?"

Everyone turned to look at Kelly and me.

When a teacher says something like that, he's not usually doing it because he wants to encourage your budding friendship. I tried to catch Kelly's eye but she wouldn't look at me.

After everyone else had left with smirks on their faces that said, "Someone is getting in trouble and that person is not me", the teacher looked at us and sighed.

"Who wants to talk first?" he asked. I looked at his desk and noticed that he had my test and Kelly's test sitting next to each other. It didn't take a genius to put two and two together. I felt a rush of rage, and I turned to Kelly.

"You *cheated?*"

"Actually, Miss Blunt," said Mr. Barrett, "Miss Svancara told me yesterday that she saw *you* looking at *her* paper during the test." He raised his eyebrows and steepled his fingers like some sort of villain.

"Well, Miss Svancara is quite the liar," I said.

"Look, I know it must be hard to move to a new school and everything," said Kelly with the most demure little smile, "but I really don't think that excuses you cheating off of me, especially when Mr. Barrett gave you a chance to actually learn the material later on."

"And why would I have agreed to take the test unless I already knew the material? He gave me a chance to get out of it and I turned it down!"

"Because if you wrote the test alone during lunch there'd be no one to cheat off of, obviously."

Mr. Barrett waved his hand. "Okay, settle down, you two. Kelly, can I ask you to wait out in the hall for a minute while I speak to Stella alone?"

Apparently, the "Miss Blunt" and "Miss Svancara" names were only necessary during the intimidation stage of this maneuver.

Kelly smirked and flounced out of the room.

I turned to the teacher in a fury. "That sneaking Janus cheated off of me but I can't effing prove it."

"Please calm down, Miss Blunt." Oh, it was "Miss Blunt" again, now. "Listen. I know that you knew this material. Your answers were much more coherent and well organized than Kelly's, and you finished your test a good ten minutes before anyone else. Your mistake was waiting twenty minutes to hand it in, and triple checking your answers while Kelly helped herself. You can invite her back in now."

"Cheating biznitches in the hall are welcome to return!" I announced loudly, opening the classroom door.

"MISS BLUNT."

"My name isn't Miss Polite, Mr. Barrett!"

Kelly rolled her eyes at me and walked past me to stand in front of the teacher.

Mr. Barrett gave Kelly a charming smile. "Well, I've spoken with Stella, and I think I've come to a conclusion about what to do. I am afraid I'll have to give you both a zero on this test."

"WHAT?" we both shouted.

"Or," he continued, "I will offer each of you a chance to write the test again today at lunch. At separate desks."

"That's not fair, either, Mr. Barrett," said Kelly. "She deserves a zero. Now she's probably had more time to study and she'll do better than she would've yesterday. That's practically like rewarding her for cheating."

"Oh, I doubt she would've studied last night, considering that she had just written a test on the subject. Did *you* study for English last night?"

"I... no, but I didn't have to!"

"Besides," I snarled, "I've *never* had to study for an English test. What's to study? You just read the goddamn book."

"Not to worry. I won't be giving her a new grade. Whoever does best will get their original grade. Whoever does poorly will get a zero." Mr. Barrett grinned and spread his hands.

I started to like him.

"But she learned the answers from my test!" Kelly insisted.

"But surely she didn't learn enough to be better than you? Besides, you don't have to worry. I wrote a totally different test last night. It took up a lot of my evening. I'm sure I'll find you suitably grateful."

Kelly sniffed. "Grateful that I have to waste a lunch hour proving something I already know?"

"I'm giving up *my* lunch hour to vindicate you. Don't you want that?"

"Fine by me," I said loudly. "I like it. I love spending my lunch hours writing tests to prove corrupt pieces of crap wrong."

"Language, Miss Blunt."

"I'm well versed in the language arts, Mr. Barrett."

"You're hardly speaking Shakespeare's English, Stella."

"Thou whoreson zed! Thou unnecessary letter!"

"Have a seat! Your test starts now."

I threw myself into my chair, which skidded slightly on the floor. That bitch! That utter, complete, evil, bitch! She was nice to me, then cheated off of me, and then *blamed me*. Somehow, the niceness was the worst part.

Mr. Barrett handed me a test and I started scribbling angrily. He sat Kelly on the other side of the room and laid her paper in front of her.

This test was more challenging than the one we did before, and I found it hard to prevent my anger from affecting my answers.

Why do you think John Wyndham named his story "The Chrysalids"?

A chrysalis is a cocoon. David and the other characters are cocooned by their outwardly "normal" form. The story ends just as they fly away from their problems, having finally accepted and unleashed their full selves, like butterflies leaving their cocoons.

.By contrast, there are some people who seem to remain permanent grubs hiding in the cocoon of normalcy, and never transition to anything better because they are and always will be nasty little grubs.

My pen was leaving deep grooves in the paper.

Kelly raised her hand. "Mr. Barrett, I don't think these questions are fair. We haven't covered this stuff in class."

"This test isn't for a grade, remember? It's to test your overall knowledge and comprehension of the subject matter. Anyone who does well on this test would've had no need to cheat on yesterday's test."

I went back to my test and added some clarifications.

(LIKE KELLY).

I moved on to the next question with a smile on my face.

The test was short and I didn't spend any time looking it over. I was done before lunch was half-over, and when I finished I stood up so fast that I sent my chair clattering over backward. Kelly snorted but I ignored her. I stomped to Mr. Barrett's desk, plunked it down, and stormed out the door and almost directly into Howie.

He didn't hold up his hands to block me or anything, just stood there as I nearly plowed right into him.

"Watch out!" I snapped, stopping myself about an inch from his face.

"You're mad about something."

"Brilliant deduction, Sherlock. What are you doing here?"

He looked confused. "I go to school here."

"I mean now. Right here. In the hallway. At lunchtime. Outside of my English class."

He didn't answer, just gazed at me dreamily. His glasses were slightly crooked.

I squinted at him. "What's your problem? Are you hungry again?"

"You have no idea."

"Okay, well, me too. I'm going to go eat. Bye. Glad I didn't knock you over."

I walked off toward the cafeteria.

"Stella?"

I spun. "WHAT?"

"Do you want to talk about it?"

"TALK ABOUT WHAT?"

"Why you're so mad."

I started to feel bad. It was like talking to a wide-eyed five-year-old. I hesitated.

He gestured down the hall. "We have fifteen minutes till the bell rings. Why don't you bring your lunch outside and tell me about it?"

I did have a packed lunch and a pop in my bag. Our kitchen had recovered to the point where my father was able to make sandwiches.

"...Okay."

"Do you want to sit on the bleachers?"

"Sure. Fine. Lead on."

He looked disoriented for a moment, then led me out a side door to a field with bleachers.

He sat and pulled a thermos out of his bag. Did this guy live on liquid lunches?

"Talk," he said.

I don't know why it's so damn hard to talk when someone says "talk", but it is. I guess it's like someone saying "be funny". Some things are meant to happen organically in conversation. But he just kept looking at me and sucking from a straw. I tried to fill the silence.

"Kelly Svancara, you know, the girl I sit with in Social Studies?"

He nodded.

"She copied off of me in English and then told the teacher that *I* copied off of *her*." Funny, it had felt like a longer story in my head.

"Did he believe her?"

"Pff. No! He said it was clear that I knew the material and he said her answers seemed more patched together than mine. But he made us write a second test to prove we knew the material, so no one could say it was her word against mine."

"How did you do?"

"Fine, I think."

"How do you think she'll do?"

"I have no idea, but she complained about the questions not being fair. So hopefully she'll bomb."

"So, then you'll be vindicated."

"Yeah, I guess."

"Then why are you still so furious?" He was leaning forward now, focusing on me entirely. His drink was sitting forgotten next to him.

"Because... because I can't believe what a bitch she is!" I exploded, slamming the bench. It made a loud *twunnnnng* sound. He didn't even flinch. He just calmly bent down and picked up my pop bottle, which had fallen over, before it could roll onto the ground.

"Why not? There are people like her everywhere."

"I guess it stings because she started out being really nice to me," I admitted. "It's not like we were about to become best friends or anything, but I thought she was nice, and then this happened."

Howie nodded slowly. "Oh. She hurt your feelings. Yes, I can understand that."

"I mean, someone is nice to you and then just turns around and makes you out to be a cheat and a liar. Wouldn't that piss you off?"

"Maybe, but you shouldn't let it bother you. She's just jealous."

"Jealous because I know more about *The Chrysalids* than she does? Please."

"Jealous because you're smarter and more attractive than she is."

I took a swig of Diet Pepsi. "I seriously doubt that she envies my looks. She probably despises me because I spoil her view in class. In fact, that's probably why she got me to sit next to her, so I wouldn't be in front of her."

"If she doesn't envy you, she should."

"Don't give me that bullshit!" I stood up. "Look, I don't know what kind of trick you're trying to pull, but the whole 'you're beautiful' thing is getting hard to believe. You have *eyes*, and so do I."

He furrowed his brow. "Don't you know how stunning you are?"

"I know what society considers beautiful, and I know that Kelly fits that ideal way better than I do, okay?"

"Why?"

I seriously wanted to punch him. I knew that it was okay to be bigger, that there were lots of kinds of beauty, but there's such a thing as reality. I struggled to control my breathing, the way I learned in kung fu.

"Because modern society values people who are THIN," I said. "And I am NOT."

"Okay, so she's thinner than you. That only makes her more attractive to people who like stick figures. I think your curves are way more beautiful. Your face is way more beautiful. Your mind is way more beautiful. Your beauty is more global than her lack of adipose tissue."

I couldn't believe I was hearing those words coming out of anyone's mouth, let alone hearing them aimed at me.

"Who says stuff like that to people?"

"What do you mean?"

"Don't you know how bizarre this is for me?"

He looked me in the eyes. "I know I seem strange. I'm used to hearing that. There's nothing I can do about it. But that doesn't mean that you shouldn't believe the truth when I tell it. You don't have to like me. It's natural to dislike me. But you're stunning, mind and body, and you should know it, and I stand by that."

"Why would it be natural to dislike you?" He threw me off with this change in tactics. I thought he was supposed to be convincing me how eminently dateable he was or something.

"It just... is. I have a... medical condition."

"Can you be more specific?"

"I don't really like to talk about it."

"Okay... but this condition makes people dislike you? What do you have, hate-me-itis?"

"Hate-me-itis would imply an inflammation. This is more like hate-me-osis." His voice was as toneless as ever but there was a twinkle in his eye. Then he went back to looking serious. "People avoid those who aren't "normal" or appear unhealthy. That's why the kids with developmental delays, and the kids in wheelchairs, and the kids with Crohn's Disease don't get voted into Student Council, even though they might be great people."

He was right there.

"It's not right, but it's how things are. You instinctively want to avoid me, and in my case, it's a good instinct."

"Are you saying I should stay away from you?"

He looked back up at me.

"I'd rather you didn't," he said softly. "I'm harmless. You won't catch it from me."

"Wait... did you say that I won't catch it, or that I can't catch it?"

That made him wince. All my raging and shouting and banging and he didn't blink an eye – literally – but this made him flinch?

"It's catching, but you almost definitely can't catch it from me."

"ALMOST definitely?"

"It's complicated, but yes."

"So, if you don't know whether or not someone can catch it, then how can you be so sure I won't catch it?" If this condition was contagious, that seemed like an excellent reason to stay away.

"Because it's not like a common cold. It's not like, I sneeze and you catch it. I just don't know if you could catch it if we decided to swap blood or... something. And since I don't plan on sharing needles with you, you won't catch it."

I felt minimally reassured.

"Stella," he said, sitting upright and leaning forward, "I would never hurt you. Do you believe me?"

When someone urges you, unprompted, to believe that they'd never hurt you, it makes you think that they're thinking about hurting you.

"I think I should go inside."

He looked at his feet again and heaved a sigh.

"I understand."

Damn straight, I thought, standing up. The bell rang as I stepped down from the bleachers, and I used that as an excuse to break into a jog. Getting the hell out of this awkward situation.

When I glanced back he was still sitting there.

It started to rain.

5

I fumed all through Physics, completely oblivious to anything except the battle of conflicting feelings inside me. I was furious with Kelly, but whenever I thought about how Howie let me rant, I felt grateful. When I thought of the nice things he said to me, I felt good. When I thought about the creepy "I won't hurt you/give you diseases" stuff I felt uncomfortable, so then I'd think about Kelly instead, and the whole thing would start all over.

The teacher noticed and called on me. I asked her to repeat the question. She told me to pay attention and people laughed.

I felt like walking out and never coming back.

Howie was waiting for me outside the Social Studies classroom door. If he was upset at me for storming out earlier, he didn't look it. He looked entranced and reached out his hands as I approached.

"Sit with me today," he said.

Hmm. Sit with a lying cheater, or sit with a diseased weirdo? My friend options were becoming increasingly stellar.

"Well, I'm not sitting with that vapid-faced shit goblin, BUT," I levelled a finger at him, "this doesn't mean that I'm okay with your sycophancy or your possibly contagious disease."

Howie smiled, did the pulling-out-a-chair thing again, and I sat down. Kelly walked past us and smiled angelically.

"Maybe you belonged with the losers all along," she said.

"If that were true, I'd still be sitting with you," I said. I had a few more things I wanted to say, but the teacher was present. So, I just thought them in my head. ALL THROUGH CLASS.

Howie didn't stare at me. He paid attention to the teacher, as far as I could tell. But at one point he shifted his notes toward me slightly and I saw that he had written in the margin,

You are smarter and more lovely than she will ever be.

I didn't know how to react to that, so I pretended I hadn't seen it. But I had. And I glanced at it again and again.

When I came home from school, I tried to work up a good rant about Kelly and the whole test incident, but I couldn't seem to find the steam. Howie and his open flattery had somehow undone my rage.

"So you rewrote the test? Good." Dad said.

"Yeah, I rewrote it. What a waste of time."

"Otherwise your lunch hour would've been spent doing... what, exactly?"

Getting insanely complimented by a cute geek, I thought. "Yeah, yeah," I said out loud. "I'm just pissed off, okay?"

"Pissed off, but not shouting? I'm surprised. You seem to be taking this almost calmly. For you, anyway."

"I blew off a lot of steam when I got out of the classroom. I went out the bleachers and shouted." Why didn't I tell Dad who I shouted at? For whatever reason, I was feeling secretive about Howie.

"How unusually sane of you." He patted me on the shoulder. "Don't worry. It sounds like this teacher had Kelly pegged from the start. Take pleasure in that – after having you in his class for only two days, this guy trusted you over one of his regular students."

Dad recounted the story to Mom when she came home, and I actually sat there and let him tell it. She just shook her head sympathetically.

"And here you thought she might be a new friend. What a rotten thing for her to do. I'm sorry, sweetie."

"Yeah. She seemed nice at first, but now I know she's a complete cunt."

"STELLA!"

"Well, she *is!*"

"Stella, WHAT HAVE I SAID about using misogynistic words to insult people? Having a vagina does not make someone a bad person!"

"That's not my point!"

"Language matters, young lady!"

"The vagina is a wonderful organ," chimed my Dad.

"WHAT WOULD YOU LIKE ME TO CALL HER?"

"Shitface, asshole, two-faced twit, crapbag," Dad ticked off on his fingers.

"Llamabreath, dingweasel, fart-brained dillhole..." Mom added.

"DINGWEASEL?"

"Or you could just call her pathetic and witless and feel sorry for her because she had to cheat on a test about a book that you read for pleasure when you were ten years old."

"Seriously, though, dingweasel? Where do you come up with this stuff?"

Since my only prospective non-weird friend had turned out to be using me to boost her English grades, my parents suggested that they take me to a used bookstore and then treat me to a nice dinner.

They knew their audience. I love used bookstores.

While new bookstores pipe pop music through their speakers and have shelves full of toys and picture frames and all sorts of things that don't actually have anything to do with reading, used bookstores are usually run by hardcore book lovers. The stores have the deep hush of a library. The floors are almost always made of wood, and they creak a little, so you find yourself almost tiptoeing. They're slightly musty, with lots of that delicious book smell.

Dad wanted to check out an RC hobby shop down the road, so my parents left me at the bookstore and told me they'd be back in a half an hour.

The quiet booky-smelling store felt peaceful, and I was in desperate need of peace. My thoughts kept bouncing from anger at Kelly to confusion over Howie.

On the one hand, he talked like a robot, sporadically turned into a drooling moron, walked in a strange and lurching way, and had a possibly contagious disease. On the other hand, he said wonderfully flattering things, was occasionally brilliant at Chemistry, was a good listener, and had an adorable smile.

I had no idea why I got rude with him whenever he started saying complimentary things. I got rude a lot in general, and I knew this about myself, but surely it was not normal to keep being reflexively rude to someone who repeatedly applied the adjective "beautiful" to you.

On the other hand, what was the appropriate reaction to this kind of situation? Was I supposed to giggle girlishly and bat my eyelashes like an idiot? But the truth was that some part of me was giggling and batting her eyelashes. What had he said? "Your body is way more beautiful. Your face is way more beautiful. Your mind is way more beautiful"? Oh, God, just remembering those words made me feel all… all… giggly. I'd heard of butterflies in your stomach, but this felt more like fucking Christmas in my chest.

That pissed me off because he made me feel that way without my permission.

You want to make me feel all warm and happy? You should find out if I *want* to feel that way.

No, that sounded stupid.

Here's the thing: the son of a bitch – sorry, the son of a woman who was probably *perfectly nice* and not at all responsible for the peculiarities of her progeny – made me like him, and I resented having my mind changed just because he threw superlatives in my direction.

I browsed the shelves as I seethed, but slowly the dusty comfort of old books seeped into my soul and I began to feel calmer. Then I turned a corner and nearly walked bang into Howie. *Again.*

"Howie!" I hissed. "What are you doing here?"

"Looking," he said, holding up his hands in mock surrender. "I looked, and I saw you. So I was coming to say hi."

"You couldn't have called out and given me some warning?"

"That would've felt wrong in here."

Fair point. I respected his respect for the bookstore.

"What have you found?" he gestured at the books in my hand.

I reluctantly held them out. For some reason, I had been attracted to Jane Austen and decided that I should really pick up copies of *Northanger Abbey* and *Persuasion*.

"What about you?" I asked.

"Nothing has really caught my attention yet." He was gazing deeply into my eyes again, and I felt like he was trying to send a subtext of "except you," but didn't dare say it out loud. "Don't let me stop you from browsing," he said, his eyes not leaving my face. "I don't want to get in the way."

"You're not getting in the way," I muttered because it was socially obligatory. Really, all I could think about right now was how I wished he wasn't here – but also how I wanted to feel his arms around me. It was a complicated swirl of contradictory emotions.

"Good," he said. He stepped back to let me pass, bowing his head like an obedient servant stepping aside for his master.

I went back to scanning book titles, but with a high degree of self-consciousness, because he continued to stand within eyesight. He didn't follow me closely, but as I moved down the aisle, so did he. If I glanced at him, he looked up right away and smiled at me.

So I stopped glancing at him.

My parents came back in just as I was moving on to the children's fiction section. Really, I was just appearing interested to avoid a conversation with Howie.

"Ready to go, Stella?" Dad spoke slightly too loudly for a used bookstore.

"Yeah, Dad."

Howie followed behind me. Mom and Dad looked at him oddly.

I looked at him. He looked at me. I sighed. "Mom, Dad, this is Howie. He's, uh, my Chemistry partner."

Their facial expressions were priceless. There was non-recognition, and then there was recognition, and then there was the frantic effort to keep their faces straight, which resulted in them looking very surprised and very pleased.

"OH! HOWARD! How nice to MEET you!" my mother said, offering her hand.

He took her hand in both of his hands, and said gravely, "Mrs. Blunt, how do you do?"

"What brings you here, Howard?" my father said.

Damn you both. I introduced him to you as Howie and you both called him Howard. Now he knows I've told you guys about him.

If Howie drew that conclusion, he didn't show it. "Oh, the usual," he said, glancing at me.

Please tell me that he just means this is his favourite bookstore. Because if he doesn't, I officially have a stalker.

"We're just about to go to dinner. Would you like to join us?" my father asked. There was a twinkle in his eye.

Goddamnit, Dad, my life is not a practical joke.

"Oh, I wouldn't want to intrude." Howie was looking at his feet, which would surely egg Dad on. He loved to make people uncomfortable.

"Nonsense," said Dad, "Stella's new and doesn't have any friends yet..." *Thanks for that.* "...And we'd be happy to get to know her Chemistry partner. We're still just settling into Vancouver, you know. Why don't you come to dinner with us? Or do you have other plans?"

"I'm not very hungry, but I'd be delighted to join you. I'm not expected back home."

"Sound good, Stella?" Dad's grin was positively evil.

"I guess," I said. Howie shot me a sheepish glance and I felt unwelcoming. "If Howie doesn't mind getting the third degree from you two, I mean."

I was hoping that might scare him off, but Howie shook his head.

"We were going for Indian food. Is that all right with you?" my mother asked with a smile, taking my father's arm.

"If it's that restaurant down the road, it's supposed to be very good. I have a medical condition and a rather restricted diet, so I may not eat much."

"Is there somewhere else we should go instead?"

"No, I'd rather not come at all than disturb your evening, but I am happy to get to know Stella and her family better. I really enjoy your daughter's company in class. She's so smart."

"She is, isn't she?" my mother beamed, but she had a twinkle in her eye too.

"Congratulations on your new job," he added. "Stella told me about it. I hope you like it as much as you had hoped."

"I do," she said, with a bemused expression on her face.

"Well, Stella, let's see if your mother's new salary can cover your book expenditures," Dad said, reaching for my books.

Howie brought a couple of books to the cash, too.

"What did you get? I showed you mine, so show me yours," I said, pointing. He smiled and offered them to me. One was a mock survival guide about weathering the zombie apocalypse. The other was a book of poetry.

I raised my eyebrows. "Interesting combination."

"I am a host of contradictions."

Howie walked with us to the restaurant, chatting with my parents while I squirmed. Part of me, yes, I admit it, was secretly delighted that he was there.

It's an odd feeling to be worshiped. On one hand, it's slightly offensive. I felt like shaking him and telling him every bad thing I knew about myself – my short temper, especially with those intellectually inferior to me, my love of a good argument, my waist size. After all, what was he basing his adoration on? My looks? On the other hand, it's sexy when someone thinks you're sexy. Even if he is a little weird. Okay, a *lot* weird.

But there was also the fact that my parents were about to have a field day with this poor guy, and while I knew it'd be embarrassing for me, I was more concerned for him. What if they humiliated him utterly and he never wanted to see me again? I mean, this guy thought I was awesome, and I didn't want my parents to put him off.

That was my job.

Oddly enough, it turned out okay.

Howie didn't flinch at anything my parents threw at him. He drank water and ate about two bites of lamb and calmly answered their questions. He told them that his father was a scientist at SFU (which I knew), that he was adopted (which I didn't know), that he had a brother and sister, and that they lived fairly close to us.

"It's an old house, not one of those new mansion homes," he said, "but there's more of them being built around us every year. It used to be you couldn't hear traffic at our place, despite being only a ten-minute drive from everything. Now we hear construction."

I eventually re-introduced the topic of Kelly, because I wanted a reason to be angry. Anger is a good emotion. It wipes out the less comfortable emotions like anxiety, shame, and hunger. I know where I am when I'm angry. I'm *good* at angry.

My mother sometimes said that I got my temper from her, which made no sense because she almost never got angry. My grandmother, on the other hand, was a flaming ball of unadulterated snark. So maybe Mom meant that I got it through the maternal line. I was usually too angry when she said stuff like that to pursue it rationally.

"Do you know this Kelly, Howard?" Dad asked.

"Not very well, but well enough," said Howie. "She's clearly damaged in some way, but she's very popular at school."

"Well, it doesn't sound like this Mr. Barrett ever seriously entertained the idea that Stella was the one who cheated."

"I think Stella's acumen and honesty shine through, Mr. Blunt. I can vouch for them and I've only known Stella for a couple of days."

Howie didn't sound real. Even at his most animated, like now, his sentences just sounded like lines he was reading from a script.

Only his eyes were really real.

Between answers, he would look at me. For just a second, I'd feel like I had known him forever, and that everything was going to be okay. Then I'd get confused and look away. My parents noticed, of course. They weren't idiots. They were probably killing themselves laughing inside.

As the dinner wore on, he seemed to slowly lose some of his vitality, and he talked less and stared at me more. It wasn't the vacant staring of that first day. Instead, he seemed to be looking deep inside me. All I could do was blush like a moron. For some reason, I didn't feel the need to mock him or scold him or be mean to him in front of my parents. Maybe some part of me knew they'd see through it, and I didn't want them to know how flustered all of this made me feel. Some emotions you just keep from your parents, even if it's the emotion of wanting to decapitate a cute guy who keeps ogling you.

When dinner was over he thanked them for the pleasant evening (those were his actual words – he sounded like an etiquette manual from the 1950s) and promised to see me in school tomorrow. Then he slipped both of his books into my hand and whispered in my ear, "They were for you, really." The chemical smell that I associated with him seemed to have followed him out of the lab.

"Do you need a ride home, Howie?" my mother asked.

"No, thank you, Mrs. Blunt, I have my own car. It's parked just up here."

"Well, it was nice to meet you," she said, eyes dancing impishly.

He smiled at her. "The pleasure was all mine," he said. And then, I swear to God, he took my hand in his and, watching me closely, he kissed it gently and walked away.

"HE JUST KISSED MY HAND!" I said as soon as I thought he might be out of earshot. I could still feel the cool touch of his fingers on mine, and the place where his lips had brushed the skin of my hand. "DID YOU SEE THAT?"

"What a peculiar young man," my mother mused.

"That was great fun. Did you see him drooling over Stells? I need to get me that Nerf rifle."

"Dad!"

"I have to say I'm disappointed," said Mom. "His gazing lacked the slack-jawedness that I had pictured from your stories, Stella."

"I told you, he varies from day to day. He says it's something to do with a medical condition. Like, when he gets hungry, except I almost never see him eat. Mostly he drinks out of a thermos."

"I did notice that he started out using words like 'acumen' and by the end of it was down to normal teenage vocabulary," said Mom, "but no worse than that."

"He speaks a little funny," said Dad. "Do you think he might be mildly autistic?"

"I don't think he's in Special Ed," I said, "but maybe."

"If he's functioning well he might not need it. Is he any good in Chemistry?"

"Yeah, actually, better than me really, although that's because I'm behind in the material."

"Definitely autistic."

"That doesn't explain the whole 'I can only eat out of a mug' thing."

"He ate that lamb."

"No, he didn't, Dad. He picked it apart. Maybe he had a bite or two. That's it."

"Well, I like him."

I boggled. "You DO?"

"Sure," Dad shrugged. "He was polite, well spoken, and he clearly thinks the sun rises and sets on you."

"Are you implying I have a large gravitational mass?"

"Brush it away with jokes all you like, Stella, but you've got an admirer. It's up to you whether you want to do something about it."

"But he's a slack-jawed, staring admirer with a strange disease!"

"Not tonight, he wasn't. Give him a chance. When we first met you, you were bald and you screamed incoherently for hours on end. But we got to like you anyway. You grew on us, you could say. You can't go by first impressions."

"Did he give you his books?" my mother pointed to my hand.

"He said he bought them for me. Look, it's a book of classic poetry and a book about surviving a zombie apocalypse! Doesn't that seem like an odd combination to buy for a girl you hardly know?"

"Maybe he gave you the wrong two."

"He only bought the two books."

"Autistic. That's what I think. You have to be autistic to think that giving a girl a book about zombies is a romantic gesture."

Except autism isn't contagious, I thought. But I didn't tell my parents about the contagious thing. For some reason, I wanted to keep that to myself until I knew more about it.

When we got home, I hid in my room and opened the book of poems. They were all love poems. I scanned the index of first lines.

"She walks in beauty, like the night"

"Let me not to the marriage of true minds admit impediment"

"Come live with me and be my Love"
"I dwelt alone in a world of moan"
"My true love hath my heart and I have his," and more.
On the frontispiece, someone had written in pencil:

When I met you, all of these came true.

Had Howie written that? Surely not – when would he have had the chance? I mentally tried to compare it to his "you are lovely" note from Social Studies. I thought they were the same.

Part of me was freaking out at the incredible romance of being kissed on the hand and then given a batch of love poems. I never thought of myself as the romantic type, but *love poems*.

The other part of me was panicking because I didn't know what to do. I mean, probably the correct thing to do was to walk into school tomorrow and kiss him or take his hand or something, and boom, I'd have a boyfriend. A bit of a weirdo, but probably worth a chance.

It sounded simple, but it didn't *feel* simple to me. Whenever Howie was around I went on the defensive and kept pushing him away because that was easy. That was safe. Can't be rejected if you're the rejecter. Can't be laughed at if you're the one doing the laughing.

To unbend and say, "Yes, okay, let's give this a chance, I've never kissed a boy but you have eyes that feel like home and you have been so nice to me and you're damn good at chemistry..." I didn't know if I could do that. No, I was pretty sure that I couldn't do it. Just thinking about it felt impossible.

On some level, I was positive that if I let my guard down, if I took his hand or smiled at him, if I was *soft* –

then someone would jump out from behind a bush and point their finger at me and laugh and laugh and laugh. That same part of me kept saying that this must be an elaborate joke, that Howie would laugh too and say, "Did you really think anyone could be obsessed with *you*?"

Just the thought of it was more humiliation than I could bear. Okay, all the Kelly stuff, that pissed me off, but it didn't really hurt too much. Anger happens on the outside, if that makes any sense. It didn't make me feel vulnerable. But this romance stuff made me all kinds of vulnerable, and I hated it – and loved it.

When I finally set aside the poetry book, I had accepted three basic facts: First, that Howie was in *no way* normal. Second, that he had a mysterious disease which I really didn't want to catch. And third – that I had a massive fucking crush on him anyway.

Before I turned out the light, I picked up the zombie book. On the first page, under the price, someone had scrawled,

Just in case.

6

Howie met me as I got off the bus the next morning. My parents had finally insisted that I try to navigate the transit system. I survived it despite massive anxiety. I stepped off the bus, and BAM, there he was beside me, holding an umbrella, which he immediately held over me.

"Morning," he said as if he did this every morning.

"Uh... hi," I said.

"Can I carry your bag?"

"No, that's all right. I carry it all the time."

"Please?"

"Are you for real?" Okay, maybe I did have a crush on him, but that still didn't translate into being nice to him.

"Sometimes I wonder," he said, holding out his hand. And again, for a second, I had a comfortable sense of familiarity, like maybe he did do this every morning and I had just forgotten.

I decided to make an effort to be kind to him. Come to think of it, the last time I had a crush on a guy I had badgered him until he hated me. I handed Howie my bag.

"Thanks," I said grudgingly.

He followed me up to my locker and held the bag open so I could take out my homework books out and put the morning's school books in. He didn't say a word. He just stood there, like a servant.

"You're being weird again," I told him.

"I'm sorry. But to be fair, you're being beautiful again."

"Stop calling me beautiful!"

"Would you prefer radiant? Stunning? Brilliant? Altogether lovely?" He raised his eyes up to mine briefly and I felt my heart respond again. One glance from him and I melted. What was that about?

"I would *prefer* you talk like a human being and not like a bad poem." The nicer he was to me, the meaner I was to him. That was messed up. There was probably some kind of mental pathology there.

I tried to summon an apology on the way to our classroom. I'm not good at those. "Uh… thank you for the poetry book, by the way."

"The masters say it all better than I ever could," he replied with a shrug. He pulled out my chair.

I opened my mouth to ask him why he had given me a comedic zombie survival guide when someone whispered behind me.

"That's the one that cheated off of Kelly Svancara's test."

I stiffened and turned around. The girls who wouldn't let me sit with them the other day were looking right at me. When they saw me turn they immediately looked away, but then looked at each other and burst into giggles.

"Excuse me, I need to take some names," I told Howie, barely controlling my simmering fury.

I marched up to the girls and leaned right over them. They leaned back and tittered nervously. I gave them a bright smile.

"I'm sorry, I don't think we've been introduced. My name is Stella, I know kung fu, and Kelly is a lying bag of leprous snakes. I'd go into more details, but class is about to start and I'm a keen student. However, if you want to continue to spread malicious lies about me, I'd be happy to dismember you after class."

I turned away before they had a chance to rub their three or four collective neurons together to come up with a comeback. Chair Kicking Guy whistled and laughed as I stormed back to my seat.

"Diplomatic as well as beautiful," said Howie. His voice was as deadpan as ever, but there was an ironic twist to his smile. It was the first time he had said anything even slightly negative about me, and I appreciated it. If he had said something soppy, I might have done something violent.

"I don't take people's crap very well," I said. My heart was pounding with rage. I wanted to smash beakers.

"They don't know you. They're just repeating what they heard."

"What they heard was WRONG."

"I know that."

"You don't know shit, Howie! You don't know me either," I snarled.

"I have absolutely no doubt in my mind that you are telling the truth. How do you feel about the deus ex machina at the end of *The Chrysalids*?"

"You had your breakfast this morning, didn't you?"

"I had an extra helping. Answer the question."

"I think it's asinine, and I think that the whole 'different species need to fight to the death' thing is just Waknuk all over again."

"See, you didn't cheat on that test."

"That doesn't change the fact that someone who I thought might be a friend is spreading lies about me."

"It bothers you that people are thinking bad things about you." Sometimes it was really hard to tell if he was asking a question or making a statement.

"No, it bothers me that people are thinking WRONG things about me."

That was when the teacher, whose name, I had learned, was Mr. Nguyen (which was apparently pronounced "Wen" because why the fuck not), finally decided to stand up and start teaching so our conversation had to end there since I was seated right under his nose. I began to understand why people never wanted to sit front and centre. I had more fuming to do, and taking out my anger on covalent bonds wasn't very effective.

I don't think I have ever dreaded a class the way I dreaded going to English that day. At first, Howie followed in my wake until I asked him sharply where his next class was and it turned out to be in a totally different part of the school. I sent him off but felt strangely desolate without my adoring acolyte.

My heart was pounding when I walked into that classroom. Never mind that I'd have to find somewhere new to sit, *again*, but I wasn't sure that I could see Kelly's face without attempting to destroy it.

It was definitely the betrayal that bothered me. The more I thought about it, the more I realized that she had orchestrated the whole thing. The whole class heard me tell Mr. Barrett that I knew *The Chrysalids* well. She then invited me to sit next to her in English in time for the test. With the exception of inviting me to sit next to her in class, there hadn't actually been much friendliness on her side. I mean, when I was talking to Howie, he asked me a bunch of stuff about myself, but Kelly had never asked me anything except my name and how I managed to take such efficient notes.

I asked to sit with her at lunch. I tried to make conversation. I was the one desperate enough to take a seat invitation and try to turn it into a potential friendship. I was now humiliated, and I wanted to either kill her or disappear down a hole forever, or both.

Now, the smart thing to do would probably have been to slink into class, seat myself in a corner somewhere, and stay under the radar, thus avoiding all potential confrontations.

The smart thing was probably *not* to walk into class with my middle finger held out in front of me, aimed at Kelly's seat without even checking to see if she was there yet.

She wasn't.

So, I just middle fingered a bunch of strangers. Great.

I sat down in my original seat from my first day at school, and when Kelly came in, I flipped her off. She just smiled demurely.

"You're so immature," she said to my finger.

"And you're such a lying bag of toxic gas," I said. "Isn't it wonderful how many different kinds of people there are in this world?"

She just held up her hand and sat down calmly. Her serenity was driving me crazy. I needed a blow-up fight. I wanted yelling. I wanted slapping. I wanted to kick her nose cartilage into her brain. I wanted her ability to be so unruffled and morally corrupt.

"If you two keep this up, I'm going to send you both to the Vice Principal's office," said Mr. Barrett from his desk without looking up. "As it is, I want to see you both after class."

When the bell rang I went and stood at Mr. Barrett's desk with my arms folded while the mindless morons all shuffled out. Kelly remained in her seat, leaning back. Her blonde friend waited with her.

"Miss Cichon, you can wait outside," said Mr. Barrett. The blonde cast Kelly a sympathetic glance and left.

"Well, girls, the results are pretty conclusive. Stella's answers showed a considerable need for anger management classes, but no lack of understanding of the subject matter. Kelly, on the other hand, made some fairly serious errors. I'm afraid I'm going to have to accord Kelly the zero and allow Stella to keep her grade."

I smiled broadly at Kelly.

"I know what I saw, Mr. Barrett," said Kelly, "and I saw Stella cheat off of me."

"I'd respect you for sticking to your guns if I had any reason to think you might be telling the truth. I've been more than fair, Kelly. You get a zero. Stella, thank you for going through this rigmarole."

When we were dismissed from the classroom, I expected Kelly to slink off in defeat. Instead, she turned to me and said, "I feel sorry for you."

"You what now?"

"I pity you. Because you are scum, and no one will believe you over me. I hope you enjoy being known as a fat, cheating slut." She raised an eyebrow, gave me a little smile and walked away.

Filled with fury, I barged through the halls to the cafeteria and looked at my lackluster lunch. It's not that Dad didn't make good sandwiches. He did. It's just that no sandwich tastes good after four hours in cling wrap.

To hell with it. I had some cash.

I was standing in line minding my own business, by which I mean mentally ranting and raving about my business to an audience of suitably appalled imaginary people, when two of Kelly's friends walked by. They saw me, then whispered in each other's ears, then looked right at me, and then giggled. Then they grabbed some other chick, whispered in her ear, and pointed.

They weren't being subtle about it, so I decided not to be subtle with my middle finger. Finesse is often lost on such people. I was about to step out of line to go tell them to stuff it up their rectums when Howie lurched into view. He didn't even stop to take in the scene. He went straight up to me and gave me a concerned look.

"Do you need to go out on the bleachers again?" he asked.

"Yes. Right after I have a word with these two mindless fuckwallops."

"Wow, it's like one loser attracts another!" said one of the girls loudly. "It's turning into a whole pile of worthless."

"They aren't worth your time or your wit," said Howie. "You're almost to the front of the line. What are you getting?"

"Angry!"

"She's just so big that she's sucking people into her or-bit!" said one of my new little friends.

"They're nothing a good kick in the face wouldn't solve, Howie," I snarled.

"You know you wouldn't attack them unless they at-tacked you first, and these aren't the violent types unless you mess with their boyfriends."

"Hey, Fatty, how does it feel to know that your cankles are bigger than your IQ?" teased another girl.

Whoa, whoa, whoa.

I had been teased about my weight all my life. The last couple of years I finally escaped it because I flipped a bully over in the playground. After that, people left me alone, although my parents threatened to take me out of kung fu if I did it again.

But never, ever, had anyone ever suggested that I was stupid.

My intelligence was all that I had. I didn't have popu-larity. I didn't have charm. I didn't have a size 0 figure. You know what I had? Brains. That girl had crossed a line.

I pushed Howie to one side. "I'm sorry, did you just call me STUPID? Because if you think I'm STUPID, then you are dumber than a sack full of nematodes, without the nematodes."

The girl just smiled at me, although she stepped back a little. "I didn't say your IQ wasn't big. I was just saying that your cankles are even bigger."

I flushed with anger and shame and I wished that I could kick her in the face without getting suspended from school and deeply disappointing my parents.

I felt a cool hand touch mine. "They aren't worth it," said Howie. "Look, I bought you pizza and a Diet Pepsi. Come outside and eat it."

Howie didn't lead me out of the school. After spewing a final round of creative insults at the bully trio, I led *him* out, blasting my way through people while he followed me doggedly, clutching the plate of pizza. The moment we were outside I whirled around. Howie offered me my pizza with a dazed expression.

"What the hell is wrong with these people, Howie? Do they really seriously think that Kelly's telling the truth?"

"I don't know."

"VERY HELPFUL."

"You're radiant when you're angry."

"EVEN LESS HELPFUL."

"Why does it bother you? Some stupid girls in a stupid clique, harassing someone who got the best of their friend."

"It just does!"

"Did Mr. Barrett officially clear you of cheating?"

"Yes. But that doesn't make it better, Howie. That doesn't make me feel better when people are whispering about me in class and teasing me in line for lunch. Frig. Which reminds me, I need to pay you back for my lunch."

"It's on me."

"I'm paying you back, Howard." I wasn't going to be bought. I dug out a bill and handed it to him. He wouldn't take it.

"It's just a lunch. You can buy me lunch some time to make it up."

I stuffed the bill down his shirt. "You don't eat normal food. What DO you eat, anyway?"

"It's a sort of a shake."

"Sounds appetizing."

"Really, really, not." He smiled at me, and I found my-self smiling back. My anger was dissolving. Damn him. How did he do that? He was like some kind of emotional fire extinguisher. Now I just felt confused.

He leaned forward and looked at me over his glasses. "I'm sorry Kelly hurt your feelings, and that she's trying to turn people against you. But don't let her get the satisfaction of knowing that she gets to you. She's just a vapid, socially aggressive twit who probably has some serious personal problems. You're worth ten of her."

"But why did she do it, Howie? Why me?"

"You were there. You knew the material. She saw an opportunity. She knew that the teacher didn't know you, she figured he'd believe her over the new girl. She was wrong. I feel sorry for her."

"Well, I still want to punch her."

"Can I ask you one favour?"

"What?"

A shy smile spread across his face. "If you do... can I watch?"

And then Physics happened, and oh my God. The teacher handed back the results of our assignment, and I got all except one of the honors questions right. She didn't go over the questions in class or anything though – she just moved on to refraction. So after class, I went up to her and asked her how the last question should have been an-swered. Normal enough thing to do, right?

"If you were having trouble with that question, you should have come to me before you handed it in," she said.

"But I thought I had it right, and I want to know what I did wrong," I said, trying hard not to explode.

"Then you're going to have to figure it out. If I just give you the answer you won't learn," she said.

Was this woman for real?

"Why did you become a teacher when you clearly loathe teaching?" I growled at her. She looked shocked, then purposely turned her face away from me.

Hah. It looked like I had been added to the "not-being-spoken-to" list. The short-haired girl caught my eye and smiled.

I think you can imagine that I didn't arrive at Social Studies in the most chipper of moods. My scowl didn't seem to faze Howie in the slightest.

"Why are you so thrilled to see me?" I said, walking up to him, "You just saw me at lunch, and I feel like killing people."

"You'll have to tell me what happened this time, but anger looks good on you."

"What? Anger is my glory?"

"It becomes you, in any case."

Before I could pursue this tidbit more, I saw the sign on my chair.

There was a "Beware of Dog" sign stuck to my seat. At least, my seat as of yesterday, since now I wasn't sitting with Bitchy McAsswaffle.

I stopped and stared at it for a moment. I heard a few chuckles. The classroom was only half full, but obviously the people already there had seen the sign. Someone pushed past me and laughed and pointed.

Howie swiftly sat down in my seat, covering the sign.

"You can sit here today," he said, pointing at his usual chair. I sat, my face hot with shame which I quickly transferred to the more comfortable emotion of "fucking pissed off."

"Where is the worthless bag of beaver dung?" I asked him, turning in my seat. "I don't see her."

"One of her buddies probably did it. Stella, let it go. It's just high school drama stunts. It doesn't mean anything."

"It doesn't mean anything GOOD. I'm trying to make friends in a new school and I'm quickly becoming a pariah. That's ASSTACULAR, HOWARD."

"I don't even understand it. Why call you a dog?"

"They're implying that I'm ugly, Howie, and/or a bitch."

"But you're beautiful and intelligent, and I think that underneath all your brash talk, you're kind and caring, too."

I looked at him. "You're making me into the person you want me to be."

"No, I can sense it. It's sort of a vibe. You can debate with me point by point, but I'd win."

Kelly arrived. She glanced at the chair, looked surprised to see Howie in it, and then glanced at me. I ignored her, hoping that she'd think that Howie had sat in the chair before I even had a chance to see her little sign. I didn't want her to get the satisfaction, although someone would probably tell her soon enough.

When the bell rang at the end of class, I motioned Howie out of the chair and waited until Kelly passed us, sending me a disparaging glance. Then I whisked the sign off of the chair and stuck it to her bag as she went by.

For about two seconds, her book bag said "Beware of Dog" and she didn't notice and it was great. Then it clattered to the floor and she turned around.

"Pathetic, Stella," she said. "I think you dropped something."

"Let's go, Stella," said Howie.

"Yes, Stella, go with the freakazoid. He's clearly your soul mate," said Kelly. "He's almost as big of a loser as you. But then, no one's bigger than you."

"Is your family a happy one?" I snarled, "Or do you go home at night?"

She took a moment to think about that one, and I swept out of the room before she had untangled its complexities.

I struggled to get my binder into my bag as I walked, fighting the burning sensation behind my eyes. I knew it would be like this. I knew I'd end up at the bottom of the social strata. But that didn't make it easier to deal with. I slowed down and stood against the wall, taking deep breaths.

Howie reached out his arm as if he was going to put it around me. I stiffened, and his hand paused in mid-air, then changed direction, reaching for my bag instead.

I hitched the bag onto my back and started walking again.

"I don't need you to carry things for me."

"I know. I want to." He followed me along the hall and down the stairs. He tried to open the school doors for me but I pushed through myself.

"I don't need you to do stuff for me! Look, I don't know if you're trying to suck up or what, but I don't need to be treated like a delicate princess, okay? I'm far too aware of the irony."

"Why is it ironic to be treated like a princess?"

"Because I'm big and tough, and I could probably kick your ass."

"Stella, I don't think you're weak. If anything, I admire your strength. I just want to be helpful to you. Tell me what you'd like me to do, and I will do it."

"Why?"

"Because I like you. Because you, you're..." he held his hands out wide.

"Fat?"

"No, you're... amazing. I want... I want you to be useful to you. I want to become someone you want in your life, even if it isn't in a romantic way."

"Are you telling me that you'd settle for being *used* by me?"

He shrugged his lean shoulders. "Yes."

"That's seriously messed up, okay?"

How could I have considered dating this guy, even for a minute?

Yes, okay, his attraction for me was attractive, but this guy had issues. You can't date someone with issues. It's a bad plan. I started to feel better about being completely unable to be nice to him.

I grabbed Howie's arm and pulled him aside, out of the crowd of students all heading to their cars or down to the bus. Part of my brain squealed girlishly with the thrill of actually touching him but I shut that down fast.

"Listen," I said, "I don't know anything about dating or romance, but I'm pretty sure that it's not normal to just tell someone, 'I'll do whatever it takes to make you like me'. It comes across as a little desperate, you know?"

"You do like me," he replied frankly, and his eyes looked steadily into mine, "I know that. We have a lot in common. You can talk with me. If I eat often enough I can keep up with you intellectually, and I'm the closest thing to a friend you have here so far. I know all of this. But I can't make you feel more for me than that, and I don't want to force you into anything you aren't comfortable with. I just want to be helpful to you, to be useful to you, to make you more comfortable, and not less. I want to make your days better, and not worse.

"So I am telling you now – tell me to jump, and I will ask how high. Tell me to carry your books, fetch your lunch, sort your notes, and I will do it. Tell me to leave you alone and never talk to you again, and I will do that too. Anything you ask... and I will do it. It's not a plea, it's not a bribe. It is what it is."

He was so calm. Not desperate or crazy or anything, just serene and still slightly monotone. He held me with his eyes and I was transfixed. His hands closed over my arms, gently drawing me in until our bodies were almost touching. I thought I felt a tingle where we touched, as though there was a current running through us. The burble of voices around us and the whoosh of traffic going by all seemed to fade into the background as he held me.

"Tell me," he whispered. "Tell me what you want, anything, and I promise I will do it."

This is the moment, I thought.

I could tell him, "Kiss me," and he'd do it. I paused, trying to work up the words. I was trying to reconcile who I was with who I could be.

No, Stella Blunt had never been a sap for soppy romance. No, Stella had never done the kissy face stuff. Yes, Stella had always been the "ugh, get a room" type.

But Stella could change, right?

I opened my mouth, and I seriously thought I was going to be able to do it. My whole sense of self was about to change. This would be a moment I'd remember for the rest of my life.

My first kiss.

Then I felt a spasm of panic and instead my mouth said, "So, what, like if I asked you to step in front of a speeding car, you'd do it?"

And the moment broke, and he smiled and stepped back, and while I was wishing I could grab those words and stuff them back into my mouth, he took another step off of the curb and

BAM.

A car appeared where he had just been standing, and there was a shout of shock from all the people around us. I heard a wet thud as Howie's body landed on the pavement.

Oh, *shit.*

7

My memory of the next few minutes is pretty blurred.

There was a lot of running and screaming, and the driver of the car was freaking out and saying, "I didn't see him! He just stepped in front of me! Oh my God, I'm a murderer," and lots of other unhelpful things.

I ran to Howie but there was a bunch of other people around him and I couldn't get to him properly. People were shouting stuff like, "Is he breathing?" and "don't move him!" and "sick, look at his arm!" and other things that made me even more convinced that I was the murderer.

I clenched my hands.

"Everyone, get the hell out of my way!" I said and everyone did. Howie was lying on the ground with his eyes wide open and for one hideous heartbeat, I was sure he was dead. Then his eyes turned to meet mine and he smiled.

"I promised," he said.

"What the hell, Howie! What did you do that for? Are you alive?" I leaned over him and grabbed his shoulders, but then stopped myself before I shook him. If getting him to step in front of a car hadn't killed him, shaking him with a potential back injury might do the trick.

"I'm not sure," he said.

I scanned for pools of blood, protruding organs, bones sticking out of his neck. No blood, but his arm was doubled under him in a funny way.

"Well, your arm is sure as hell broken," I snapped. I felt a gush of relief and horrible guilt, which made me angry. "Pro tip, okay? Don't kill yourself just because someone said so. EVER."

"I'm tougher than you think."

A teacher appeared and tried to push me aside, then went around me.

"Are you okay?"

"I feel fine." Howie began to sit up and the teacher made him lie back down. I picked up his glasses off of the street and handed them to him. He put them on with the hand that wasn't pointing the wrong way.

Someone called an ambulance, paramedics showed up, and I just sort of stood there. I realized that I was going to miss the bus, but I needed to know that he was okay, for my own sanity.

Rationally, I knew that if a nearly-adult person decides to step in front of a car, then that is really their decision and not the fault of any sarcastic orders that may have been issued. Even more rationally, I knew that I hadn't even really issued the order. I had just asked him what would happen if I told him to step in front of a car. It was entirely his decision to go ahead and give me a fucking demonstration.

But if you can suggest that someone step in front of a car, and then watch them do it, and not feel some guilt, then you aren't a proper human being.

Besides, I had managed to take a potentially big romantic moment and turn it into a scene full of paramedics.

Way to go, Stella. Howie wasn't the only one with serious issues. Maybe we were right for each other. One thing was for sure – People don't deliberately pull suicidal stunts as a practical joke. The tiny part of myself that kept thinking *this is all a joke, this is just how they haze the new kids* was finally silenced.

On the other hand, the part of me that kept thinking *this guy is a lunatic and you should not date him* was even louder now.

He refused to go to the hospital, insisting that he was fine. They were going to bully him into it, but then his father showed up and backed him up. He felt Howie all over and said there were no breaks.

"His arm *must* be broken. Arms do not bend at that angle," argued the teacher. But Howie showed everyone that he could move both arms comfortably, and even did a couple of jumping jacks. The paramedics felt the arm carefully and couldn't find anything wrong with it, but they still wanted to take him to the hospital to get looked at by an actual doctor.

"No, he's fine, I'm taking him home." Like Howie, his father spoke in a bored drone, although he certainly *looked* concerned.

"Sir, your son could have a concussion or internal injuries. His heart rate seems a little irregular, and he looks pale, so he may be going into shock. We won't know until we get him back to the hospital. I strongly advise you to let us take him for assessment."

"His heart is irregular because he has a cardiac arrhythmia. I know all about it, and he's on medications for it. He looks pale for the same reason."

Howie's dad had grey hair and a three-day-old unshaven scruff. He was gaunt and pale. The Mullinses didn't seem to be a get-out-in-the-sunshine type of family.

Howie's siblings also showed up (probably the whole school was buzzing about a kid being hit by a car, or maybe someone actually thought to fetch them). They agreed with their father about keeping Howie out of the hospital. The paramedics didn't want to leave, though.

"Listen, he's adopted, and he's had some traumatic incidents in hospitals," said the father eventually. "Try to sympathize. I will monitor him carefully. I'm a Medical Virologist. I am familiar with signs of concussion or internal bleeding. I am familiar with his medical history, and I know what is and is not normal for him. I will arrange to have him seen by his regular doctor. I'll even sign a release. Just don't make him go to a hospital. I don't want to put him through any more than necessary, and I think you can agree that he does not appear to be severely injured."

That got the paramedics acting more understanding, and after getting Howie's dad to sign some paperwork, the ambulance drove off. Howie's family gathered around him and started to lead him to their car. Then Howie turned back and looked at me and said something to them.

Oh my God, what was he saying? They all turned to look at me, and then they pulled him away.

I was walking down to the bus stop in a daze when someone tapped me on the shoulder.

"Howie said to give you this."

What was it with this family sneaking up behind people? It was his sister, a scrawny little thing with light brown hair and dark circles under her eyes.

She was looking at the ground and holding out a piece of paper. I took it automatically, and before I had thought of something to say that was smoother than, "I'm sorry I was indirectly responsible for your brother's near-death", she slipped away.

I opened the folded paper. Inside, written in pencil, was a phone number.

I may have slammed the door coming home.

"Stells?" Dad was up to his arms in dishwater. I think he did most of the cleaning and tidying ten minutes before I walked through the door every day. "You're late, I was starting to get worried. How was your day?"

"I don't want to talk about it!" I walked past him. Then I turned around and came back.

"Yes, I do! Do you know what that freak did today?"

"Howard? Charming boy. What now? Offered you a bouquet of worms?"

"He started going on about how he'd do anything I asked him to do, so I asked him if that meant he'd jump in front of a car if I asked, and do you know what he did?"

"Stepped into the road?"

"And got HIT BY A FUCKING CAR."

"Are you serious? Is he okay?"

"He's fine, shockingly! BUT WHAT THE HELL, DAD."

"Seems like the correct thing for you to do would've been to suggest that he kiss you."

"I don't want to talk about it!"

I turned around again and marched off to my room, grabbing the landline phone on my way. I was calling my friends *now*.

It took me half an hour to tell Liz about everything properly. By the end of the story, she was screeching her head off.

"Oh my God, you should totally go for it!"

"Are you nuts? Did I not describe to you what a freak he is?"

"Stella, he jumped in front of a car for you. Okay? Unless he has herpes on his face or child porn on his computer, you need to date him RIGHT NOW." It felt so good to hear Liz's voice again. I could picture her lying on her bed with green eyeshadow and fishnet stockings.

"Liz, either he stepped into the road to call my bluff, in which case he's an idiot, or he knowingly stepped out in front of a car, in which case he's insane."

"He didn't even look, though, right?"

"No, he didn't look, obviously, or he wouldn't have been knocked right off his feet by a seventeen-year-old bimbo in an SUV."

"So it's not like he checked, knew it was safe, and stepped into the road. He just stepped back with pure trust? That's SO HOT."

"Are you serious?"

"YES!"

"Okay, how about the fact that the pure trust was shattered into more pieces than that chick's windshield?"

"Whatever, he'll forgive you, guys think with their dicks. What did you tell him to step in the road for, anyway? You could have ordered him to buy you diamonds or give you hours of cunnilingus, and instead, you came up with 'jump in front of a car'? What's wrong with you?"

"I just want to say thanks for all the loving support."

"Fuck that. I'm here to tell you that you're being a moron."

"I can't help it! When he says all that flowery stuff I just can't NOT say something mean. It's a problem. I mean, do you think I really believed 'jump in front of a car' was my best option for replies?"

"What other criteria do you use when deciding what comes out of your mouth? Oh, right, THIS IS YOU I'M TALKING TO."

"What's that supposed to mean?"

"Stella, you've always been so tough on people who try to get close to you. The only reason Jeremy and I got through is because we were willing to take your shit until you finally let us in. Everyone here knows that you're a smart mouth and a good bet in a fight, so they left you alone, but on the other hand, *they left you alone*. How are you going to make friends if you're rude to everyone who is nice to you?"

"Hey, I tried." I started to tell her about Kelly, but Liz cut me off. "Yeah, okay, so she's a bitch and you're ten times smarter than her. But now she'll turn the whole school against you, and here you have this guy who thinks you're sex on legs and you're pushing him in front of cars."

"I didn't push him!"

"Semantics, Stella, semantics. You know what Graeme said about you once?"

I liked Graeme, her grungy, bearded, artistically gifted off-and-on boyfriend.

"What?"

"He said, 'Stella knows what she's worth but she doesn't think anybody else does.'"

"What the hell does that mean?"

"You know what that means, Stella. Use your brain – your IQ is fucking higher than mine, and I'm no Slow Joe. Maybe that's half your problem. You think the entire world is too stupid to find you likable, so you just push them away before you've even given them a chance."

"Yeah? Well, what about Kelly? I was nice to her and look what happened…"

"Shock and surprise, the popular girl is a snot. Who gives a tiny rat's ass? Meanwhile, you've got some guy giving you books of poetry, offering to be your slave, writing compliments in his notes, and you PUSH HIM IN FRONT OF A CAR. Jesus H. Merciful, Stella, if you don't do something about this, you're going to die alone, surrounded by cats. Just wait till I tell Jeremy about this guy. He is going to kick your ass when he hears how you're screwing it up."

"Jeremy couldn't kick my ass if I had both hands tied behind my back."

"He is going to *flip his shit*. Just you wait."

"So what do I do now?"

"You need to talk to this guy, and not at school where people can hear you. Maybe if you spoke to him privately you wouldn't be such a dillweed."

"He gave me his phone number."

"What? *When?*"

"Um, he had his sister bring it to me after they put him in the car to go home."

"And you didn't mention this? Why were you going on about how he'd never forgive you if he's handing out his phone number?"

"I don't know for sure it's *his* phone number. It's *a* phone number. Maybe it's a number for a self-help line because he thinks I have serious issues."

"He wouldn't be wrong, but I'm thinking that's his number. Call him and fucking apologize and then tell him you love him."

"I don't love him!"

"Well then tell him you think his geeky science routine is hot, or that you want his hand on your clit or something."

"Fine, I'll think of something, which will definitely be NEITHER OF THOSE THINGS."

"Whatever, Stella, just call him and then Facebook me and tell me how it goes. Don't screw it up or I'll post that photo from Grade Three Hallowe'en where you went dressed as a basketball."

I laughed and we said goodbye. Good old Liz. She and I both had "don't give a shit" attitudes but we carried them in very different ways. You'd never guess that she cries whenever furry animals die in movies. She wouldn't even watch *I Am Legend* because she saw a German Shepherd in the cover photo and said, "No, because the dog will die. They always kill off German Shepherds."

We both hid our feelings in a lot of bravado but she used sex as a shield the way that I used anger. Maybe I needed to borrow a page or two from her book.

Just a page or two.

Should I call Jeremy and go through the whole thing again, or just call Howie?

Fuck it.

I picked up the phone.

I dialed the number while my brain supplied all kinds of alternatives for who could pick up the phone. Maybe it wasn't Howie's number at all. Maybe it *was* some kind of self-help line, or the police, or a sex line. And even if it was

Howie's number, was it a home number, or a cell? What if his father picked up? What do you say to someone after you've prompted his son to jump in front of an SUV?

Then Howie answered.

"Hello."

"Uh..." I felt like hanging up. Damn you, caller ID. "Howie?"

"Stella. I'm so glad you called. How are you?"

"Fine. Uh... more to the point... how are *you*?"

"I'm fine."

"How can you POSSIBLY be fine?" My discomfort was turning into aggression. I definitely had a problem.

"I'm tougher than I look. Dad knew that or he would have made me go to the hospital."

The question "So, what happened in hospitals that traumatized you when you were a kid?" presented itself, but I decided that it was too nosey.

"Howie?"

"Yeah?"

"I need to know what the hell happened this morning. When you stepped into the road."

"I was demonstrating my willingness to do whatever you asked."

"Did you know a car was coming? And I have to warn you, there is no good answer here. Either you thought the coast was clear and were just trying to manipulate me into begging you off the road, or you deliberately walked in front of a car."

"So in your mind, I'm either an ass or suicidal."

"Basically. And Howie? Neither of those is really on my Perfect Guy Attributes list."

"Fair point. The truth, honestly, is neither of those – I did it because you suggested it. Whether a car was coming... well, that didn't matter."

"So, suicidal then."

"No, because I wasn't trying to get hurt. I wasn't hoping to be hit by a car. I just act without thinking sometimes. The worst you could accuse me of is thoughtlessness, and I would plead guilty. I am sorry if I caused you pain. Were you worried about me?" His speech was always so toneless that I couldn't be positive, but I thought I heard a playful tease in his voice.

"Was I worried that I might be implicated in your death? HELL YES. But I wouldn't let that go to your head. Not wanting to be a murderer is not the same as caring about you."

"It's a start. Not wanting me to be dead is a start."

"Of course I don't want you dead! I just want you to be less... intense."

"Done. What else do you want?"

"Besides world peace, flattering clothes, and cheesecake, you mean?"

"Yes."

"I need to know, really know, what the hell is going on with you."

"Define."

It was hard to encompass the constellation of weirdness that was Howie, and everything I needed to know about it all.

"Like, why are you so... persistent? Are you usually like this with girls? Are you just going to, like, drop this craze and move on to the next big thing someday? What is it about me that you like so much?"

"I'm persistent because that's who I am. No, I'm not usually like this with girls, and there could never be anything bigger than you."

"I hear that a lot."

"Don't make fat jokes about yourself. If you could see yourself the way I see you... trust me, there is no one who holds a candle to you. You don't have to be afraid that I am going to drop you just as I win you over. Did I miss anything?"

"Why do you like me so much?"

"I don't know, Stella. I just feel like the rest of the world is black and white, and to me, you're in colour. You stand out. Something about you calls to me. I like how you talk, I like how you act. I even like your tough-girl act, when I can tell that underneath, you're afraid of being hurt. You're smart. You're strong. And I don't know if I have mentioned this, but you are devastatingly sexy. I would go on, but you don't want me to get too intense, and trust me, this could get very intense."

I can't explain to you how strange it is to hear this stuff said to you by someone who sounds like they're reading the phone book. When Howie was in front of me, he had that passionate, unblinking gaze. But on the phone, he sounded distant, detached. Even so, I was loving it. God, I *loved it*. I loved it when he said these awesome things to me. I wanted him to go on and on.

"Okay, so maybe I'm okay with you being a little intense."

He laughed.

"Good. But I'd rather tell you in person. It's harder to do this over the phone. Ask me something else."

"My parents think you have Asperger's Syndrome."

"Interesting, but that's not a question." Apparently, he wasn't going to take the bait.

"Fine. Give me a brief version of your life story."

"Okay. My life, the edited for time version. Born a baby, grew into a child. Caught an illness which killed my parents. Ended up in the hospital. A scientist tried some risky, experimental cure on me and pulled me through – I'm not cured, but at least I'm not dying. He adopted me and my sister Hazel, and he adopted another boy, Ray, under similar circumstances. He's a good Dad. We're all a little messed up but we fit together. Then you walked into class."

"Yadda yadda, I'm a vessel of light, yadda yadda."

He laughed again. "Pretty much."

"I hate to keep asking you about your medical condition, but..."

He sighed. "You deserve to know, it's okay. It's a very rare disease, virtually unknown. Dad's sort of a specialist. It's contagious in its original form. It's deadly. Dad hasn't found a cure yet, but he found a way to fight it. I have to keep nourished and I need to get injections, but it works."

"So, you're NOT dying, right? Because I'm not interested in becoming a character in a John Green novel."

"No. I'm not. The dying part is over with if that makes sense. It's kind of... dormant. And likely to remain that way forever, assuming I take care of myself, which I do."

"You said I might catch it? I mean, not to be selfish or anything, but..."

There was a long pause. Was he deciding how much to tell me? That would piss me off. *Tell me a name, let me Google the damn thing. It's not up to you to decide how much I do or do not get to know about a potentially contagious, deadly disease.*

"I am not contagious. Obviously, Dad wouldn't be sending me to school with everyone if you could catch it. I am not shedding the virus. If we stopped taking our medicine and didn't eat regularly, the virus could get the upper hand and become contagious again."

My God, I thought. *He has AIDS. Do people even still get AIDS?* Pretty much everything I knew about AIDS came out of health class in grade seven and from being forced to watch *Philadelphia* with my parents.

"...How is it normally spread?" He was going to say through the blood. Hadn't he mentioned needles before?

"Through saliva. It's related to rabies, actually."

"TO RABIES?"

"Look, I'm not rabid, okay? Obviously." There was a pause. "Although you may find me drooling over you."

"Hey, you said it, I didn't."

"I had to. The joke was there."

"So, basically, you have something that isn't rabies in your saliva."

"No. I have something that isn't rabies and isn't in my saliva. I'm not contagious. But it's possible that I could be if I didn't care of myself."

"That's... comforting."

"Stella, I'm not trying to convince you that I'm the pick of the litter. I just... hope you'll let me be your friend. Can we be friends?"

"Yes, of course." What I wasn't sure of was whether I dared kiss someone who might give me rabies.

"Stop wondering if you're going to catch some foul disease from me. You aren't."

"Prove it."

"I'll get you to come over and look at Dad's research. He can talk to you about it. Better than hearing it from me."

"Maybe, yeah."

"Do you want me to tell you how spectacular you are some more?"

"Well..." I waved a hand, which of course he couldn't see, "if you insist."

And so I lay back on my bed and listened to the Song of Stella.

Why not? You can't catch rabies from a phone.

Rabies.

Fucking Christ.

8

Howie said he wouldn't be back to school until Monday – Father's orders. So that left me free to daydream about him all day at school without the inconvenience of having him actually be there, acting weird and pissing me off. That being said, knowing he wouldn't be there, making life complicated, really took a lot of interest out of my day.

Without the zest of the Howie Problem, all I had left was the Kelly Problem, and that was growing at an alarming rate.

I was hissed and barked at multiple times in the hall. "Hey, there's the cheating slut," "Hey, fatty, think you're smart?" "woof woof!" "bow wow wow!" "Here, doggy doggy," and so on. I found a nasty note in my locker – with the i's all dotted with precious circles – suggesting that I do some biologically improbable things and then die.

It didn't feel great.

As far as I could gather, the story Kelly had spread around was that I had cheated and then had sex with Mr. Barrett so he'd blame Kelly instead.

I was quickly going from an unknown and undefined quantity to a scapegoat. It presented a harsh contrast to Howie's elaborate compliments the previous night. I almost called him again when I got home, but instead, I focused on doing useful things, like homework, and tightening my Facebook privacy settings to keep out the bullies who were already starting to send me hate messages.

I nearly cried in bed that night. I wanted to go home.

When someone beckoned to me as I walked through the cafeteria the next day, I ignored them. I wasn't going to be lured over for another smartass remark or dumbass insult. I walked past without a glance and sat down by myself.

A minute later, someone plunked down in a seat next to me. I looked up. It was the girl from Physics class with the short hair and mischievous eyebrows.

"Hey, I'm Kate. You're Stella Blunt, right?"

"Yeah..."

"I heard people talking about you."

"Fuckers."

"Listen, Kelly Svancara is a bitch. What's your side of the story?"

I shrugged. "Wrote a test, she cheated off me then tried to rat on me to Mr. Barrett, he figured out who cheated on whom by not being a total moron, he got us both to rewrite the test, I passed, she failed, he considered his theory confirmed, and now I'm a pariah. Fun times."

"I figured it was something like that. Listen, why don't you come sit with me and my friends?"

"Seriously?"

"Sure. Hey, any enemy of Kelly's is a friend of ours. Come on."

I picked up my lunch and followed Kate to her table. She introduced me to her friends, Michelle and Amy. They greeted me and we had a good time abusing Kelly for a while. It felt good. They asked me politely about Halifax, and I asked them some polite questions back.

Then they brought up Howie. Apparently, Amy was in my Chemistry class and knew all about the Stare Boy fiasco.

"You have not had good luck, have you? Not only did you manage to make enemies with Kelly Svancara almost immediately, you're getting stalked by the school's biggest loser, too," giggled Michelle.

"Yeah, he's a strange, strange guy," said Kate, making a face. "The whole family is weird. My mom works at SFU and she knows his dad. She says he's a zombie."

"A zombie?"

"Well, not an actual zombie, OBVIOUSLY, but he's like a robot or something. He's, like, emotionless and really focused. He doesn't take normal lunch breaks or socialize much. I guess a lot of his research involves diseases of the brain or something so she jokes that he probably eats brains too, and calls him The Zombie."

I laughed politely. "Howie is weird, but I don't know. At least he's been nice to me. He's sort of growing on me."

"You call leering at you constantly 'nice'?"

"No, that's creepy as hell," I admitted. "But he says nice things in between the creepiness."

"Careful – That's what they say about psychopaths," said Kate with a grin.

"Were you there when he got hit by that car? What happened?" Michelle asked.

"I'd rather not talk about it," I said. Michelle and Amy looked insulted. Kate just raised her eyebrows and looked at me with this really speculative expression. I wondered what she was wondering.

"Fine," said Amy a little coolly.

There was an awkward pause, and then the bell ring. We started to stand up.

"Thanks for letting me sit with you guys."

"Sure thing," said Kate.

Kate invited me to sit with Michelle and her in Physics. Since Ms. Bond wasn't speaking to either Kate or me, it was like sitting in a strange bubble of invisibility, which was actually a nice change from being constantly targeted. It left me free to think about Howie.

The word "zombie" kept nagging at me. It stayed in the back of my mind, tugging on my mental shirt sleeves.

Zombie.

It was just such a perfect description for Howie. That mindless vacancy that first day. His emotionless speech. His slightly-cloudy eyes. Hah! Don't forget that random zombie book he gave me.

When I got home, I idly Googled "zombie", and it just got weirder and weirder. Because the word "virus" came up a lot in the context of zombies.

Virus.

Hadn't he compared his disease to rabies, a virus that turned animals into drooling, vicious, deadly monsters?

Oh, and do you know what else was freaky? Apparently respectable government bodies, like the American Center for Disease Control and even the Pentagon, have web pages devoted to preparing for a zombie apocalypse. It was meant as a joke, but of all of the weird pop-culture apocalyptic stuff out there, why zombies? Why not vampires, or Nostradamus, or alien takeovers?

And then, *and then*, I found out that British Columbia, the *very province* I had just moved to, also had a zombie preparedness section on their emergency info website. *Why*? No other province, *just BC*. I mean, it was all clearly tongue-in-cheek and while the CDC and the Pentagon's zombie stuff was pretty deadpan, the BC site had disclaimers on it making sure we knew that it was just for fun.

Because zombies don't exist, and if they did, they wouldn't be talking and drinking out of thermoses and declaring undying (undead?) love to high school girls. Howie had done a lot of weird stuff, but he had made zero attempts to eat my brains.

So then I start trying to find his actual disease, and do you know what I came up with?

Bupkes.

Well, no, I found a lot of references to Lyssavirus and diseases that were related to rabies, but if his case was as exceptional as he had claimed, I kind of thought I might find his name in an article somewhere as the first person to survive such-and-such disease or at least reference to a specific disease for which a new treatment had recently been discovered.

Nothing.

"So, I think Howie's a zombie," I announced over dinner.

"Hah, talk about a special diet – the restaurant we took him to didn't serve human flesh," Dad snorted. "Why is he a zombie?"

"Oh, this girl at school said her mom works with his dad and called him a zombie. It makes sense, eh? Pale skin, mindless stare, droning voice, gives me a book about zombies..."

"I don't think zombies talk. Do zombies talk?" Mom asked.

"Okay, so my theory has some holes."

"Hey, the zombie apocalypse is no laughing matter," said Dad, waving a finger.

"That's why I'm on the alert for potential zombie activity. The province of British Columbia would approve." I told them about the zombie preparedness site.

"Maybe he really wasn't drooling over your boobs. Maybe he was drooling over your delicious brains."

"That's probably it, Dad. That's probably it."

"So, how is Howie?"

"Alive, but still not in school."

"I don't want to upset you, but can I suggest that you do something nice for the boy? I mean, call me an old fuddy-duddy, but in my day, when a person stepped in front of a car at someone else's request, it was polite for that someone else to buy flowers or similar, at the very least."

"I called to apologize, okay?"

"You DID?"

"Well, not apologize. More like yell at him. But it's the thought that counts."

"And what did he say?"

"He told me about this virus he had when he was a kid."

Dad raised his eyebrows. "A zombie virus?"

"The exact nature of the virus, zombie or otherwise, remains unknown."

"How did he get from jumping in front of a car to telling you about his childhood diseases?"

"I don't remember the sequence of logical leaps."

"But he doesn't blame you for ruining a potentially romantic moment? This may be a boy to hold on to."

"Okay, who says the moment was romantic? Does 'tell me what to do, I'll do anything for you,' sound romantic? OR CREEPY?"

"Creepy," admitted Dad.

"Romantic," said Mom.

"Seriously, Mom?"

"Look, for tens of thousands of years, women have been trying to wrest control from men," my mother said, waving her fork. "Ever since men figured out the connection between sex and babies, they have tried to control women's choices. We've had to fight for every right we have, from being counted as human beings to working in any job we choose to perform. When a man hands you the power rather than trying to control you? That's romantic in my book."

"Is that why Dad's home cooking dinner while you're out working at your dream job?"

"Hey, I have an interview for Monday," said Dad in an injured tone of voice.

"No, but I doubt I would've married him if he wasn't the kind of man who'd do that for me," said Mom coolly. "Look, if you don't like Howie, then you don't like Howie. I don't have any real opinion about him one way or another. But if you reject him and then go off to date some controlling, overbearing bad-boy, I'll be a little disappointed in you."

"In other words," said Dad, "if he doesn't pop your toast, that's one thing, but don't let the fact that he's a little odd get in the way if you like him."

"POP MY TOAST?"

"Sizzle your steak? Boil your corn?"

"Tune your piano?" Mom suggested, "Wet your whistle?"

"Please stop."

"Charge your phone? Change your channel?"

"LOOK. Do you guys like Howie or not?"

"Does that matter?"

The phone rang just as we were clearing our plates. Mom answered it and then smirked at me.

"Just a moment, Howie, she's sitting right here."

Frig.

"I'll take it in my room," I said with dignity and then carried the phone upstairs.

"My parents think I should buy you flowers or some shit," I told him on my way up.

"Aw, shucks."

"Do you want me to buy you flowers?"

"Not especially. I'd prefer the bloom in your cheeks to all the roses in the world."

"Too much like Edna St Vincent Millay."

"Sorry."

I decided to bite the bullet. "Do you want to do something tomorrow?"

There was a split second that lasted an eternity. This was it. If I was rejected by a love-sick zombie, my self-esteem might be severely damaged.

"You know I do."

I felt a wave of relief which was closely akin to excitement. "What do you want to do?"

"Whatever you like."

"Damnit, Howie, make a decision."

"Let's go for a walk. I hear it won't be raining tomorrow."

"Fine. At one pm. I don't know where people walk around here."

He gave me the name of a park. "Do you want me to pick you up?"

"No, I don't trust someone who walks in front of cars to be safe behind the wheel. We'll meet there."

"I can't wait."

"Now leave me alone, I have homework to do."

"Good night, then. And Stella?"

"Yeah?"

"Thanks."

He hung up.

I left my room, hung myself over the banister on the stairs, and hollered "We're going for a walk tomorrow. I HOPE YOU'RE HAPPY."

There was no direct answer, but I swear I heard some giggling.

It was actually sunny that Saturday. I purposely arrived a little late because I didn't want to be standing around waiting for him. I seriously don't know why I was so afraid of being rejected by someone who wanted so badly to accept me. I just was.

It was cruel to show up late because *he* had good reason to think that *I* might reject *him*. He didn't look worried, though, when I stepped out of the car. In fact, he was reading a book and casually leaning on a tree. As soon as I pulled into the parking lot, he looked up, closed his book, and stood.

I was pleased with myself for navigating the roads in Vancouver by myself for the first time. Vancouver drivers are batshit insane. I saw three people turn left on red lights, and the park that Howie picked was only a five-minute drive from my house. I got out of the car and walked over to Howie.

"Hi," he said with a smile. God, that dimple. I scanned his face for bruises, scratches, etc. Other than the fact that his glasses were a little crooked, he looked fine. He was dressed in preppy slacks and a button-down shirt, neatly tucked into his pants. I glanced at the book in his hand. It looked like more poetry.

"So, I've decided that you're a zombie," my mouth said. Howie seemed understandably surprised by my non-sequitur.

"Oh?"

"You've got the zombie virus and you drink brains out of your metal thermos," I said.

"But you came out for a walk anyway?"

"Well, how often do you get a chance to interview a zombie?"

"Maybe I am a zombie."

"Maybe."

"If you're going to walk with a zombie, you might as well take a zombie's arm. How often do you get a chance to do that?" he offered me his arm, so I took it. Why the hell not?

Somehow, the "let's pretend he's a zombie" joke took the pressure off the situation. Maybe because it distracted the conversation from all the 'you're beautiful' stuff which I clearly couldn't handle rationally. We began to stroll down a wide gravel path through the park. Holy hells, the trees were tall here. They towered high above us, and the sunlight filtered down through the branches.

"So, tell me," said Howie after a minute of comfortable silence, "if I'm a zombie, why aren't I lurching through a graveyard somewhere?"

"Well, you said your dad cured you."

"If I was cured, would I still be a zombie?"

"Well, but you weren't really cured, were you? You're, like, in remission."

He smiled. "Ah, so I'm a half zombie."

"Sure, well, you can talk and seem to think occasionally, so I guess so."

"Occasionally?"

"That first Thursday, you didn't show much sign of life."

"That's not fair. I was undernourished and overwhelmed by your radiance."

"That's something I haven't figured out. I don't know why a zombie would start drooling over a random new girl." I shook my head.

"I was drooling over your brains, obviously."

"But you can't see my brains."

"Oh, but we zombies, you see, we can sense brain waves. That's how we find more brains."

"Oh, so it was my beautiful brain waves that transfixed you."

"Naturally." He smiled at me.

"But shouldn't it have sent you into BRAINS NOM NOM mode?"

He shrugged. "Well, I'm in remission, right? Presumably, I can control myself."

"I guess so, or you wouldn't be in school."

"Right. Too dangerous. What if I got hungry and started a zombie apocalypse?"

"That wouldn't be good."

"You think?"

"I don't know why a zombie would be in school at all, though," I said.

"Well, you know, when you're constantly replenishing your brain supply, you need to keep yourself stimulated."

"High school is stimulating? That's a new one."

"Well, university is better but we zombies aren't known for our erudition."

"What about your zombie dad? He works for a university so he must be pretty well educated."

"Oh, sure, but see, he was already a scientist before he became a zombie."

"What does that have to do with anything?"

"Lots. The zombie virus eats away at your brains. Once you stop it, you get to keep whatever it hasn't eaten. Anything else has to be constantly replaced with fresh brain matter."

I was impressed by how fast he came up with this stuff. "So, you wouldn't remember new things from after you got bitten?"

"Oh, we do, but we have to keep reminding ourselves. High school, attempt some university, then sometime in the real world, and you start to realize you've forgotten calculus again."

"As opposed to real humans who remember calculus all their lives?"

Howie frowned briefly. "I assume so. Wouldn't it be depressing to assume that we're learning all of this for nothing and will have forgotten most of it in a few years' time?"

"Um, YES."

"Well then. That must just be a zombie problem."

"So how many times have you repeated high school?"

"I could tell you, but then I'd have to eat your brains."

"You know you want to, anyway."

"You do have the most delicious-sounding brains I have ever encountered, it's true." He tightened the arm that I was holding a little.

"How can brains *sound* delicious?"

"It's a zombie thing. Your brain waves sort of... thrum... and it stimulates the appetite so it all gets very confusing. Yours would be a symphony of strawberries and chocolate with drum solo sauce."

"What would Kelly Svancara's brain waves sound like?"

"Like a child playing a song about Cheetos on the recorder."

"Ugh."

"You see my point."

Apparently, I could flirt with Howie fine as long as we were constructing elaborate fantasies. Maybe, since I knew all of this was nonsense, it meant that anything I said could also be considered nonsense. It was like, "Oh, we didn't mean any of that, did we?" and that made it okay.

"Who has the next prettiest brains to me?"

"No one even comes close."

"There have to be lots of smart girls at school."

"Smart, sure. But there's flute-and-asparagus smart, and trumpet-and-licorice smart, and even brass-and-onions smart. Then there's you."

"You know, I don't buy the strawberry symphony thing. I'm far too angry."

"You haven't heard *In the Hall of the Mountain King?* That could be your theme song."

"What about the chocolate and strawberries? They don't sound angry."

"You do have a lot of anger, but it's just your way of being loud about things that make you uncomfortable. That's what drums and brass are for. But you also have a piano, and a strings section, and woodwinds. And the chocolate is a dark chocolate – rich, intense, addicting. And the strawberries mellow it out into a perfect combination of dangerous and sexy."

"And you got all of this out of brain waves?"

"It's a zombie thing, I told you. A mere human couldn't understand."

"A mere human? Hah. At least I'm alive."

"Hey, I'm walking and talking."

"Yeah, that does poke a hole in my zombie theory, since I don't actually believe in the undead."

"We prefer the term 'differently alive.'"

"There's zombie political correctness, now?"

"Well, political correctness is part of life, why not part of undeath?"

"Let's get back to my attractive brain waves. I'm supposed to believe that my thoughts are so special that they sent you head over heels?"

"Well, they certainly make you stand out. Add that intoxicating brain of yours to that stellar body and it's a combination that I'm helpless to resist."

"Have you always been big on the fat chicks?"

"I've always appreciated curves. Remember, I've been through high school a few times. In my day, women worried about getting too skinny."

"So, what, you're super old? Not hot, Howie. I don't date creepy pedophiles."

"Okay, but my brain doesn't age, right? It's constantly being replenished by all the brains I'm drinking. So, I'm still young at heart. I mean, at brain."

Our feet scrunched in the sand on the path as we walked through the trees. I felt like the conversation was getting a little weird.

"If you're old, why hasn't your body rotted yet?"

"In remission, remember? I'm only partly dead."

"Which part?"

He smiled wryly. "None of the parts that really matter."

"So, you don't age? You'll just be a teenager forever?"

"I'm in a sort of stasis. The hope is that once properly cured, I'll age again."

"Nice save."

"Thank you."

Howie's monotone was perfect for deadpan conversations. He was really convincing. I stopped, and he turned to face me.

"Howie? You *are* joking, right?"

He paused, looking hunted. "What if I weren't?"

9

He looked totally serious. I backed up a bit. He reached out, as if to catch my hands, then pulled back at the last second.

"Don't be scared. We were having fun," he begged.

Then I felt like an asshole because I had ruined the game. I ruined romantic moments, I kicked people, and I couldn't tell jokes from mental illness. Because I was an asshole.

I looked at him right in the eyes. "I'm sorry." Finally, I had apologized. I tried to put a lot of things into that short sentence, but I'm not sure it got across.

He reached out again for my hand, and I let him take it. His fingers felt icy in the late winter air.

"You need gloves or something. Your fingers are freezing!" We started walking again.

"Well, I'm a zombie, remember?"

"Right." I appreciated that he was trying to pick up where we left off as if I hadn't gone all weird on him.

"Besides, they say 'cold hands, warm heart.'"

"Does that work for the undead?"

"Um, in general, I have to say absolutely not. But in my case, sure. Figuratively speaking."

"Not literally?"

"I've never taken the actual temperature of my heart, although I suppose I could."

"I guess it wouldn't kill you."

"Exactly."

"So, wait, does that make you immortal?"

"Nah, nothing's immortal. If you destroyed my brain, I'd die pretty fast."

"What about that car hitting you?"

"Didn't get my brain. The virus pretty much repairs me anywhere else."

"Why not when your brain gets wrecked?"

"Because it controls things out of the brain. A body can't survive without a brain."

"What about plants?"

"There aren't zombie plants."

"Besides, I thought you were in remission, but the virus is in your brain and body?"

"Definitely."

"Then why aren't you contagious? I don't really want to be a zombie. I don't feel there's a career in it."

"Because the virus's first goal is to destroy my brain and convert my body into its perfect machine. Then it starts trying to spread itself to others. There's an incubation period."

I was impressed by his ability to make up stuff on the fly. Then again, maybe the incubation period bit was true for his real disease, and he was just tacking on the zombie stuff. Even so, it made a crazy kind of sense.

"I see."

We walked in silence for a minute or so. Howie squeezed my hand and looked at me seriously.

"You keep asking questions about how you could catch this. You must know that I'm not walking around infecting everyone at school by breathing their air. What are you afraid of?"

"Just... I just want to know the risk factors, that's all."

"Risk of what?"

"Just... risk."

"You mean, the risk that I might lose my mind, bite you, and start a zombie outbreak?"

"Something like that."

He slowed down and turned to face me. He scanned my face, as though memorizing it. The wind ruffled his hair. It was such a pale blonde that it was almost white in the sunlight.

"Are you afraid that you'll get sick if you kiss me?" he asked gently.

Frig. Yes! Why did he have to cut right through to the heart of the matter like that?

I looked away and shrugged. "Should I be?"

"No," he whispered. "You won't get sick." We were standing so close, now. I could feel his body just barely touching mine. My heart was racing. I wanted to lean into him. I also wanted to run away. So, I stood still.

He took both of my hands in his. "Hey," he whispered. I looked into his face. "You don't have to kiss me if you don't feel safe. I'd... boy, I'd love for you to kiss me, but I'm happy just to have you here with me." He smiled. "You and your beautiful brain."

Kiss him, said my beautiful brain. *Aaargh, I don't know how*, said my idiot body.

He squeezed my hands again. He still smelled slightly chemical, a little like our chem lab. Or did the lab smell like him? Anyway, I sort of liked it. I had never thought of dating someone who smelled like science.

Then he leaned into me. He tilted his head forward, and I thought he was going to kiss me, and I froze because part of me was like, *holy shit, he's going to kiss me* and the other part of me was like, *that fucker said I didn't have to kiss him!* But he just rested his forehead against mine.

"Mind meld," he whispered with a sideways grin. "My God, you're beautiful."

"You keep using that word," I whispered back. "I don't think it means what you think it means."

"I may need a thesaurus, but I don't need a dictionary. I'm no Vizzini."

He even got my *Princess Bride* reference. I couldn't help but like this weird guy. "Are you the Man in Black?"

"Are you Buttercup?"

"Buttercup is a useless bint."

"I agree. You're infinitely superior to her. Are you ready to kiss me yet?"

"No."

He chuckled and sighed. Then he bent his head down and his lips brushed my ear. "As you wish."

We continued walking down the path, hand in hand.

"Do you want to come over to my house?" Howie asked as the path finally looped around and the parking lot came into sight.

"Uh. Why?"

"So you can meet my family. Not so that I can eat your brains."

"You want me to meet your parents?"

"I've already met both of yours, and I just have the one."

He had a point.

"I guess. I can follow you in my car."

"Oh, I walked here, it only took about twenty minutes. You can walk back with me, or we can drive. Up to you."

I decided that we'd drive. Not that I objected to walking, but if things got uncomfortable, I wanted to be able to leave quickly.

He climbed into the passenger seat and directed me to his house. As he had described, it was an older house set far back from the road, with a lot of trees around it. The properties on either side were probably multi-million dollar homes.

I parked behind a rusted little blue car that Howie said was his. He ushered me inside where we were greeted by a large and friendly shepherd mix dog.

"This is Army," said Howie, patting him. I greeted the dog and got a big lick on my face. Their house was clean, but a little bare. The walls were plain white, with no decorations. There were a lot of bookshelves, though. I approved.

"Dad. Hazel. Ray. I brought Stella home," Howie called.

"Oh, great," said a voice by my shoulder. I jumped and turned. His brother, a tall gangly guy, stood at the base of the stairs. He looked nothing like Howie, except for the weird bits: His brown eyes had the same cloudy look, his skin had the same sallow colour, and he had the same monotone voice. I couldn't tell if he was being sarcastic or just not emoting properly. Then he turned and went up the stairs.

Well, I felt welcome.

I heard the sound of someone coming up a set of stairs, and a door opened into the front hall. Howie's father stepped out.

"Hello, Stella," he said, offering his hand. "I'm Morton. Howie has told us a lot about you."

"Stella has decided that we're all zombies since we have a mysterious virus," said Howie. His father paused thoughtfully and studied me for a moment, still holding my hand.

"Interesting conclusion, Stella."

"Could you explain to her how the virus works?" Howie prompted.

It was like listening to two robots talk to each other. I felt distinctly uncomfortable. I pulled my hand free.

Howie's father nodded. "I think that's important. Come on down to my lab in the basement, Stella."

I looked at Howie and he nodded. Part of me was thinking that I was about to be murdered and buried in the floorboards, or possibly fed to the dog. As we went down the stairs, though, I found that the basement wasn't very basementy. It was above ground, at least on one side (since the house was built into the slope of a mountain) and fully finished. There was a microscope in the corner, a big deep freeze, a very large sink, a full kitchen, and a computer workstation.

Dr. Mullins sat at his computer and gestured vaguely at a second chair. I perched on the edge of it, looking around warily. The dog nudged my hand until I rested it on his head, and he leaned heavily on me. I scratched his ears idly while Howie's father talked.

"The virus that affects all of us is extremely rare but quite dangerous. Knowledge of it is technically considered a government secret, but for a friend of Howie, we're willing to share important information for health and safety reasons. I have to ask you not to share anything more than a general gist with other people, though."

It sounded like he was reading a script.

"Okay."

"It is a retrovirus which acts by quickly spreading and incorporating itself into every cell in the body, becoming part of the cell's DNA and altering the way the cells function. Once there, it is impossible to root out. That is, I have not been able to find a way, and nor has anyone else. I feel confident that someday, however, a cure will be found." He pulled up a diagram of the brain. "The virus alters metabolic processing and progressively destroys brain tissue, starting with the frontal lobes, memory and language centres. As the disease progresses the person begins to act erratically, starts to mumble, suffers cannibalistic urges and may become aggressive. At this point the virus begins to replicate itself, preparing to spread to the next host. Infection is usually spread by saliva – through bites – but in rare cases has been known to be spread through the blood as well."

"You keep calling it 'the virus'. Does this thing have a name?"

Howie and his father exchanged looks.

"Not a common name. Just a code," said his father.

"What is it?"

There was a very long silence. Then Howie spoke. "We call it Z0381E."

I looked from one face to another, but I didn't see a flicker of humor. Howie looked distinctly anxious, as though he expected me to run away screaming.

I'm not the run-away-screaming type.

"...Is that name a joke?"

"No," said Howie quickly. "Well, sort of. But that's really what we call it."

"Okay, I need to hear you say that you're not zombies."

There was an awkward silence.

I heard footsteps on the stairs, and Howie's sister limped into view. She stared at me.

"Stella, this is my sister Hazel," Howie said. "Hazel, you remember Stella." She nodded and licked her lips.

"Hi," I said shortly. I turned back to Howie. "I'm still waiting."

He looked imploringly at his father, who fiddled with his computer for a minute, then cleared his throat.

"Well, that depends on your definition of 'zombie'," he said. "For example, we are clearly intelligent, capable of speech, and not attempting to eat you alive. Nor are we fictional. Does that violate your definition of a zombie?"

"Yes."

"Well, then." He went back to staring at his computer screen, and I wasn't sure if he was thinking, waiting for me to respond, or if his brain had just switched off.

"Okay... now tell me the parts that make you say that it 'depends' instead of just answering 'no'".

He cleared his throat again. "If you were to ask me if we suffered from a real disease which can result in loss of higher brain function, the craving for human flesh, and reanimation after apparent time of death, then I would have to answer, 'yes'."

I stood up. "Are you FUCKING SERIOUS?"

"Oh, yes. Now, the existence of this disease is considered top secret information, so I would ask you to kindly refrain from publicizing it. Not that anyone would be likely to believe you."

"So, if I tell anyone, you have to kill me?"

"Of course not. But you might be detained by certain government authorities, and I would be in a great deal of trouble since we are allowed to live on sufferance of my research advances."

"Allowed to *live*?"

"Surely you know that the most important aspect of preventing the global disaster commonly known as a 'zombie apocalypse' is destroying all carriers as quickly as possible."

"Is that an actual risk?"

"Oh yes. The truth about the virus is kept secret for several reasons. The first reason is fear of misapplied vigilante action. If people start shooting other people in the head whenever they suspect that they may be zombies, it could cause a significant breakdown in law and order. Schizophrenics, itinerants, and drunks would be mistakenly killed. Then there's the risk of rioting. A simple brutal murder could incite a full-scale panic. Instead, by carefully releasing information disguised as jokes and popular culture, they have disseminated the requisite knowledge into the collective consciousness without causing any particular panic. In the meantime, government health authorities monitor for signs of outbreaks and deal with them swiftly."

"Isn't that risky? Do doctors know to look out for it?"

"Most don't. But a few do. And we pay those few to keep tabs on suspicious-sounding cases. If a case is too suspicious, a surreptitious saliva swab is taken."

"That sounds risky. Wouldn't it be safer if everyone knew?"

"No. If the Z0381E virus were made known to the public, doctors would be even less likely to see suspicious cases."

"What? Why?"

"Imagine for a moment that you knew someone you loved – your mother, perhaps? - was infected with a deadly disease, and that the prescribed way to deal with it would be to shoot her in the head. The right thing to do would be to do so, immediately. But could you? Or could you even put her in the car and drive her to someone who might do just that?"

I thought about it. "Probably not."

"Now imagine it is a mother whose daughter has been bitten. That mother is not going to take the risk of a doctor forcibly removing and possibly killing her child. The fact is that when people are presented with an incurable disease that involves significant risk to society, they do not put the safety of society over their own family. They still try to protect the loved one for as long as possible. Furthermore, it can be very hard to convince someone that their child is dead when said child is still walking around."

"But it's treatable! Why not just tell people that, so they bring their loved ones in for treatment as soon as possible?"

"Our treatment is not approved by the government."

"Why not?"

"Because of the potential ramifications. I hadn't discovered a cure, or a prevention, only a way of halting the progression of the disease with regular treatment. That is not an ideal state of affairs. All of us are zombies in potentia, you could say. We are considered a problem and a potential risk."

"Howie says you aren't contagious."

"We are not. The treatment halts the progress of the disease, and all of us were treated long before the infectious stage, which occurs after the brain is destroyed and the heart stops beating."

"The HEART stops BEATING?"

"Yes," said Dr. Mullins, looking impatient.

"But your hearts are beating, right?"

"Yes, and will continue to do so unless we halt all treatment for a prolonged period of time."

I stared at Howie for a while, trying to wrap my mind around all of this. I tried to see him as an honest-to-goodness-for-real zombie, and I just couldn't. He looked like a skinny kid with a health problem and an anxious expression on his face.

"What is this treatment, anyway? Some kind of drug?"

"No. It's cruder than that."

"How crude?"

Howie's sister Hazel spoke up. "We eat brains."

Howie's father went on to explain that when he was bitten, his first thought was to stave off the onset of symptoms by consuming brains. He knew that the virus attacked the brain, and assumed that this is why zombies prefer brains when presented with choices of different body parts. I didn't ask how he knew about these preferences. This whole conversation was enough of a mindfuck already.

Since the virus could be spread through any kind of a bite, there was no reason for the virus itself to target brains. He figured that this preference must be that of the body and not the disease, in an attempt to replace that which was being destroyed. So he ate a lot of brains.

I made a mental note to ask Howie later where one found brains on short notice. I didn't ask right then because I wasn't sure whether I wanted to hear the answer.

"I found that consuming brains did seem to delay the onset of my symptoms, which I had confirmed already in experiments with infected rats. However, I knew that it did not slow the progress of the virus, only allowed the infected host to retain use of mental faculties for a longer period of time. When I began to detect symptoms in myself, I attempted suicide by injecting myself with formalin."

"Why not shoot yourself in the head?"

"Like many civilians in Canada, I did not have a personal weapon. I also hoped that by injecting myself with a known tissue preservative, I might be able to halt the virus in its tracks. Formaldehyde penetrates the blood-brain barrier."

"Oh. So you hoped to sort of preserve your brain."

"Destroy it in a way that would still allow others to study it, yes."

"And?"

"It turns out that the virus is capable of metabolizing formaldehyde, albeit slowly. I was unable to commit suicide with this method. However, the formaldehyde treatment seemed to distract the virus, forcing it to re-fold proteins to keep my body usable. As long as I re-administered the formaldehyde at regular intervals, and continued to provide neuronal material to repair damage to my brain, my disease no longer progressed. You could say that my body and the virus are caught in a stalemate.

"I presented evidence based on my experimentation with rodents and requested permission to perform it on human subjects. We were fighting a rather large outbreak, and I hoped to save some of the victims. I was denied."

"They just let people die?"

"Yes. They claimed that insufficient evidence existed that it would work on humans – I hadn't wanted to inform them that I myself was affected. Then I heard that two children had been brought in, both only recently bitten. Howie and Hazel had been chained to their beds until the virus could take hold strongly enough that it became morally acceptable to kill them."

I looked at Howie, who was staring fixedly at the floor. "They were chained to the bed? That's terrible!"

"Yes. It seemed cruel to me, too, but it violated their ethical principles to shoot two children who were still acting normal and human."

"But withholding a possible treatment..."

"I felt the same way. So, I obtained access to their room. I was supposed to take tissue samples before their disease had progressed to the point where they became dangerous. Instead, I brought them my experimental treatment. I did the same for an older boy who was brought in the same day, named Ray. I was severely reprimanded for that decision."

"You saved them."

"In a manner of speaking. Once the effect had been proven to the medical staff, they could not in good conscience deny them or myself the right to continue living. So, we are, at least, alive, although my treatment is formally banned and I am no longer permitted access to recently infected individuals. However, we aren't cured. We don't function normally. We have all suffered certain amounts of brain damage. Our senses and perceptions are altered. The metabolic process is entirely different."

"How?"

"It's complicated. But if you think about it for a minute, you will realize that neural tissue is made of the same building blocks as any other kind of tissue. Normal humans do not need to eat brains in order to maintain their neural networks. The human body breaks things down into their constituent parts and rebuilds them again. Bodies under the control of the Z0381E virus tend to shortcut this, taking proteins and applying them where they are needed as directly as possible. We do not have a normal bloodstream and the blood supply is a sort of nutrient sludge directing things where they are needed most. Oxygen is less important. Zombies do not suffocate. The cells can function anaerobically. Does this make sense?"

"I understand the words you're using, but it sounds like pseudoscience crap."

He shook his head irritably, but his voice didn't contain any more emotion when he continued. "Well, it works by magic, then. You can call it that if you prefer. 'Magic' is only a word for that which we do not understand."

"You mean, like, if you don't know how light switches work you might as well call it magic."

"Yes."

"That's a cop-out answer."

Howie's father stared at me for a minute. His grey eyes had the same foggy look as Howie's eyes. "You're rather cynical for your age."

"I told you she was smart," said Howie proudly, reaching for my hand. I glared at him. He backed off.

"I can feel it as well as you can, Howie," said his father, eyeing me in a way that made me feel uncomfortable.

"What does that mean?"

"I told you," said Howie, "you have really fantastic brain waves."

"Are you serious?"

"Your brain waves are strong and complex, which is an attractive combination to zombies," said Dr. Mullins. I edged away from them slightly, and almost bumped into Hazel, who was standing uncomfortably close to me.

"What are you saying?"

"Don't be afraid," Howie reached out his hands imploringly. "You're feeling scared and you shouldn't be."

"I'm not scared, I'm PISSED and UNCOMFORTABLE! I've never had a man old enough to be my father tell me I have 'attractive brain waves'!"

"Oh, no, it does sound creepy when you put it that way," said Howie. "It's not like that. We're... we're sensitive to brain waves, and we appreciate nice ones, the way you would appreciate good music or might flip through a cookbook just to look at the pretty dishes."

"Are you calling me a pretty dish?"

"'Pretty' isn't strong enough to describe you."

"Can you ask your sister to STAND THE HELL BACK?" As we were talking, Hazel had slowly edged closer and closer, until I could feel her breathing behind my earlobe. When I shouted, she blinked once, and then took a deliberate step backwards.

"Sorry," she said.

"I'm old enough to be your grandfather, actually," said Dr. Mullins suddenly. "And that's only counting pre-infection age. For the amount of time I have been in this suspended state, I could be your great, great grandfather. Don't worry, we don't all see you the way Howie does. But he does have good taste. I'm afraid that you would need higher levels of protection should a Z0381E outbreak occur."

"What?"

"Dad's trying to compliment you," said Howie. "Listen, do you want to come to my room?"

"Are you going to EAT ME?"

"Absolutely not. You can even call your parents to let them know where you are."

Now, how did he know I had been fretting about that exact thing? How many times have my parents told me to call them and let them know when I go somewhere I hadn't planned on going? Then I go and walk into a house full of zombies without so much as sending them a freaking text.

"Are you giving me PERMISSION to call my parents?"

"No, I was suggesting you do it to put your mind at ease. And then will you come with me? I think we need to talk away from my family for a bit."

"FINE."

I texted my parents as I followed Howie upstairs to his bedroom.

—

Howie invited me home to meet his family. If I don't come home by five it's because they murdered me and ate my brains.

—

There. That made me feel a little better.

Howie's room had more personality than the rest of their house, though not much. There were no posters, no decorations. There was a bed, neatly made, two bookcases, a dresser with a vinyl record player sitting on it, and a neatly arranged desk. His book bag sat on the floor next to the desk, and there was a teddy bear sitting on a shelf next to a small framed black and white photo of a family. It looked old. Howie gestured to the picture.

"That's my family – me, Hazel, and our parents. It was taken a couple years before it happened."

Howie looked nine or ten years old in the photo. His hair was pale blond and ruffled, and he was wearing glasses similar to the ones he wore now. Hazel looked younger, maybe seven. They were standing on the porch steps of a wooden house with their parents.

"What happened?"

"The virus," he said simply. "I try not to remember it. As far as I'm concerned the virus can finish eating those memories. I prefer to remember before."

I had a million more questions. I bit back my next sentence before it came out of my mouth, and replaced it with, "I'm sorry."

"They were good parents. But Dad is good, too. I have a family, and I still have Hazel. She doesn't remember as much. The virus got further with her, plus she was younger when it happened."

We were silent for a moment. I looked at the family photo again. It looked old, like a photo of your grandfather when he was a kid. The clothes looked old fashioned. The photo looked like grainy black and white film.

"Howie? How old are you?"

"It's hard to say."

"Numbers are pretty easy to pronounce, Howard."

"No, I mean… When it happened, I was younger than I am now."

"That's how time works, Howie."

I wouldn't have blamed him at all if he had blown up at me. I sort of wanted it. He was so calm all the time. I was nervous and uncertain, and I could have used a good fight. You know where you stand in a fight.

Howie sighed. "It's been sixty-eight years since I was born."

"Bullshit."

139

"You see? Do I look sixty-eight?" He gestured at his boyish face.

"Of course not, that's horse manure."

"That's because I'm not sixty-eight, not maturity-wise. As far as we can tell, in the last fifty-six years, I have aged by maybe five years. About the same for Hazel and Ray."

"And your dad?"

"He hasn't changed at all that we've noticed. We don't know if he's ageing slowly, too, though. A few years here or there don't make such a difference to someone who was fifty-eight to begin with."

"Are you trying to tell me that he's, like, a hundred and fourteen?"

"Good mental math," Howie said with a smile. "Yes, in years since he was born, but in actual physical age we figure he's more like sixty-something, if that."

"Just because you look young doesn't mean you aren't the age you are. I mean, Cher didn't actually lose ten years per facelift."

"Do you really think I'm a developmentally delayed old man who just happens to look seventeen? Because I've got to say, I don't feel sixty-eight. I live with my father. I've never had sex. I can't even vote."

"But if you have lived for sixty-eight years, which I'm not saying I BELIEVE..."

"Fifty-six years of living with a virus that keeps trying to destroy my sense of self. Listen, I remember specific events from the last sixty-eight years. I saw Neil Armstrong walk on the moon. I remember the Kennedy assassination. I cried for John Lennon when he was shot. I saw *Jaws* when it first came out in theaters. I can tell you where we have lived, what we have done... but it feels like all of that was crammed into a few years. Things change so fast.

I remember when boom boxes were a big advance, and now people carry their entire music collection in their pockets. I remember when you needed a dime for a pay phone, but you just used a phone to send a message to your parents without even breaking your stride. I feel like it all happened overnight. I don't feel old, or jaded, and when I see other kids, they look like my age. If I stop to think about it, I know I have lived a long time, but I also feel like that was all a dream, and that maybe I actually was born seventeen years ago."

"Which is much more likely the case. I think you're all delusional."

Howie pointed at the picture. "How old does that photo look? Isn't that me, there?"

"You can get old-timey looking photos, or that could be your father or grandfather in that picture, and you just take after him."

He put his hands on his head and then dropped them at his sides. "You can believe that we're delusional if you want. Maybe that'd be better. My family said I couldn't tell you the truth, but you guessed anyway."

"I was JOKING."

"Because you didn't think it was possible. But you still guessed."

"You wanted me to guess. You gave me that book."

"See? You are starting to believe me."

"Or this is all an elaborate practical joke and you were just planting the seeds. Jesus, Howie, you expect me to believe that there is such as thing as zombies? The living dead?"

"Would you rather believe it's all a joke? I won't keep on trying to convince you if it's making you unhappy." He looked pretty unhappy himself, and it made me wonder if he was unhappy that his trick wasn't working, or unhappy that I didn't believe what he really believed was true.

"I'd rather you told the GODDAMNED TRUTH. I can't stand lies."

"Okay, then, I'll prove it to you," he said, looking desperate. "I'd rather you hate me for what I am than for something I'm not. Wait here."

He left me in his room.

There was an awkward space of a couple minutes where I just stood there, looking around nervously. I noticed that the teddy bear looked antique, but that didn't mean anything. There were two shelves of vinyl records, but some people still collect those. I looked at the books and found a wide variety, from *The Princess Bride* and *Harry Potter* to *World War Z* and *The Hunger Games*. There were lots of classics like *To Kill a Mockingbird*, *The Grapes of Wrath*, *Dracula*, that sort of thing. There was a whole shelf of poetry and another shelf of *Hardy Boys*.

Then Howie burst back into the room, carrying a *fucking cleaver*.

10

I reacted.

I kicked him in the stomach, then again in the chest, and he fell over backwards. Then I stepped on his wrist to make him let go of the cleaver. Once I had him down, I took the time to freak out.

"What the HELL is wrong with you? I am so calling the police!" I fumbled to dig out my cell phone. My hands were shaking a little.

He didn't drop the cleaver.

"Okay, so that was stupid," he said. "I wasn't trying to hurt you, Stella, I swear. It didn't even occur to me."

"You run at me with a giant knife and then say that you weren't trying to hurt me? I can't believe I liked you, you disturbing, messed up, lying little freak!"

He looked close to tears, possibly because I was standing on his wrist, and I had a lot of poundage to bring to each square inch.

"I'm such a moron. I didn't even think how scary that would look to you. I just wanted to show you something that'd prove what we've been telling you."

"And HOW, exactly, were you going to do that?"

His eyes met mine. "I was going to chop off my hand."

"*That's* the best excuse you can think up?"

"No, really, I was going to chop off my hand. Just let me show you, and you'll know that I haven't lied to you."

"Hmm... let you up with a big knife because you swear you're going to use it to turn yourself into Captain Hook, so you can disembowel me and eat me alive?"

"See? You do believe that I'm a zombie. Just let me prove it."

"I don't believe that you're a zombie. I believe that you're crazy and may want to feast on my flesh."

"Then chop off my hand."

"No!"

"What have you got to lose? Either you can claim self-defence against a dangerous cannibal, or you get solid proof that I'm a zombie."

"Just how is cutting off your hand supposed to prove anything?"

"Because then I'm going to reattach it."

He really was insane.

You know, for a while, they had me. When I was listening to all that pseudoscience coming from a scientist's mouth, it had seemed credible. Now I couldn't believe how far they had drawn me in. An hour ago, I had been falling head over heels for this guy.

This is what happens when you show emotions. The guy you like turns out to be dangerously psychotic.

"Give me the knife," I told him. He opened his hand and the cleaver clattered onto the floor. I bent down and picked it up, with my foot still on his bony wrist.

"Just give it a good chop," he said, lying there calmly.

"I'm not chopping anything, I'm getting the hell out of here," I told him.

It was then, while I was standing over Howie with a big knife, that his brother appeared in the doorway. We stared at each other for a moment.

"Are you going to chop off his hand?" Ray asked. He had a sort of hick-drawl. I half expected him to call for "Pa" or tell me that I had a purty mouth.

Howie turned his head. "Ray, tell her I'm not insane."

"I warn you, I'm predisposed not to believe you," I said.

Ray folded his arms. "Nope. Watching this should be fun."

The dog came pushing past Ray and stood next to me, tail waving, looking not at all concerned by the fact that I had one of his masters pinned. There's loyalty for you.

I narrowed my eyes and glared at Ray. "How did you know he wanted me to chop off his hand? Does he make a habit of bringing girls to his room and asking them to chop off his hand?"

Ray laughed shortly. "Nah. I just figured it'd be a good way for him to prove to you that he's telling the truth."

"I'm leaving."

"Oh, just chop off his hand," Ray said.

"No!"

"D'you want me to do it?" He held out his hand.

I tightened my grip. "I'm not handing anyone this knife."

Ray rolled his eyes. "Oh for gawd's sake. Howie, I don't know why you're bothering with this chick. Look, lady, if you get to keep that knife, can we chop off Howie's hand with another one?"

"Am I on TV?"

Howie chuckled. "Because she's great, Ray, isn't she?"

"Dad? Can you bring a cleaver up here?"

It was Hazel who showed up, lugging an even bigger cleaver. She was so waif-like that it made the thing look even more enormous. I backed up warily, and Howie sat up. You'd think he'd rub his wrist or something but he didn't. He seemed much more concerned about my reaction than the fact that I had been standing on his arm bones for the last five minutes.

"Okay, Stella? Don't be upset. They're going to chop off my hand, but it'll be okay."

"You're all insane." I held my knife up in a defensive stance. Did Howie know that I knew kung fu? I couldn't remember if I had told him. Anyway, I knew how to handle a blade.

Ray took the cleaver from Hazel, and Howie held out his hand, bracing it with his other arm. Ray brought the cleaver down swiftly through the air and there was a meaty schliiiick, and then a heavy thud.

Howie's hand was *lying on the floor.*

I couldn't have screamed even if I had wanted to. When something that surreal happens right in front of you, you just freeze up. At least, that's what I did.

Army bent down to sniff the hand and gave it a little lick. There wasn't any bleeding, just some blackish goop. There was more goop on the stump of Howie's arm. Howie seemed entirely unconcerned.

"Get rid of the knife. It's scaring Stella," he said. "I'm sorry I ever started this."

Ray tossed the knife out into the hall, barely missing the dog, who didn't even flinch.

Howie looked at me pleadingly. "Stella? Do you want to come look and confirm that this isn't a trick?"

"What?" I felt stupefied.

"I don't want to reattach my hand and then have you claim that it was all a magic trick. I'm sorry I upset you this much, and I at least want to make sure it isn't for nothing."

I held my knife tightly. I edged closer. None of them moved. A drop of black goop dropped stickily to the floor from Howie's wrist. It looked gorily, viscerally real.

"You can touch it," said Howie, watching me closely. "It doesn't hurt. We don't feel pain."

"Why not?"

"The virus eats away at our senses of self-preservation, including things like pain. It gets rid of things that might stop us in our pursuit for new humans to bite. Can you imagine if zombies just said 'ow' and backed off when you shot them in the arm?"

That would've ruined the plot of a lot of bad movies, it's true.

I ran my hand cautiously down Howie's arm, feeling for the edges of a prosthetic. How would a magician have done this? I ran my hand under his sleeve and felt his skin.

"Let me feel your other arm to compare."

"Happily," he said dreamily, offering me his other arm. I drew up his sleeve and felt his skin. The skin on both arms felt the same. I felt along the stump arm right up to the stump. The same.

"Take your shirt right off."

"Yes, ma'am." He couldn't undo his buttons with one hand, and Hazel stepped in to help. Howie with his shirt off was better looking than I expected, if you ignored the gory stump. He didn't have a rippling six pack or anything, but I had been expecting a 98-pound weakling kind of chest, and it looked fine. It was smooth and hairless and he didn't have scary massive nipples like some guys have. These things are important.

There was no sign of a prosthetic to fake the stump.

Howie knelt down and picked up the hand. "Do you want to hold my hand?" he asked, flashing a dimpled smile.

"I seem to be doing that a lot today." I gingerly took the thing. It seriously felt like a hand. It was heavy. It was dripping goo. Close up, I could see that the goop wasn't actually black. It was just really, really dark blood. No spurting or active bleeding. It was like it had clotted a long time ago.

"The virus clots the blood instantly to preserve function in the remaining limbs," said Howie. Then the hand twitched and I threw it away from me instinctively. It landed with a thump.

"Oh, I forgot to warn you. The virus continues to control the hand for a while."

"Am I going to get the virus from this?"

"Only if you rub the blood into an open cut, and even then, I'm not sure."

I wiped my hands on my jeans.

"Satisfied?"

"I guess."

"Okay, now watch." Howie went across the room and picked up his hand. He brought it back to me. "Watch."

He pressed his hand back into place on his arm. For a moment, nothing happened, and I imagined myself on a talk show with a subtitle reading, "My boyfriend cut off his hand for no reason!". Then the skin began to seal. Before my eyes, in a matter of a minute or two, his hand fused itself back to his arm.

"Fucking unreal," I breathed. Howie pulled a white cloth out of his pocket, wiped off the blood, and tossed it in his laundry hamper. Then he held out his arm for me to inspect. I ran my hands all over his wrist. There was no scar or scab where he the hand had been severed. I could actually feel it knitting itself back together under his skin.

"How...?"

"Regeneration."

"Zombies can regenerate?"

"Not once you hit the drooling, lurching, undead, rotting stage, no. But before then, the virus puts self-repair into overdrive. Hides the original bite wound, and makes up for the fact that we feel no pain and have no self-preservation instincts. Makes sense if you think about it. Otherwise, we'd die the death of a thousand cuts."

"Huh." It all sounded so crazy, but when you've witnessed a biological miracle right before your eyes, it tends to help with the suspension of disbelief.

I ran my hand over his wrist and down his arm again, then looked up at his face. He was gazing at me seriously through his glasses. If he wasn't lying... then he must be telling the truth... about everything, including how he felt about me.

"I'm so sorry I scared you, Stella. I feel awful. When you don't have a sense of self-preservation, you forget that other people do. I never meant you any harm. I'd die first. And you know I mean that because I have no sense of self-preservation."

"Define *no* sense of self-preservation. Does that mean... and this is PURELY HYPOTHETICAL... you'd shoot yourself in the head?"

Howie shook his head. "I do have a brain. I'd rather not die, and wouldn't voluntarily do it without a good reason.

I have a logical preference for self-preservation, but that instinct, that 'don't do something stupid because you could get hurt' voice in your head... mine is pretty much broken. I have to THINK about self-preservation. Does that make sense?"

"Of course not, it sounds completely moronic, but whatever."

"Do you forgive me for scaring you?"

"Well... you sure know how to get a girl's heart pumping, Howard."

"I'll take that as a yes," he whispered. I looked around. His brother and sister must have crept out of the room. The bedroom door was discretely closed.

Howie held out his arm one more time. It looked like a normal, slightly-gangly, teenage boy arm. "Do you believe me now?"

"Humph. Let's just say maybe."

"Do you at least feel safe again?"

"Well, I *am* still holding a big old cleaver."

"You can keep it if you like. We have more."

"Not comforting, Howie."

He smiled. "We go through a lot of pig and cow heads in this house."

"Not human?"

"No. Less ethical and harder to obtain."

"Oh, well, it's good to know that governmental red tape prevents you from committing cannibalism."

"Did you know that I love your sarcasm?"

I raised my eyebrows. "Are you being sarcastic?"

"No."

"Humph."

"Do you have more questions still, Stella? You've been putting me through the Spanish Inquisition today. Complete with dismemberment."

"What did you expect?"

"No one expects the Spanish Inquisition. So, do you have more to ask me?"

"I'm temporarily exhausted. I'll think of more in a minute."

"I'll take it." He reached out and touched me gently on the elbow, and my skin tingled at his touch. "I love that you don't mindlessly accept startling information. I love that you ask questions. I love that you kicked me over and stood on me rather than bursting into hysterical tears. Everything you do, I seem to love. In fact, I think I'm falling in love... with you."

He was only slightly taller than me. He smelled like chemistry. My heart was still thumping so hard that it felt like it was trying to burst out of my chest.

"I am in love with you," he said.

What the hell, I thought. I leaned in and kissed him.

I bet you're all wondering what it's like to kiss a zombie. My problem is, I hadn't kissed a non-zombie before, so that makes it hard to compare.

What I can tell you is how smooth and soft his lips felt on mine, and how he gasped slightly as our mouths met. His hand tightened on my elbow for a moment, and then he put his arms right around my waist and pulled me close. I felt a warm glow like a light had gone on inside me.

Then he shuddered and pulled away.

"What's wrong?" I asked, feeling my cheeks grow hot. Did I kiss wrong? Oh my God. A half-dead zombie was going to reject me. I was going to kick his ass.

"Nothing in the world," he said quickly, reaching out to stroke my cheek with his hand and tuck a stray lock of hair behind my ear. The gesture was so gentle and tender that it did squirmy things to my insides. His hands weren't freakishly cold, but comfortingly cool to the touch, like the fresh side of a pillowcase. His lips were parted and he was breathing heavily.

"...Is everything okay?"

"More than okay, but I need a minute," he said, his voice slightly raspy. He gazed intently at my face, staring at me as though he wanted to drink me in. I realized that he probably wanted just that.

"Are you thinking about eating me?"

He laughed shakily, staggered, then slowly bent his body to sit on the bed. He picked up his shirt and slipped it back on, and looked up at me while he fumbled with the buttons.

"Let's just say certain desires were starting to get the upper hand."

I started to feel concerned for my safety again, and I tightened my hold on the cleaver, which had been dangling loosely in my hand. "Do you actually crave people, or do your cow brains or whatever fill you up?"

"No," Howie looked down. "Human brains are what the virus is most attuned to, so the brain waves of a person are much more attractive than those of, say, a bird or a dog. And don't forget, the brains thing is actually the human in us, trying to stay human. The virus just craves flesh - ideally, human flesh."

"Should I go, then, if you're having urges to bite me? I don't want to turn into Van Gogh."

"No." He took my hand in both of his and massaged it adoringly. "I have never hurt anyone, and I will never hurt you. I give you my heart. Literally, if you want. You still have a cleaver."

"That won't be necessary, but thanks." I put it down.

"It wouldn't even kill me. How many boys out there could literally offer you their hearts?"

"Not many, but I bet some would offer their hearts figuratively while misusing the word 'literally'."

"Well, I know the difference when I'm not too hungry, so all the more reason to be with me."

I put my hands on my hips. "You're saying that if you were 'too hungry', you could misuse the word 'literally'? That might be a deal breaker."

"I should probably make this clear. My smarts are directly related to how much I've had to, uh, drink, lately. That first day we met, that's me when I haven't eaten a whole lot. The second day, slightly more. I've basically been stuffing myself ever since to keep up with you."

"Okay..."

"So if I say or do something stupid, just chalk it up to needing more nutrients. Give me a swift drink and I'll be as smart as you want me to be. I'm no moron. I'm just... brain damaged. As the virus eats away at things, I get dumber."

"I wish I could drink a nutrient shake and suddenly get smarter."

"Stella, you're smart all the time. No complaining. Smart, and sexy, and swift to kick a guy in the chest when he comes at her with a knife. Am I the luckiest guy on the planet or what, huh?"

He reached out and pulled me down to sit next to him on the bed. He looked me up and down and took a heaving breath. "God, I'm so lucky."

I leaned in to kiss him again, and this time the warm glow filled my whole body and burned hotter and hotter.

The rest of that afternoon is a bit of a blur.

I was home by five. Dad was cooking some kind of stir fry while Mom sipped coffee at the kitchen table.

"So? How was it?" Mom asked the second I walked in the door. "You were gone a long time."

"It was fine."

"Oh?" The subsequent pause was so heavily pregnant that it nearly had silence puppies all over our floor. That metaphor needs work, but you know what I mean.

"Yep. I'm going to go call Jeremy."

Let them wonder. Maybe there are girls who come home and give their parents graphic details of their love lives. If those girls exist, I had no intention of joining their weird little club.

Instead, I called Jeremy and told him everything.

Well, except the zombie stuff.

I told him the family was "creepy" and that Howie had a disease that meant he had to eat a special diet.

"Oh God, Stella, that's not going to do anything for your popularity at school. You're dating the loser kid who can't eat chocolate and is allergic to everything? NO ONE DATES THAT KID."

"I know, I know," I moaned. "But Jeremy, he's just so... he's so into me! Does that sound wrong? Is it wrong to date someone just because they are completely obsessed with you?"

"That depends. Does he have a shrine to you in his bedroom?"

"Not that I saw."

"Is he stalking you?"

"He showed up at a used bookstore randomly. He might have followed us there. It also might have been a coincidence."

"So, he hasn't broken into your room to watch you sleep or anything?"

"No! At least, not that I know of!"

"Then go for it. He's nice, you think he's cute, why not go for him?"

"I don't know. I don't want to date someone just because they're the first person to show any interest in me."

"Better than dating someone who hasn't shown that much interest. Besides, I'm pretty sure Devin Schofield had a thing for you in grade nine."

"Yuck! He smells bad AND he's thicker than two short planks."

"See? You don't jump for just *anyone* who might have a crush on you. Stop trying to talk yourself out of being happy, Stella. Jesus. Do you know what I'd do if I found a guy who was that into me? You'd better sit back because this is going to get graphic."

"That's quite all right, I get the picture."

"It would involve teabagging and a lot of sweating."

"That's quite all right!"

"Possibly snowballing."

"THANK YOU!"

"Why are you such a prude when you hang out with people like Liz and me?"

"Maybe it's rebellion against you guys."

"And maybe you're so repressed that you enjoy our sexual abandon."

"I'm not repressed. I have dignity and a tendency towards pickiness."

"So... in other words... you're repressed."

"I'M NOT REPRESSED!"

"Are you getting angry?"

"A little!"

"That's all part of your repression. Listen, Stella, you've only ever let Liz and me in. You push everyone else away. I think you should stop trying to talk yourself out of it and let this Howie guy in. And I mean that literally as well as metaphorically."

"I miss you guys."

"Come on home. But bring Howie with you. Alternatively, post pictures ASAP... Of his penis."

When I came back downstairs, my parents were watching TV.

"We ate without you. Dinner's on the stove."

"Thanks, I wanted to call before it got too late back home."

"How's Jeremy?"

"He's good."

"How's Howie?"

"Subtle, Dad. Slipped it right in there and I DIDN'T EVEN NOTICE. He's fine too. No signs of being hit by a car." I went and got myself a plate of Dad's stir-fry. I was ravenous. Howie hadn't offered much in the way of refreshment.

"So, did you find out if he's a zombie?"

"Yep, he's a zombie."

"He admitted it?"

"Yup, his whole family admitted to it. They're actually relics from the 1950s and they can regenerate, which is why the car didn't kill him. They've had the zombie virus for decades so they're all really old. Howie's robbing the cradle."

"Forget the Nerf rifle, it sounds like I'll need a shotgun. Isn't that the weapon of choice against zombies?"

"Oh, it's okay, they're recovering zombies. They won't be starting the zombie apocalypse because of something to do with science."

"I prefer the term 'zompocalypse'," said my mother. "I love a good portmanteau."

"Noted."

"I remain unconvinced," said Dad. "You'd better warn Howie that if he starts drooling over you in our presence we may need to take steps to prevent the end of the world."

"I'll be sure to pass that along to him." I took a bite of dinner and wondered how long it would take for my parents to get tired of my zombie joke. Until then, I could tell them the truth. Not my fault if they took it all as playful banter. I judged Howie less now for just rolling with it when I thought it was all a game. It made things easier.

I heard my cell phone go off, and I hopped out of my chair to check it.

-

Hope I put your number in right. I'll see you in my dreams tonight. I am in love with you.

-

I put the phone back in my purse and sat back down, trying not to smile. My parents watched me closely.

"So," Dad said overly-casually, "when will you be seeing your zombie friend again?"

"I haven't decided. What are our plans for tomorrow?"

I woke up feeling girlishly giddy. I had drifted off to sleep replaying the memory of Howie's lips on mine again and again, and when I opened my eyes in the morning, the memory came flooding back. I felt almost dizzy. I had a boyfriend. *Me.*

At least, I assumed. I mean, a guy cuts off his hand and tells you he loves you, and then you make out – that basically means you're dating, right?

And sure, okay, so he was brain damaged, socially stilted and had a potentially contagious virus which was so horrific that the world thought it was fictional. But he was smart, and he was gentle, and he had the shyest, sweetest smile, and when he put his arms around me I felt like springtime.

I know that doesn't make any sense, but it was how I felt.

I was eating cereal dreamily in my fuzzy kitten-and-puppies pajamas, trying to think of a better way to mentally describe the bubbles of excitement in my chest, when there was a knock at the door.

My mother opened it to reveal Howie, standing on the stoop and clutching a bouquet of red roses.

"Mrs. Blunt? How are you this morning?"

"Fine, thank you, Howie. Uh, do you want to come in?"

"Mom! I'm in my pajamas!" I hissed. There was no escape. I'd have to pass the front door on my bolt from the kitchen, and Howie was already stepping inside. He looked right at me and his eyes lit up, and for a moment he just stood there, staring at me and swaying slightly.

"Howie, it's ten in the morning," I said. "FYI, I don't do mornings."

"Sorry, Stella."

"Why are you here at such an ungodly hour, and *when did I tell you my address*?"

He glanced awkwardly at my mother, and she slipped out of the room with an annoying little smirk on her face. He sat down next to me at the breakfast table, laying the roses next to my cereal bowl.

"You didn't tell me. I just followed you." His speech sounded slightly slurred.

"You mean when I left yesterday? That's fucked up, Howie."

"No. You. Your mind. This morning. I followed you. Are you happy?"

"At the moment, Howie, I have to say, I'm a little cheesed. My hair is a mess, I'm in my pajamas, I just woke up, and I have a stalker. I'm not really ready to entertain socially peculiar guests."

"When I woke up this morning, I felt like the whole world was singing. I followed it to you."

"I don't even sing in the shower, Howie."

"All I can think about is you."

I hoped to God my parents weren't eavesdropping. "Not now, okay, Howie?"

He nodded and continued to stare at me, entranced.

"Sooo... I'm going to go get dressed and brush my hair."

"No, eat your breakfast. I'll be quiet."

"It's not a matter of noise, Howie, it's the fact that I don't have clothes on."

"I think you look wonderful. Please eat."

So I ate while he rested his head on his hands and watched me with adoration. I felt like the Mona Lisa but with bed head. It's impossible not to be horribly self-aware when someone is staring at you that intently.

"Howie?"

"Mmm?"

"Have you… eaten today?"

"They cut me off. I ate two weeks' worth of food in the last seven days."

"They cut you *off*?"

"Mmm hmmm."

"Won't you… I mean, can't you… um… get sick?"

"Oh, I'm not cut off for long, but then I'm going to be rationed for a while. I'm sorry."

"Why are you apologizing?"

"I won't be smart 'nough for you. Probably should've stayed home, but I was so happy and I wanted to see you."

"I… see."

He lapsed into reverent silence again. I crunched my cereal and stared at the flowers. Then I decided that this was stupid, and if he was going to stare at me, I could damn well stare back at him.

He might not be at his most alert, but his face was as earnest as ever, his smile as sweet, and his button-down shirt looked ironed and his hair was freshly washed and still damp.

Maybe he didn't care how I looked, but he had taken a shower and dressed carefully before coming to see me. Hypocrite.

When I scraped the bottom of my cereal bowl, he stood up and took it from me.

"Let me get you more."

"No, I'm finished."

"No more?"

"No, thank you! Why are you offering me hospitality in my own house?"

"I just want to be useful."

A few minutes later I met my mother on the stairs.

"I'm going to take a quick shower."

"Where's your friend?"

"Washing our breakfast dishes."

By the time I came back downstairs, with clothes on and everything this time, Howie had finished the dishes and had moved on to cleaning the counter. He was moving the microwave to clean underneath it when I walked in. My mother's eyebrows were climbing into her hairline. When she saw me she rolled her eyes at him and mouthed, *"Is he for real?"*

I mouthed back, *"Not really sure."*

"Is there anything else I can do, Mrs. Blunt?" he asked robotically as he wrung out the dishcloth and hung it carefully on the faucet to dry.

"No, uh, thank you, Howie."

"Stella, if you've no other plans, d'you want to go out with me today?"

"I dunno. Where to?"

"Wherever you like."

"Can you take me to Paris?"

He frowned thoughtfully. "Prob'ly not today. I'd have to check available funds and flights."

"Howie, I was kidding."

"Oh. Then so was I."

For frig's sake. Why did my mother have to see Hungry Howie? If it wasn't for the fact that part of me wanted to get him alone so I could run my hands over his body again, I think I would've gotten fed up and kicked him out. But there was just something about the dishtowel flung casually over his shoulder that I was finding irresistibly delicious.

"Mind if I go out, Mom?"

"I guess not. Call if you're going to be home after supper, will you?"

"I will."

"Take care of her, Howie," said Dad, walking into the room.

Howie looked at him with mild surprise. "She can take care of herself, Mr. Blunt."

"Not if you're the one driving the car."

"I swear I'll value her life over my own."

"Good man." Dad glanced quickly at my V-neck shirt. "Stella, don't you want to wear a sweater?"

"NO, DAD."

"Ah well." Dad sighed and winked at Howie, who looked non-plussed.

"I don't understand."

"GOOD, LET'S GO." I gave him a little shove toward the door. He dragged his feet, turning to wave goodbye to my parents.

"Thank you," he called.

"Howie, shut up! They're going to think you're weird."

"D'you get cold easily? Is your coat not warm enough? Maybe your father was right about the sweater."

"He was teasing me that my cleavage was showing because he DOESN'T LOVE ME."

"Based on his brain waves, he loves you very much."

"Based on his... wait, can you read minds?"

"Not really. Just brain waves."

"Pretend for a minute that I don't know what brain waves sound like."

"You can tell if someone's asleep or awake, anxious or relaxed, that sort of thing. Your father feels love looking at you. I can't tell you what he was thinking. Your mother felt surprised and amused."

"Do you have brain waves? I mean, can your whole family feel each other's... whatevers?"

"Zombies brain waves feel different."

"How far away can you feel these? You said you tracked me from your house? Because you should know – that's creepy and stalkerish."

"Sorry. I knocked and came in. It's not like I hung outside, peering in the window."

Fair point. "That's what you did at the bookstore, isn't it? You stalked my brain waves?"

He shook his head no. "Uh-uh. I was going to get you a book. Thought you'd like a book as a gift. Felt you there when I got close."

"Hmm. Okay. So you can't just follow me all over town? You have to be close by?"

"Different people have different strengths of waves. They get louder or quieter sometimes. Yours felt 'specially loud this morning."

"Why?"

"I'd explain better if I wasn't hungry. I think maybe because I was tuned in to you? Or maybe you're happy and that is making you loud. You get loud when you're angry, too."

I *was* happy. Even with my zombie boyfriend being all weird in front of my parents, even with him showing up at my house slurring his words like a drunk, I was happy.

He was cute, he loved me, and I had successfully kissed a boy without anything terrible happening.

"Kiss me, Howie."

He stopped, turned, and heartily obliged. It was as awesome as I remembered it being.

After a minute he pulled back and took a deep breath. "I love you. I could do this all day."

"Fine by me. Maybe not so close to my parents' house though."

"Mmm. I parked my car around the corner."

"Then let's get out of here."

He took my hand and we half-ran around the building to the street corner, where we ran into something grey, lurching, and scary as hell.

11

The person wasn't walking right, and when we came around the corner he – it – sped up, and reached out for me, and its mouth opened and this moan that wasn't really a moan so much as rattling expulsion of air came out.

It was indescribably terrifying. If you've ever watched a horror movie that made you want to go home and scrub your brain, this was worse.

I freaked out and kicked it in the chest and then again in the stomach, and it fell back, but it didn't fall over. Instead, it kept moving forward like a puppet on strings, and I backed up with my hands up in a block and my mouth open in a silent scream.

Then Howie stepped forward, pulled something shiny out of his pocket, placed it against the back of the person's head, and the thing dropped to the ground, twitched once in a way that I felt would haunt me for years, and lay still.

I found my voice. "WHAT THE HELL IS THAT?"

Howie licked his lips. "Undead. I need to call home."

"YOU THINK? WHAT THE EVERLASTING FUCK?"

He put the shiny thing away and reached out to me. "Are you okay?"

"NO!"

He looked surprised, then frightened. "Where? Where did it get you?" He spoke quickly. His voice sounded more emotional now than it had in all of his professions of love.

"It didn't *get* me, it scared the figurative crap out of me!"

He sighed with relief, pulled me close, then yanked out a tiny cell phone, and dialed a number. "Dad? Z0381E alert. YES. I just put it down. It nearly got Stella..." his voice cracked, and I thought I saw him shudder. "Okay. Okay. Please hurry, Dad..." He hung up. "Stella... Dad says to call 911. Tell them you saw a man fall over in the street. Tell them you think he might be dead. Then hang up."

"THAT'S NOT WHAT HAPPENED, HOWARD. HOW THE HELL DID YOU KILL IT?"

"Stella, can you do me a favour? Please stop shouting. You'll attract attention."

"Howie, can you do me a favour and explain to me why no one I know has ever run into a zombie in the history of ever, but I walk into one less than twenty-four hours after learning that they even exist?"

"No."

"Fuck you."

"I don't mean I won't, I mean I've no idea. Cases are so rare."

"Are you saying this could possibly be a coincidence?"

"Must be."

"I don't buy that."

"Please call 911, Stella. They won't believe me if I call. I... I wouldn't sound convincing."

I tried to imagine a 911 operator hearing Howie's monotone voice blandly reporting a sudden death in the street.

"Fuck."

I pulled out my new cell phone and dialed 911. The automated system wanted me to choose between police and ambulance, and I picked ambulance.

"911, what is your emergency?"

"I need an ambulance!" I said, glancing at the body. "I think a man just died."

"What is your location?"

I gave the address and told the woman that he'd just fallen over in front of us and that he wasn't breathing. Then I hung up, giving Howie a dirty look.

"I'll be in trouble for that. I don't think you're supposed to just hang up on 911."

"Probably happens all the time," said Howie. "Dad said to fake CPR till they get here."

"Oh God, Howard, that's gross. I'm not going near... THAT."

He gave me a shocked look. "Course not. It's infectious. I'll do it."

He lifted the body effortlessly and carried it to the grass. He began to do chest compressions with occasional mouth-to-mouth breaths. The dead zombie's eyes were open and staring. Every time I saw its chest rise with air from Howie's lungs, I felt sick.

"Howie... what about the paramedics, when they get here? Won't they... couldn't they..." I wondered if paramedics were at a high risk of getting zombified from saliva.

"They'll have masks and stuff," Howie answered.

A car pulled up and I panicked. What do you say to a neighbour when they find your boyfriend doing CPR on someone who looks like they've been dead for over a day? But Dr. Mullins hopped out and went to bend over the body while Howie worked away mechanically on it.

Ray and Hazel climbed out of the car, too. Great. Just what this scene needed. More zombies.

I could hear the wail of an ambulance in the distance and soon it blasted up the street and pulled up near the body. The paramedics jumped out and Howie stepped aside. Sure enough, they had a mask to put on the body's face and they started attaching electric paddles to the chest to try and stimulate the heart.

Howie came and put his arm around me. I wasn't sure if he was trying to comfort me or seeking comfort.

"Howie, could… could they…?"

"Brain's dead. Nothing they could do'll wake it up."

Then a couple came out of their townhouse and looked in our direction.

"Oh, good, just what we need: Spectators," said Ray, joining us.

"Let them watch," said Howie.

But then, a black car with a police siren came screaming up and screeched to a stop next to the ambulance. Three men in black swat-team style gear jumped out and ran up to the paramedics. They quickly cleared a perimeter and shooed people away. One of them stopped to talk to Dr. Mullins, while another started to talk to the paramedics.

"Wow, they really don't trust us," said Ray.

"Who? Why? *What the fuck is going on?*"

"Nice mouth your girlfriend's got, Howie," said Ray. "Real genteel."

"Did you stick to words like 'gosh' and 'darn' the first time you saw one of those?" Howie asked, pointing to the body.

There was a moment of silence. Ray's mouth twisted. "No."

I tried again. "So, who are those guys?"

Ray cleared his throat. "Virus Response. Dad called them, but it's not like you have a squad sitting in a car ready to go in every city in Canada twenty-four seven. If they got here that fast, that means they must keep our local area manned with more people, in case we go bonkers or something."

Dr. Mullins walked over to us. "Howie, we need to get Stella out of here before they find out how much she has learned. They're already asking me questions."

I folded my arms. "Why in the name of God's goopy rectum are they asking YOU anything? You weren't here," I said.

Dr. Mullins nodded at me gravely. "Good morning, Stella. Your mind was in fine tune this morning."

Oh for fuck's sake. I was going to have to get a tinfoil hat or something.

Dr. Mullins cleared his throat. "Stella, I am going to have to ask you to dissemble when the squad gets here. It would... make our position more awkward if you appear to be in possession of classified information. Do you understand?"

"I hate lying."

Howie held me tighter. "Please, Stella."

One of the Zombie-SWAT team guys was swaggering our way.

"Fine!" I snapped.

The man squinted at Howie and me suspiciously as he approached.

Howie nodded at the man. "Hi, Agent Baum."

I tried to look surprised and perplexed, but it may have just come across as constipated.

"Who's this?" the man asked, gesturing at me.

"This is Stella," Howie said, moving in front of me slightly as if to hide me, which was stupid because it was like trying to hide an elephant behind a telephone pole. "She's... a little confused."

The man looked at me. "Do you want to tell me what happened? I understand you called 911. Good for you! That's good civic spirit." I half expected him to pat me on the head and offer me a lollipop.

"We were heading to Howie's car and this man came out of the bushes and... started to fall, and Howie went to help him, I think," I sent a glance at Howie, "but he fell. I called 911 and Howie gave him CPR."

"Isn't that nice of him," said the man, eyeing Howie as if he were a particularly large and pungent dog turd. "Now, I need to have a few words with him, too, if you would excuse us."

I gave Howie a dirty look and walked away.

After a couple of minutes, the SWAT guy went back to the others. They climbed into their car and followed the ambulance out of the parking lot. No sirens now. The body had probably been declared very, very dead.

Dr. Mullins, Ray, Howie, and Hazel walked right over to me.

"Okay, what did I just miss?"

"He needed the real version of events," said Dr. Mullins. "Which Howie gave him."

"I HATE playing dumb, and I hate lying, and you just asked me to do BOTH."

"I know you hated it," said Dr. Mullins, "but it was necessary."

"HOW do you know what I hate? YOU JUST MET ME!"

Howie tapped his head. "Remember?"

"We appreciate it, Stella," said Dr. Mullins gravely, "Agent Baum was extremely interested in you and your relationship with Howie and was openly disapproving. It would have been very…"

"CAN SOMEONE ANSWER MY QUESTIONS NOW?"

"I doubt that we can, but we will endeavour to do so," said Dr. Mullins. "But not here. Somewhere private."

So that's how I ended up back at Howie's house again, getting drooled on by a large dog while I barraged them with questions I never thought I'd ask, like, "What was that thing you used to kill the zombie?"

Howie pulled something small and silver out of his pocket. It looked like a bullet vibrator that Liz bought online last year. "Brain disruptor."

"It sends a jolt of electricity deep into the brain and permanently damages the neural tissue," explained his father. "Aimed at the right spot, it works instantly."

"And you just carry this around?"

"Yes. Just in case. Technically they're for use on ourselves or each other in case we suddenly begin to progress in our disease again. Government orders."

"Is that LIKELY?"

"No."

"Are you sure? Are you sure that this doesn't have anything to do with the fact that Howie is slurring his words and having difficulty with sentences with more than three words in them? Maybe he went crazy and bit people on his way to my house!"

"Nonsense. Howie has only missed two meals, and he is still taking his formalin injections on schedule. Even if he was infectious, and attacked a person, the infection takes hours and sometimes days to take hold in the victim."

"Why have you cut off his meals, anyway? I could use him coherent."

Howie gave me a wounded look.

"Howie consumed double the normal number of rations in the last week, trying to impress you," said Dr. Mullins. "We don't want to 'cut him off', but the fact is his rations are now reduced."

"Rations? What is this, war?"

"We can't exactly pop out to the Seven Eleven when we get low on brains," said Ray. "We stock up once a month. That's it."

"Okay, then can you tell me why everywhere I turn lately, there's zombies? Is British Columbia just, like, crawling with them?"

"No. Cases are very rare in all provinces. It is an extremely unlikely coincidence."

"THEN MAYBE IT'S NOT A COINCIDENCE."

"I am open to suggestions, Stella," said Dr. Mullins. "But I have no further explanation."

"THE ZOMBIE APOCALYPSE COULD BE STARTING AND YOU HAVE NO EXPLANATIONS?"

"This is not an apocalypse. This is an isolated case."

I opened my mouth to yell some more, but Howie roused suddenly.

"I was going to take Stella on a date."

"I think that's a good idea, Howie," said Dr. Mullins. "Until she calms down."

"I HAVE NO INTENTION OF CALMING DOWN."

"Then let's get in my car and you can be loud there," said Howie. "D'you want to get some lunch?"

I allowed myself to be ushered to Howie's ancient, rusting beater. He yanked the passenger door open for me.

"Are you even okay to drive?" I asked.

"I drove you here."

"Yeah, but A, that's like a two-minute drive and B, I was too busy freaking out to remember that you have no self-preservation and that you are having trouble making simple sentences right now."

"I'm hungry, not drunk. I'd never put you in danger. Ever."

"Except for all the zombies."

"Hey," he said. He looked hurt.

I got in the car. "Okay, but if I don't like how you drive I'm making you pull over."

"Deal," he said, giving me a little smile. "Where d'you wanna eat?"

"I'm not hungry for lunch, Howie. I just saw you kill someone who was already dead. I'm a LITTLE upset."

"Just want to get you away. No point dwelling on it."

"Do you always drop your personal pronouns when you're hungry?"

"Dunno."

"Seriously, Howie, when are you going to be able to speak full sentences? Because I need to talk to someone about this, and not your freak show family."

"Hey," he said again.

"Okay, I know, they're nice enough but they're zombies, and they're weird, and WHY THE FUCK WAS I JUST ATTACKED BY A ZOMBIE?"

He let me rant. He drove and he listened while I shouted and demanded answers to questions that he didn't know the answers to, and I know he was actually listening because he'd put in something small but pertinent every now and then, just to show that he cared.

His driving was fine, too. I'd almost call it robotic. No rolling stops. No running yellow lights. He followed all the rules of the road with precision, from shoulder checks to stopping for pedestrians, without even seeming to think about it. Maybe mindless driving isn't always a bad thing.

By the time I calmed down, the car had made its way up a mountain, and was pulling into a parking lot near a lot of totem poles. Beyond the totem poles, the city of Vancouver spread out below us. Beyond the city was the ocean, and snow-covered peaks.

I have to say, Nova Scotia didn't have views like this one.

Howie pointed. "That's a restaurant at the top of the hill. I have a thermos."

"I'm still not really hungry."

"They have cheesecake."

"You're on."

Howie drew some nasty looks from the staff for bringing his own drink, but he explained that he had special needs and encouraged me to order as much as I wanted, and they let it pass.

Once he started drinking, his intellect picked up significantly and we could actually have a real conversation.

"Do you have any enemies?" I asked.

"What do you mean?"

"Enemies, Howie. People who don't like you. People who are not friendly."

"Most people don't like me. I don't count them as enemies. Why?"

"I dunno. Just, maybe someone created a zombie and sicked it on you and your girlfriend for a joke?"

"There are people out there who'd use the zombie virus as a biological weapon, but not against me and my family. Very few people know what we are – only the relevant government officials and upper members of Z0381E Intelligence, Research and Control. Besides, it's not like you can just aim a zombie where you want it. Once they're in that state, they're mindless attacking machines. They go toward anything with human brain function."

"Like you?"

"The virus announces itself in our brain waves. It wouldn't prefer me as a victim, but since they bite practically anything that gets close, I'd also be at risk. Of being bitten that is. Not that it'd really matter."

"Well, I don't think it's a coincidence. I mean, what are the chances of me running into a zombie just DAYS after meeting you?"

"Gambler's fallacy."

"What's that, now?"

"The gambler's fallacy. Gamblers often think that their past luck influences their future luck. 'Oh, I've rolled a seven three times, so it'd be very unlikely to roll another seven.'"

"Oh, I get it," I said. "When really, the chances are the same each time. Like, the chance of a woman having four sons in a row is really low, but if she already has three sons, the chance of having that fourth son is still fifty-fifty."

"Right," said Howie. "So, the chance of you meeting me is incredibly small. But having done so, your chance of running into an infected person is still the same as anyone else living in a major city."

"Which is?"

"Still very, very, very slim. You get maybe a case a year in Vancouver. Less."

"And I got to meet that one case within days of meeting you. It still seems like very bad luck."

"Do you feel like we talk about zombies a lot? Because I do, and I feel like there's more to talk about in this world." He rubbed his foot against mine and my heart thumped in response. "Like you. Your favourite books. Music. Math. Whatever you like to talk about."

"See, now, how can you tell me you love me and not know whether I'd rather talk about math or books?"

"Knowing you, it'd probably depend on your mood. After all, we just had a conversation about statistics. Before this weekend, would you have expected to spend so much time voluntarily discussing zombies?"

"Point taken."

We talked about books. *Jane Eyre* vs *Pride and Prejudice*. I liked *Jane Eyre*. He preferred *Pride and Prejudice*.

"*Jane Eyre* is more feminist," I argued.

"Jane is an excellent feminist character," agreed Howie, "But Mr. Rochester is a dominating liar. Mr. Darcy is a better person, and I like romances better when I actually respect both people involved."

"Rochester is awesome! He falls in love with his unattractive governess based entirely on her wit and inner strength, and he isn't afraid to flaunt society to do it. That's real love."

"Mr. Darcy loves Elizabeth just as much. He just doesn't run around roaring her name and threatening to shake her, and he doesn't weave elaborate fictions just to toy with her emotions."

"Darcy was ashamed of loving a pretty woman because she had embarrassing relatives. You call that love? Darcy is a snob."

"The fact that he overcame a life of snobbery to fall in love with someone like Elizabeth shows how deep his love for her was. What does it matter that Rochester was willing to flout social convention to be with Jane? He hated convention. The man had already married a lunatic and had serial mistresses."

By the time I finished my cheesecake, we had moved on to disagreeing over whether Wilbur the pig had deserved everything that Charlotte the spider did for him. I thought that Wilbur was a useless layabout who had never held up his side of the friendship. Howie said that friendship isn't about keeping score.

I was loving the argument, so I scowled when Howie's ancient phone went off. I pointed at the phone. "Is that a Nokia? Did you know there's a whole meme based on those phones? I've never actually seen one in real life."

"I don't know what a meme is. Sorry, I need to take this. It's Dad." He pressed a button - it had *buttons!*- and put it to his ear. "Dad? I'm out with Stella. What's up?"

He looked increasingly agitated as his father talked.

"Okay, yeah, I'm coming," he said. "Bye."

He put the phone away and looked at me.

"So, date's over, then?" I asked.

"Family emergency," he said grimly, dropping some bills on the table and standing up.

"Your family is immortal. What kind of emergencies can you have?"

"Really, really, bad ones."

"Are you going to tell me what this is about?" I asked as we rushed out of the restaurant. But before he could answer, we ran right into two more zombies.

You can safely assume that we were taken by surprise. You can also take for granted that I lost my shit. It's almost impossible to explain to you how goddamn terrifying these things were. "Oh, zombies, haha," you might think, but let me tell you, when you see something that should not be alive coming at you with unstoppable hunger in its eyes, it kicks you in three instincts all at once: The natural fear of death and dying, the instinct to stay away from the contagious and the mentally unstable, and the instinct to get the fuck away from whatever is coming to eat you.

The zombies were aiming directly at me. One of them seemed to have lost half of its face somehow, and bone and flesh were baldly exposed on that side. The other one had no shoes and the feet were bloody messes. Neither seemed to be at all unhappy about their injuries, which made it even scarier. Their mouths were open and their teeth bared, and they were doing this creepy fast shuffle that would've been hilarious in a normal human being.

Howie let go of my hand. "Stay here," he ordered, and he ran to the first zombie and used his device against its head. The other one turned and grabbed at him, and for a moment they wrestled before Howie got his hand on its head and it dropped, too. Then he looked back at me and shouted something, pointing over my shoulder.

I turned just as a foul smell reached my nostrils, and a hand grabbed my shoulder in an iron-strong grip. There was a gurgling moan near my ear. I spun and crouched, wrenching myself from the zombie's clutches, and brought my leg up in a spinning kick to the head. There was a sickening crunch and the zombie opened its mouth once more, let out a sigh, and toppled like a felled tree.

"Eat that!"

"Are you okay? Did he bite you?" Howie snatched me and pulled me backwards. I elbowed him automatically but he didn't even grunt.

"I'm fine. He didn't bite me." I stared down at the body which now just looked like a sad old man. A very dead sad old man. I took deep breaths, trying to calm down, while Howie held me.

"Stella, we have to split. This is so bad."

"Don't we have to wait for your SWAT team to show up again?"

"There's no hiding this. A restaurant full of people saw it happen. They've likely called the cops."

"Let's get in the car."

"Yes. Now."

We sped back down the mountain, leaving behind three dead people and a lot of people who had been put off their lunch.

"You realize what this means?" asked Dr. Mullins, pacing. "It can only mean an outbreak of epic proportions."

As I had already guessed, the reason Howie had been called home in the first place was that another zombie had turned up somewhere which was considered to be *very bad*.

"There was your encounter this morning, a second incident downtown, and then you ran into three more? Disastrous."

"So, one zombie and you guys aren't concerned, but five and you're in a panic?"

I wasn't ranting or raving this time. This seemed like it was beyond the scope of ranting and raving. Before today, I might not have thought that possible.

Dr. Mullins raised his eyebrows. "We were always concerned, Stella. But one is an isolated incident. Five people in three different locations is an outbreak."

"Like, zompocalypse level?"

"No. An outbreak. It will be contained as quickly as possible."

"So, your secrecy thing is going to be in tatters, huh? I mean, a whole restaurant full of people saw us get attacked by zombies."

"It will be hushed up."

"How can you POSSIBLY hush up something like that?"

"It's done all the time," said Howie. "The zombie wasn't a zombie, he was a schizophrenic on a day pass from the mental institution, or he was on drugs, or he had rabies…"

"Isn't it a problem when the zombie in question turns out to be a well-respected family man or someone's grandmother?"

"Money solves a lot of problems. Even better, they give out a fake name for the "official" report and tell the actual family a totally different story. If the person was thought dead already, it's really easy. Just bring the body back and don't say anything about a connection to that attacking-schizophrenic story in the paper."

"I still think it'd be better to stop trying to keep this a big secret."

"And have people killing strangers in the street? 'Oh, he was walking funny, I thought it was a zombie.' Have you driven through the parts of Hastings Street where all the homeless are? It'd be a bloodbath. Meanwhile, people would be hiding their schizophrenic teenagers in the attic in case the doctors decide that it's not schizophrenia, it's the zombie virus."

"They'd only hide family members if the only 'cure' is death. But there IS a cure. Or at least, a treatment."

Howie threw up his hands. "Okay, so now you have a bunch of people who actually want to get the zombie virus so they can become immortal, and now you've got street zombie virus being sold along with jars of formalin, and people who live for forty or fifty years before they forget to inject themselves for a couple of weeks and end up starting a plague. No, no matter which way you look at it, the government stands to lose by letting people know it's real or allowing access to our treatment."

"Besides," said Ray, "They'd rather not end up with a bunch of senior citizens who can collect the government pension for eternity."

Dr. Mullins glanced at his phone. He had placed several calls and was waiting for an update. Then he sat at the kitchen table and looked back at me. "You need to understand, Stella, that outbreaks are usually small and easy to contain – an incident of one infected person biting another person, and a 911 call. It is hard to get a true 'apocalypse' rolling because people generally call the police when someone attacks them. I haven't seen five turn up in a single day for... well, for a very long time."

"They'll blame us," said Ray.

"They will not blame us. They trust us," said Dr. Mullins.

"You think Baum trusts us?" Ray asked.

"Maybe not, but Agent Hunt and I have worked together for many years. In any case, it is a simple enough test to prove that we are not infectious."

"If not you, then what starts outbreaks?"

Dr. Mullins shrugged. "Most of the time, the origin point is not identified. It has sometimes been found in small animals in the wild – usually submitted for rabies testing and then diverted to our department. Outbreaks are more common in certain third world countries and occasionally travel via tourists. There is also always the concern of deliberate release by terrorists or a hostile nation."

"What about, like, accidental release? I read in the news once that they found, like, vials of smallpox in the back of some fridge in a totally not-approved lab. Could that happen? Or… do researchers ever get infected and go on the rampage?"

"One of the more fortunate outcomes of my accident in the lab has been the fact that they now have a lead researcher who cannot be infected. I am in charge of the more dangerous experiments, and access to my lab is strictly limited to a few high-level personnel for that reason. Viral sample vials exist but are even more strictly controlled. I find the paperwork to access them tedious and prefer to simply maintain an infected population in my lab, and spread the virus directly from lab animal to lab animal."

"And they couldn't get out, right?"

A cell phone rang, and Dr. Mullins reached for it quickly. He fumbled with it for a moment, as if trying to remember how it worked. Howie reached out and swiped the screen. His father nodded thanks and put the phone to his ear.

"Morton Mullins speaking." He listened intently. Then he sat upright. "That... that is not possible," he said. His fingers gripped the table tightly. "I... Michaela... I don't know how... I was there yesterday morning to feed them and check their progress and they were all... no, of course not. I log all experimental procedures with you... absolutely not, why would I... you can test the brain mash in the dispenser..." I could hear an angry woman's voice now. Dr. Mullins visibly wilted under the tirade. "Of course. I completely understand. I can't see how this could happen... Please ask Agent Baum to check the entry logs. Which one is it? Number Twenty-Two? I'm so sorry... It makes no sense... Yes, I will. Yes. Goodbye."

He hung up and stared at his phone with a haggard look.

I folded my arms. "One got out, eh?"

12

The Mullinses were in uproar. Except, they couldn't actually sound angry or upset so they were just talking in loud, unexcited voices.

"Are you sure they were all there yesterday?"

"Raymond, I may be over a hundred years old, but I am not senile. Of course, they were all there. According to Agent Hunt, when she sent a team to check the lab they found Number Twenty-Two's cage bars bent open and he was gone."

"It's probably hiding under a table or something," said Ray.

Dr. Mullins looked at Howie. "You said the second attack happened on Burnaby Mountain?"

He nodded.

Dr. Mullins ran his hands through his hair and then covered his face. "I can't understand it. They're sending someone over to interrogate all of us, and then I'll go to the lab and help them figure out how this could have occurred."

"They're coming here?" Howie stood up. "I should take Stella home."

"What, and miss all the excitement? I'm not going anywhere." I put my hands on my hips and frowned at Howie.

"You know too much, and even if I hadn't told you by now you probably would've figured it out. That means you know confidential information."

"It's not my fault zombies attacked me."

"I'd still rather you stay out of their sight. They're going to be wrapped up in figuring out how the hamster got out, so..."

"Hamster? It's not a rat, it's a hamster?"

"Yes," said Dr. Mullins, "I began using hamsters instead of rats for several reasons. First of all..."

"Not now, Dad," said Hazel.

"She might as well stay. They're going to have to talk to her at some point. They're not going to just forget," said Ray to Howie.

"Her parents will notice if I don't bring her home tonight. I promised her dad I'd deliver her home safe."

"You make me sound like a parcel," I snarled. "No one DELIVERS ME anywhere."

"Then please allow me to escort you to your home before angry government officials show up and want to know how much you know."

"Fine. You know, today turned out a lot different than I expected."

"Life is full of surprises," said Howie with an attempt at a smile. "And undeath even more so."

Howie pulled up at my house and we sat in silence for a minute.

"I guess I'm supposed to thank you for a nice day out," I said, "but I've got to say, it's not the first thought that comes to my mind."

He covered his face with his hands. "Today has been like something out my nightmares."

"You have nightmares about zombies? You ARE a zombie."

"And if you had been attacked by the reanimated corpse of someone you loved, you might have nightmares about it too."

"Oh, God. I'm a gigantic bitch. I'm sorry."

"And zombie hamsters escaping from Dad's lab and possibly causing the death of who knows how many people? That's not exactly in my favourite fantasies list."

I realized that for all my fear and grumbling, that I wasn't taking it as seriously as Howie was. And if you're wondering how I could have two terrifying encounters with the living dead, and actually kill one myself, and still not be taking it seriously, well – you're underestimating what a severely skeptical disposition can do to a person.

I had been presented with a lot of unbelievable stuff this weekend. It all just started to blend together after a while, you know?

My admirer has the zombie virus. My admirer is a good kisser. My admirer and I got attacked by a flesh-eating undead monster. My admirer treated me to a lovely dessert at a fancy restaurant. My admirer and I ran into more zombies. My admirer's father lost a zombified hamster from his top-secret laboratory.

Somewhere in all of that, I forgot to take things seriously, partially because I still expected someone (alive) to jump out from behind a tree and go, "Gotcha!"

Howie looked like he was taking things *really* seriously.

"Hey," I said softly, putting my hand on his thigh. "Things will be okay."

"You're basing that on which facts?"

"I dunno. It's just what you say, isn't it?"

His hand reached down and laid his hand on mine.

"Hmm. You sure know how to distract a guy from thinking about the zombie apocalypse."

"Oh?"

"You also helped me remember something."

"What's that?"

"There's something I was hoping to do today." He leaned forward, looking deeply into my eyes, his lips slightly parted. His hands held mine, and his thumbs played gently over my knuckles. He really was damn cute. I leaned in to kiss him.

And that's the moment that yet another zombie chose to go THUNK on our windshield.

"Shit-mother-fuck-piss-damn-hell-Christ," I said as the zombie pressed its face against the windshield and moaned. There was another thump, and the car rocked slightly. I twisted around and saw another one dragging its tongue along the rear passenger window.

I glanced over at Howie. He was frozen.

"We're trapped," he whispered. "I can't open the door to fight them without risking letting one in. What am I going to do?"

"Fucking kill them!"

"I'm scared one of them will hurt you while I'm trying."

"You're IN A FUCKING CAR, HOWARD. Turn it on and run them OVER."

He blinked and stared at me. The front window zombie was trying to bite the glass, while the rocking motions set off by the rear window zombie suggested that it was either trying to flip the car over or humping it.

"You are brilliant," Howie breathed.

"No, I apparently just have more brains than you at the moment. Turn the car back ON!"

He fumbled for his keys and the engine sputtered to life. The zombies continued to be utterly useless at getting into the car.

Howie smiled grimly, shifted the car into drive, and pressed on the gas. We lurched forward and the zombie was crushed into a tree. Howie shifted again, put his arm behind my seat and turned to look over his shoulder as he backed up, shaking off the rear zombie, and spun the wheel to swing smack into it. It tumbled over, arms flailing, and there was an uncomfortable bump as the wheel went over it.

The front zombie was recovering from its tree smoosh, and rising to its feet, so Howie drove forward again and knocked it down a second time. Then he unbuckled his seat belt, leaped from the car, slammed the door, ran up to the front zombie, stuck the metal vibrator thing against its head, and as soon as it had collapsed, moved on to the rear zombie, which was just rising to its feet. It twitched and collapsed.

I switched the car off and got out, holding the keys in my hand. Howie walked back to me and kissed me gently on the cheek. "You should get inside, where you're safe. I'll deal with this."

"Who says inside is safe? What if my parents got eaten by zombies while I was gone?" I was suddenly nervous. Howie's reference to his own zombification had filled me with worry. What if I walked into the house and found both of my parents turned into zombies? "Howie? How long does it take to turn into a zombie?"

"From hours to days, why?"

"If… if my parents are bitten, can you…"

He reached out and hugged me. "Let me make a call, and then I'll come in and check with you."

I looked around nervously while he phoned the Zom Squad or whatever they were called. Then I helped him move the bodies under his car, to hide them from passers-by. Of course, a zillion people had probably seen what happened and were calling the police as we spoke.

Howie held my hand and we went to my front door. I opened it slowly.

"…Mom? Dad?"

"Hi, honey!" Mom called from the living room. "We're just playing a game."

We ventured cautiously in. My parents had finally gotten around to hooking up their ancient N64 console and were trying to destroy each other in a game of GoldenEye.

"Did you kids have fun? DIE, DAMN YOU, DIE!" said my Dad.

"When will you learn that when it comes to weapons, size doesn't matter? That giant thing of yours isn't compensating for anything. Lasagna for dinner; sound good?" said Mom.

"Um, yeah."

"Stop hiding and come out where I can kill you! Do you want to stay for dinner, Howie?" asked Dad.

"Thank you, Mr. Blunt, but we have a bit of a family emergency, so I have to run home." Howie squeezed my hand. "Stay inside, okay? I'll call you in a bit."

I watched my parents explode things for a couple minutes, and then asked casually, "So, anything exciting happen around here today?"

"Not that we've noticed, why? Are we missing world breaking news?"

"Maybe. Howie and I saw some… strange people out on the street. Fighting. Maybe it's the zompocalypse."

"Should we go out and stock up on bottled water?"

"No, I think we should stay in and lock everything."

"We aren't going anywhere with that lasagna in the oven anyway," said Mom firmly. "Not even for the zompocalypse. Lasagna is a pain in the butt to make."

"Once I've killed Elaine, I'll turn on the news and we'll see if they mention anything," said Dad, mashing buttons frantically.

"That might take a while, I don't go down easily," said Mom.

"You're telling me."

"DAD! I'M GOING UPSTAIRS NOW."

After dinner, my parents went back to their vintage video game, but they caught a few minutes of the news when they turned on the TV.

"This must be what you were talking about seeing when you were out with Howie!"

The newscaster was standing in front of a swarm of police cars.

"The violence is being blamed on the dissemination of a toxic chemical which is tainting certain imported foods. Officials say they are unsure of just which foods need to be avoided, or how this may have happened. What they do know is that people who have been affected by this drug show a loss of coordination, an inability to speak, and violent tendencies. If anyone believes that someone they know may be showing symptoms, they are encouraged to dial 911 or call Health Canada immediately. If you encounter someone who has become violent, officials urge you to stay away, as the person may be extremely dangerous. In the meantime, it is recommended that we eat local, Canada-made produce."

"Thank you, Catherine. And now, we move on to this Mosque in Surrey, which has reported an alarming new trend – the theft of worshipers' shoes."

"That's it?" I said. "It's some 'drug' that's supposedly tainting some food, but they don't know which?"

"That's not very comforting, is it? Did the lasagna taste okay to you?" Mom asked.

"I'm sure we're all fine," I said firmly.

"So, I guess it's not the zompocalypse after all," sighed my father, "just big business tainting the very food we eat again."

"It's a fine line, really," said Mom. "Come on, Tim, you're just putting off getting your butt kicked again."

I rolled my eyes. "I'm going upstairs, you guys."

"You want to play the winner?"

"No thanks, I have an essay I should work on."

Upstairs, I picked away at my essay while nervously glancing at my phone off and on. Why hadn't Howie called? What the hell was going on out there? Why the fuck did I get shuffled off home and then kept in the dark?

Eventually, I sent him a text message.

—

What the hell is going on?

—

A lot of stuff. I miss you xxx

—

Damnit, give me some details.

—

Sorry, I'm under surveillance and I don't want them to think too much about you.
They came up with an explanation to feed to the media.

—

I saw that. Toxic chemicals? Really?

—

People will buy it. It's more plausible than zombies.

—

YOU'RE more plausible than zombies.

—

What?

—

Never mind, I'm tired and worried about the zombie apocalypse.

—

We should have it under control, only a few other people have reported incidents, and those zombies were all contained.

—

Got to go, want me to call when I get a chance?

—

Damn straight, you better call.

—

As you wish. I am so in love with you.

—

I grinned at my phone. I wasn't ready to say "I love you" back to Howie, but he didn't seem to care. I still loved to hear it, or, in this case, see it.

I could hear my parents going to bed. I got into my pajamas and then went downstairs for a drink of water. You know that nervous feeling you get when you walk downstairs in your house at night when it's dark and you can't be bothered to turn on the lights? You start remembering your childhood fears and think about how you used to worry about something climbing out of the hall mirror when you passed it in the dark?

Or is that just me?

Anyway, I was definitely rattled by the day's zombie encounters. I was trying not to remember them, and I was really trying to convince myself that there was nothing to be afraid of at this particular moment when I heard a thunk on the kitchen window.

I froze.

There was an unpleasant squealing noise, like the sound of someone's finger on a clean plate – or someone's face sliding down a window pane.

Two minutes later I was back in my room with the door shut and holding my phone to my ear.

Howie picked up on the fourth ring.

"Stella?" he whispered, "Officials are still here. What's wrong?"

"You'd better send those fucking officials over here RIGHT NOW, Howard, because there's a HORDE OF FUCKING ZOMBIES at my front door."

I could look down from my bedroom window and watch the zombies, and that's what I did while I waited for help to arrive. There were at least seven or eight of them. I couldn't make out any details, but they were definitely zombies, and they were piled outside my door.

Why *my* door? I heard a thump as another one pounded on the door. Then one of them looked up and looked right at me. I jumped back, but curiosity overcame me and I went back for another look after a couple of seconds.

I sent another text.

—

Tell them to hurry because the zombies are trying to climb
up my wall.

Okay now one of them is standing on another's shoulders.
I thought you said they didn't have brains.

Howard, one of them HAS A ROCK.

—

With the sort of timing usually reserved for badly written television dramas, the authorities pulled up in a swarm
just as a rock crashed through our kitchen window. The
men burst out of the cars and began zapping the zombies,
who were distracted from my house and stumbled towards the Zom Squad instead.

My parents heard the window smash and came bursting out of their rooms. I tried to tell them that a bunch of
toxin-crazy ruffians were outside and that they should stay
inside.

Then we heard Howie shouting loudly, but still emo-
tionlessly, downstairs.

"STELLA. STELLA."

We rushed down the stairs.

"I'm right here."

"You're okay?" He grabbed my arms.

"Howie, what on Earth?" my mother began.

"Stella told me there were... people outside, and I came
over," he said. "I'm sorry for showing up unannounced at
such a late hour."

Dad stared at the shattered glass inside our kitchen. "We haven't owned this place a month and already we have to make repairs."

"The strata are responsible for windows, I think, my love," said Mom distractedly.

"Howie, how did you get past all of those cops?" Dad asked, looking out the window and then taking a dramatic step back.

There was a growl as someone half-threw themselves over our window sill. There was a shout, and the zombie was yanked back outside.

"I ran fast," said Howie.

"Are they actually tazing those poor people?" said Mom. "I mean, it's not their fault they ate imported foods."

"Now, dear, you know the importance of eating organic," teased Dad. "You can't tell me they didn't know they were taking a risk."

"And they don't deserve to be electrocuted!"

"Everything okay in here?" asked one of the uniformed men, opening the door unceremoniously. "Have any of you been hurt?"

"No!" said Mom irritably. "I hope you have ambulances on hand."

"We do. They are being loaded into them as we speak." I saw bodies being slung into the white vans. "We use the minimum force necessary, ma'am, but these people are extremely dangerous. Tazers are necessary."

"*Tazers* are dangerous!"

"But better than allowing these fine people to commit murder. I'm afraid the results of this toxin result in murderous rage and even cannibalism."

"Cannibalism!"

"Yes, ma'am. If these people had managed to reach you, they would've attempted to eat you alive. It's far better to incapacitate them and get them to the hospital as safely as possible."

"But what were they all doing outside our door?"

The man hesitated. "We have no idea."

Some more people in uniform came in to "debrief" my parents and "take a statement", which I think was really more like "brainwash" and "make a good record of who these people are."

Howie hovered over me anxiously, with an awed look on his face.

"We need to speak somewhere privately," he whispered in my ear. "Can we go to your room?"

"Oh yeah, take my boyfriend up to my room in the middle of the night when I'm wearing nothing but pajamas. My parents will be totally fine with that."

Howie gave one of his shy grins. "I know you're being sarcastic, but it just makes me happy when I hear you call me your boyfriend."

"Is now really the time for lovey-dovey, Howie?"

"Every time is the time for lovey-dovey, but I really do need to speak to you."

"Well, everyone seems preoccupied at the front door for now; let's just go into the living room, and talk fast."

Howie sat next to me on the couch and leaned in close.

"The zombies are tracking you, Stella."

"Well, it certainly looks that way, doesn't it? But WHY?"

"I told you that your brain waves are really attractive. I noticed it; my whole family noticed it. You're luring every zombie who happens to be nearby."

"Bullshit!"

"Shh!"

"Howie, there's nothing that special about my brain. Are you actually trying to suggest that these zombies are ignoring all other prey to come to ME? Because that's nuts."

"Listen, I can't explain exactly what it is about you – your confidence, your intelligence, maybe even your cynicism. All I know is, it draws me like a beacon, my whole family agrees that you're overwhelmingly attractive, and now there's a bunch of dead bodies on the lawn."

"First of all, if I were that self-confident, I'd have no trouble believing that I'm some sort of special snowflake that zombies love to nom on. This is clearly not the case. Second of all, I do well in school but I'm not a genius. The cynicism I will buy, although I'm not at all sure why cynicism would be an attractive trait."

"Cynicism involves thought – you're not mindlessly accepting the world around you. You question everything."

"I've met mindless cynics."

"Are you one of them?"

"I hope not!"

"Well, then. Stella, we can argue about why there were eight zombies outside your door tonight, but the fact remains that there were eight zombies outside your door tonight. I think we need to take you somewhere safe."

"Like where?"

"A bunker or something."

"Why don't I just wear a tinfoil hat?" I said sarcastically.

When I climbed into bed that night, I was wearing a tinfoil hat and a scowl. According to Howie, a government zombie-killing dude was stationed outside in the bushes, in case the tin foil hat didn't work.

It turns out that Howie's dad must have been sitting around with his thumb up his butt all those decades because it had never occurred to him to check the efficacy of tinfoil hats. They knew that it blocked certain radio waves, but they weren't positive about the kinds of brain waves that attract zombies.

So, this was an experiment.

I couldn't very well stick on a tinfoil hat and prance around in front of Howie with my parents right there, so he told me just to sneak some tinfoil upstairs once they went to bed.

Newsflash: Tinfoil is not comfortable sleepwear. It kept falling off of my head and making really unpleasant crackling noises whenever I shifted.

My phone dinged at two in the morning.

—

It's not working, I can feel you loud and clear.

—

Thank God. I'm taking this off then.
I folded the tinfoil into a shape. What is it?

—

You know I can't read your mind. That would be disturbing.

—

But "your mind sounds delicious" isn't disturbing?

—

Very – I could never argue otherwise.

—

> Don't you forget it.
> By the way, I folded the tinfoil into a swan.

—

Goodnight, you talented beauty.

—

I drifted off to sleep, trying to think about Howie's lips, instead of zombies.

13

I lay in bed the next morning, trying to force myself to get up. I kept playing the memory of Howie's hands on my waist and thinking *mmmmm*. Then I thought, *do I really remember fighting zombies yesterday?* And then it hit me. *Oh, fuck.* It was Monday, and that meant I had to go back to dealing with The Kelly Problem. My stomach clenched. The zombies felt too nightmarish to be real, but Kelly felt painfully real, and so did the social rejection.

I was stewing about it in the shower when I heard the screen door slam downstairs, and a murmur of voices. I shut off the water and stepped on the mat, dripping as I listened. Yes! That was Howie's voice!

I ran back to my room in my bathrobe and hurriedly got dressed. When I got downstairs I found Howie making pancakes in the kitchen while my parents sat at the table exchanging incredulous glances. There was a cereal box taped over the broken part of our kitchen window.

"What the hell are you doing?" I asked. Howie glanced up and smiled briefly, then went back to flipping over a perfectly golden pancake.

"Good morning yourself," he said. "Your parents let me use their kitchen so I could make you breakfast. I thought the pancakes'd get cold if I cooked them at home." He glanced at my parents. "Don't worry, I'm sure none of this is tainted. I'm making them from scratch."

"He just... came in the door with a bag of groceries and asked if he could make you breakfast," said my mother. "Why has this never happened to me?"

"I come home with groceries and cook all the time," my father pointed out testily.

"Well, yes, but you live here."

"Would you rather I didn't?"

She stuck her tongue out at him and went back to raising her eyebrows while Howie added the last pancake to the stack and busied himself laying out butter and real maple syrup.

"Please, help yourselves," he said. "There are three each. I hope that's enough."

I watched my parents glance at the nine giant pancakes and four people and get error messages on their mental calculators.

"Aren't you having any, Howie?" my mother asked.

Howie was already washing the bowl and pan that he had used. "No, thank you, Mrs. Blunt. I don't eat pancakes."

The pancakes were frigging delicious, too. Fluffy and melt-in-your-mouth good. Howie put all the ingredients in the fridge and cupboard, insisting to my parents that he didn't want or need them at home. When I finished he scooped away my plate, stacked it on my parents' dishes, and started washing them.

My parents were uncharacteristically silent, and that bothered me a lot more than the zombie who was swishing suds in the sink with his sleeves rolled up.

"So... I guess I'll go grab my school stuff," I said. "It's almost time for my bus. I'm assuming we still have school? Does anyone know if school was cancelled due to zompocalypse?"

"I think it'll take more than a few people being poisoned to justify shutting down the entire school system," said my mother. "Head for the bus, kid."

"I hope you'll let me drive you to school," Howie said, glancing over his shoulder. His glasses were slightly fogged from the hot water.

"...Sure?"

I disappeared from the awkward situation, leaving my parents smack in the middle of it. Maybe I should have felt guilty about leaving *Howie* smack in the middle of it, but after all, he was the only one who didn't seem to think he was being weird.

I took my time shoving my homework and stuff in my bag and then thumping downstairs. I dreaded the uncomfortable silence of the kitchen. But I heard my father chuckle as I came down the hall. I found Howie in my seat, the kitchen looking spotless, and my parents looking amused. Howie jumped to his feet when I walked in.

"Well, have a good day, you two," Dad said. I gave him a swift kiss on the cheek.

"Ha, right. Kelly, remember? Also, cannibalistic crazies on the street. Good luck on your interview today, Dad. Bye, Mom. Don't get eaten."

"See you later, honey. And, thank you for breakfast, Howard."

When the door shut behind us, I imagined my parents bursting into hysterical laughter. I even paused to listen for a moment but I didn't hear anything. If they were laughing, it was either quietly or the door was good at blocking out sound.

"Stella?" Howie asked. "You coming?"

"Yeah, what the hell was that about, Howard?"

"What?"

"You... you show up in the middle of the night, show up first thing in the morning, take over the kitchen... what are my parents supposed to think? It's embarrassing!"

"I've made you uncomfortable again. I'm sorry. Did you at least like the pancakes?"

He looked so disappointed that I felt bad, so I punched him. Gently. "They were delicious. Where the hell did you learn to cook like that if you haven't eaten normal food in fifty years? But also, that's entirely beside the point."

"I spent some time as a cook in a diner. Why isn't it the point?"

"I'm just... I want my parents to like you, and they're going to think you're weird."

"I am weird. I'd just rather they think I'm weird in a cooks-their-daughter-breakfast way than in an eats-brains kind of way. And your evening guard had to go home – he couldn't very well stand outside in broad daylight – so I thought I had better take over."

"Wait, I thought you couldn't remember new things well, but you remember how to cook pancakes?"

"It wasn't that long ago, and if you do the same thing over and over for a few years, you remember. For a while, at least. Today was a good chance to practice."

He walked up to his battered old car and held open the passenger side door for me. "Madam," he smiled. But I wasn't done having an argument yet.

"Do you want to stop treating me like a delicate flower? I can open doors for myself."

"I just like doing things for you."

"It smacks of chivalry."

"Isn't chivalry a way to demonstrate respect for women?"

"No, it's anti-feminist." I squinted at him. "You had your breakfast this morning. I thought you were rationed."

"I skipped dinner last night instead. Better to be stupid when you're not around. Anyway, I don't understand why chivalry is anti-feminist. Chivalry was all about taking orders from women, and serving them."

"It implies we can't do shit ourselves."

"If a CEO hires a secretary, does it mean that he is incapable of answering a phone? Having people serve you doesn't mean you're incapable. It means you have power."

"Where is the agency, Howie? You drop me off, pick me up, guide me in and out of doors, kill zombies for me... That's not respect. That's treating me like a pet puppy. Except for the zombie thing."

He smiled. "Well then, catch."

He tossed his keys at me. I snagged them out of the air and stared at them. "You're giving me your car?"

He laughed. "Gee, I love you. You can have the car if you want it, but I was going to let you drive and, if necessary, run over zombies yourself."

"Oh. I think that's better." I eyed the car. "I'm not sure I'd want the car if you offered it to me."

"Why? Because it's a cheap piece of junk?"

"Yep."

"I'll have you know that this is a 1994 Dodge Shadow," Howie said. "When I bought it new it was… well, it was still a cheap piece of junk but it was shinier. Besides, some of those dents are fresh. We ran over some people yesterday, remember?"

"Oh, well then," I said, climbing into the driver's seat. "I will at least try to show it the respect that I owe to my elders."

"How strange is that?" he said as he sat next to me. "I've owned this car longer than you've been alive."

I was quiet for a moment while I tried to coax the engine to life. It finally sputtered and roared. I glanced at Howie before backing out of the visitor parking spot. His cheeks were pale but smooth. His face was still boyish. It was completely impossible to believe that he could be older than me, older than this ancient piece of shit little car. But then again, it was also hard to believe that the dead walked and were trying to eat me.

"Apparently three more zombies came by your house last night."

"Well, that's better than eight. Where are they all coming from?"

"The local hospitals and a couple funeral homes are panicking really quietly about bodies going missing, and some of their staff haven't turned up for work."

"Zombies who died and walked off the mortuary table, then ate the attendants?"

"Must be."

"And one freaking hamster did all of this? HOW?"

"We… don't know. It seems impossible, but what else could have started this?"

"How did it even get out?"

"We still don't know. Agent Baum said he was going to see whose key cards were used to unlock the door recently."

"Is there no surveillance video?"

"No. There's no videos inside the lab. It's top secret."

"And there's no, like, tracking devices on these potentially deadly little beasts?"

"No… a hamster can't open doors, so how far could one get?"

"Yeah, but, like, what about animal liberation fronts?"

"They'd go for bigger labs than Dad's."

"And now there's a zombie apocalypse, and it's possibly your dad's fault. Have they, like, arrested him?"

"Not yet. But they might." Howie ran his hand through his hair. "This is really, really bad."

"And we're just off to school like normal?"

"Well, how are we supposed to hunt for a hamster that has gotten far enough to create dozens of zombies?" his voice almost sounded emotional.

"And what are your Zombie Squad peeps doing about all this?"

"Scouring the city. A few will stay in our area since they seem to be drifting toward you. The rest will be driving around, looking for suspicious lurching figures or responding to 911 calls that sound like they could relate to zombies."

"Fun. Is it wrong that I sort of hope the zombies catch Kelly?"

"Definitely. But I like you anyway."

Howie reached for my hand as we walked toward the school and for one shameful moment, I resisted. What would people think when they realized that I was dating

Stare Boy? But Howie cast me a sweet smile, and that dimple sold me. I took his hand and he squeezed it.

On the way to class, everyone around us was talking about the "zombie" poison, and trying to out-do each other with how organic and local their lunches were. I wondered what they would do if someone who did eat only organic managed to come down with the "toxicity".

It wasn't until we walked into Chemistry that people noticed that we were holding hands. Chair Kicking Guy spotted it, nudged his friend, and started to laugh.

"Nice catch," he said to me.

"Mullins landed a whale!" snorted his buddy. There was a ripple of laughter.

Cheeks burning, I waved my middle finger around, because that's how I deal with things. Howie didn't seem at all bothered.

"I should be telling everyone how lucky I am to be with you." His breath tickled my ear. I stifled my embarrassment.

"I think that you should definitely NOT do that because they'll probably kick your ass."

Mr. Nguyen started the class with an announcement that public health nurses were going to be taking cheek swabs from all of the students to test for exposure to the rage toxin, so we were to report to the gym immediately following lunch.

That led to class being partially hijacked by questions about the "rage chemical" in our food. Our teacher, unsurprisingly, said he had no idea what chemical might be doing this. He did mention some new kinds of drugs that had turned up in the States a while back that caused a similar kind of problem.

"Also fiction to cover zombies," Howie whispered in my ear.

"How comforting," I whispered back.

Mr. Nguyen quickly redirected the class back to organic chemistry and things went back to normal – except that Howie kept reaching for my hand and squeezing it under the table, and every time he did, it made me feel feelings.

When the bell rang and I had to leave Howie to go to English class, those feelings changed to dread. But who knew, maybe Kelly was off roaming the countryside, groaning for brains, and I wouldn't have to deal with her.

When I walked into English class, everyone started hooting and pounding their desks. Whoa. This wasn't about Howie, was it? I mean, the news that we were holding hands couldn't be that big, not when there were zombies around.

I followed their eyes and turned my head. Stuck to the whiteboard with scotch tape was a piece of paper that said:

"I SUCK MR BARETT'S COCK"
- STELLA BLUNT

Mr. Barrett looked up from his desk at all the noise, saw me, and followed my gaze. He stood up and strode over to the board, but before he got to the sign, I ripped it down myself and tore it in half.

"Okay, you mentally deficient dung-meisters," I said loudly, "If you're going to insult me you could at least have the self-respect not to do it in COMIC FUCKING SANS."

"I WILL HANDLE THIS, STELLA, THANK YOU," said Mr. Barrett, pointing me to what was now my seat. I kicked over a chair and threw myself into mine.

"Careful, or you'll break it!" shouted someone.

"Silence, please," Mr. Barrett said. "Where is Kelly Svancara?"

"I'm here – sorry I'm late, what's up?" Kelly asked sweetly from the doorway.

"Just get in your seat, Miss Svancara," he said coldly. He looked back at the class. "I want to remind all of you that this school has a zero-tolerance policy toward bullying. Now, I can't know who put that sign up there, but I want to let you all know that if I had happened to spot you doing it, you'd be getting detention right now. And I want you to ask yourself if a simple-minded, un-clever moment of bullying is really worth giving up your lunch hour for." He pointed at me. "If I hear another outburst of language like that, you'll be joining them in detention."

"No! Why punish us twice?" some guy hollered from the back. Everyone laughed. Mr. Barrett pointed at him. "Detention, Mr. Sandhu."

The guy slammed his arms on his desk and looked mutinous, but didn't say anything else.

Kelly Svancara raised her hand. "Mr. Barrett, I don't think it's fair to hold Stella *or* Ravi accountable for their actions today. Maybe they've been poisoned by that toxin. That would explain a lot of Stella's behavior recently."

Oh, you AIDS-Nazi.

Mr. Barrett raised his eyebrows. "The symptoms are physical violence and cannibalism, not insulting wordplay, Miss Svancara, but if it turns out later that they tested positive, I will take it under advisement. I suggest you stay quiet for a while: Just because you were not in the room

209

does not mean I have eliminated you from my list of suspects."

Kelly looked shocked and insulted.

I smiled.

Mr. Barrett began to talk about George Bernard Shaw.

After English, I waited outside the classroom for Kelly so I could give her a piece of my fist, but Howie arrived before she emerged.

"What happened this time?" he asked. "I felt it over in Biology."

"I'll tell you later," I growled. "I'm waiting for the Princess of Evil."

Kelly came out the door, chatting calmly with her blonde friend. I grabbed her arm and pulled her aside. She looked at me and calmly raised her eyebrows.

"Can I help you?" she asked sweetly.

"Listen, I know you were behind that fucking sign, and if I catch you doing anything like that ever I will make you eat your own entrails," I snarled at her.

"I didn't touch that sign, Stella," she said with a smile, "Have you considered anger management classes? Besides, maybe you did it yourself and forgot – I hear the rage poison causes insanity. Now, please let me go, you're getting your fat on my Forever 21."

"And if you try to lay a hand on her, you'll regret it," said the blonde. We were quickly being surrounded by several other girls and guys.

"Fatty."

"Loser."

"Whore."

"Dog!"

"Teacher fucker."

"Cheat."

"You're all just jealous of Stella. Let her go, beautiful, she's not worth it," said Howie in his usual bland tone.

Everyone started to laugh, but I let go. Somehow, his calmness made me feel silly, like a two-year-old throwing a tantrum. Jesus, how many decades had he taken shit like this for?

They turned on him, now, calling him a freak and a faggot and bunch of other standard words that just mean, "You don't belong and we shun you."

Howie totally ignored it. He just took my hand and suggested we go to lunch.

"I don't want to eat, I want to kick in some heads," I scowled, pulling away. "Listen, you mealy-mouthed ass weasels…"

"STELLA," Howie said loudly, and I stopped and looked at him. He put his finger to his lips and jerked his head toward the classroom door. I looked over, and a moment later, Mr. Barrett stepped out, shuffling some papers in a folder. He saw the people crowded around Howie and me, and he sighed.

"Okay. What's going on?"

"Nothing, Mr. Barrett," said Kelly, "I was just meeting up with some friends for lunch."

"Well, then, go. To lunch. Now," he said.

We went.

Howie insisted on buying me lunch, and this time, I let him do it. He suggested I go and find a seat and promised he'd join me in a minute.

"Will you find me in this throng?" I asked dubiously.

He sighed and shook his head. "I could probably find you in the middle of an international airport during a blackout. Your mind would call me." He smiled. "Especially when you get mad."

"That makes you sound a little stalkerish, Howard."

He put his hand on his heart. "I swear that I wouldn't find you if you preferred to remain lost in an international airport during a blackout," he promised.

"Damn straight."

I started to head to the back of the cafeteria, but Kate caught my eye and waved me over.

"Hey, come sit with us," she said. "I hear you had another epic incident with Kelly Svancara."

"Word travels fast."

"It travels at the speed of text," she said, holding up her phone with a smirk. "Michelle's in your English class, too. You should look for her next time."

"It's a good thing it happened with Mr. Barrett and not Ms. Bond," I said. "He's pretty fair."

"Yeah, he is. Oh my God, did I tell you? I went to Ms. Bond after class on Friday and asked for an extension for our lab assignment because I had a band trip this weekend, and she told me that people who take Physics shouldn't be in band because they won't have enough time to learn science properly or something."

"What? Is that normal? Back home the band kids get away with murder! Did you point out to her that music involves sound waves which is totally Physics-related?"

"No, it totally isn't normal, and yes, I did! And then I suggested she consider it extra credit and she told me to get out of the classroom and that I had better turn in my lab on Monday."

"Are you serious? I have never met a teacher who was so childish."

"Yeah, well, the joke's on her because Physics is cancelled for this saliva test thing. Apparently, everyone went crazy while I was in Seattle?"

Michelle arrived at the table and nodded to me. "Hey, sorry about the bitches in class. I didn't see who put up the sign either, sorry."

"One of her henchmen, no doubt, probably from the class before ours. She's careful not to do crap like that herself," I said.

"Hey, at least if rumour is going around that you slept with one of the teachers, it was one of the better-looking ones. It could have been worse. It could have been Mr. Philips."

They all shuddered.

"I don't know him."

"Oh, he's the gym teacher. He's fifty, red as a lobster, always sweaty and his chest hair is always peeping over the top of his shirt collar like a pet rodent."

"Charming."

Then Howie arrived with a tray of food for me. "Here you are, gorgeous."

"Oh, my God, leave her alone already!" said Kate. "Doesn't she have enough problems?"

Howie just stood there, looking lost.

"No, it's okay," I said awkwardly, "I... told him he could buy me lunch."

"You shouldn't do that, Stella, it just encourages him."

"No, we're... we're friends. Howie, sit down."

Howie didn't sit down. He just looked at me quietly, and then said, "No, it's okay, I should go sit with my brother and sister. You stay here. I'll see you later."

"No," I said crossly, "Just... just sit down, will you? Or, I can come with you if you want."

"No, I'm glad you've made some friends," he said in his usual calm, unemotional tone. "I'll see you after lunch."

And he put down my tray, gave me a little smile, and he left me feeling like a bag of stinking sheep shit.

"Oh, man, you do have shitty luck," giggled Amy after he left.

I flushed. "Look! He's nice, and he's smarter than he looks. He's one of the only people here who hasn't treated me like something that came out of a cow's anus. Lay off, will you?"

"Whoa," said Kate. "In case you haven't noticed, we're *also* being nice to you, so will you cool it?"

"Sorry," I mumbled. "Just... lay off Howie, okay?"

"Okay, but you need to know – being hated by Kelly Svancara, well, that's bad. She's popular and she has a lot of clout. On the other hand, the rest of us hate her guts and root for anyone who stands up to her. But hanging around with Howard Mullins... well..." she waved her hand. "The Mullinses are, like, the lowest of the low."

"I know, I know," I said.

"No, like, below the level of the special needs kids," said Michelle.

"Yeah, yeah," I said.

"No, like, the other losers wouldn't be caught sitting next to him," said Amy.

"Look," I flared, "Kate, you said your mother works with his Dad. He's a scientist. Howie's good at science, too. It's not like he spends his days in detention or thinks reading is a waste of time, like some of the losers out there. He's... well, he's a little strange..."

"Those eyes," said Amy. "How can he see, even with glasses?"

"And he doesn't eat. Those thermoses they drink out of," reminded Michelle.

"So? Is having a medical condition a crime?"

"And his Dad isn't just a normal scientist," said Kate, "he's weird. He's like a mad scientist from the movies. No one knows exactly what he studies, or even where he gets his funding from. He doesn't even have to go through the university ethics board when he does his experiments – he has some kind of letter of dispensation. My mother would love to get inside his lab sometime and figure out what he's up to. He probably, like, vivisects his poor rats."

"Hamsters," I said. "He uses hamsters. And I am SURE he doesn't do anything to them while they are still alive." *They might still be moving, though,* I thought.

Kate stared at me, open-mouthed. "Okay, you know more than my mother does. Hamsters? God, that's worse; they're *cuter*."

"I really don't think he does anything bad to them. But apparently they're super infectious, so your mom might want to stay away," I said.

"Hey, has Howie told you what he used to keep in his top-secret fridge?"

"His what, now?"

"Apparently he used to have a top-secret fridge with its own key code and everything, but the university ordered the contents removed, and it disappeared a couple years ago."

"Nope, don't know anything about that," I shook my head. Was it full of brains? Vials of virus? Who knew? "I think I've already told you everything I can." *Just not everything I know.*

"Anyway, this isn't about his Dad. This is about Howard and the fact that he and his brother and sister are considered to be less than dirt. Look, I have nothing personal against the guy, and you can do what you want. I'm just saying, it's social suicide," said Kate frankly.

I sat there and fumed.

On the one hand, I knew what they were trying to say, and I knew they were right. Hadn't I known it from the moment I saw Howie? He had "loser" written all over him, from his vacant, milky blue stare to his unhealthy complexion to his shuffling, aimless way of walking and his droning, monotonous voice. What was it Jeremy had said? "NO ONE dates that kid"?

And seriously, ever since I had started dating Howie – all of three days ago – my life had become a clusterfuck of undead.

Now here I was, sitting with Kate, who I really liked, who made me laugh in Physics class, who talked straight and didn't believe the Kelly Svancara bullshit… and she was basically telling me that if I stayed with Howie, that she wouldn't dare be seen with me.

But on the other hand, I remembered pancakes and a good listener who always turned up when I needed someone to yell at. Someone who liked me despite, or possibly even *because of*, my temper, and who thought that my size eighteen body was stellar hot.

Sometimes, don't you just wish the entire world would just go screw itself with a rusty hammer?

As soon as I was done eating, I picked up my tray and told Kate and company that I had something I needed to do. "I'll see you in Physics," I said to Kate and Michelle.

"No, we all have to go to the gym and get swabbed, remember?"

"Oh, right. See you later, then."

I walked away. I needed to go scream at someone or something. I considered hunting Kelly down and shoving sushi up her rectum, but instead, I headed outside.

Some part of me was imagining Howie's voice, telling me to calm down, come outside, and tell him all about it. Except I couldn't tell him all about this. How could I tell him that while part of me was still giddy about him, the other part of me was asking myself what the hell I thought I was doing.

Not only was dating Howie social suicide but honestly, what could come out of it? He was going to be a teenager forever, pretty much. What good would that be to me in two or three years?

Christ. I'd become even more outcast, even more hated by basically everybody, and in a year or two I'd start wanting to find someone my own age and all of that suffering would've been wasted.

But what was I going to do? Tell Howie, "I still like you, but I don't want to be seen with you and our relationship has no future"?

I wasn't that shallow. I was still feeling like shit for letting him get shooed away from me at lunch.

I was just an all-around shitty person who had no idea how to make basic life decisions. Fuck all the fuckety fucks!

I slammed my fist on the bleachers and tried not to cry.

Moments later, a hand landed on my shoulder. I looked up and was relieved to find that it was attached to an arm. Howie's arm. He was looking extremely concerned.

"I'm sorry, Howie, but I don't want to talk about it this time," I said, wiping my nose.

"We have to leave," he said.

"What?"

"We have to leave NOW."

"What? Why?"

"The zombies are here."

14

I jumped to my feet. "How many?"

Howie just pointed. Around the corner lumbered a clump of zombies, probably ten or fifteen of them.

"SHIT!"

I grabbed Howie and dragged him back inside and slammed the door.

"Can they open unlocked doors?"

"Sometimes. It depends on how long they've been dead… they start to forget stuff…"

A zombie hit the door with a thump. The door did not open.

"Thank God. How does anyone get bitten by these bozos?"

"Gorgeous, we have to get out of here."

"What? Why? We're safe inside."

I felt fingers claw at my arm and I instinctively shrunk away, shifted my weight, spun and kicked.

Ms. Bond, my Physics teacher, stumbled back against a row of lockers with a loud bang. Her face registered no pain. Her eyes, completely fogged over, stared avidly in my direction without blinking. As she rose and dove to-ward me, I realized how young she looked. In class, her sour face had made me think of her as a nasty old crone, but her blonde hair was untouched by grey, and while frown lines creased her face, her hands were smooth and young-looking as they tried to grasp at my shirt.

Her body chattered its teeth and lunged at me. I backed away in shock but bumped up against the door. There was another thump as the zombies outside threw themselves against the glass.

Howie stepped forward calmly with his silver bullet thing and knocked Ms. Bond out. There was that terrible twitch, and her body lay still.

"That... that was..."

"I know."

"She was a shitty teacher, Howie."

"I know."

"But she didn't deserve that."

"No one does."

I heard screams and shouts coming from the cafeteria, and occasional gurgles.

"More?"

I ran to the cafeteria while Howie desperately tried to tug me back. It was a madhouse. Zombies tumbling down the stairs. They must have broken in through the upstairs doors. Our school – like most Vancouver buildings, it seemed – was built into the side of a hill, and had doors on both levels.

Some kids were standing on tables hitting zombies with binders and shielding themselves with chairs.

"They seem to be holding their own," I said. Then a kid almost slipped off the edge of the table when a zombie grabbed his leg. He screamed and pushed a chair in its face while it pulled him down.

"Oh, FUCK burgers!" I started forward to help him but someone else kicked the zombie in the head and yanked the kid to safety.

"STELLA," said Howie, giving me a little push. "We need to get you out of here NOW."

"Howard, they need help; get your disruptor out and help me go save them!" I said, plowing him out of the way.

Howie looked really freaked out. "Stella, they're going for anyone they can reach, but I think they were drawn here to you. We need to get you away from the school."

"Are you serious? I can't just skip school."

There was a loud smash and a lot of girlish shrieks from down the hall.

"Think, Stella," Howie was near tears. "If they are here for you, then you are basically putting all these kids in danger. This isn't about dragging you to safety. This is about keeping you away from other human beings."

Oh.

"Okay, let's go, then," I said, "but let's kill as many as we can on our way out."

So we ran through the room, me kicking zombies in the head and Howie bending over to finish them with his disruptor. The cafeteria was emptying rapidly, so the zombies lumbered in our direction, which made it easier.

I pulled one brave moron off of a table and told him, "Just run. Lock yourself in a classroom, you idiot." Once he was gone the last zombie came for me instead, and Howie disrupted it.

We darted for the exit and hit another clump of undead.

"Just dodge them, get to my car," said Howie.

My basic grip on reality had made me doubt that I was somehow attracting zombies from all over town, but as statistically improbable as it might be, I'd have to be an idiot to deny what I saw on our way to the car – a group of zombies pulling away from the school and moving towards us instead. We threw ourselves into the car and locked the doors.

"Give 'er," I said, fumbling for my seat belt. Howie didn't bother with his. We blasted out of the parking lot as fast as that ancient little Dodge could go, leaving the shambling horde behind.

"I thought it was just a little outbreak?" I said. "What do you call all of that?"

"Really bad," said Howie, wiping his eyes.

"Okay, here's what I don't get," I said.

"What?"

"If I'm so damn attractive to zombies, why have I never met zombies before? Why have I encountered ALL THE ZOMBIES within days of meeting YOU?"

"Zombies aren't a dime a dozen, you know, or humanity would be pretty much done by now."

"You could have fooled me."

"The outbreak and your meeting me are an unfortunate coincidence."

"Unfortunate? Can you imagine if all this were happening and you weren't around to explain what was happening?"

"You'd figure it out."

Howie took me back to his house. His logic was that it was the only place he could take me that didn't have humans in it.

"Do you mean I am dating outside my species? Because that's a little gross."

"Well, you know, by 'human' I mean 'not the living dead.'"

"And you are... what? The dead living?"

"I'm in the grey zone."

"So, what're we going to do when all the zombies get to your house?"

"Kill them."

He pulled in to the driveway and I marched inside. Dr. Mullins was arguing with the same government agent I had met yesterday – what's-his-face. Baum.

"I don't know what you expect me to do about it, George, since you have placed me under house arrest and refuse to admit me to my own laboratory."

"The laboratory that we fund, which you have been using to conduct secret experiments."

"I have done no such thing."

"Oh? Then how could a simple-minded lab animal bend the bars of its cage and escape a sealed room without a trace?"

"I cannot explain that."

"Because you won't admit that you have been adding a little something to its food."

"I haven't tried any new treatments other than those documented in my most recently submitted experimental procedure plan. If that treatment had an untoward effect, then I am as surprised as you. I cannot explain how it became infectious so quickly."

"Can't you? I can. And Agent Hunt will be forced to agree with me, given the devastation you have wrought. If it were up to me I'd be arresting you right now."

"Dad," Howie interrupted. Dr. Mullins turned and grasped his son's arms.

"I'm glad you're here, son," he said. Everything he said made him sound like a robot pre-programmed with fake emotions. "I heard about the school. I see that you chose to bring Stella here. Was that wise?"

"We have to keep her away from people. They all came after us when we drove off."

"They left a school full of minds to follow Stella?" Howie's father raised his eyebrows. "Impressive. But I would hardly qualify our neighbourhood as 'away from people'."

"Maybe I should take Stella right out of the city."

"That may change the direction in which they head, but it won't do anything for the individuals caught between them and Stella."

The front door opened and Hazel and Ray walked in.

"Well, you sure caused a ruckus," said Ray to me.

"The zombies caused the ruckus," I snapped. "I was moping well away from other humans."

"Not well enough away, clearly."

Ray was an asshole, but somehow I didn't mind him. Maybe his simmering hatred toward everything and anyone struck a sympathetic note with me.

"What happened, anyway?" Howie asked, reaching for my hand. "You were so sad."

"I don't want to talk about it."

The agent guy cleared his throat. "The rat, Mullins. We were discussing your rat."

"It is a hamster, George, and I think we need to discuss Howie's news, don't you?"

"You will address me as 'Agent Baum,'" said Agent Baum, who was clearly a bullying jerk. "There are no hordes marching toward your house. My squad is hunting down infected targets around the school property. The remaining infected in that area will be eliminated. Stop trying to change the subject."

"That was my first attempt to change the subject, George."

"AGENT BAUM!"

"Agent Baum, then. I apologize. You know how I forget these things."

"Yes – your poor memory. Even if we trust you to stick to your experiment protocols, how do we know we can trust your memory when you say that you checked your lab on Saturday? We can't help but wonder if the virus is beginning to damage your brain further."

"The virus is not progressing. Our saliva swabs were negative, as always," said Dr. Mullins with a hint of "we've-been-over-this-a-million-times" in his otherwise passive voice.

"You may not be contagious, but your brain might be falling apart. Once this situation has been neutralized, we require you and your family to present themselves for full fMRIs, CT scans, and extensive testing. It may no longer be safe to allow you to live among the general public."

"When have you ever considered it safe?" muttered Ray.

"I heard that."

"You can perform whatever tests you like on me as soon as you have the available staff do so," said Howie's father, "but right now we need to talk about Stella."

"Who would REALLY appreciate being addressed in the second person," I added. "Since I'm RIGHT HERE."

Agent Baum looked at me and sighed.

"Hello, Miss Blunt," he said wearily. "I'm sorry you got mixed up in all of this."

"I think the whole city has gotten mixed up in this, Agent Baum, but don't really know what it is they're mixed up in," I said. "Don't you think they should be told?

"I wasn't referring to the outbreak, specifically," he said, "and the truth is kept secret to protect the public. I will be telling Agent Hunt how well informed you are." He glanced at Howie. "Divulging confidential information is a federal offense."

"They didn't need to divulge much. I'm a good guesser," I said.

"You guessed, did you? You guessed that your boy-friend was actually the walking dead?"

"If I hadn't, then you would've just told me," I said. "I thought we were talking about the zombies out there." I waved my hand at the window. "Not in here. But thanks for divulging that confidential information."

His pompous face flushed red. "I happen to know a lot more than you think, so watch your mouth, Miss Blunt."

"What the hell does that mean?"

Howie lay a hand on my shoulder and shook his head warningly. I glared at him.

"Considering the way that she has been drawing the in-fected, she should be informed, George," said Dr. Mullins.

"WE should be the judge of that," snapped Agent Baum with a curl of his lip. "Maintaining the secret of Z038IE is of vital importance: not only to the safety of the Canadian public but also to national security. I think Canada did right to exile you back in '69. But you wormed your way back in. America sent you back."

"The American government did not want me living within their borders, but that is largely because I refused to help them find ways of adjusting the disease into a potent biological weapon for use on the Vietnamese."

"And where is the cure you promised us? When you brought us news of the American conspiracy to make this cursed virus more infectious, what good did it do us? Without a cure, we are at risk daily of being destroyed by our American enemy!" He was starting to look a little crazed.

Dr. Mullins was impassive, as always. "America is not your enemy, George, you keep forgetting. We are at peace. We have trade agreements. We have the world's longest undefended border. Furthermore, we share the same land mass. Canada would not be a good target for this kind of weapon because the infected would be able to cross freely into the U.S. and bring a crisis down on America. If it were ever used, and I hope it would not, it would be in a country that is well separated from the United States, such as North Korea or an island like Cuba. Furthermore, it is very unlikely that they would do so even then until they had developed a cure to be released upon negotiation of a peace treaty."

"You are so naive," snarled the agent. "Can't you see the attack on Canada that's being perpetrated by America on a daily basis? They infiltrate our culture with their big box stores, their dark roasts, and their phonetic spellings! They steal our creative talent, lure us into their wars, and our citizens are more invested in presidential elections than in our own! Canada is being weakened from within, and we must stand with our beloved nation and fight against everything that threatens its sanctity!"

"What the…" I said but Howie squeezed my arm and I shut up.

"All of that aside, George, let's talk about young Stella. Everything suggests that she is a strong draw. You will need to protect her."

"Perhaps you should have done the same, instead of allowing one of your infected wards to pursue a romantic relationship with her," snapped Baum.

"Are you going to protect Stella or not?" Howie interjected.

"Are you all going to start speaking like I'm in the room or not?" I demanded.

"What do you suggest?" Baum said, ignoring me entirely. "I can't spare personnel to stand around and neutralize the occasional infected arrival like we did last night. I need the manpower elsewhere. You can do it yourselves. In fact, you'll be less at risk than my staff since you are already infected."

"I'm not suggesting that," said Dr. Mullins, polishing his glasses. "I'm suggesting that we intentionally allow a large horde to build up in order to attract as many as possible, and then eliminate them in one stroke."

There was a pause.

"No," said Howie loudly. Everyone ignored him. Baum seemed frozen in place.

"You realize that this places you at a certain amount of risk? The girl, too."

"My name is STELLA. I'm sitting RIGHT HERE," I said. "Can I participate in the conversation? What the hell are you all talking about?"

Howie looked furious. "They want to use you like cheese in a giant rat trap."

"I'm cheese?"

Dr. Mullins turned to me. "For once we know where the horde will gather in advance. Let's take advantage of that fact. We clear a perimeter, place you in a building in the center, wait for a large horde to build up outside and then eliminate them." He turned to Baum. "It makes the most sense to do this from headquarters or some other location which is secured against the infected."

Baum shook his head. "I'm not risking government property. What if we need to detonate explosives?"

"You'd do that?" I asked. "How do you cover THAT up?"

"Natural gas explosion, very sad," he shrugged.

"You know that explosives are a dubious method of elimination," warned Dr. Mullins. "Often the brain is still not destroyed, and you just end up with infected walking around on fire."

"Sure, but most of them at least end up on fire with no arms or legs. Much easier targets," said Agent Baum dismissively. "I'm not surprised that you'd try to talk us out of vital measures to protect the sanctity of our populace."

"In any case, Agent Baum," said Dr. Mullins, "I believe that Stella can and will draw an extremely large horde, which you can then eliminate in a single attack. Isn't that a better option, as opposed to seeking small groups all over the city?"

"Makes sense to me," I said. "Count me in. Not that any of you have actually asked me."

Howie looked troubled but said nothing. Agent Baum glowered for a minute while shifting his weight from foot to foot. Then he sighed. "Yes, I suppose so. I will clear the plan with Agent Hunt. Then we will arrange an evacuation of the houses in your neighbourhood, to protect the innocent Canadians. YOU will all be fitted with GPS units to assure us that you have not broken house arrest. That includes you, Miss Blunt, since you are in possession of our beloved Canada's national secrets and are unnaturally attractive to the foul souls of the tainted undead."

I wasn't sure how to respond.

"We will send a helicopter to monitor your situation occasionally. When we think it's big enough to be worth the staff effort, we'll eliminate the problem. If you encounter difficulties, contact me immediately. You know my number."

The moment the door slammed behind Agent Baum, I exploded.

"WHAT IN THE NAME OF JESUS HEPATITIS CHRIST...?"

"Just let it go, Stella, he's always like that," said Howie.

"He's crazier than a syphilitic Republican!"

"He's a passionate nationalist. Everyone just waits for him to simmer down and goes on like nothing happened because he's very good at what he does."

"Which is what – channeling Glenn Beck?"

"No, security – his paranoia is an asset," said Dr. Mullins, inspecting his ankle bracelet gloomily.

"Paranoia? I think he passed paranoia and left it in his dust fifty klicks outside of Crazytown."

"It doesn't help that Dad riles him up," said Ray. "All that calm, reasonable arguing drives him bug nuts, and Dad knows it."

"Man's a fool," said Dr. Mullins.

"If he wanted to, he could lock you away, Dad. You shouldn't provoke him," said Hazel softly.

"Oh, under all his prejudice he knows that I'm their best hope for finding a cure," said Dr. Mullins.

"You better hope so, Dad, because this is bad," said Howie softly. "A whole outbreak, all from your lab?"

"It doesn't make sense," said Dr. Mullins. "Stella, I hope you can attract a large number of infected. The more that come here, the fewer there will be out attacking the public."

"Besides, I think Agent Baum will wait until the horde gets as big as possible before they come in," said Howie.

"I still don't get why he didn't want to leave guards here when you already know that all the zombies will be coming here," I said.

"Well, not all the zombies. There are going to be pockets all over the city."

"You think there will still be other groups?"

"Of course," said Dr. Mullins. "Zombies naturally tend to gather in hordes. As I've said, one or two zombies are largely ineffective, but a large horde is extremely dangerous."

I felt like I was missing something.

"I thought the whole point was that the zombies were all going to group around me, so you could kill them all at once."

"Yes, it's an excellent advantage to know where they will gather so we can evacuate the area beforehand."

"But if it's such a big deal that you're going to have a horde around me, why does Agent Explode'em feel so sure that he'll have other hordes to deal with?"

Howie and I stared at each other in mutual befuddlement for a moment. Then he sat up straight, made a little "Oh" with his mouth, and then kneeled in front of me and took both my hands in his.

"Stella, I think I haven't been clear. You are not the only person to have this kind of effect on zombies."

Oh. I wasn't?

"Zombies tend to drift toward the most attractive minds, and these serve as a sort of beacon to lead them into groups. But there will be lots of minds around that attract them."

Okay, this is going to sound stupid, but I was a little hurt and disappointed. I really had let myself become convinced that I was some sort of super-special snowflake with the best mind in the universe. I felt a stab of embarrassment. I mean, obviously. Duh. I couldn't be THAT SPECIAL. Sure, I was smart and savvy and all the things that Howie liked to enthuse about. But obviously, I wasn't that frigging unique.

"So, how many people?"

"It's hard to say because it's not a cut-and-dried thing, you understand," said Howie with an earnest look on his face, "The more attractive the mind, the more likely zombies are to drift toward it."

"In rural areas, one in every two or three hundred may attract a group, while in cities, it tends to be more like one in every two or three hundred thousand," explained Dr. Mullins. "The goal is for any local zombies to congregate to the most attractive mind in a given area. Cities provide greater diversity, and so they are able to choose from a much larger range of minds. A mind that might attract a crowd in a small town might be relatively overlooked in the city."

Humph. So I could still feel smug, at least, that my mind was the nicest in our general vicinity, then.

"Okay, so if there are lots of people like me, then why are you making a big deal about me?"

"Because we don't usually know who those people are until the zombies have already eaten them. It's great to have some warning, clear away the local people, and lure as many as possible to a relatively safe location."

Howie pulled me into the living room, invited me to sit down, and then brought me a Diet Pepsi. Apparently, he had stocked up just for me.

"Stella, can we come up with a good reason why you aren't at school and have to stay with me for the night?"

"No."

"There has to be something we can think up."

"My parents are pretty easy going, Howie. They trust me, and they're left wing. But I can pretty much guarantee you that if I tell them that I skipped school and want to sleep over at my boyfriend's house on a school night, they will have a problem with that." I looked at my ankle GPS. "Do you think I could get this off?"

"No. And they will know if you go even as far as your house. So you have to stay here."

"What am I supposed to tell them? I can't just *not* go home. They'd panic!"

"We'll think of some story."

"No!" I shouted at him. "You don't know my parents! I've *always* told them the truth! I might tell incomplete truths, withhold information occasionally, but I've never out-and-out-lied to them because they *never* lie to me. I can't break that now. I'd feel guilty forever."

Howie frowned. "Then there's only one option."

"What?"

"We actually tell them the truth."

15

My parents sat close together on the couch in the sterile living room and sipped their Diet Pepsis while Dr. Mullins went through the whole lecture, including the chopping off and re-application of his left hand. They went from amused, to incredulous, to angry, and then, after the hand thing, to worried.

"So... you're seriously telling me that there is a zombie attack, that you're all zombies too, and that the zombies are all hunting Stella?" Dad asked.

"No, no," said Dr. Mullins in what I think was supposed to be a soothing tone. "We are all infected with the Z0381E virus, but in a state of permanent stasis, so that we are not yet fully zombies, but possess some of the qualities of the infected. An outbreak is currently in progress, and while the zombies are hunting anyone with a brain, your daughter's mind is particularly attractive to them. So any nearby tend to move in her direction, although they will stop to attack anyone in their path."

"Stella's mind is attractive to zombies?"

"Very."

"Are you telling me young Howard here is only interested in Stella because of her brain?" Dad turned to look at Howie.

My mother looked at my father with a furrowed brow. "That's supposed to be a good thing."

"Well... well... not when you think about it from the point of view that he's a zombie!"

Dr. Mullins shook his head. "May I remind you that this whole family is infected with the same virus as Howard, but that he is the only one interested in a romantic relationship with her? We are all... aware of Stella's attractive qualities, but we merely wish to eat her."

There was a long pause. Hazel whispered in her father's ear.

"Ah, yes, I realize that may not have been as reassuring as it was intended to be. Allow me to rephrase. We would never actually eat Stella or any human. We are strongly morally opposed."

Hazel whispered to her father again.

"On further reflection, I understand that I did not so much rephrase my point as place an addendum to it. I hope, however, that my point is nonetheless made."

"I love everything about Stella," said Howie, "and I am physically attracted to her body, not just her brain."

I put my head in my hands. My mother looked like she was trying very hard not to laugh. Dad closed his eyes for a moment, breathed deeply, and opened them again.

"So what's this plan about using her as zombie bait?"

"Ah, yes," said Dr. Mullins. "Since we suspect that any zombies in the immediate area will be drawn to your daughter, it seems prudent to expect them."

"So, you're waiting for a zombie horde to show up and annihilate our daughter?"

"Oh, no, they're likely to show up one by one or in very small groups."

"They why aren't you planning to kill them off as they show up? I'm no expert on the zombie genre, but aren't they supposed to be more trouble when they pile up?"

"If our concern was only Stella's safety, eliminating them individually would be the ideal method," admitted Dr. Mullins.

"Our only concern *is* Stella's safety," snapped my mother.

"I can appreciate that. But I ask you to think about this: zombies naturally gather into hordes because they are stronger in groups. One zombie, drifting toward Stella, will likely join another zombie drifting toward Stella. A third zombie is then more likely to join them, which in turn makes it more likely that a fourth and a fifth will appear. The attraction grows exponentially based on the number of other infected individuals in the area. In other words, if we pick them off as they arrive, we may stop a dozen. Meanwhile, the rest of the infected will be menacing the general populace, getting snagged into hordes elsewhere, and so on. On the other hand, if we allow them to build up here, more and more infected will hasten to join them. We could clear a large portion of the surrounding city."

"Ants," said Hazel.

We all looked at her.

"Ants," she said again, wiping a spot of drool from the corner of her mouth. "If you put down a pile of sugar and kill off the ants one by one when they come by, you won't see a lot of ants. But if you leave it there and you come back in an hour, there will be hundreds of them crawling all over it."

"But I don't *want* hundreds of undead crawling all over my daughter," complained my Dad.

"You are willing to let them into the path of other people's children, instead?" Dr. Mullins asked.

My parents looked mutinous, as if they were thinking "yes," but knew it was socially inappropriate to say so.

"Guys, this is not up to you," I said finally. "It's really obvious what the moral choice is. And it's not like they're talking about tying me to a stake in the middle of a field and leaving me there."

Howie shuddered and moved closer to me.

"There will be people with guns and crap ready to kill them all off when it's time," I pointed out.

Howie nodded. "I don't want anything to happen to her either. But if the infection keeps spreading, and more and more people get infected, and more and more of them show up at her door..." he trailed off. "They're coming. Let's kill them off as efficiently as we can, before it gets worse."

His father nodded. "Yes, officials will be monitoring our situation and will come in and destroy the horde when it becomes dangerously large."

"And when can we expect the undead to start showing up, exactly?"

There was a bang on the door.

"Ah," said Dr. Mullins, rising. "That may be them now."

My parents rushed to a window. There were only two outside. Not too bad.

"We'll need a lot more'n that," said Ray.

"So, how many will it take to get the government in here and protecting our child?"

"It depends mostly on proportions. Obviously, if we only have a few, and there are hundreds somewhere else, we won't be high on their triage list."

"So, they think there aren't many zombies coming?" I asked.

"No, but I'm sure that there are. They don't understand your draw, Stella. I heartily agree with Howie that you are a fairly strong beacon for them. However, unless we draw excessive numbers, they are leaving us to deal with the situation ourselves."

"So what are you doing to do?"

"I'm going to trust in Stella to draw excessive numbers."

My parents looked at me. I could see them mentally calculating how alluring I might be to the undead, and coming up doubtful.

"Can't we go back to the kill'em one-by-one plan?" Dad asked.

"Even if we did, there's no guarantee that we would be able to handle them all by ourselves, nor is it the morally correct decision. Our best bet is to simply keep safe until they have time to come help us."

"Well, let's at least get Stella somewhere safer. What's a good anti-zombie location?"

"A zeppelin," suggested my mother.

"Stella is not allowed to leave the premises," Dr. Mullins reminded them, gesturing at my GPS anklet. "You are welcome to stay or leave. If you do stay, please be aware that you are putting yourself at risk, since the chance of encountering zombies at your home without Stella present will be much lower than here with Stella in close proximity."

My parents gave him a really dirty pair of looks.

"Of course we aren't running off and leaving our daughter!" My mother folded her arms.

"I definitely think we should stock up on zombie killing supplies, though," said Dad eagerly. "How long does it take to get a gun permit?"

"We should not need to defend ourselves. In that eventuality, we have a wide range of cleavers. They are intended to help us extract brain material from the livestock heads that we buy in bulk. We also have some electric gardening tools, and they will serve as weapons in an emergency. We are also equipped with a few neural disruption devices. We are each supposed to carry one with us always, in case one of us suddenly develops advanced symptoms. We are supposed to neutralize ourselves or each other the moment it appears necessary."

"Is that a risk?"

"Not so far as I can discover, as long as we take care of ourselves."

Dad looked disappointed that he wouldn't get to shoot a gun. "Are you sure a shotgun wouldn't be good? I thought shotguns were the weapon of choice."

"I assure you, obtaining a shotgun in Vancouver at a few hours' notice would involve breaking several laws, even in the case of a zombie outbreak. Our best bet is to bunker down and wait for the horde to reach a point that the authorities will consider worth eradicating on our behalf."

In the end, my parents decided to run home to get some supplies, like food and pajamas, since Howie's family agreed that it would probably take all night to build up a reasonable collection of zombies. Dad originally suggested ordering pizza, until it was pointed out to him that the unwitting pizza delivery person might get savaged by a horde of the undead.

"In that case, know any Jehovah's Witnesses we can call?"

"Dad!"

"Sorry, I couldn't resist."

"I guess we better get rid of those two on our stoop, so you can leave," said Ray, standing up. Hazel went with him to the front door. There were some eager, rattling moans, and then two thumps. Ray stuck his head back inside.

"We'll just take these down to cold storage in the basement," he said.

My parents watched with open mouths as two bodies were dragged down the basement steps. They left with promises to be very careful.

I couldn't really relax until my parents got back. I kept picturing them getting eaten the moment they pulled back in the driveway. I sat in the window and watched anxiously, while Howie offered me Diet Pepsi and back massages, which he was surprisingly skilled at.

"It's all about knowing anatomy," he said, "I've sat through a lot of anatomy classes."

Another shambling body came lurching up the walk just as my parents' new car turned the corner. Dad drove right into the body, causing it to cartwheel into the bushes. Dad jumped out eagerly, and I ran out to meet him.

"Did I kill it? Did I kill it?" he asked. I went to the bush to check, and a hand shot out and grabbed my ankle. I stepped on the zombie's neck with my other foot, and my mother ran up. She looked down, shuddered, and stabbed the zombie deep in the eye with a pen from her purse, and actually disabled it before I could do any damage myself.

I stared gape-mouthed at the pen sticking out of the zombie's eye socket. Eyes ooze, did you know that?

"You just stabbed someone in the eye," I said. "Without hesitation."

"I thought it would look like a person. But that just looked like a nightmare. For God's sakes, Stella, stay in the house. You know these things have it in for you," she said.

"Mom. They're *zombies*. They have it in for everybody."

"I'd feel *much* better if you were in the house. Zombies are coming from miles around to eat my only child. This was *not* in any of my parenting books."

Dad followed us inside, looking sulky. I think he was sorry that he missed out on the kill.

Mom and Dad had packed pajamas, toothbrushes and toothpaste, books to read, and a lasagna from the freezer. Everything you need when preparing to weather the zombie apocalypse.

They also remembered to bring my little teddy bear that I got when I was six and have slept with ever since. Because, you know, parents are morally obligated to embarrass their offspring.

"He's cute. What's his name?" asked Howie.

"Howard!" my mother said with a grin.

"I named him that when I was SIX," I said firmly. "Can I have my bear please?"

Howie handed him over, carefully smoothing his bow. I shoved him unceremoniously into the bag with my jammies.

"Okay, so where am I putting this stuff?"

It turned out that a bunch of zombies with no friends don't have a lot of spare beds in their house. On the bright side, it also turned out that zombies don't have any difficulty losing consciousness whenever they want and don't mind sleeping on the couch.

Dr. Mullins gave up his room for my parents, and Howie gave up his room for me.

My parents insisted that they could sleep on the couch/floor, but Dr. Mullins wouldn't take no for an answer. I mean that. He just totally ignored their polite protestations in a decidedly rude manner.

Howie finally just put a hand on the shoulder of each parent and said, "We could sleep standing up. He really doesn't mind. Just go with it. Besides, since we'll be waiting for angry undead to pile up at our front door, I don't think any of us are going to get much sleep tonight. So just let us play host to the first guests we've had in fifty-five years, okay? Now, why don't you go get settled, and I'll get started on that lasagna. What temperature should I pre-heat the oven to?"

"I hope that oven still works..." said Hazel.

It was a weird dining experience. We sat around eating our lasagna while the Mullinses watched us. The only one that didn't seem fascinated by the sight of us eating was the dog, who slumbered at my feet.

Eventually, I burst out irritably with, "Howard, don't you guys have some brains to eat or something? We're not used to an audience when we have dinner."

"We didn't want to put you off your food."

"Are you going to spoon it directly out of some poor pig's skull?"

"No, we have pre-prepared portions in the fridge."

"Then EAT THEM."

"Besides, I ate sheep brains once," said my mother. "In Greece."

"Gross!"

"Hey," said Howie.

"Fine. How delightfully cultural that must have been, Mother."

"Yeah, it really was quite disgusting."

"Even we don't really like them," Howie admitted.

"Really?" said Dad, "then what's the idea?"

"Well, you see," said Dr. Mullins, "pre-prepared, already-deceased, non-human brains are not our ideal diet. But for obvious reasons, we make do. They work to provide us with what we need. A neuron is a neuron, really."

"But it doesn't satisfy in the same way?"

"No. The virus programs us for human flesh. But in order for us to maintain brain function, we need brains, preferably human brains."

"So you could eat meat and other things, too?"

"Oh yes, and we do occasionally as a treat, but we consider the most vital thing to be brains. If we fill up on bacon, the virus wins, you see?"

"Hmm, give up bacon or become a zombie. Difficult decision," said Dad, shoveling another heaping spoonful of cheesy lasagna into his mouth.

The zombies sat back down at the table with thankfully opaque thermoses. There was a chorus of slurpy straw noises.

"See, this is much more friendly," said Dad cheerfully. "Would you like some lasagna with your brains?"

After dinner, we checked the front door. It was dark out now, but Ray switched on the porch light with a flick of his finger and five haunted faces were illuminated by the glow. They looked at the light and started milling around a bit.

"They're hoping we're about to come out," said Ray with a sneer.

"Why are they just standing there? I thought they'd be knocking down the door or something," I said.

"Hey, you had eight outside your house last night before you noticed 'em," Ray pointed out. "They just gather and wait, at first. The more of 'em there are, the more desperate they get. Not sure if it's competition or maybe a sorta collective consciousness thing. We don't really know because we've never been this far gone, obviously. Anyway, when there's a lot of 'em, they get a lot more determined. And violent."

That sounded just wonderful.

"Should we go out and kill them?" asked Dad.

"The more there are, the faster more will arrive," said Dr. Mullins. "It's a sort of domino effect."

"He means snowball effect," said Hazel.

"How stupid do these zombies have to be?" I said. "They could be off eating lots of human brains but instead they're hanging around outside our door? How does that make sense?"

"Yeah, well, there's a reason it's never called the Rocket Scientist Apocalypse," said Howie, taking my hand in his. "Think of your mind as a bright light. When you look up at the sky under a street light, can you see the stars as well as when you are in a dark field? Your mind is like that street light. It makes the others fade into the background."

"I always knew she was bright," said Dad, giving me a cuddle, which was awkward since Howie was still holding my hand. Man sandwich.

It turns out that sitting inside while zombies line up at the front door is surprisingly boring. There was no smashing of windows or clawing at the door. They were oddly calm. I mean, which was good but didn't really represent my recent experiences. Dad seemed a little disappointed. So did Ray.

"Where the hell are they all?" Ray muttered. "Howie, I thought you said she was a big draw."

"She is; can't you feel her?"

Ray sent me a look that I found deeply uncomfortable.

"Sure, but I'm right next to her." He stomped downstairs to the basement.

The rest of us spent some time sitting around the living room, watching the news, which was managing to skillfully downplay the fact that there were undead gathering at multiple points of the city, instead making it sound like a few isolated incidents of toxin-addled rage attacks. My school was on the news, though, which was cool.

Then Dr. Mullins went down to his lab, and Hazel drifted away to her room, and my parents pulled out their books. So Howie and I went off to talk in his room.

"Don't do anything I wouldn't do," called Dad as we went upstairs.

"Would you pee sitting down, Dad?"

"I might!"

"Would you wear a V-neck top, Dad?"

"MAYBE!"

"Would you have long chaste conversations with your boyfriend?"

"Yeah, yeah. Just don't have unprotected sex."

"Thank you for the reassurance that you wouldn't have unprotected sex. I'll leave you and Mom to work out the mystery of my paternity and go upstairs, shall I?"

I grabbed Howie's hand and pulled him up the stairs.

We actually did do homework. We had our school bags, and we needed to kill time, and I was very aware of the fact that my parents were downstairs. So, homework.

Howie was fired up on brains and told me a lot about the 1950s that wasn't in my textbook. I have to say, writing an essay on the post-war era was a lot more interesting when you could talk to someone who remembered it. Especially when that someone was cute and wearing glasses that made him look sensitive and scholarly.

He also demonstrated his vinyl record player, picking out records from the 1950s to go along with our homework.

"This one was a favourite of mine when I was a kid," he said, putting on a new song. "Doesn't it make you want to dance?"

"Nothing makes me want to dance," I said. "But it *is* catchy. Sh-boom, sh-boom. Simple, but catchy." I listened for a while as Howie bobbed his head to the old-timey music. "It's kinda date-rapey."

Howie looked startled. "What?"

"Listen to it! He's trying to talk this chick into having sex with him."

Howie opened his mouth, then closed it again. And then he covered his face. "I'll never hear it the same way again."

"You didn't know that it's a sex song?"

"I did but... I thought it was cute until you said it that way and then I heard it how you heard it..."

"Sorry. I didn't mean to wreck your favourite song."

He shook his head. "There have been a lot of great hits since this one. But this one was, like, probably the first Rock 'n Roll big hit song."

"Okay. So it's sort of like your car – kind of crappy by today's standards, but worthy of respect."

Howie grinned. "Exactly."

"So, what great hit do you think would actually stand up to the test of time?" I asked.

Howie's face got serious. "Good question." He browsed his shelf for a while. "Ah." He took off his fifties record and carefully placed a new one on the turnstile. There was a crackle, and then the unmistakable voice of Louis Armstrong filled the room, singing *As Time Goes By*.

"Okay," I said. "Fair point. But 'woman needs man'?"

Howie grinned again. "Tough customer. Hmm." He spent a long time flipping through records. "Got it."

There was a thump and another crackle, a couple of false starts as he tried to find the right track... and then Aretha Franklin's *Respect* blasted out. Howie looked up hopefully and smiled when he saw me smiling.

"*Now* you're playing to your audience," I said.

My parents came upstairs around 11 p.m.

"Kids?" said Dad, sticking his head into the room, "We're headed to bed to get a bit of shut-eye before the hordes of the underdark make their move. Howie, Ray said to tell you that he thinks there's around twenty out there now."

I got the creeps thinking about twenty dead bodies just handing out on the stoop, so I turned to my half-dead sixty-eight-year-old boyfriend for comfort as soon as Dad closed the door.

"Twenty? Shouldn't we be calling in the Zom Squad?"

"Oh, no. I think that at this point they're not likely to come out for anything under a hundred."

"A HUNDRED? How many zombies are there in this town?"

"It's bad. We're not at the turning point yet, but it's bad."

"What's the turning point?"

"When there are more zombies than people."

"That's the turning point?"

"Well, that's more the point of no return. Anyway, it's important to get as many as possible together and then take them out all at once."

"Won't this really suck for the people who live around here? I mean, I know they evacuated your street, but there are other streets. What if they spill over to other people's houses? You said that a group of zombies is really dangerous."

"My lovely, you are so overwhelming in your presence that I can't even tell that there are other minds nearby."

"Seriously?"

"I am very serious." He leaned forward and held my eyes with his. "When you walked into school that first day," said Howie in a quiet voice, "I knew it immediately. It was like a blinding light had just turned on. You electrified me."

"What, just all of a sudden? Not gradually as I got closer?"

Howie frowned. "No, you took me by surprise. It was like a shockwave going through me. I was completely overwhelmed." He paused. "I mean, your brain waves aren't the same all the time. They fluctuate based on your mood. Like when you're angry." A dreamy look passed over his face. "I love it when you get angry. I think that those zombies last night got riled up when you saw them and panicked. They were calm enough until you spotted them, right?"

"So if I go to sleep, will they all drift away?"

"Apparently a couple of zombies still drifted to your door last night while you were asleep, so I think it'll be fine. You have brain waves when you sleep, they're just calmer, more relaxed. Except when you dream."

"And my asleep brain waves are still good?"

"Well, I've never felt your sleeping brain waves, have I? It's not like I hang around outside your window listening to you sleep. But maybe if you're sleeping it'll just help keep them calm. If it isn't working, and they stop gathering, we'll wake you up again."

I stifled a yawn. Howie stood up with a smile.

"Try to get some sleep, gorgeous. I'll be downstairs, guarding the door."

He kissed my hand and left.

Believe it or not, even in my pajamas and with my teddy bear, I had difficulty getting to sleep in a strange bedroom with bloodthirsty walking dead gathering outside my window. I just lay there with my book, glancing at the black and white photo on the shelf and wondering about the disaster that blew that family apart.

How did the parents get infected? Did Howie or Hazel have to kill their own undead parents? How did the authorities know about it in time to take Howie and Hazel into custody? Was there a big outbreak? Was it an isolated incident?

Those are the questions you never ask someone, for many different reasons.

After a while, I gave up and went to look out the window. I was looking out the side of the house, so I didn't expect to see much, but then something moved. I could see a multitude of forms gathering outside my window, clawing at the side of the house.

Those assholes wanted to eat me!

I felt a flood of rage. I hated being penned up in Howie's weird house, with his weird family, with the threat of a zombie apocalypse.

Why did the first semi-intelligent, caring, worshipful guy I had ever found have to turn out to be a zombie? And why did he have to have a creepy half-dead family? And WHY did there have to be zombie outbreak? And why the *hell* was I some kind of beacon for the undead?

I mean, Liz once snitched a book off her mom's bookshelf that claimed that women attract a certain kind of person to them, so a woman who has been in a relationship with several abusive alcoholics will naturally tend to attract other abusive alcoholics. What did it say about me that I apparently attracted diseased, mindless, murderous corpses?

Fuck this. Fuck the everything.

I threw Howard (the bear, not the boyfriend) across the room. He hit the door with a thump and then landed on his head. I felt bad and picked him up and hugged him as Howie burst into the room.

I hastily tossed my bear onto the bed.

"Christ on a waffle, Howie, I could have been naked or something!"

Howie looked momentarily baffled. "Is that meant to be encouragement?"

"NO!"

"I came up because you just got all excited. What happened?"

"I'm pissed off!"

"You just got angry?"

"Yes, angry!"

"Why?"

"Because I'm getting really bored of waiting until the zombies decide to come eat me! Because I'm pissed off that they chased me out of school. Because I'm pissed off about the fact that this many people have DIED and are going to have to die AGAIN. Because fuck the fuckety fucks, that's why, Howard."

Howie went to the window and looked out. "There's more coming down the street. Keep it up and we'll draw in zombies from all over town."

I scowled. "'Oh, don't get upset, Stella, you'll rile up the zombies!' Why are men always trying to suppress female emotions?"

Howie knelt at my feet. "I love your emotions, gorgeous, I find your anger overwhelmingly attractive, and I am encouraging you to keep it up. Why wait around all night when we can get you in a rage and turn you into the brightest mind in the city?"

I was mollified, then realized that it was the wrong emotion.

"Then you're going to have to piss me off some more."

"Or we could see if other strong emotions do the same trick," he said breathlessly.

Hmm.

"When you light up like that, my whole soul sings," he whispered. "You are so strong, so brilliant. Those zombies out there aren't half as attracted to you as I am. I unconditionally surrender to you. I want to serve you every day for the rest of my life. I love you."

I pulled him up and kissed him. When I opened my mouth to him, he gasped and pulled free for a moment. I could feel him trembling.

After a deep breath, he pulled me close and we kissed again and again, running our hands up and down each other's bodies, exploring each other. He pressed against me and I could feel his erection digging into my leg.

I couldn't help it. I glanced down, and Howie looked embarrassed.

"I'm blaming that on rigor mortis. Comes from being half-dead." Then he gave me a shy grin. "But with you, I'm half-alive."

"Oh, God. That's beyond corny."

I was breathing heavily. I had never felt quite like this. Acting on impulse, I pushed him onto the bed and he toppled willingly. He looked up at me with parted lips and ran his fingers gently through my hair.

"You are amazing." His voice was soft.

"Shut up and let me kiss you some more."

My heart was pounding as we pressed ourselves into each other. I could feel his heart pounding too, in a funny, irregular kind of a way. His chemical smell felt clean and safe, and he radiated desire. He ran his hands over my hips and pressed me close against him, and then moaned under his breath.

"We're just making out, Howie," I warned.

"I know. That's all we'll ever do."

"What does that mean?" I said, pulling away. He moved his arms as if to stop me, then dropped them, chest heaving.

"You don't have to worry that I'll... take advantage of you," he said quietly.

I almost laughed. "Howie, I've already proven I can take you in a fight. I haven't been worrying about that."

"I didn't fight back, you know," he reminded me with a wink, "but yes, I am sure you could. You know what I mean. I am just saying that I... I would never want..."

"You don't want to have sex with me?" My emotions were switching back to "pissed off" again.

He gave a little laugh that was also a groan. "That might be the first stupid thing I have ever heard you say. You have no idea what it is like to be a teenage boy for fifty plus years."

"Then what? Some sort of chivalrous 1950s values?"

"Maybe... a little. I don't think it stopped a lot of people back then, though, either. I just... I'd worry all the time that it wasn't safe." Howie sat up and stared at his feet.

"Sex Ed class scared you?"

He looked uncomfortable. "It's just a conversation I've never really had. Can you imagine asking your Dad to test your... your... to see if it... carried the virus?"

Ew.

"Oh. Well. There are condoms, you know."

"Not what they were designed for. Would you want to take that risk?"

There was a long silence.

"No."

He rubbed his face. "Welcome to my life."

"So, none of you have..."

"I think Ray may have... occasionally... with... protection." His blue eyes met mine. "But I could never take that kind of risk with someone's life. With people's safety."

"Maybe Ray asked your Dad..."

"I don't think so. I think he just assumed. I don't know if Dad's ever thought about it. And I don't know how to start that conversation."

Sixty-eight years old, and still so innocent. I felt a gush of affection for him. He was good at science, he thought I was some kind of goddess, and most importantly, he was just a good person. It was beginning to dawn on me that zombie stuff aside, Howie was a real find.

"Well. It's way too early in the relationship anyway. As long as it's not that you aren't interested," I teased. His eyes opened wide.

"You. Have. No. Idea." He whispered huskily into my ear. "But it isn't worth your safety. I love you."

I wondered if I could say what I was feeling. I wondered if what I was feeling was real. Maybe it was teenage hormones, or pheromones, an accident of neurons and biochemistry. Maybe it'd be an accidental lie. Maybe I'd regret it in a month, or a year. Maybe I'd open my mouth and say something horribly inappropriate instead.

Fuck it.

"I think... I might... love you, too," I whispered, and I waited for the world to end. Instead, his lip trembled as if he was going to cry, and then he pulled me tight against him. He kissed me fiercely and I kissed him back, fiercer, each of us trying to overpower the other with proof of our passion.

That's when the zombies decided to start smashing windows.

16

There were shouts from the living room at the sound of breaking glass, and Howie and I pulled apart, dizzy and disheveled. Howie smiled, and even with the sounds of mayhem coming from downstairs, I wanted to kiss his dimple. Or maybe lick it. Hormones are bizarre.

"Is it just me or do zombies have a real sense of timing?" I asked. "That's twice, or three times that they've interrupted us?"

"I guess your emotions work on more than just me," he said. He rolled off the bed and stiffly lumbered to the window. "I think the crowd out there has more than doubled."

"And they're angry. Are you sure that was a good idea?"

"You're asking whether the best moment of my life was a good idea? Besides, the more zombies outside our door, the fewer there are to attack other people. It was selfless," he said, flashing me another smile. "Come on, let's go see how bad it is."

He stumbled down the stairs. I followed him, feeling strangely light-headed.

The living room window was broken, but Ray was already hammering a board in place. Fingers curled around the board.

"You happened to have a board and hammer and nails prepared?" I said.

Ray turned and smirked.

"I knew what to expect, especially since you started lighting up like a Christmas tree up there. I hope you two were having fun. They've been coming running and piling up six deep. Look out there!"

He threw another board up and started to hammer. A finger got in the way of one of the nails but he just kept hammering. After a moment, the finger ripped itself free, leaving shreds of flesh pinned to the board.

I looked out the front door peephole and almost jumped back again. Corpses crammed on the porch and trailed down the driveway, and more lurching figures were appearing under the streetlight.

"How did the window break?"

"One of the smarter ones brought a rock." Ray gestured at a stone on the floor surrounded by broken glass.

Howie calmly got a broom and started to sweep things up.

"Zombies are breaking windows and you're *sweeping*?"

"Floor has to be cleaned."

"What's going on?" My parents were coming down the stairs. I noticed that they were fully dressed, unlike me. Why was I always getting caught in my pajamas?

"I'm going to go get dressed," I said. "I think the zombie wars are picking up."

When I came back downstairs, dressed, Dr. Mullins was on the phone. Howie went right to my side and reached for my hand. I felt a probably-imaginary tingle on my skin where we touched.

"Dad's calling the authorities. He thinks it's about time we started wiping these guys out. They're getting out of hand."

There was a gurgle, and a thump of a hand beating on the board over the window. More hands scrabbled at the other, unbroken window. Ray started hammering boards over that one, too.

Dr. Mullins hung up the phone.

"George Baum says they cannot possibly come for several more hours."

"Is he fucking serious?" I stared at him.

"It would appear so," he said blandly.

"So, what? We just hold out until they can wander up this way?" I turned to Howie. "You said the more zombies the better, but what if there's more than we can handle before they get here?"

Howie pursed his lips. For the first time since we met, he looked angry. For a shocked moment, I thought it was at *me*.

"Agent Baum doesn't give a darn about us," he said. "They probably planned this. Let zombies kill off the zombies."

"What about me and my parents?"

"Stella, my love, they value human life but look at all of the lost human life standing outside on our porch. A few more... I just don't think you're high on their priority list."

For a moment we stood there and contemplated our probable demises. Death. I could actually die. Die being ripped apart by zombies. I could have my brains eaten. I wondered if you were still alive when that happened.

"Well… I'll bring up some tarps to cover the furniture," said Ray.

Howie's family raided their basement for defensive supplies. A chainsaw for trimming branches in the garden. The four brain disruptors. A hammer. A lot of meat cleavers. Some protective laboratory glasses to keep blood out of our mucous membranes.

Ray lectured my parents in self-defense while they tried out the different weapons.

"Aim for the head. Nothing else matters. Unless the brain is destroyed, the zombie keeps going."

"So what about if we chop off its head?" Dad asked.

"The body stops but the head'll still bite."

"For how long?"

"Long enough."

"I can't believe that," I said. "If the head has no heart to pump blood, no stomach to digest with, no lungs to breathe with, then how can it stay alive?"

Ray rolled his eyes. "They aren't alive, Stella. They're dead."

"In all the ways that matter, anyway," said Howie.

"But *they're walking around!*"

"You have a very critical mind, Stella," said Dr. Mullins in his usual drawl, "I really think that if our Lord Jesus Christ rose from the dead before you and turned your water into wine, you'd refuse to accept the evidence of your own eyes until he explained the science of how it was done to your satisfaction."

"Damn straight. Zombie Jesus doesn't get any worship from me without some really detailed answers about basic physics and biology."

Ray made an irritated gesture. Howie squeezed my hand and walked out of the room, idly swinging a cleaver. Dr. Mullins rubbed his temples.

"You'll just have to take our word for it for now. When we actually survive this caper and you graduate from school you are welcome to come research the virus until your understanding of it has met your rigorous criteria."

"Maybe I will. Okay, riddle me this – you're still alive, right? The virus hasn't totally taken over?"

"Correct."

"So what happens if *your* head gets chopped off? How long could you live as just a head?"

"Without the ability to ingest and assimilate brains and flesh, we would slowly progress to full-zombie-ism and enter the state of suspended death involved therein."

"So, why do zombies who are already past that point of no return still crave flesh and brains? Can it do them any good?"

"No. No amount of human tissue can revert them to what they were. Otherwise, we would be focusing on feeding the poor souls out there, not destroying them. The zombie instinct to bite anything is a mechanism to spread the virus. We view the urge to consume human brains after the virus has fully taken over as an instinctual remnant of the human self, trying to save itself from what it has become. It's tragic when you think about it."

We all thought about it.

There was a crash outside as one zombie pushed another off of the porch, or something like that. They were past the point of saving, but still craving the thing that could have saved them, if they had just given in and eaten it earlier – well, that and some highly toxic chemical preservatives.

Damn. Those poor fuckers.

That's when Howie walked back into the room with no shirt on and a gaping, bloody wound in his chest. He swiftly knelt at my feet and wordlessly offered me his heart, no longer beating, in his blackened hands.

"HOWIE? What the hell?" I shrieked, standing up. He continued to kneel calmly, and he looked up at me with eyes that burned with passion or, possibly, insanity.

"In my hands, I offer you two things," he droned. "Proof that our bodies do not function in the way of normal bodies, and a literal version of the expression 'to give someone one's heart.' My heart is yours, my love, my skeptic. Are you convinced?"

"Today has been a highly original day," commented my father in the silence. My mother elbowed him and covered her mouth with her hand.

Howie didn't budge. He was still as a statue, his heart held over his head, his chest sliced open clumsily like the top of a jack o lantern. A line of blackish red goo slowly trickled down his chest.

"Do I have to touch it?" I asked eventually. Howie smiled.

"You have touched my heart, more than you know," he said.

"I really hope you mean metaphorically because I have to say, this doesn't ring a bell."

"Yes, metaphorically."

"Okay. I accept that your bodies are fucking bizarre. Do you feel satisfied?"

"Satisfied? No. I will always be hungry for closeness to you. But I can put my heart back now, if you don't want to accept it."

"I accept your heart as a metaphor, but I want it literally back in your fucking chest!"

There was a stirring outside, and a thump at the door.

Howie spent a minute or two arranging his heart to his satisfaction.

"Hazel, can you check this? I don't think I have my aorta lined up right."

"You've got your heart faced backwards, bozo."

"No, it's still not working, come and have a look."

She ended up needing to fetch a flashlight so they could get a better view of the whole thing.

Eventually, after they replaced the hacked-out portion of his chest, it sealed itself up and Howie put my hand on it to prove to me that his heart was beating, of a sort, again.

"If your body doesn't need your heart to beat, why does it?"

"The virus doesn't need my heart to beat. In order for me to maintain my humanity through diet, I need to keep my systems intact."

"So you were risking turning into a zombie when you did that? Uncool, Howie."

"No more so than I am risking turning into a zombie every second that I'm not drinking a brain smoothie or taking shots of formaldehyde. That's when I really need those systems. It would take probably days of heartlessness, or hunger, or what-have-you in order to have a real effect, and the formalin slows the process down even more so I could probably even go a couple of weeks."

"Could formalin do anything for those guys outside?"

Howie looked at his dad, who shrugged.

"It might slow down their decomposition process, so they'd last ten years wandering around outside instead of three or four."

"Not what we're aiming for."

"No so much," said Howie.

"Can I go back to my killing lessons now?" asked Ray.

The preparations continued while the noises against the side of the house got more frequent and more violent. Another window got smashed, but Ray slapped on a board immediately and had it half-hammered into the wall before the zombies even tried to reach in.

The estimate was at least a hundred zombies, possibly more.

I can't believe this many people died, I thought. *More, since apparently there are other spots around the city. Jesus. How many people got bitten? How many are dying now, denied a saving drink by the authorities who don't want half-zombies around?*

My parents insisted on my taking the chainsaw. They figured it was the best weapon and that I had the strength to wield it. Howie backed them up. Ray made sure I knew how to use it. Dad originally tried to explain it, but he kept getting stuff wrong.

I had handled weapons in my kung fu classes, but never a chainsaw. Unsurprisingly, the chainsaw is not an ancient weapon commonly used in stylistic forms of Chinese martial arts. Still, I hefted it in my arms and swung it back and forth experimentally. I could pretend it was a badly balanced broadsword or something.

Mom and Dad both took cleavers and declined the brain disruptors from Howie's family.

"It looks like those things take some finesse," Mom pointed out. "And I'm not sure there's time to really get comfortable with finesse."

"Will you be comfortable putting a cleaver into another human's brain? It's harder than it sounds," said Dr. Mullins.

"I'm pretty sure that we're both programmed to put a cleaver through the head of anyone who wants to hurt Stella," my mother replied with a grim expression.

"Will the zombies be ignoring my parents to get to me?" I asked.

"No."

"Why not? What happened to I-am-a-shining-beacon - of-overwhelming-light?"

"They won't need to hear your parents' minds. They'll be able to see them and smell them. Human flesh won't be passed up."

"You guys, too?"

"We don't smell appetizing, but if we're in the way, yes, we'll get attacked as well. In fact, I suspect the authorities are hoping for that."

"Will they eat your brains?"

"Possibly."

"And then you'll die."

"Yes. But since we can lose other limbs and take damage to vital organs without getting hurt, we're in much less danger than you. Not to mention that the slightest bite will result in infection for you, whereas that is no longer a problem for us."

The Mullinses proposed that we normal humans try to stay as far back as possible, preferably upstairs or even on the roof if necessary. They'd destroy as many zombies as they could, and we'd have to kill the ones who broke through.

"Howie, stay near me," I said.

"I can't let my family fight up front without me, Stella."

"You say you love me, DO WHAT I ASK."

"Okay, Stella."

The zombies were getting more and more restless, and their numbers were getting bigger and bigger. The more of them there were, the more aggressive they got. My parents and I positioned ourselves at the top of the stairs. Howie stood close to me.

Dr. Mullins tried a last call to the authorities. They weren't even answering their phones. Another window smashed. Ray grabbed a plank, but before he could get to the window, there was a smash from the kitchen and another from the bathroom. Arms groped inside. The gurgling moans became louder.

This was it. The ravening undead were breaking into the house. They were coming for me. My heart was thumping frantically. I couldn't believe this was actually happening. My Dad sniffled suddenly, and pulled me close, while my mother stroked my hair and patted Dad's back. Howie leaned close to me, and wrapped his arm around me, and whispered, "Whatever happens, I want you to know that you are the best thing that ever happened to me. I love you."

"Fuck that shit," I said. I grabbed my chainsaw with both hands and held it up in front of me. "Let's slice off some heads."

"Actually, my love, remember, you need to destroy the brain, not just decapitate the body..."

"JUST START KILLING ZOMBIES, HOWIE."

"Yes, my queen."

17

The zombies swarmed in like hornets pouring from their nest, except slower and completely uncoordinated. So, really, they just tumbled in, clawing their way in the windows while more and more pressure was put on the front door until the deadbolt snapped in the wooden door frame and burst open.

The good part was that the door hit the doorstop, bounced back, and knocked the first zombie backward into the zombies behind her, so we got a minor dominoes situation. The zombies behind trampled those zombies, though, in their lust for my delicious mind.

I could see Dr. Mullins and Ray and Hazel knocking out zombies with their disruptors at first, but then the swarm passed them and reached the stairs and my focus shifted. I held up my sputtering chainsaw as they tumbled toward me.

And then everything just seemed to slow down. I sliced the first zombie's head in half, and brains splattered everywhere. I saw Howie lick his lips and then make a face. I saw my mother cleave a zombie in the face, and my father miss and hit one right in the cleavage, which became much more cleaved than before.

Howie took out a zombie that was coming for me, but totally ignored another one coming for him. No self fucking preservation. This is why I wanted him close by.

I took down the one behind Howie and sawed at another one while Dad tried to shake his cleaver loose from the woman's chest. Mom took out the woman, shoved her cleaver into his hands with a dirty look and grabbed another from the pile behind us while I swung my chainsaw again and took out a row of undead in a satisfying bloodbath.

I kicked the brainless bodies and shoved them into the zombies coming up behind them, knocking them all down the stairs. I followed, swinging madly, kicking, elbows – I was in the zone. I felt graceful, like a fairy with a magic wand, except my wand was a chainsaw that scattered brains instead of sparkles.

Time lost all meaning. There was no past or future: just now, and killing zombies. I saved Dad from another zombie after he missed again, and Mom took one down just as it reached for Howie. Howie was zapping zombies with his brain thing every time they came near me, ignoring bites and threats to himself.

And me? I was in my element. I was chainsawing and spinning and kicking and knocking zombies away from Howie and my parents. I forgot to stay up on the stairs. I forgot about keeping safe. All I remembered was KILL ALL THE ZOMBIES. I chopped my way through more than I'd ever remember or count.

Then things started to fall apart.

Figuratively, I mean, since things were coming apart quite literally already.

You know how, in the movies, enemies gather around the protagonist and attack one at a time? Yeah, well, the zombies weren't doing that.

They were attacking three deep, and climbing over each other, and going around each other, and they were starting to get behind me and on my left and on my right.

Howie got shunted to the side. My mother was up on a coffee table and I think she might have been shouting instructions at me but my mind was too busy trying to stay alive to actually process sound. I think my father was behind me, somewhere, because I heard fleshy sounds that I desperately hoped were made by my father cleaving zombies and not his brains being slurped out of his head through his ears.

"Dad?" I shouted in a panicky voice, and I thought I heard him call back, but I was worried and I wanted to turn and check but more zombies were coming. I was feeling increasingly desperate and the chainsaw was starting to feel heavy.

Then a zombie almost got me. I yanked my arm closer just in the nick of time and I heard the sound of dentures snapping together. I used my elbow to bonk that dead old woman on the head while kicking away someone who looked a lot like one of the Real Housewives of Vancouver gone terribly wrong.

I tried to back up but I heard a growl in my ear and whirled in the nick of time, and I think it was around then that I began to cry. Howie turned and fought his way closer to me and we ended up back to back.

"Is my Dad okay?" I shouted, and I thought I heard him say, "Yes!" but I couldn't be sure. Everything was too surreal. For a moment I felt a surge of hope as I pressed my shoulders against Howie's. Together against a world of zombies, fighting like a synchronized pair, my chainsaw and his disruptor destroying the brains of the diseased undead.

Then I felt him knocked away from me. I glanced over my shoulder and saw him go down.

"NO!" I shouted. Zombies closed in around me and I couldn't see what was happening with Howie. I tripped a zombie, killed it, and then tried to turn and get to him. I spotted my father. He was backed into a corner but holding his own. Good thing zombies were even clumsier and less coordinated than my dear old Dad. I killed another zombie and I could see several more bending down where Howie should be. The disruptor had been knocked from his hand and from the bits of him I could see, he was curled in the fetal position.

I jumped forward but another zombie got in my way, and another, and another.

"NO!" I screamed. "Dr. Mullins, Ray, Hazel, someone, HELP!"

But everyone was fighting their own zombies. There was no one to save Howie, and I couldn't save him either.

Then, with a loud bark, Army jumped past me and fought to get to Howie. His barking distracted the zombies going after Howie, and they turned toward him. I watched helplessly as the dog was literally torn to pieces in front of my very eyes.

Another one of those memories that will haunt me for the rest of my life.

"NO!"

I had to get through. I was picturing the zombies doing to Howie what they had just done to his poor dog. The skin coming off the bone, the organs exposed - Oh my

God. I needed these goddamn zombies to get OUT OF MY WAY.

"MOVE!" I bellowed, and I wasn't sure if I was shouting to the zombies or to Howie or to those goddamned authorities who didn't mind letting the Mullinses go down with the ship. I just needed those dog-killing undead mother fuckers away from my GODDAMN BOYFRIEND.

"GET OUT OF MY WAY!"

It's just another crowd, I thought. I can do this.

And I turned it on. I pictured myself going through a busy store or the halls at school, and I just started to move toward Howie.

I am here. Make way for me. Get the HELL out of my way.

The response was instantaneous.

The fighting stopped.

The zombies all froze and turned to look at me. There were some wet schlicks as my parents took advantage of the moment's peace to slice more zombie brains. I glided through the horde like a ruling monarch strolling past the peasants, while they turned and stared at me with a vacant, enthralled expression that reminded me of someone very dear to me.

Howie was curled on the ground, his hands covering his bloodied head. His shirt was hanging in shreds, exposing bite marks down his back which were slowly closing up again. An ear was missing. I spotted it in the gaping mouth of a zombie who was crouched next to him. I reached for it but as my hand came close the zombie chattered its teeth and reached its tongue out toward me. I pulled back. The ear dropped to the floor.

I AM HERE. Make way for me.

I picked up the ear and pressed it to the blackened side of Howie's head. It twisted in my hands, aligning itself as it healed. After a few seconds, I let go. It stayed on. Howie turned his head to look at me with helpless adoration. I raised him up as he stared with a slack-jawed, worshipful gaze.

That was the look I had come to know and love.

"Mum?" I said carefully, "Dad?"

"Yes, darling?"

"Kill more zombies, please."

I held Howie's hands and we looked deeply into each other's eyes as I tried to hold the spell, or whatever it was, for as long as I could. My parents grunted as they chopped down zombies like trees in the otherwise deathly silent room.

Make way for me.

I didn't need to hold the spell long. Zombies are clumsy and easy to eliminate at the worst of times, but when they stand still for the slaughter the challenge rating decreases significantly. Within minutes, the hacking and chopping noises died down. I tore my eyes from Howie and looked around. My parents were standing, blood-spattered and panting, in a sea of carnage. The Mullinses all seemed to be experiencing some kind of moment of eternal bliss, although Ray and Dr. Mullins kept shaking their heads, half-lifting their disruptors, and then seeming to get lost in thought again.

"What is going on?" Dad asked. "Stella? Does this have something to do with you making googly eyes at Howie?"

"It's not about googly eyes," I said with dignity. "I froze them with my mind powers. Did you get them all?"

"Think so. Are you okay, honey?" my mother asked.

"I'm fine. Are you?"

"Yes, thank God," she said. Dad staggered over and held on to both of us.

Slowly, Howie's family came back to life. Ray revived first, shaking himself awake with a violent shudder and then looking at me like I was the devil.

"What was that?"

Dr. Mullins rubbed his face. "It was certainly effective. An unsettling experience."

Howie sank down and knelt on a torso. "Oh... Stella... do that again..." Then he shook his head and took a couple of deep breaths. He refocused on me. "Are you okay? Did they get you? Are you bitten?" As always, the questions came out in a robotic, neutral tone but he looked frantically worried.

"*I'm* fine. Look at your sister."

Hazel was still staring off into space. One of her arms ended in a stump. Howie squeezed my hand and then stumbled his way over to her. He laid a hand on her shoulder. She looked at him vacantly.

"It's over," he said gently. Hazel blinked.

"Can you help me find my hand?" she asked. "Stella's dad cut it off. I think it was an accident."

"Sorry," said Dad. No one looked at him.

Howie shook no. "Army needs help first."

"Oh, no..." said Hazel.

"I think he's past help, Howie," I said gently, committing a gross understatement. But there's no nice way to say, "Your dog got eaten by zombies and only pieces of him are left." I automatically glanced down at the remains and quickly looked away.

"What do you mean?" said Ray, jumping over bodies towards me. He bent down and looked at the bits of Army. "Don't scare us like that. Look," he said, picking up Army's head, which was missing half of its skin, and brandishing it. "He's perfectly fine."

"Oh, good," said Hazel.

Then my parents and I watched while they put their dog back together.

They picked up part of the torso, and the other part of the torso, both of which had big chunks missing. They pulled his liver out of a dead zombie's jaws. They stuffed the remains of the intestines back inside his body cavity and added the liver. They attached the head to the body and stuck on his tail.

For a minute nothing happened.

"Uh... guys...?" I started to say, and then I looked more closely. The skin began to regrow over the bite wounds and flayed sections. Then he twitched and jumped up, and shook himself. His tail fell off again and Howie calmly re-applied it. A minute later, it was wagging.

"Holy shit," I said.

"Did I know the dog was a zombie?" asked Dad. "I don't think I knew the dog was a zombie."

Army leaned on me adoringly. He began licking blood off of my hand.

"Don't tell Agent Baum. He doesn't know. We just got tired of our pets dying on us, and then there was a small outbreak and we found this one covered in bites, holding the arm of his old master..." said Ray.

"You can't keep a good dog down," said Hazel, hugging him. His tail thumped. My parents both tried to collapse on the couch and then jumped up again when they realized that five or six other people had done that already in a very messy fashion. I understood why Ray had laid down a tarp.

"We can look for your hand now, Hazel," said Howie.

So, while Dr. Mullins and Ray carefully investigated the yard and street for straggling undead, the rest of us rummaged through dead bodies looking for a hand. It sounds horrific, and it was, but we were temporarily desensitized, I guess.

"I think I found it!" Mom called, hoisting her find into the air. Howie looked at it and shook his head. "Too much arm on that one. She lost hers at the wrist."

"This one could be it," I said, pulling one out from under a staring head with a smashed-in skull. "Oh, never mind, wrong skin colour." I turned over another body and something moved. I stared at a thin, scraggly, bloodstained albino hamster crouching on the floor.

I froze.

"I've found the hand," announced Howie from across the room, tossing it to Hazel, who didn't catch it in time and had to bend down and pick it up off someone's face.

I looked back down. My voice trembled as I said, "Yeah, well, I've found your hamster." It was staring at me with beady red eyes. Then it scuttled toward me and I staggered backward, nearly tripping over bodies.

"Don't touch it," said Howie.

"Howie, do you think I'm an idiot?"

He bent down and caught it in his hands. It squeaked and tried to escape his grip, its little eyes bugging out of its head. Howie frowned at it.

"You're hurting it," I said automatically.

"It doesn't feel pain," Howie said.

"Dad..." Hazel went to the door. "Come here."

Dr. Mullins and Ray showed up at a run. Howie held up the hamster wordlessly. His father strode over and took it from Howie's grip, expertly dangling it by the scruff of the neck. It continued to struggle, staring at me.

"Stella, can't you freeze it with your mind powers?" Dad suggested.

"No," said Ray, Dr. Mullins, and Hazel together.

"We need to… talk about how Stella managed what she did, but right now, I need to be in a functioning state," said Dr. Mullins. He peered closely at the hamster. "Hmm. That's worrying."

"What?" asked Mom.

"It doesn't look like a zombie," I said. Dr. Mullins nodded.

"Really?" asked Dad. "It sure doesn't look healthy or normal in any way."

Dr. Mullins raised his eyebrows at me. I felt like a student being quizzed by a professor, which, of course, Dr. Mullins was.

"It squeaked," I said. "And it's struggling. And it looks… alive. It's breathing."

"Okay," said Dad, "So it's not a dead zombie." He paused. "I never thought I'd be making that distinction someday."

"It does not appear to be undead," said Dr. Mullins, "which indicates that the formaldehyde treatments are still in effect, and the disease has not progressed to the point of apparent death."

"But it's contagious anyway?" my mother asked.

"Well, it's got to be, right?" said Dad. "Because, you know, all this." He gestured around us.

Dr. Mullins nodded slowly. He looked almost scared.

"Maybe the formaldehyde makes you contagious earlier. Oh my God," said Mom, looking at Howie and then at me.

"No, it doesn't," said Dr. Mullins firmly. "I've studied this hamster for ten years, and we ourselves are swabbed regularly."

"Then, how…?" I said.

Dr. Mullins was running his free hand through his hair agitatedly, shaking his head.

"This is really fucking bad," said Ray. "Isn't it? If it's alive like us, but contagious, then that's got to mean…"

"Dad, look into this later," said Howie. "We need to check Stella and her family all over for bites."

"Also, I need to shower," I said.

"Not if I get there first," said Mom.

They decided to stash the hamster in a Tupperware container, and then put it in the freezer.

"That should prevent any further progression of the disease until I can investigate," said Dr. Mullins. "I would like to know all the facts before I surrender it. I am quite concerned about the implications. Depending on the reason for its premature contagiousness, my family's freedom could be put in jeopardy."

"Because it could happen to you?" Dad asked, somewhat unnecessarily.

No one dignified his question with an answer. I watched Hazel tuck the hamster into a container and carefully burp the air out of it.

"Freezing it really won't kill it?" I asked.

"Stella," said Howie.

"But if the water in the brain froze, then doesn't it…"

"No, it doesn't seem to," said Dr. Mullins. "I actually investigated that once, because I was wondering what would happen in the Northern Territories should an outbreak occur there. I noticed a correlation to season in reported incidents, and…"

"Some other time, Dad," said Hazel.

My family and I picked our way over the bodies and up the stairs. Howie made it his personal mission to make sure each and every one of us was okay, starting with me.

He carefully inspected every inch of my exposed skin while gently dabbing away a lot of blood (none of which turned out to be mine) with a washcloth. When he finished, his eyes met mine and we stood just looking at each other for a moment. I thought he might kiss me, but instead, he stroked my cheek briefly, handed me a towel and my unbloodied pajamas, and then sent me into the bathroom with my mother to have the rest of me just as carefully examined and declared bite-free. Then I was given the all-clear to have a shower.

I covered myself with soap and lathered my hair for a very long time. I could have stood under that hot stream forever, but after all, there were other people who wanted to wash the death off of them, too. When I had changed, stuffed my bloodied clothes into a plastic bag, and wrapped the towel around my head in a turban, I opened the door and my parents rushed in to check each other over and shower.

Mom found a cut under Dad's arm, but he swore up and down that he had done it to himself with a cleaver. Dr. Mullins examined the wound and agreed that it was not a bite mark and was likely "self-inflicted".

"If zombie blood got into the wound, could he get sick?" I asked nervously.

"The cut is located in his armpit and does not appear to be contaminated."

"But if there was zombie blood on the cleaver…"

Dr. Mullins frowned. "Perhaps we should feed you some brains immediately, just in case."

"It was a clean cleaver," said Dad hastily. "I fumbled it when I saw them coming at us and... I should have changed before I came here," he added regretfully, gesturing with a bloody piece of fabric in one hand. "I liked this shirt."

"Peroxide will probably get it out, dear," said my mother absently, while trying to pick crusted blood out from the links in her watch band.

"No, love, I believe that it is beyond the help of peroxide," said Dad, "unless peroxide mends multiple rips."

They closed the door again and soon I heard the water running. I looked at Howie, who was trying to clean himself off. I took the cloth from him and started swabbing at the bits in his hair and on the back of his neck which he had missed. Dr. Mullins watched me in a way that I found unnerving.

Dad opened the bathroom door and found himself caught between our stares. He looked at me, looked at Dr. Mullins, then ducked down and dramatically tiptoed between us.

"Stella," said Dr. Mullins finally, "I need to know what it was that you did to us."

"I just... turned it on," I said.

"Turned what on?"

"Howie," giggled Hazel. Howie stomped on her foot. She didn't seem to notice.

"Do I want to hear this?" asked Dad.

"It's just a trick I use to get through crowds. You know, you just make yourself seem... *bigger*, and you make eye contact with people and they make way for you," I said. "I kind of yell, 'Here I am! Make way!' in my head and people let me through."

"Interesting," said Dr. Mullins, except his zombie drone made him sound more bored than fascinated. "Your mental focus during that exercise seems to project your brain waves in a certain way which is extremely potent towards infected persons. It was certainly a very unsettling experience."

"Why, what'd it feel like?" asked Dad.

"Like something out of fucking *Trainspotting*," said Ray.

"I would more describe it as being similar to a deer in headlights," said Dr. Mullins. "With the senses overwhelmed, decision making becomes difficult."

"Zombies don't make decisions," I said.

"But when it's coming from all around you, which way do you go?" asked Howie.

"Very unsettling," repeated Dr. Mullins.

"That's what you do at school, isn't it?" said Howie. "Trying to get through the crowd?"

"Yes," I said.

"No wonder you rendered me into a drooling mess that first day."

I didn't like the way this conversation was going.

"Are you saying that I... like, love-spelled you? That the only reason you were so captivated by me is because I had just fought my way through a crowd?"

I think I may have been a bit of a mess after the late night and all the fighting, and bloody corpses, and the sorting through umpteen severed hands, and the disemboweling and reassembly of a German Shepherd, because I found myself in tears.

It just hit me so hard when I realized that all of Howie's love for me, his obsession with me, had all just been the side effect of a psychology trick. It wasn't real love, in that case, was it? And if it wasn't real love, then I didn't want it. I think I might have sobbed as much.

"You're an idiot," said Ray, blandly cutting through all my dramatic anguish. "You just 'love spelled' all of us, and I don't see me or Hazel or Dad swearing eternal devotion to you."

Howie reached out and cupped my face in his cool hands.

"You are stunning and you stunned me. But there is more to you than just that. I love you for you. How could I not love you? The way you can wield a chainsaw, the way you karate chop your way through every problem to cross your path? You are vibrant, and capable, and brilliant. So, no, it's not just some kind of diseased attraction to a trick of your brain waves. It is so much more. I want to listen to your opinions, and make you pancakes, and buy you used books, and be your Chemistry partner – shut up, Hazel – for all eternity. So, you're just going to have to accept that I love you and you can also render me into a drooling mess at the drop of a hat."

"But feel free to NOT do that around me," muttered Ray.

I wiped my eyes. "It's kung fu, not karate," I said. "It's a style of wu-shu and it's Chinese, not Japanese. And I don't chop much. I'm more about the kicks and the hand blocks."

Howie's dimple appeared again. "Just kiss me, please."

So, I did. Howie wrapped his arms around me and pulled me close against him. Dad whistled and I stuck my middle finger up at him. Then Dr. Mullins cleared his throat.

"We need to decide what we're going to tell the agency about this."

"About what?" said Howie, not looking away from me.

"Stella can overwhelm a horde of zombies, Howie," said Ray. "Don't you think that's kind of a big deal?"

"I've been telling everyone that she's a big deal from the beginning," said Howie, nuzzling me.

I became aware that Hazel was standing uncomfortably close to me again. I pulled away and Howie turned and looked at her. She put her hand on Howie's arm.

"Howie. They'll take her away."

"What do you mean, take her away?" demanded Dad. My mother opened the bathroom door.

"Over my dead body," she said. "Take her where?"

"They won't take her away," said Ray. "But they'll test her to pieces."

"To pieces?" repeated Howie.

"They will not remove Stella from her parents," said Dr. Mullins. "She's still a minor. But Stella, they will want to study your technique and see if it can be duplicated. If it can, it could give us a powerful tool against further outbreaks."

"And if it can't?" asked my mother grimly.

"Then they will no doubt be rather pressing that she contribute her services when necessary."

"That's not so bad," I said.

"And possibly require you to submit to extensive testing to figure out why you possess this unique ability," continued Dr. Mullins.

"How extensive?"

They exchanged glances.

"There's no point worrying about that at this moment," said Dr. Mullins. "However, until we've thought out all potential consequences, I suggest we downplay Stella's role in our success here tonight."

"You mean, lie?" I said harshly.

"No, just word things carefully."

"You mean, not saying 'Stella has magic brain waves that can render us completely helpless in a way that we have never experienced before'?" said Ray.

"Yes, let's not phrase it quite that way."

I closed my eyes and rubbed my face.

"You should get to bed; you must be exhausted," said Howie.

"What if more zombies come?"

"Then we'll wake you up and you can hypnotize us again."

"Baby, wake up." Howie's voice sounded far away, and my pillow felt soft and near. I decided to go back to sleep. Besides, I hate it when people call their romantic partners "baby". It's not sexy.

I'd have told him that if I weren't asleep.

An indeterminate amount of time passed. I felt fingers through my hair again, and soft, cool lips on my cheek.

"Gorgeous," said Howie. "Loveliest, wake up." I was learning to interpret the subtle inflections in his speech. His monotone sounded urgent.

I moaned and buried my face deeper into the pillow. "G'way," I mumbled, closing my eyes tighter. Then my brain caught up with me and I shot upright, knocking right into Howie who was leaning over me. He didn't seem to mind. "Zombies!" I shouted. "Are there more zombies?"

"No, no. Well, yes. There were a couple. But one of them had no legs."

I sighed, fell back, and pulled the blanket over my head. "Whad'ya wake me for, then?"

"The agents'll be here soon. I don't really know what's going to happen. I thought you might want to be dressed for it. I brought you leftover lasagna."

I sat up. Howie was sitting at the foot of the bed in a white tee and a pair of jeans. He smiled at me and handed me the plate of lasagna which I obligingly picked at. He watched my every bite.

"Howie?"

"Hmm?"

"Are you staring at the food, or at me?"

"Can't it be both?"

"I guess, for you, I am both," I grumbled. Howie smiled, but he didn't disagree. I thought I recognized a glazed quality to his gaze.

"Howie?"

"Hmm?"

"Are you hungry?"

"Mmh hmmm."

"Can't you go get something to eat?"

"Mmm nnn. Rations, remember?"

"For Christ's sake, Howard. Can't we just buy you more brains?"

He paused. "You're right. What'm I saving up for? Be back."

I continued to pick at my lasagna. I heard a loud chunk noise from downstairs, which sounded exactly like a cleaver burying itself into a skull. I am now an expert on that sound.

A few minutes later Howie joined me holding a thermos.

"You have some blood on your forehead, Howie."

"Oh. That's not mine." He pulled a white piece of cloth from his pocket and wiped his forehead. "I just opened up a new pig head."

"Did you just pull out a handkerchief?"

"Yes, they're handy."

"Howie, *no one* uses handkerchiefs."

He smiled. "I've been no one for a very long time."

"Okay, but why this particular vestige of old-fashionedness? You have a cell phone, you wear t-shirts, but you still use a handkerchief?"

"It's a hanky. It just doesn't feel right going around without one. I never have a Kleenex around when I need one, and wiping this sort of thing on your sleeve just seems gross. Kids these days sneeze on their sleeve or their hand. That's not hygienic. You sneeze into your hanky, you wash your hanky."

I shook my head at him. He fastidiously folded the hanky and tucked it back in his pocket, and as he did this I noticed something.

"Howie, hold out your hands."

He obeyed promptly.

"Howie, where is your FUCKING FINGER?"

He looked down. "Oh. Shoot. Just a second."

I listened to him run downstairs and I heard some banging and rummaging below.

This sort of shit never happens to girls in storybooks.

When he came back in, he had ten fingers again. He spread them out for me to see.

"All better!"

I closed my eyes. He sat next to me. "Are you doing okay?"

"I'm tired, but yeah, I'm okay, why?"

"Well, you chopped about forty skulls open last night."

"I did, didn't I? I didn't have nightmares about it, even. Does that make me a terrible person?"

"No, just a very tired person." He looked at me quietly for a minute. "I didn't get around to saying thank you last night."

"Thank you? For what?"

"For freezing all the zombies before they could eat me."

"Oh, that."

"You were amazing. I was sure that... that I was done..." he shuddered. "And then you just... parted them, like Moses parting the waters of the Red Sea."

"Can we not talk about it?" I asked. It was bringing back memories that I didn't feel like processing yet. "I'm still so sleepy."

"I'm sorry I had to wake you up. But I didn't think you'd want to get caught in your pajamas. I'll step out while you change."

"No."

Howie raised his eyebrows and sat up a bit. "Uh... really? Because... I'm okay with that."

I swatted playfully at him. "I'm not ready to get dressed, yet. What time is it? It feels ungodly early."

"Nine a.m."

"Three hours, Howie. Three hours of sleep. I need a few minutes."

I curled back up in the comfy, comfy bed. My head was buzzing with exhaustion. Howie lay down next to me. "Do you mind if I stay with you? I could look at you forever." He tucked my hair behind my ear and ran his (thankfully, now intact) hand gently down my cheek. I smiled drowsily at him.

"My life was much duller before I met you," I said. "I used to go to sleep at night and not have to worry about zombies."

"That sounds like a nice life," said Howie. "I'm sorry that changed. But you know, the zombies are a coincidence. I mean, the other ones. It's just bad luck that the hamster got out on the same weekend that you found out about me being a zombie."

"It's a really bizarre coincidence," I said. "It seems contrived."

"Real life can't be contrived, Stella."

"Well, I'm having trouble suspending my disbelief of real life these days."

"I've felt that way before. Maybe this is all a dream," said Howie into my ear. "Maybe everything that's happened to me over the last fifty years has been a complicated dream."

"I'm not just a supporting character in your hallucination, Howie, I'm sure of that."

"You're the most dream-like of all," he said in my ear. "I'll wake up tomorrow and you'll be gone."

"Well, yes, but that's probably because I will be back in my own home," I said. "But feel free to visit."

"I'll see what I can do. In the meantime, I plan to enjoy every second of you being here with me."

He leaned forward and pressed his cool lips against my neck. Somehow, that seemed to reach right down inside me. I took a deep breath, and he kissed my neck again, and then again. My heart was thumping. I didn't feel sleepy anymore. I felt crazy alive.

"Stella… Just having you so close… I feel…"

He kissed my earlobe, and I felt that right down to my toes. I turned and touched my lips to his, and he took a sharp breath followed by a quiet moan. It made me feel powerful. I kissed his neck.

"Oh, God. Stella," he gasped, leaning back. I did it again. He groaned and pulled me on top of him with surprising strength. "Kiss me again," he begged. I did, on the mouth, and he kissed me back, running his hands over my body as if he couldn't get enough of touching me. I felt his fingers slip under the back of my pajama top and onto my bare skin.

"Is that okay?" he whispered.

"It's fine." It was more than fine – I felt almost on fire for his touch.

"Stella, I love you," he whispered. "Everything about you. You saved me. Remember that."

I realized that I trusted him completely. Even wearing my pajamas, I was naked with him, because finally all of my angry B.S. had been stripped away. With this boy, I could just be: he accepted me completely the way I was. No judging. No censure. I felt a wild freedom that took my breath away.

It was worth the zombies, to find this kind of a person. He was worth it.

We kissed until I began to feel like we were melding together, until he became an extension of me, until there was no more thought, just hunger for closeness. His hands were tentatively beginning to cup my breasts when a loud bang came from downstairs. Howie froze.

"Screw the zombies!" I gasped, "I'll stop them in a minute."

But the footsteps that came thump-thump-thump up the stairs were too fast and coordinated for a zombie.

"They're here," whispered Howie, sitting up. The bedroom door flew open.

18

I'm sure that most people, at some point in their life, have the embarrassing experience of being caught in flagrante delicto. But I should get bonus sympathy because *I* was caught in bed with a *zombie* by an angry *secret agent* in my *fuzzy pajamas*.

By which I mean that I was in my fuzzy pajamas, not the secret agent. Because that'd be strange.

I rolled away from Howie and onto my feet quicker than I might have thought possible if I had taken the time to think about it. My face burned as I straightened out my pajama top. Howie pulled the blankets over his pants. He looked so unhappy and vulnerable that my humiliation immediately transformed into fury.

"What the..." I began. Agent Baum interrupted.

"Howard Mullins, you are under arrest."

"What?" I shouted.

He raised his voice. "If you wish to have a lawyer, we will appoint one for you. You will be tried in closed court. Do you understand?"

Howie nodded, and Agent Baum roughly pulled him off the bed and began to handcuff him.

"Howie, don't put up with this shit! Don't they need a warrant?"

Agent Baum turned to me. "Miss Blunt, if you don't start using a more age-appropriate vocabulary, so help me, I will arrest you for obstructing justice."

"I am holding a warrant to arrest all members of the Mullins family. It was issued by the Supreme Court of Canada," said a voice in the doorway. A tall woman agent stood in the hall.

"I thought this would happen," said Dr. Mullins, coming out of the bathroom and patting his face dry with a towel.

The woman agent turned to him. "I'm sorry, Morton. You are under arrest for spreading government secrets and engaging in treasonous activities, including endangering the Canadian public."

"Yes, I understand, Michaella," said Dr. Mullins.

"Well, I DON'T! Where the hell were you last night when we were being overrun? If they released the virus on purpose why would they ALMOST DIE in the process?"

"MISS BLUNT!" bellowed Agent Baum, "You and YOUR PARENTS WHO SHOULD NOT EVEN BE HERE will report downstairs immediately for transport back to your regular place of residence. You will continue to wear your electronic tracking bracelet and your parents will be fitted with the same since they have also been given access to top secret information."

"If you had needed assistance we would have given it to you immediately," said the woman agent. I gaped at her. I didn't even know where to begin being angry at that sentence.

"What's all the yelling about?" asked my Dad opening the door to his bedroom. "Hello. Who are you?"

"They're the sphincter-ninjas who let us get overrun by undead," I spat.

"WE are the ones who just stopped your daughter from committing sexual acts with a foully infected sixty-eight-year-old!" said Agent Baum. My father cast a horrified glance at Dr. Mullins.

"He means Howie, Dad!" I said in exasperation. Dad cast *me* a horrified glance.

"Who means Howie?" asked my mother, craning her neck over my father's shoulder. "Wait, are those handcuffs?"

"Downstairs," ordered Agent Baum. Howie and Dr. Mullins meekly allowed themselves to be shepherded downstairs. I could hear Ray swearing in the living room and the clink of handcuffs. Two more agents were shackling Hazel and Ray among the wreckage of the living room while some people in hazmat suits stuffed body parts in bags.

"Why did you arrest Howie FIRST?" I asked.

The agents ignored me.

"What did they mean about sexual acts, Stella?" Dad asked.

I ignored him.

"Sexual whats?" asked my mother.

We ignored her.

"What did HOWIE do?"

"What did any of us do?" Ray muttered with a sullen expression.

Agent Baum's face was beet red. "Be quiet, all of you! Out of the house, NOW."

Howie looked longingly at me over his shoulder as they shoved and prodded him out the remains of the front door.

"Wait," I demanded, "where are you taking him? I mean, them?"

"To a secure facility," said the woman in a clipped voice.

"And then what?"

"That is none of your business, Miss Blunt," said Agent Baum.

"They will be held and possibly tried in closed court," said the woman.

"Yeah," said Ray, a trace of bitterness in his monotone, "in twenty or thirty years, maybe."

"That soon?" asked Hazel.

"I'll need someone to feed my lab animals, Michaela," said Dr. Mullins over his shoulder.

She nodded. "That has all been arranged, Morton. Your experiment will be disturbed as little as possible."

"And our dog?"

"Your dog may need to be relinquished to a shelter."

"No," said Ray. "Stella, feed our goddamn dog, will you?"

"Sure, but how…"

"There's cans of dog food in the pantry."

There was a line of sleek black cars with tinted windows parked outside and a big cube van. Howie and his family were led to two of the cars. I followed in my bare feet, hopping over stray limbs.

"Howie! Wait… I…"

"I love you, Stella," Howie said unemotionally. His face looked tortured.

There were so many things I wanted to say, so many asses I wanted to kick. I didn't know what to do. So, I stammered and fumed and followed like a puppy while they stuffed him into a car next to Hazel. Just as they were about to shut the door, I heard his voice again.

"Agent Hunt, can I give Stella something?"

The woman agent paused.

"Absolutely not," said Agent Baum.

"He asked *me*, George," said the woman sharply. "What is it, Howard?"

"Just a little thing… for Stella to remember me by," said Howie. He seemed to be fighting tears.

"Their relationship is foul and unnatural! Don't encourage it!"

"What do you mean, 'foul and unnatural?'" I asked.

"WHAT thing, Howard?" Agent Hunt asked calmly. Baum threw up his hands and rubbed his face.

"Just my handkerchief," said Howie. "It's in my pocket. We… had a smile over it earlier."

The woman agent sighed and checked her watch. "Hand it over."

Howie looked at his pants and then at his cuffed hands. "Uh…"

The woman rolled her eyes. "Miss Blunt, come here, please."

She stepped aside and let me approach the car. Howie watched me intensely.

"It's in my left pocket," he said. I leaned over him and reached for the corner of his hanky. It was folded neatly but had spots of blood on it. What a gross piece of memorabilia.

"Howie…"

He shook his head no. "Keep it folded for now," he whispered in my ear. "Put it in your pocket." I did. "I'll see you in my dreams. One last kiss?"

He leaned forward and touched his lips to mine. I could feel his lower lip trembling. I was yanked back by a firm hand on my shoulder. I spun furiously on Agent Baum.

"Get your hands off me!"

"You should be ashamed of touching that filth," he snarled, slamming the car door. I couldn't see Howie through the tinted windows. Agent Hunt got into the driver's seat, and another agent got in the other car with Ray and Dr. Mullins. I watched helplessly as the cars pulled out and drove off, carrying away the best person I had ever met.

When the cars had turned the corner, and disappeared, my mother put her arm around me.

"Come inside, honey," she said. "Come inside."

The clean-up team was tagging body parts and putting them into separate bags.

"This is disgusting," I heard one of them mutter, looking around.

"Why don't you go and get dressed," said Mom, leading me up the stairs. I went where she directed me. I felt numb.

Howie's bed was all mussed up, the sheets half hanging off the bed. It looked wrong. Howie kept his room neat, his bed made. I started to make the bed.

"Get dressed, sweetie, I packed a spare shirt and pants in here... good thing..." she laid the clothes out on the bed like I was a little child. "Now, I'm going to get dressed too, and then we'll go home, okay?"

I nodded and she closed the door. I slowly stripped off my shirt and pajama pants and pulled on my clothes. The memory of Howie's hands on my skin was fading. It seemed surreal. What Howie? There was no Howie.

Then, as I stuffed my pajamas and Howard the Bear into my bag, I saw the photo. I picked it up and looked at it again. A family on the steps of a farmhouse. A young Howie, and a younger Hazel. Their faces were unmistakable. Howie was already wearing glasses. I looked at the parents, a tall and stringy man with a crooked smile and a housewifey looking mother. For the first time, I noticed a baby on the mother's hip. It was looking away from the camera, hiding its face in her ample arms. What happened to that baby? Maybe I didn't want to know.

I felt my anger starting to come back. I was angry at the virus, for taking away Howie's family. I was angry at the zombies that almost killed us all last night. But most of all, I was fucking furious with the goddamn feds who didn't help us and then took Howie away.

I stomped down the stairs with my bag. I was going to have some words with Agent Baum.

He was standing in the doorway watching the clean-up crew with a look of disgust on his face.

"Smart of them to lay down a tarp on their furniture, eh?" I heard Dad say to him. Agent Baum ignored the comment.

"So, what the hell are you playing at, arresting Howie anyway?" I demanded, charging through the wreckage. "Howie wasn't even in the lab; he wasn't responsible for letting that damn hamster out."

Agent Baum rubbed his temples. "He also gave you top secret information about his condition and the existence of the Z0381E virus."

"Well, there was an outbreak after all. I mean, when zombies are attacking you from all sides, it's sort of hard to deny their existence."

"He told you about himself *before* the outbreak, Miss Blunt, which is part of what I need to talk to you about. But not here. I will escort you home and then you and I need to have a conversation."

"How do you know when...?"

"NOT NOW, MISS BLUNT."

Agent Baum walked us to our car. Army followed us, tail waving. Dad opened the back door and the dog hopped into the backseat.

"You know we can't keep that dog," said my mother.

"We'll talk about that later. For now, let's give the poor mutt a place to sleep that isn't full of hazmat suits and zombie bits," said Dad. "I grabbed a couple cans of his... food."

"I will be following behind you in my squad car," said Agent Baum.

"And I will be angry with you for leaving my daughter to be eaten by angry, flesh-eating corpses last night," said my mother breezily. "It's important to get these things out in the open. Get in, Stella," she added. I slid in next to Army. I knew that I should be feeling emotions, but I was out of them.

I was still processing the fact that I might never see Howie again. I couldn't make it make sense in my brain. No. In my brain, it made total sense. In my heart, maybe? Anyway. I wasn't feeling it. I wasn't feeling anything, except Army's drool on my arm.

The short ride home was almost entirely silent. At one point Dad cleared his throat and said, "So, uh, when that Baum guy said he interrupted you and Howie..."

He was cut off by a combination of my glare and my mother's hand on his knee.

"Now isn't the time," she said to him quietly. He nodded. I stared out the window.

Part of me felt a dull surprise when we walked into our house and found everything to be completely normal. Somehow, after last night and this morning, it seemed like the entire world had fallen apart. My life was supposed to be full of dead bodies and shattered romance. The roses on the kitchen table and the clacking of Army's nails on the laminate seemed offensively mundane.

Baum came marching up our steps and into our kitchen right behind us. My parents met him with folded arms and squinted eyes.

"I need to speak to your daughter privately," he said shortly.

"Absolutely not," blazed my mother. "First, you let her nearly die, then you yank away her boyfriend possibly forever without allowing so much as a proper goodbye, and now you want to... what? Scold her? Verbally abuse her? She is not legally an adult, and anything you say to her will be in our extremely disapproving presence."

"Yeah," my Dad said.

"Good for you," said Baum. This seemed to throw my mother off her groove.

"Uh... what?"

"I applaud your dedication as parents and your attention to legal niceties," said Baum. "Our great nation is fortunate to have citizens such as yourselves."

He doesn't talk like a real person, I thought.

"…Thanks?" said Dad.

"Let me assure you that I have only goodwill towards all of you. You seem to be labouring under some misapprehensions, no doubt due to falsehoods spread by those foul creatures who you know as 'the Mullins family'. First of all, I did not knowingly risk your daughter's life. My squad was on standby. No one contacted us to let us know when the horde of infected became large enough to require assistance."

"What?" we all said. My anger began to flicker again. How could he stand there and lie like that?

"They called," said Dad. "We saw them call."

"You saw one of them speak into a phone, I presume."

"Well, yes, of course, that's what I…"

"Do you consider that sufficient evidence?"

"Well… I did… until you put it like that…"

"There are some truths I need to make evident," said Baum. "Some of them may be embarrassing to your daughter, and I'd prefer to give them to her privately. Of course, you have the legal right to insist on being present."

My parents looked at me, then at each other, and back at Baum.

"We're staying," said Dad firmly, while my mother said just as firmly,

"We'll go."

They looked at each other again in mutual surprise, and Mom raised her eyebrows.

"I mean, we'll go," Dad corrected himself meekly.

"Call if you want us, honey," said Mom. "We'll be upstairs in our room."

"Unpacking," Dad added.

"Thank you. I will need to speak to you two as well, once our private conversation has finished," said Baum. "There is some paperwork I need you to sign."

I glowered at Baum from the couch while he struggled to sit in Dad's recliner and still maintain an upright posture. After a minute, he got up, marched from the room and returned with a kitchen chair, which he placed a few feet away from me.

We looked at each other in silence for a minute.

Baum sighed.

"I feel that we got off on the wrong foot," he said. "You met me at times of... particular tension. As you may have noticed, I do not get along with your infected friends."

"Obviously," I said. "I also noticed that you're nuttier than a chocolate bar."

"I'm going to let that slide since you have been through an incredible amount of trauma over the last forty-eight hours or so," he said. "But if you're going to sling insults at me, I'd prefer that they be more appropriate to your nationality. 'Crazy as a loon' has a nice Canadian ring to it."

I almost smiled.

"I may come across as... a little overzealous. But you need to trust me when I say that I have only our great nation's best interests at heart. It makes me sad that in America, patriotism like mine is considered admirable, and much more commonplace. What does it say about Canada, and Canadians, that people question my sanity, just because I love my country?" he stared at his hands while he mused. "You know, in many American homes you can find portraits of Washington, Lincoln, even generals like Robert E Lee. So why do Canadians giggle about my portrait of the Right Honourable John Diefenbaker?" He looked up at me. "You, like most, probably think I'm wrong to call America our enemy."

I didn't even dignify that question with an answer. I was still waiting to hear what the crazy loon wanted to tell me so privately.

"You know that my job involves maintaining our homeland security from this terrible virus. Can you accept that I have access to many inside sources and a lot of covert information?"

I shrugged.

"Then let me assure you – I know things about America which would shock you. Oh, yes. They're our friends – we have NAFTA and an undefended border. They own our businesses and sell us their clothing, their oil, their television programs. Do you think America needs a law about how much American content must be played on their radio stations? Of course not. But we do, or Canadian content wouldn't be played at all. If it weren't for laws like that, America would have swallowed us up. Cultural invasion. It's only the beginning.

"Now, what if I told you – not that I would, of course, you already know too much – that I had proof that America is gathering inside information from us on the Z0381E virus? That I knew for a fact that they had contacts in Vancouver who are sending them samples of the virus? That I had evidence that an army of infected people – not corpses, but living people like the Mullins family – was slowly being assembled across the border? An army of near immortal, intelligent beings. What if I told you that your new friends were the ones who were involved in this?"

Before I could come up with an intelligent response, he suddenly changed subjects. "There were a lot of bodies in that living room. The windows were broken in. My team hasn't given me a final count, but I am guessing that there were more than fifty, maybe even a hundred infected souls lying dead in and around the premises. Quite the gory sight. My newer team members may need counseling. But you all survived."

I said nothing.

"You know, outbreaks aren't as rare as you might think, especially in less developed countries, where superstition and poor media access prevent lockdowns from happening quickly. So, this has been studied a lot: Did you know, Miss Blunt, that the chance of a handful of people surviving an onslaught of numbers like you experienced last night, in hand-to-hand combat, is statistically improbable? In fact, I'd say... impossible?"

"Well, we did. You can send in nurses and doctors to check us. We didn't get bitten," I said. "The Mullinses did, but obviously that didn't count."

"It's too late to check you. Any bites would likely be completely healed by now. But you all seem calm, not feverish... You don't look bitten. It happens quickly, you know."

"So? We did survive. No thanks to you."

"We'll get to that. Now, tell me this – how?"

I folded my arms.

Baum went on, conversationally. "Now, what if I were to tell you – but I wouldn't, of course, it's completely confidential – that I have received reports of rare cases of individuals who, if they concentrated properly, were actually capable of freezing zombies in their tracks?"

I know I jumped – just a little. Just a twitch. It was enough. Baum saw it, and he went on, speaking more quickly.

"What if I told you that only a couple governments in the world had gotten their hands on such an individual and that neither Canada nor America is among them? Not because they don't exist – they must. They may even be common – but they aren't exactly easy to identify except in the case of an outbreak, and even then, people like that are probably gobbled up before they have a chance to discover that they have any such talent."

I opened my mouth, but he held up a finger. "I'm not done," he said. "Now. Imagine what such a person could mean to a government that was amassing an army of infected persons. Imagine what it could mean to the government they meant to overthrow." He paused. "It could completely alter the outcome of the war." He went on, softly. "Isn't it strange that the Mullins family didn't tell me what you are, right away?"

"They did. They tried to. You didn't listen…"

"They told me that you can draw in a horde. So what? People like that are a dime a dozen. But they knew you could do more than that."

"No, they didn't… We almost were overrun. It was an accident that I discovered it. They were surprised," I said quickly. But doubts were beginning to form in my mind. How could they have been surprised? I did it at school daily, without even knowing I was doing it.

"Yes, let's talk about the horde that almost overran you. The outbreak that started within two weeks of you moving here. The outbreak that started within twenty-four hours of Howard Mullins wheedling a kiss from you. The first patient practically stumbling onto you, taking you by surprise. That's quite a coincidence."

I opened my mouth again and closed it again. Then I frowned. "How the hell do you know when Howie and I...?"

"My job is the security of our nation, and you ask me how I know when one of our nation's greatest threats suddenly gets cozy with an innocent young girl?" he leaned in closer, and there was sympathy in his gaze. He spoke quietly. "I realize that to you, Howard Mullins looks like a boy your own age. But you need to understand that he is older than I am, participating in the leaking of secrets to another government, and carrying a deadly disease. You think I don't monitor him? My only regret is not monitoring more closely. I didn't see Morton Mullins sneak the hamster out of his lab. I didn't figure out why they would start an outbreak – risk exposing themselves – in their own city. I didn't figure out the connection to you."

I felt like the room was spinning. Was it because I hadn't had any sleep? Or was my world getting turned upside down... again?

"When they wanted to use you as some kind of a lure, I thought it seemed suspicious, but I didn't make the connection. I thought maybe they wanted to take my team out of action, distract us from the real threat – whatever that may be. I thought maybe the Americans would be making their move. I had people watching the border. When we didn't hear from the Mullinses, I thought I was right. I didn't send the helicopter because I didn't want to fall into their trap. I should have realized that the trap wasn't for me. It was for you."

"No..." I shook my head. "They defended me."

"Did they? Did they put you in a bunker, where you belonged? Did they suggest putting you to sleep, to mute your brain waves?"

"No... they wanted to make the horde bigger... to pull them away from other people..." I rubbed my temples. I was trying to remember. It had made sense at the time.

"Howard Mullins claimed that he loved you, and then put you at the center of a horde of zombies in numbers that you couldn't hope to fight against."

"Howie loves me..."

"They are all, *all* of them, fascinated by you. There is no doubt of that. But love you? I realize you are a teenage girl, so you may not know this, but love doesn't happen in a matter of days."

"If they'd wanted me dead, they could have just killed me. They carry murder weapons in their pockets... they keep cleavers in their basement."

"Oh, they didn't want you dead," he said smoothly. "No. Trial by fire. They lure you in. They prove your power. They smuggle you to the U.S."

"But... but..." It didn't make sense. Did it?

"Think of it this way," he said gently. "What do *you* think is more likely? That Howard Mullins *just happened* to fall in love with someone who governments would fight tooth and nail to get their hands on, and that this *just happened* to be right before an outbreak that gave them the chance to test and prove your power? Or... They found the kind of person that both frightened and fascinated them – someone who could control them if she wanted to, someone who the American government would love to get their hands on, someone who was new, and lonely, and innocent. They lured her in – easy enough to do with an overweight, bullied outsider – won her trust, tested her talent... and if one of them got some tail in the process, all the more fun for him..."

He spread his hands.

I felt like I was falling.

"I'll call your parents now," he said, as the first tears began to spill down my cheeks.

19

I wiped my eyes hurriedly as my parents came down the stairs. I wasn't going to cry in front of Baum and I didn't want my parents to feel sorry for me.

They looked at me curiously. I avoided eye contact. I felt like my stomach was being squeezed and wrung by the shame of it. Stupid girl. I thought he loved me. He fooled me. After I was so determined not to be fooled.

Dimly I heard Baum talking to my parents as he laid papers on the coffee table.

"Since you have received top secret information from traitors, I need to inform you that the disclosure of that information to any other person could result in criminal prosecution. These forms indicate that you acknowledge that fact."

"If we don't sign it?" my mother asked with a raised eyebrow.

"I've verbally informed you of the confidential nature of the information, so refusal to sign isn't going to help you much. It'll just ensure that we keep even stricter surveillance on you," he said with a shrug. My parents ex-changed glances and began reading the papers carefully.

I looked at the forms dully and tried to muster the energy to care.

"Stella doesn't have to sign, though, does she?" my mother asked, pointing at the third pile in front of me. "She's under eighteen. It wouldn't be legally binding."

"We ask her to sign as a gesture of trust. You'd be legally responsible for her if she were to disclose privileged information."

I signed my non-legally binding contract without reading it. I just couldn't summon a single shit to give. Howie took away my shit.

After a lot of nit-picking questions from my parents about whether discussing *The Walking Dead* on Facebook or calling themselves a zombie when they were really tired would fall under section two paragraph three or whatever, they signed the paperwork.

Baum stood up. "We will be in contact with you. Stella, your school is closed until further notice for repairs. We ask that for the present you remain within the Greater Vancouver area. Do you have any questions?"

"Yes. What is going to happen to the Mullinses?" my mother demanded.

I looked up.

Baum hesitated. "The Mullins family have been determined to be too high a risk to the Canadian public. Quite honestly, the result of their trial, if it ever convenes, is irrelevant. The family will be officially listed as casualties of the food contamination epidemic."

"You're going to declare them DEAD?"

"Essentially," he said, looking away. He pulled open the door and stepped outside. "I'll be in touch."

The door shut behind him.

My parents turned to me, but I stood up and walked up the stairs without saying a word.

I never thought that I'd be the type of person to ball herself up in the fetal position and just stare at the wall. I didn't do that when I found out that we were moving. I didn't do it after my disastrous first day at school. But now all I could do was fold up and try to keep out the waves of pain that kept washing over me, leaving sour humiliation in their wake.

Stupid, stupid, stupid. How could I have been so stupid?

They say your first instinct is usually the correct one. Hadn't he bothered me from the outset? Wasn't his stare, his obsessive behaviour, his dogged friendliness all unwelcome at first?

It seemed so obvious now. How he had been overwhelmed and fascinated. How he must have gone home in the middle of class when he figured it out. How he must have talked it over with the family – what to do about me. How he had returned with the resolve of winning over my trust. How he had flattered his way into my confidence – he laid it on thick, too, no subtlety there – and even put himself in front of a car when he saw me resisting his advances. How he had used guilt to get me alone with him. How he had brought me right home to his family to be inspected like a piece of meat. How he had rushed in with that cleaver.

Did they intend to kill me? Did my self-defense take them by surprise? Did they change tactics mid-stream?

But no. Why kill me? If I hadn't known about zombies, I never would have known that I could control them. My own ignorance would have protected them. No, Baum was probably right. They wanted to deliver me to the U.S.

And the outbreak. Was that to test my power? But then – I squeezed my eyes closed and tears leaked out between the lids. I couldn't concentrate on political intrigue. I couldn't make that come out straight because my thoughts kept wandering back to memories of Howie. The delicately pale skin. The hazy blue eyes. The way his glasses tended to sit slightly askew. The look of concentration on his face as he made pancakes. The way his fingers looked intertwined with mine. The feel of his lips on my neck.

Oh, the feel of his lips on my neck.

And each memory came with a fresh stab of unbearable pain. It was all tainted by the truth. I had been fooled and then used. I fell for pretty words like a love-sick school girl, which I guess I was.

The moments that I had loved most – now I realized how stupid they were. Howie telling me how sexy my obesity was. Did he laugh himself sick over that after I went home? Howie telling me how he'd do whatever I asked of him. Hah – to win my trust so he could use me and probably kidnap me.

He held out the metaphorical lollipop and I stepped right into his creepy van.

The worst part, the absolute worst, as I tried to squeeze away the pain, was discovering that love can't just be turned off again because you found out something terrible. When I could feel anger again, I'd probably be glad that Howie was locked away forever, glad that he was being declared dead. I'd probably want to spit in his face and then put a cleaver in his skull.

But right now, I still wanted Howie to comfort me, to kiss me, to wrap his arms around me and tell me that it was lies, all lies. I was in love with the fictional character that he had created for me, and I clung to it, even though every moment that passed made me realize more sharply that I was an idiot.

My parents tried tapping on my door a few times, but I didn't respond. I could hear Army moving around outside my bedroom door. I didn't want the goddamn dog, now. I'd tell Baum that it was a zombie – maybe he already knew. Baum would probably have the poor thing destroyed. I couldn't just keep a zombie dog forever, could I? He'd be a constant reminder of the betrayal.

Then the pain would come again and I'd ball up until the wave passed. Had I really been upset by Kelly's crap? Had I called *that* a betrayal? How could I? What a stupid thing. What a stupid, minor, inconsequential thing. It was nothing, absolutely nothing, compared to this.

But it was me, it was the kind of shit that happened to me. Someone was nice. I was suspicious. I gave them a chance and then look what they did – they used me, and betrayed me.

I should have seen it coming.

At one point, I remembered how it had felt to see the dead swarming in at us, to watch the stuff of fiction coming to destroy me. I wondered why *this* felt more like the end of the world than the zombie outbreak had.

My mother knocked on the door again. "Supper's ready, honey."

Hell, it was getting dark. But I wasn't hungry.

I could hear the news playing on the TV downstairs. I wondered what they were saying. I didn't care enough to heave myself off the bed. I could hear my parents' voices, too. This house sure carried sound.

Then I heard footsteps on the stairs. There was a knock.

"Stells? Do you want to come downstairs?"

I shook my head no as I lay in the dark.

"Do you want to know what they're saying on TV?" He listened at my door for a minute. "It's interesting."

I didn't answer.

"Can I come in?"

It took me a moment to talk around the pain. "Do what you want."

My door opened and Dad sat on my bed. "Okay. That's it. We need to talk."

"What's there to say?" I said softly.

"You and I need to have a talk about the fact that you were caught by secret agents having sex with a boy you'd known for barely more than a week."

I shot upright. "Excuse me?"

"We trusted you, Stella, and you go and sneak around behind our backs like that... I am deeply disappointed in you. Listen, your mother and I understand what it is to be young. We'd have made sure you were on some birth control, made sure you knew how to protect yourself. You didn't give us time for any of that. And if you end up pregnant..."

"EXCUSE ME?" I roared. "You take ONE THING said by some asshole you have never even met before and you blow it TOTALLY out of proportion without so much as ASKING me if it was even TRUE? And don't you think I'd KNOW to use proper birth control without you having to FUCKING COACH ME ON IT? Don't you think I FUCK-ING LISTEN to ANYTHING you and Mom and a VERY sweaty sex-ed teacher ever said to me?

"I fucking ORDER my BOYFRIEND to tell you CON-FIDENTIAL INFORMATION just so I don't have to

FUCKING LIE TO YOU and then you say you can't TRUST ME?" I was starting to run out of breath. The rage had come on hot and fast, but for once, it wasn't pushing away the other feelings. It was just heaping on top of them.

My mother appeared in the doorway.

Dad just nodded calmly, and then looked over his shoulder at my mother. "I told you it'd work, Elaine," he said. She smiled at him, and then at me.

"We do trust you, Stella. Your father just wanted to snap you out of your funk," she said, "which he seems to have done quite well. Now," she sat on the bed next to me and put her arm around me. "Do you want to tell us what *did* happen with you and Howie before all the arresting started?"

I started to cry. Not just the little tears running down my cheek that I had been fighting all day but big, ugly wracking sobs. The kind with slime pouring from your nose and hair sticking to your face.

My parents were shocked. I don't know when they last saw me cry like that.

"What... Stella..." Dad said. "I didn't mean it. Really. We trust you. Well, you know, as much as anyone can trust a teenager. So probably not TOTALLY. But enough."

"It's.... not... that..." I managed to say between uncontrollable sobs.

My mother wrapped her arms around me. "Oh, honey, I can't imagine how it feels. You and Howie had so little time together. But you know, someday..."

"It's... not... THAT... either..." Oh, I wished I was only missing him. I wished I was only faced with never seeing him again. I wished the memories of him were happy and not tainted.

My parents didn't ask any more questions, possibly because my cry talk was barely intelligible anyway. They just held me while I soaked their shoulders and snotted up their necks.

I finally ran out of tears but it took me a long time to get control of my breathing. I really tried, too, because my loud, spasmodic breaths just added to my humiliation over the whole situation.

Finally, my mother said, "I think you need to tell us what on Earth that Baum man said to you."

"Do I need to kick his ass?" asked Dad.

"Not his... Howie's..." I said, and another shuddering breath passed through me.

"Howie?" my parents said together.

Slowly, and interrupted by hiccups, I told them what Baum had told me. I told it to them with my face hidden in my mother's shoulder, because I didn't want to see their faces. I didn't want to know how they looked when they realized that their daughter had been a total moron. Then I waited for them to scold me.

"I don't believe it," said Dad.

"Me either," said my mother. "He had me fooled too. Stella, honey, you have nothing to feel ashamed of."

"No, I mean I literally DO NOT believe it," said Dad. "Something is not right about this story."

"It all fits, Dad," I said. "It makes sense."

"*Nothing* about it makes sense," Dad said. "I saw how that boy looked at you. I watched him cut out his heart for you."

"It's not like it hurt him," I said dully. "It was just a big show."

"Stella, my beautiful girl, I know your dear old Dad has his flaws, but trust me on this one thing – I can tell a nice guy from a jerk."

"He can, it's true," said Mom. "Long ago, when we were first dating, my friend had a boyfriend, and we all thought he was a great guy. But Tim hated him, kept telling me that he didn't care about my friend at all. Then we found out that he had been cheating for months..."

"Yeah, well, maybe zombies are different," I said. "It's not like you can listen to his tone of voice. He could be telling you that the sky is green and his voice would still be deadpan serious..."

"It's not about that," said Dad. "It's about how he looks at the girl. That guy Elaine's talking about, he was always checking out waitresses..."

"Dad, YOU check out waitresses."

"No, this was different. Look, a waitress with big boobs comes by, and every straight male is going to notice them, okay? But does he glance at them appreciatively and then forget about them again? Or does he watch them and look like he's trying to figure out how to get to know them better? There's not a woman in the world who I'd give up Elaine for. But this guy didn't do the mindless glance. He was still shopping around. That's how I knew. But Howie... that boy looked at you and no one else. I'm not even talking about whether he looked at other girls. He looked at YOU and only YOU."

"Yeah, well, don't forget that about a hundred other zombies looked for me too," I said. "Fascination is not the same thing as love." I had no more tears, but my eyes burned.

"But Ray didn't do that. What's her name... Hazel, didn't look like that. They're as zombified as Howie, right?"

My mother laid her hand on Dad's arm. "Tim... it's nice what you're trying to do..."

"No, seriously, Elaine, think about it. It makes no sense. If Stella is so valuable, and if they orchestrated some outbreak just to prove it, why not tell her what she could do? Stella was almost killed by all those zombies and at no point did they say, 'Hey, did you know you could stop them all with your mind?' Their house was DESTROYED last night. Why not just take Stella to the Americans and say, 'Hey, she can do it, she does it whenever she's in a crowd'? Why start an outbreak just to see what happens?

"It doesn't make any sense. If this was a book, I'd be leaving snarky reviews on Amazon about major plot holes. It's worse than the fourth Harry Potter book."

"J. K. Rowling's explained that," said Mom. "The rules about portkeys..."

Dad waved his hand. "Look, we didn't know the Mullinses very long, and maybe they *are* the world's best actors, and maybe I'm wrong," he said. "But their every action, their every *word* last night had me convinced that they were completely committed to stopping the outbreak, that young Howard was completely dedicated to Stella in every way, and that they were taken completely by surprise when she froze them all with her magical mind powers or whatever that was."

We were silent. I sniffed. I had a headache from crying. I wanted to believe Dad. But how could I?

"Stella, I'm not being nosy, really, but why don't you tell us what was going on in Howie's room when Baum and his buddies came bursting in?" Dad said quietly.

I took a deep breath and thought back.

"He brought me lasagna. He wanted me to wake up because he thought that the agents would be coming soon." I thought more about that. "Shit. Maybe he even knew they'd be coming to take him away. He wanted me to get up and get dressed."

"He wanted his girlfriend to get dressed? What a singular young man," said Dad. My mother gave him a light slap on the arm and shushed him.

"See? Further proof that he didn't actually... well, whatever... anyway, you know how easily I wake up in the morning, so I didn't do what he asked, and that's why I was still in my fucking pajamas when the feds came roaring in."

"Do we have feds in Canada?" Mom asked. "I suppose they were federal agents. Secret ones."

"So, if you didn't get up and get dressed, what DID you do?" Dad asked.

A 'none of your business' was born and then died in my throat. I glowered. "We were making out, okay? Baum walked in on us kissing. That's IT, end of STORY." I paused. "But IF WE DID have sex we would have used protection, so don't give me bullshit about trust ever again."

"Even if I want to piss you off?" Dad asked. "Because it does the trick so beautifully."

"I wonder why he called it sex when you were just kissing," mused my mother.

"He said 'sexual acts'" I corrected, "He probably thought Howie was taking advantage of me."

"Was he?" asked Dad.

I glared at him.

"No, I mean, at any time, did you feel that he was pushing you to do something you didn't want to do?"

"No," I said after a minute. *No wonder he didn't want to have sex with me*, I thought. *He was probably never attracted to me at all.* "But Baum said…if he got some…" I didn't want to repeat it again.

"I could kill Baum for that crude comment alone," my mother muttered to herself. "I should have stayed."

"Stella, tell us honestly," said Dad. "What convinced you that Baum was right? Why are you so sure that Howie couldn't possibly have been honest with you?"

I sighed. "Let's look at it practically. On the one hand, there's a fairy tale of love-at-first-sight, where he falls head over heels for me, reveals the truth about himself, yadda yadda, just in time for a zombie apocalypse to hit the city which his family *may* have been responsible for. And I *just happen* to be a secret weapon capable of stopping it. On the other hand, there's a cohesive explanation that ties everything together and seems much more probable."

"In other words, you find it more likely that he was using you than that he was genuinely attracted to you, or that he could genuinely care about you," said my mother.

I nodded.

"Stella, you're an idiot," said Dad.

"What?"

"Look, I know that you haven't always had… a lot of positive treatment from your peers and it's given you a fairly significant chip on your shoulder. But honestly – you think that a teenage infatuation and a coincidence are less likely than a complicated conspiracy theory with some gaping plot holes?"

My mother was giggling. "Okay, honey, this isn't something one normally points out to one's teenage daughter –

I don't think – but conspiracy or no, Howard Mullins is attracted to you. Okay? I'm pretty sure simulating at least two fairly prominent erections in public was not part of his elaborate plan to ensnare your affections."

"What?"

"Yeah, I saw those too," said Dad. "It was awkward. God, I would never want to be a teenager again."

"When? Which times?"

"Well, in the bookshop, for starters," said Dad.

"It was glorious. I didn't know where to look," said Mom.

"And that day he made pancakes," said Dad.

"You mean the day he just showed up and cleaned the kitchen," said Mom. They looked at each other.

"Make that at least three awkward public erections," said Dad. "You didn't notice?"

"Well, not those particular times..." I grumbled.

"So. Maybe we'll never know whether this Baum guy had it right. But I can promise you, Howard Mullins was, I mean *is*, attracted to you," Mom said.

"Or, possibly, to me, I suppose," added Dad. Mom punched him.

I felt some of the pain seep out of my chest. I could handle the rest. I could handle the betrayal. If only it wasn't *all* an act.

Dad stroked my hair. "Stella. Love can't be proven. You can spend your life looking for proof that people love you, but you're going to find it thin on the ground. Some people will say they love you when clearly they don't give a crap about you. Other people will swear they don't care but would cross a mountain for you. The only thing you have to go by is a person's actions. Do they act like they love you? Or do they act like they don't? Now, I never saw

Howie do a damn thing that made me think he didn't care about you. Did you?"

I stared at him.

"What about putting me at the centre of a zombie horde?"

"Oh. Well, that."

I rubbed my forehead. Mom patted me. "Let me get you some water and an ibuprofen. Do you think you can sleep?"

I shrugged, but then I nodded. My parents kissed me and brought me water and headache medicine, and the door closed. Then my Dad knocked again.

"Uh... Army *really* wants to sleep with you. Is that okay? I fed him. Get this: they feed him canned pork brains in milk gravy. I didn't even know that was a thing."

"Send him in."

The door opened and shut again. Army stood next to my bed and breathed heavily. I patted the bed and he jumped awkwardly on to it and collapsed almost on top of me.

"Please don't eat me, okay?" I muttered.

Army's tail thumped against the wall happily.

He loves me.

He loves me not.

He loves me.

He loves me not.

He loves me.

I sat in the dark of the winter morning, ripping apart one of the roses Howie had given me. I'd woken a few minutes before, my leg crushed by Army. Then everything that had happened came flooding in and I couldn't get back to sleep. So here I was, desperately looking for an answer. I plucked the last petal off the rose.

He loves me.

No. That couldn't be right. I threw the rose stem in my garbage and grabbed another one.

He loves me.

He loves me not.

He loves me.

I plucked the petals savagely, scattering them over my bed cover. The second rose came out to 'he loves me', too, so I grabbed a third and started with "he loves me not" this time.

He loves me not.

He loves me.

He loves me not.

I plucked the last petal and stared at it. *There*, I thought. *Validated.*

It didn't make me feel better.

I felt like I was losing my mind. Sometimes I'd start to think that Dad was right and that Baum's story didn't make any sense. But then I'd remember something odd, like the fact that they had hidden the hamster instead of turning it in, and realize that Baum had to be telling the truth. Besides, why would he lie?

Then I'd think of something else, like Howie getting torn apart by zombies without even yelling, "Hey, Stella, stop them, will you?" and Baum's story would stop making sense. But then I'd remember that Howie had no sense of self-preservation so maybe they really didn't care... But then why...

It was like looking at a hologram. I could turn the story one way, and see Baum's version, and turn it another and see Howie's version.

I remembered the handkerchief, and I rummaged in my jeans for it. If it was all an act, why give me this weird, gross memento? I looked at the neatly folded square, which still smelled a little like formaldehyde. I was hit with a vivid memory of how safe I had felt with him. For a few minutes, I relived the desire, the closeness, and complete trust.

Howie.

Then it faded and I was left alone on my bed again.

I'd never know for sure. Love me or love me not, they'd declare him dead, and that'd be the end of it.

Probably after proof of his treachery was brought forth in closed court.

I unfolded the handkerchief, noticing that it had a poorly embroidered HM on it. They were hand stitches, all knotted and ragged in the back. I wondered if he had embroidered it himself.

Then I saw it: A small scrap of paper had fluttered out of the handkerchief and landed on my lap. I picked it up and read Howie's last message to me.

Main and Fifth Vancouver.

Brown building. No sign.

I love you forever.

H.

20

At 6:30 the next morning, my father stumbled into the kitchen, yawning, and started to make coffee. He grabbed a box of cereal out of the cupboard, rattled some into a bowl, turned toward the kitchen table and almost dropped his bowl in surprise when he saw me sitting in my chair.

"Jesus, Stella," he said, as Cheerios scattered over the linoleum, "you nearly gave me a heart attack."

"You faced the living dead, but *I* nearly give you a heart attack? How bad is my bed head?"

"I think the idea of you voluntarily rising in the morning is actually more startling than the idea of people involuntarily rising from the dead," he said, sitting down next to me. "What's up, buttercup?"

"I've just had a lot to think about." I had been thinking furiously, and making plans, ever since I found Howie's note.

"Tim! Stella's bed is empty!" My mother came thumping down the stairs, throwing on her housecoat. "And she's not in the bathroom, either. Do you think we should... Stella, what on EARTH?"

"Okay, if everyone could stop acting like my getting up early is some kind of completely unprecedented event…" I said.

"We've been dragging you out of bed for over a decade," said Dad. "Don't expect us to act like this is normal. You stayed up all night, didn't you? You didn't get up. You're STILL up."

"I slept. Some," I said.

My mother poured a coffee for herself and another one for Dad. "You need to get some rest, honey."

"I will," I said, cracking open a Diet Pepsi. I don't drink coffee. "Later."

"Where's the dog?" Dad asked.

"Under the table," I said. "He makes a good footrest. Don't you, boy?"

Army thumped his tail.

"He must be hungry. Want some food, big fella?" Dad asked him, getting up and rummaging for the can opener. My feet slid onto the floor as Army surged out from under the table. "Check it out – *pork brains in milk gravy*. It's actually a human food product. I think."

"When Baum or whoever comes back to check on us, we're giving them this dog," said Mom.

"Aw, Elaine…"

"Tim, we can't keep an immortal, brain-eating dog. Where do you plan to get more pork brains?"

"Maybe we have to order them on Amazon or something once a month. Must be doable. The Mullinses managed it. The cans must be cheaper than real brains, or they'd feed him the same thing they eat themselves."

"Uh huh, and what about the formaldehyde injections? Or do we just buy it from some lab and dump it in his food?"

"We'll figure it out. How hard can it be? Elaine, this is the perfect dog – no vet bills, won't die on us…"

"No, he could just wander off and then accidentally cause a zombie apocalypse. PERFECT DOG."

"So we don't let him off leash on hikes."

"Oh, and if the government finds out that we've been harboring a secret zombie dog, they'll lock us up and declare us dead," my mother added.

"Then we say, 'Oh, we thought you knew,'" shrugged Dad. "They don't want to look stupid."

They glowered at each other.

"Do we have to decide this right now?" I asked. "Did you take all the cans at the house, Dad?"

"No, I only grabbed a few. There were lots more. Are you thinking what I'm thinking?"

I shrugged, trying to look casual. "There were some things I wanted to pick up over there, and I figure the windows might be broken still. We could probably get in. It'd buy us some time while we decide what to do with Army."

"What if you two run into agents guarding the house?"

"Then we tell them Stella left some things there," said Dad, shrugging. "I have an interview to get to at ten, so I say let's hop to it and steal pork brains fast."

"Ah, the sentence every daughter expects to hear from her father one day: 'Let's steal pork brains.' Let me just shower."

I took the stairs two at a time.

Dad drove cautiously down Howie's street. The local residents seemed to have returned to their homes – there were cars parked in driveways. Howie's driveway, though, was empty. The white vans and the black cars had left tire tracks on the lawn. There was yellow tape over the broken windows.

"Well, I feel like a burglar," said Dad, putting the car in park. "A brain burglar."

We tried the door and it was locked, but it was easy to climb in the bay window. The broken wooden boards were still nailed to the walls, but the zombie bodies were gone, and someone had cleaned all the blood off the walls and floor. I could smell the sharp tang of ammonia. The lights were off and the house felt deserted.

Dad and I walked to the kitchen. "I found the cans in the pantry..." Dad said, pulling open the pantry door. "I'll stock up. Check the cupboard for more."

Instead, I went right to the freezer, my heart pounding. The Tupperware container holding the hamster was still there, sitting next to a pig head which seemed to be giving me the stink eye.

I took out the container and peered through the clear plastic. The hamster was curled up, unmoving, unbreathing. I quickly slipped it into my backpack and zipped it up tight.

I glanced in the fridge. It was mostly empty, except for a gleaming line of thermoses.

Then I opened the cupboards. More thermoses.

"Any formalin?" Dad asked. I shook my head no.

"Maybe they shoot up in the bathroom," I said. "I'll go look."

I ran upstairs, opened their bathroom cabinets and found bottles and bottles of formalin. In the bathroom drawer next to the sink, there were stacks of needles.

My boyfriend kept heads in his freezer and needles in his bathroom. But I had chosen to believe him over a federal agent. I reached into my pocket and squeezed the handkerchief. I knew where he was. I'd find out soon enough if I had made the right choice.

"I found the formalin, Dad. Uh… how much do we want to steal?"

"They asked us to look after their dog. This isn't stealing, it's taking what he needs."

He grabbed a couple of bottles and an unopened box of needles. "Formalin should be easy enough to get online. I'm more worried about getting all the brains. I'm going to do one last sweep of the kitchen. Meet you at the car, okay?"

I nodded, and as soon as Dad was down the stairs, I rushed into Howie's room and began looking through every corner. If my theory was right, then there was some kind of spy bug in this room. There had to be. But I didn't really know what that would look like in real life. If this were a movie, I'd have found some blinking light under the bed or a tiny hole drilled in the wall. But I didn't find anything. I was running out of time.

My gaze fell on Howie's teddy bear.

I looked at the bear. It looked at me.

Then I leaned forward. One of its eyes looked sort of strange. I picked up the bear and looked closer. Was that a camera in its eye? I squished its head and felt a hard box in its head.

FOUND IT.

I ran down the stairs and out to the car. Dad looked at me curiously.

"You've been looking transformed this morning. What's up?"

"Determination."

Dad didn't ask me any more questions. Maybe he didn't want to push his luck. Maybe he just didn't want to know.

He dropped me off at home and I wished him luck at his interview, then lugged the bags of brains and formalin into the house. I dumped the bags on the kitchen floor and ripped open my backpack.

I took out the hamster. It still looked frozen. I set it on the table. Army sniffed it and I pushed him away. Then I pulled out the bear and plunked it on the table, too. Then I sat down in front of it.

"I hope you're watching, because you and I are going to have a little conversation," I said sweetly to the teddy. "You see, I've been thinking since our talk yesterday, and something struck me as strange." I paused. "Well, a lot of things have struck me as strange, but this is the important one: You knew what day Howie told me that he was a zombie. You knew what day we kissed. You knew that my parents were in Howie's house. You knew that Howie and I were making out in his room yesterday morning, and you came running up the stairs to stop us."

I chewed the inside of my lip thoughtfully, mentally re-checking the facts that I had gone over and over since I awoke that morning.

"But there were a lot of things you didn't know. For example, you say you didn't know that we were being overwhelmed by zombies. Now, maybe that's just because you were off checking the border like you said, instead of spying on the world's most monotonous family. But there are other things you don't seem to know." I stroked Army, who was standing with his head in my lap, tail waving. "Surprising things. And they're all things that happened or were said downstairs. For example, this." I opened the container and showed the contents.

"This is the hamster you've all been looking for. It came along with all of the other zombies. And do you know what was strange?" I leaned in close to the bear. "It wasn't actually a zombie. Oh, sure, it looked pretty awful, but it was breathing and trying to get away and stuff. Stuff that real zombies don't do. That really freaked out the Mullinses. They were scared that it meant something bad – like maybe that it was possible for them to turn contagious before they were completely dead. But you know what I think?" I stood up and put the container back in the freezer. "I think that the hamster never did turn contagious. I think something else started that outbreak." I smiled and folded my arms. "And I think that something else was you."

I left the bear to think about what I had said and I ran upstairs. I used the bathroom and then went into my parents' room and raided their loose cash drawer, where they dumped all their change from their pockets at the end of the day.

I left a note on the kitchen table saying,

Gone to rescue my undead boyfriend from insane government agents. IOU $15.

Underneath, I scribbled the address that Howie had given me on the note so my parents would know where I had gone. Then I plugged that same address into Google Maps on my phone, stuffed the hamster container and the teddy into my backpack, swung the pack onto my shoulders and opened the front door.

Agent Baum was standing on the front steps.

Shit.

"Hello, Stella," Baum said pleasantly, but with a dangerous glint in his eyes. "Can I come in?"

"No, actually," I said. "I was just headed out."

"Out where?"

I folded my arms and shrugged.

Baum folded his arms too. "Listen, young lady. I don't know where you think you're going with that hamster, but I can guarantee you that the only place you are actually going to go is back into that kitchen."

"You mean the harmless, not-at-all-contagious hamster?"

"It *is* contagious! Surrender it to me now. I will bring it to the laboratory for testing."

"You know, I think I'd rather take it down there myself." As I spoke I slowly shifted my weight onto my left leg and slid my right one out slightly.

"That vile boy gave you the location? His treachery astounds even me."

"He never actually said it out loud. But I'm pretty sure I can find it."

"Give me the hamster."

"Why? So you can hide the evidence? Are you worried about what they'll think when they realize it isn't contagious? They might wonder how the outbreak really started."

"If that *thing* isn't contagious, then your undead, disgusting boyfriend must have found some other way to spread the virus!"

"No," I said. "You did it. You spread it. You framed the Mullinses. You purposely let us get overwhelmed. You tried to kill them off."

"I did nothing but try to protect *you* and the rest of our nation from that foul family! Canada will be a safer place without infected undead walking around masquerading as normal people, and possibly even trying to *breed* with the normal population! THEY. MUST. BE. CONTAINED!" His face was red and his eyes bulging as he advanced on me. I took a step back, and then shifted my weight again onto my left side. My right leg was barely touching the ground, ready to go into action.

"NOW, GIVE ME THE HAMSTER!" He grabbed my shoulder and tried to rip open my backpack. I ducked and hit him with a swift, low calf kick, then brought up my elbow to hit him in the jaw. He tried to grapple me but I just broke his hold and flipped him over my back. He landed with a heavy thud in my kitchen. When he sat up, I threw a straight punch into his head.

Ten minutes later I jogged down the road to the nearest bus stop, leaving Baum duct taped into a chair in the kitchen, with Army sniffing his face.

I took the Skytrain downtown. It was my first time riding it, but it wasn't too hard to figure out. I hopped out at the station near Science World, which was a giant silver ball right on the waterfront. I might have found the experience more interesting from a tourism perspective if I hadn't been focused on trying to rescue my zombie boyfriend from the clutches of a secret government agency.

From there, my phone's mapping app directed me to walk for several blocks up a hill in the rain along a busy road until I got to 5th Avenue, and started looking at the buildings. There were several brown or brown-ish buildings on that corner. They looked like office buildings, but one had a suspicious deficiency of windows on the lower level and the windows on the upper level were heavily tinted. I looked at his note again. No signs. This one must be it. Howie was either in that building, or there were people inside who could take me to him. My heart was pounding as I marched up to the door and rattled it experimentally. It was locked. Big surprise.

There was a security camera, though.

I dropped my backpack on the ground and yanked out the lunch bag. I pulled out the Tupperware and peeled off the top to reveal the hamster, which was still pretty frozen.

"OPEN UP!" I shouted, waving the hamster in my fist. "OPEN THE FUCK UP RIGHT NOW SO HELP ME OR I'M GOING TO WAVE THIS ZOMBIE HAMSTER AT A NEWS CREW!"

It only took about five minutes of waving a frozen rodent and shouting swear words before an Asian man in a white lab coat appeared and yanked open the door. "Bring that inside," he said breathlessly, reaching for the hamster. I pulled it closer to me and swept inside with as much dignity as I could muster.

Lab Coat Guy reached out again. I held the hamster close and took a combat stance. "You won't be the first guy I've knocked out today. You can have the hamster when I see Howie."

"Don't be ridiculous, Stella, you're completely outnumbered," said a voice. Standing in a doorway was Agent Hunt. Two more people in lab coats stood behind her.

"Maybe. But I can also freeze an army of zombies with my thoughts, so it's worth cultivating my cooperation," I said. "I want to see Howie and his family, and then I want Dr. Mullins to check and see if the hamster is contagious."

"What do you mean?" asked Agent Hunt with a look of surprise.

"It's not dead," I said. "I don't think it caused the outbreak."

"It's frozen solid, and you think it's still alive?" said Lab Coat Guy. "They're not like cockroaches, you know."

"I'll explain more WHEN I SEE HOWIE!" my voice echoed in the hallway. Lab Coat Guy stepped back.

"There's really no need for the dramatics, Stella. Of course I will let you visit with Howie," said Agent Hunt.

"You will?" I said, startled.

"Yes. You found the hamster, and then you found us. I'll want to know how you did both of those things. We only have so many places equipped to lock people up, so I'll be taking you to the same room. The tricky part will be convincing us to let you out again. Now, put that hamster back in the container before it thaws and bites someone."

"It's not..."

"You may be willing to risk your life on that, but I'm not. In a container, please, and hand it to Gordon. Follow me."

I put the hamster, which had started to breathe again, back in the Tupperware and handed it to Lab Coat Guy. He held it tightly, as if he expected the hamster to force the top off and attack him violently. I followed them down a gloomy stairwell into another hallway with dismal fluorescent lighting.

My heart was thumping wildly. I was actually going to see Howie. I wasn't sure if I was excited, or terrified. Either I was about to rescue my true love, or I was about to have my heart broken and then be charged with attacking a federal agent.

It could go either way at this point.

Agent Hunt stopped at one of several solid-looking metal doors with a keypad on the door handle. She punched in a code and waved an electronic fob over the lock. A little green light appeared and she opened the door.

"Go on in," she said.

I had expected a padded room or jail cell or something. Instead, I was in a laboratory: Fume hoods. Sinks. Microscopes. Machines. Lap tops.

"Stella."

I turned. Howie was standing by the door, his eyes wide, lips parted.

"I felt you coming for me," he whispered.

My body and brain were overwhelmed with confusing emotions, so I stood frozen. Should I grab him and kiss him, or should I punch him and demand explanations?

Howie didn't seem to suffer from the same mix of feelings. He quickly closed the gap between us and reached his arms around my waist. I felt my body respond immediately to his touch.

"Thank God," he said softly, and leaned forward and kissed me with incredible tenderness. I simultaneously felt the urge to press him up against a wall and make out savagely with him, and the urge to break down and cry. I did neither. Instead, I pulled away.

"We need to talk, first," I said.

Agent Hunt cleared her throat. "Let's talk about the hamster," she said.

Howie snapped out of his dreamy look. "You brought the hamster?"

"What a fantastic way to fuck us over one more time," said Ray's voice. "Thanks so much."

Dr. Mullins removed the hamster from the container and dangled it by the scruff of its neck. The hamster had defrosted enough that it could wiggle a bit and squeak.

"Poor thing," said Hazel.

The whole family was locked up in that laboratory. The far end of the lab had two sets of bunk beds with curtains hanging over them for privacy, and a door with a men/women bathroom sign on it. Dr. Mullins had been sitting at a microscope down the far end of the room, while Ray and Hazel lay on their bunks craning their necks at a TV that hung at a weird angle in the corner of the room.

"It's a lab *and* a cell?" I murmured to Howie quietly while people looked at the zombie hamster.

"I think they've been preparing this place for us for a while," he replied softly. "They just finally had an excuse to bring us in."

"As you can see, the hamster has not yet died," said Dr. Mullins, laying a finger on the rodent's chest. "The heartbeat is quite easily palpable."

"Have you been doing any experiments on the side that we should know about?" Agent Hunt asked sharply.

"I wish I could say that I had," said Dr. Mullins. "I am as concerned as you are by the possible implications of this."

"Considering that they'll probably kill us," Ray said.

"It's not contagious," I said. Dr. Mullins raised his eyebrows.

"You sound very sure of yourself. Do you know something that we don't?"

"I know you told me that they don't turn contagious until after they die, and that hamster isn't dead, therefore it isn't contagious."

Agent Hunt and Dr. Mullins exchanged looks. "Okay," said Hunt, "but we have over a hundred and fifty dead people who would suggest otherwise. Can you explain how that could happen?"

"I have a theory."

"Do you want to tell us that theory?" Agent Hunt sounded exasperated.

"Test the hamster first. Because if it *is* contagious, then my theory is wrong, Baum told the truth, and Howie never loved me." I said.

Howie turned. "What?"

"First test. Then story."

Dr. Mullins produced a swab and stuck it briefly into the hamster's mouth. Then he handed the hamster over to Hazel, who cooed and made fish faces at it. The hamster showed no signs of being comforted by this and continued to struggle.

"You might be interested in watching, Stella," said Dr. Mullins. Goddamn zombies: you'd think we were having a slightly boring chat over coffee, rather than meeting possibly for the last time while his guilt/innocence rested on the outcome of this single test.

I went over to watch as he rubbed the swab over a little plastic stick and then dipped the stick in a series of little plastic wells filled with unnamed liquids. He carefully timed each dip, staring unblinkingly at a clock on the wall and counting the seconds under his breath. Gordon the Lab Coat Guy was watching closely.

"This is an ELISA test," said Dr. Mullins, still staring at the clock.

"I know," said Gordon. "I'm a scientist. I've done hundreds of these."

"I was talking to Stella."

"Oh."

"It uses enzymes and antibodies to identify the presence of a particular antigen in a sample. It was quite challenging to find a method of ELISA that worked on this virus, since the human immune response is so ill-equipped to fight it. Antibodies are only produced for a very short time and they aren't very effective ones. That is why we have not yet developed a vaccine for it. However, I eventually discovered that the Virginia Opossum produces quite excellent antibodies, and so we use those."

"How in hell did you discover that?"

"It's a long story," he said, transferring the stick to another well. "Now, the last well. It needs to sit here for three minutes. When I remove the stick, you will see two dots. The first dot is a control. If it does not change colour, the test was not performed correctly. The second dot indicates presence of the antigen – in this case, the virus – in the saliva."

"So… second dot is bad."

"Yes. I am expecting a second dot. The hamster must be infectious, in order to have started the outbreak."

"And if it is, they'll probably get rid of us entirely," said Ray, sending me a look of deep disgust. Agent Hunt and Gordon didn't say anything in response. We watched the seconds tick by.

"So… why does a second dot mean that I don't really love you?" Howie asked.

"Because Baum said that you released the hamster on purpose to orchestrate an outbreak just to prove my mind powers, so you could then sell me to the U.S. government to help control their zombie army."

Everyone turned and gaped at me.

"Did he not mention that to you?" I asked Agent Hunt.

Dr. Mullins glanced back at the clock. "Three minutes." He pulled the stick out of the well. "Hmm. Interesting."

"It's contagious?" I asked, rushing forward.

"The test is negative for antibodies. It would appear that the hamster's saliva is not infectious at this time," said Dr. Mullins.

I nearly collapsed with relief.

"But it must be. Is that even the right hamster?" Agent Hunt asked Dr. Mullins. "Maybe it's just… a hamster, and the real one is still running around out there, infectious."

"Oh yes, I recognize him. He's been with me for ten years," said Dr. Mullins. He pointed to one ear. "That ear has always been a little crinkled. If necessary, we can open him up, which I have done several times in the past. One of the lobes of his liver has a distinctively unusual shape. But as a simpler demonstration…" he grabbed one of the flailing legs and snapped it between his fingers like a pencil. I actually heard a small cracking sound.

"What the…" I started to protest. Howie smiled and shook his head.

"Stella," he reminded me.

Oh, right. No pain. The hamster certainly didn't seem to notice or care. Dr. Mullins held the leg carefully in his finger for a moment and then let go.

"The break has knitted."

"Also, it was frozen solid when it arrived," pointed out Gordon, "and it's still alive."

Agent Hunt nodded.

"Baum lied," I said to Agent Hunt. "They didn't start the outbreak."

"Stella... I don't know what your alternate theory is," said Dr. Mullins, "but you do realize that even if the test had been positive, it would be a far cry from evidence that we purposely released it in some sort of turncoat operation with the United States?"

"Baum said he had the evidence. Either he was telling the truth, or he wasn't."

"Wait. He said he had evidence that they were collaborating with the U.S. Government?" Agent Hunt demanded. She turned to Gordon. "Tell them to call in Baum."

"Uh... he's tied up at the moment," I said.

"Doing what? How do you know?" Gordon said.

"No, I mean, I literally tied him up in my kitchen." Everyone stared at me. "He grabbed me and tried to pull off my backpack. It was self-defense."

Agent Hunt rubbed her face. "Tell them to send an extraction team to Stella Blunt's kitchen." She pulled up Gordon's stool as he scuttled away, and she sat on it. She pointed at me, and at another stool. "You. Sit. Talk."

So, I repeated everything that had happened since the zombie outbreak. How we had called for help. How help hadn't come. How I had controlled the zombies. How Baum had shattered my universe. Howie clutched my hand tightly when I told Baum's version of events.

"Stella... you didn't believe him, did you?" Howie asked. His speech was faster than usual, which I was beginning to learn meant "intense emotion". "Please tell me you didn't. You couldn't believe that I made it all up... that I was just using you..."

I looked away. He groaned.

"But then I worked some things out," I said, moving on. "Certain things didn't make sense. Like, why did he arrest Howie first? I mean, he ran up the stairs and burst into Howie's room. Then I thought about how disgusted he was by Howie and me dating. So, I went back to the house, and I found this," I pulled out the teddy bear.

"My bear?" Howie asked.

"It has a camera in its head, Howie," I said. "Maybe you should hug your teddy every now and then. Who knows how long he's been spying on your room?"

"I didn't authorize that surveillance," said Agent Hunt swiftly to Dr. Mullins.

"I know you didn't, Michaella."

"And when the hamster found me," I said, making it sound as though the Mullins hadn't known about it, "I saw that it hadn't zombified yet. Doc said days ago that the timing was strange, that it shouldn't have become infectious so quickly even if it had somehow escaped from the lab. So then I realized that Baum could have set off the whole thing. He spied on Howie kissing me in his room and decided that Howie was a menace to society because he has this weird hang-up about zombies having sex, so he released the virus and then somehow took the hamster from the lab just to frame the Mullinses, so you'd lock them up." I looked into Howie's worried gaze. "And I realized that all of that still made more sense than Howie lying to me."

"So..." Ray said, "basically you decided that if Baum's crazy conspiracy theory was wrong, then your own crazy conspiracy theory was right?"

"Basically, I decided that either Howie had faked it all, or Baum was unbalanced enough to start an outbreak. And

I know which of those I'd put money on if I had to choose."

Howie buried his face in my hair, squeezing me tight in his arms.

Dr. Mullins cleared his throat.

"Stella, you used the word 'somehow' several times. You haven't actually said how he could have started the outbreak or gotten into the lab."

"Because I don't know, do I?" I said irritably. "Does he have clearance access to virus samples? Does he have clearance access to the lab?"

"Yes," said Dr. Mullins. "He does."

"Well then." I spread my hands.

"Get to the part where you attacked and incapacitated a federal officer," said Agent Hunt.

So I summarized my little rant into the teddy bear's camera, and how Baum accosted me before I could escape out the door.

"You do realize that even if Agent Baum did plant unauthorized surveillance, that hardly qualifies as proof that he purposely started a major outbreak just to stop a teenage romance," Agent Hunt warned me. "Baum takes the safety of Canadians very seriously."

"The bear was in my bag at the time. I hope it recorded his diatribe about how he did it all to protect Canadians from breeding with people like Howie. He practically confessed."

"We'll see. Right now, I need to decide what I'm going to do with you. Agent Baum did tell me yesterday that he suspects you may be a ZCP."

"A what now?"

"Z0381E Controlling Personality. Someone who can control people infected by the virus. Any government *would* pay a lot of money to get their hands on one." She looked at Dr. Mullins.

He raised his eyebrows. "Since you have apparently denied me access to information about the existence of such individuals, I cannot officially confirm that."

"Sorry, Morton, but it's not your research area. You know how it is."

"If I had been properly informed, I might have identified Stella as such much sooner. Simple logic should have told you that we would be your best method of identifying such a useful individual."

"Conflict of interest. They could probably control you, too. So you think that she is, then?"

He sighed and looked at me. "Yes."

"Well, Stella, I think it goes without saying that we expect you to remain in Canada," said Agent Hunt. "The upper muk-a-muks will take some time deciding exactly how to go about convincing you to do that, but I can bet it will involve a small financial incentive if you lend us your services and a legal loophole to justify arresting you if you try to leave the country."

"What, like, ever? Like, I can't go to Mexico for vacation?"

"It may depend on how cooperative you seem. You don't come across as the cooperative type, either. Especially since you attacked one of our high-level officers."

"He's a vicious man who released the virus on the city just to frame a family of peaceful half-zombies!"

"According to you."

"He lied and said that Howie was going to sell me to the U.S.!"

"How would that even work?" Ray asked. "And how much would we get?"

"He may have genuinely believed that, you know," said Agent Hunt. "Wrong is not the same as lying."

Ray folded his arms. "He refused to help us last night, and then he told Stella that we didn't call at all. Did he tell you that we called?"

Agent Hunt sighed. "No. And we could have helped you. There were minor attacks only. Baum insisted on monitoring the border. You know how it is. He said no call for help came through. After we saw the damage, he speculated that no help had been needed, which must mean that Stella was a ZCP."

"So you know at least that he's trying to hide something, since he lied to both you and us," I pointed out.

"I promise you that we will get to the bottom of that," Hunt said. "I'm not condoning his actions. I just don't see evidence that he deliberately started an outbreak. That's too big a leap."

Gordon came back into the room. "They're bringing him back. Also, uh… I checked the logs and counted the number of virus vials… and we're three short."

Everyone in the room stiffened.

"What?" Agent Hunt walked quickly across the room and then paused at the door. She looked at me speculatively for a minute.

"Before I go… In the interest of showing us how cooperative you are, Stella," she said, "would you please show me how you do it?"

"Sure, I just do this," I said.

"Aw, don't…" Ray started to say. Then he went silent.

I am here. Make way for me.

There was a thump as Hazel dropped the hamster. It stood on its hind legs and sniffed in my direction, but it didn't try to run away. I walked across the room and picked it up. The Mullinses followed me with their eyes, their jaws slightly slack. Gordon stepped up to Ray and waved a hand in front of his face.

Then I relaxed again.

"Wow." Gordon stepped back from Ray as he saw them come back to life. "She's a ZCP?"

"Apparently."

"We'll be wanting an EEG," he breathed. "And maybe an MRI. We should test to see what distance she can control them from, and how many…"

"All of which I will happily consent to… once Howie and his family are out of custody," I said, stroking the hamster absently as it tried to scrabble up my shirt.

"Stella, even if they weren't responsible for the hamster, they still broke the law when they told you and your parents confidential information," said Agent Hunt. "I have a lot of respect for Morton and his family, but the law is the law."

"Drop the charges if you want my cooperation."

"The charges have already gone to the crown. They will have to stand trial."

"So will Agent Baum, I imagine," I replied. Agent Hunt raised an eyebrow but said nothing.

"Can't they be let out on bail?" I rummaged through my pockets. "I am prepared to offer… three dollars and 15 cents. Oh, and my full cooperation, of course. If not… well… I've never cared that much about going to Mexico anyway, and my parents may be very unwilling to give permission for all this invasive testing on their only daughter. They're very protective of me, you know, and they're already a little upset, considering that no one came when we called for help and I almost got torn to pieces by a horde of the undead."

We stared each other down for a few interminable seconds. Then Agent Hunt nodded curtly.

"I need to make some phone calls," she said. "I will also need to talk to Baum. Just... wait. Wait here." She left the cell.

"Damn," said Ray, looking at me with something that resembled respect.

Howie tilted my chin up and kissed me.

"They are going to let us go, you know. You are amazing," he said.

"I know," I said.

"I am madly in love with you."

"I know that, too."

EPILOGUE

It took a week for them to open the school again. My parents made me retract my complaints about how there'd be no snow days in Vancouver.

"Apparently, you get zombie days here," Dad said. "How cool is that?"

It took most of that week to get Howie and his family officially released, but by the time school started, they were home and their house was mostly repaired.

On the first day of school, Howie showed up early at my house to wash dishes again. That no longer seemed weird to my parents, because now they knew that there were much weirder things about Howie than early morning helpfulness in the kitchen.

Walking into school felt very different that day. When you've been attacked by crazed hordes of the undead, when you've seen that many skulls smashed, when you've defended yourself against horror movie monsters, and won – some high school popularity problems don't seem to matter anymore. I didn't give a damn if everyone thought I was a backstabbing, teacher-seducing cheater.

I wasn't ashamed to be dating the school's biggest loser, either. Quite the opposite. When Howie insisted on carrying my bag and smiled shyly at me when our hands touched, I felt a glow of – pride, maybe? Pride was hard to recognize. I didn't feel it often.

The kids around me might never know it, but I helped take down nearly a hundred zombies. I chopped those bastards down like so many trees and rescued the boy who made me feel beautiful and free to be myself. I rescued him *twice*.

I used my own brain as a bargaining chip to get what I wanted and succeeded. Federal agents were dancing on my every whim and treating me like a powerful political figure.

I felt invincible, and Howie was my trophy. So what if people thought his lurching walk and his robot voice was weird? They didn't know him like I did.

When we walked into Chemistry hand in hand, someone shouted, "Oh, man, here comes the Freak and The Fatty." Instead of feeling angry, I just smiled and gave them a little wave. "Here we are!" I said.

The Chair Kicking Guy behind Howie gave me a smile.

Howie pulled out my chair and I sat down in regal splendor. He sat too and gazed adoringly at me for a moment, and then leaned in closer and said conspiratorially, "So, two men walk into a bar. The first one says, 'I'd like some H2O.' The second one says, 'Hey, I'd like that. Give me some H2O, too.'" He paused. "The second man died."

I laughed. "That may be the lamest chemistry joke ever."

"But you laughed. I have another. A neutrino walks into a bar. He orders a drink. When the bartender hands it over the neutrino asks how much he owes him. The bartender says, 'For you, no charge.'"

I thunked my head down on the desk. "It's a good thing you're cute, Howard."

"It's funny. Admit it."

"In a really, really, stupid sort of way."

"Two atoms bump into each other. The first says, 'I think I lost an electron'. The second says, 'Are you sure?' and the first one replies, 'I'm positive.'"

I noticed that Mr. Nguyen was standing near us, listening in.

"Mr. Nguyen, save me!" I begged.

He shook his head. "Hey, Howard, do you know any sodium jokes?"

"Na," replied Howie instantly with a dimpled grin. Mr. Nguyen nodded in pleased approval and went to the whiteboard to start the class. Howie reached under the table and took my hand.

"There's a dance in the spring. Will you go with me?"

"Of course not. Now, pay attention," I said, squeezing his hand.

Yep, Howie was a treasure, and goddamn, I was walking-on-air happy about it. I didn't give a shit what they said about us. All I had to do was think about slicing a zombie's brain open, and suddenly these little dipshits just didn't seem like a big deal anymore.

Besides, maybe it was just my mood, or maybe it was a side effect of the zombie stuff, but somehow the insults didn't have as much sting today. At the end of class, some guy snickered behind me, "Man, you'd think those zombies would have just eaten her and then gotten full and gone home."

"Dude, that's not cool," Chair Kicking Guy responded, "Blake's step-dad *died* from that food poisoning."

"Oh, is that why he's out today? That sucks, man."

In English, Kelly swung by just to say something nice. Oh, did I say nice? I meant vicious.

"I hear you and Howard Mullins are dating."

"Yep."

"It's so nice when freaks fall in love. It keeps the rest of us safe from them."

I shrugged. "It's your loss. Me, I like a loyal, loving guy who treats me like a queen. I guess that's not for you."

I thought she was going to explode. Then she flipped her hair and turned away.

"I understand that someone like you has to take what she can get. I'm happy for you. He's probably the only guy in the school who likes fatties."

"Then I'm glad I managed to find the only guy in the school with good taste."

She spun around. "The whole school knows that you're a cheating slut."

"Well, I'd agree with them, but then we'd all be wrong." I smiled and walked away.

I was just so happy.

On the night of the Cherry Blossom Dance, my Dad insisted on driving us there in style, which was hard for him to do with a Corolla, but he did the best he could.

He honked to let Howie know we were outside (tres classy, no doubt) and Howie came out in a powder blue tuxedo that looked like a relic from the 50s, which it probably was.

Dad held the door open for him and he slid into the back seat next to me. His eyes roamed over my new dress and its contents and his jaw worked unproductively for a moment.

"You're... stunning," he said simply.

"Thanks. What in baby Jesus's name are you wearing?"

"A suit."

"Howie, you realize the other guys will probably be wearing wife beaters and swag?"

"Well, you deserve more than that," he said. "Where I come from, we dress up for our dates."

"Where you come from, as in, fifty years ago?"

"Yep."

"Should I have worn a poodle skirt?" I was struck with the mental image. "God, can you imagine? I wouldn't be able to go through doorways."

"You would look wonderful, but this... this is very, very nice," he said, gently running his finger along the sleeve of my dress. I was pleased with it. It turned out that Vancouver had some great plus sized clothing stores. I felt fabulous in this dress, which was snug where it should be and loose and flowy where I needed it to be.

Howie's hand left my sleeve and slowly traveled down the side of my dress in a sensuous caress. I took a deep breath and tried not to purr.

Dad cleared his throat, but I could see his eyes crinkling in the rearview mirror. The jerk was trying not to laugh.

Howie sat back. "Sorry, Mr. Blunt, I'll wait to drool over Stella after we get out of the car."

"Just remember, you're dating her for her mind," said Dad sternly.

"Oh, I haven't forgotten," Howie said, looking at me hungrily.

"Thanks, Dad. Is that really better?"

"Look, I'm just saying, I'm an experienced zombie slayer now."

"You got a cleaver stuck in a woman's boobs and then cut yourself with another one," I pointed out.

"Hey, I'm a survivor! Howie needs to watch his step."

"I assure you, sir, I have a deep respect for your ability to slay me instantly should I ever keep Stella out past curfew."

"And don't you forget it," said Dad, who adored Howie's impenetrable deadpan. "You never should've let me learn your weak spot."

"Dad," I said, "his weak spot is his *head*. That's *everyone's* weak spot."

"Actually, my head's not my weakest spot," said Howie.

"Oh?" Dad raised his eyebrows and cast a curious glance into the rearview mirror.

"My real weakness is… Stella."

"NICE ONE," said my Dad.

"Oh God, I'm going to throw up. That was sickening," I groaned. "Admit it, Dad, you just wanted to drive so you could make my life miserable."

"Maybe. But hey, if you want to go to a school dance for once, then I want to make it a night to remember. I couldn't afford a limo, but at least I can be your chauffeur."

"Uh huh. We'll be the envy of the whole school," I said. "There's still a dent in the hood from when you hit that zombie."

"Besides," continued my father, "this way I know you aren't driving home drunk."

"It's a school dance, Dad, no liquor, plus we're underaged."

"Yeah, like that's ever stopped teens from getting drunk at a party. I was young once."

"Also, I physically can't get drunk," said Howie, "so you can always think of me as a guaranteed designated driver."

"Oh, yeah, the zombie behind the wheel, much better," said Dad. "Hey, what would happen if they got you to breathe into a breathalyzer, with all that formalin in your system?"

"I... don't know," admitted Howie.

When Dad pulled up at the school, Howie jumped out and came around to open the car door for me. I took his hand and stepped out graciously.

"Howie, you're staring at my legs," I said. He looked up.

"Sorry," he said. "Shall we go in?" and he offered me his arm. I waved to my Dad, and he beeped cheerily and drove off.

I used to attend school dances under protest with Liz and Jeremy. I never danced, and generally considered them opportunities to beat up people who made fat jokes at me. But after some thought, I ended up deciding that I actually did want to go to this dance after all. I liked the idea of taking Howie. I liked the idea of dancing, and drinking stupid fake punch, and acting like all the rest of the kids, instead of being a bitter outsider.

And Kate was going, too.

Oh yeah, did I mention? We were friends, now. That first day back, after I froze out Kelly, I dragged Howie over to Kate's lunch table and said frankly, "I like you, and I want to be friends, but Howie and I are together, and if that's going to be a problem, then I'll just go sit with his family."

She nodded, and shrugged, and looked at Michelle and Amy, and they shrugged, and Kate said, "Whatever. Have a seat."

So we sat. We did our moment of silence together when the principal came out and asked us to think about Ms. Bond and the people of Vancouver who had died.

Once the solemnity from that had worn off and he had finished his brain shake, Howie told a couple of his lame jokes, only this time Physics ones, and Kate laughed and that was it – he was in.

People still called him a loser, and made fun of me for being with him, and made fun of him for being with me, and occasionally made fun of Kate and company for letting us sit with them. But Howie never cared, I no longer cared, and Kate wasn't shy with her middle finger.

So, who cared?

"Howie," I said cautiously as we walked to the doors, "you know people are going to make fun of your outfit, right?"

"I don't care about them. Do you like it?" he asked. I stood back from him and looked at him critically. The powder blue matched his milky blue eyes and brought out the yellow tones in his light hair. It fit him pretty well. He looked handsome, and out of date, and quaint, and retro.

"It suits you. Yes, I like it."

"Good, then." He offered his arm again and we swept into the gym.

It was a big crowd for that kind of a space and the music was deafening. People spotted Howie's tux and started pointing and laughing, and didn't let us through.

"To hell with this," I said and turned on my crowd-blast. People made way for me as I barged through, dragging a dazed and confused Howie behind me.

"Good," I said when I reached the drinks table. I helped myself to a drink and nudged Howie. He shook his head and smiled dreamily at me.

"I like you," he said.

"Wake up, Howie. I had to do it to get through the crowd."

Kate found us at the drinks table and actually complimented Howie's suit.

"It's kind of *Gangnam Style*. You should have worn sunglasses."

"At night? I'm not Corey Hart," he said mildly. She shook her head and then whistled at me.

"Hot damn, you look great," she said.

"Why thank you, you look pretty great yourself."

Kate was normally a sweatshirt and jeans sort of girl, but she had put on a tight shirt for the occasion of the dance.

"If you aren't going to dance with her, Howie, I will," said Kate with a grin. Howie shook himself awake and smiled at Kate.

"Let me have the first dance," he said, "and then you can cut in."

"Hah. I just might. Hot DAMN!" she said, wagging a finger at me. "Oh, look, there's Amy! I'll catch you later."

The dance music had switched from frenetic, undanceable stuff to something slower. "May I have this dance?" Howie asked. He bowed to me and was promptly bumped into by two assholes.

"Watch where you're going, freakshow," shouted one.

"Nice SUIT."

"Aren't you embarrassed to be seen in public with that? I don't mean the suit; I mean the hamplanet you're with."

"She's the hottest girl here," Howie said, but I don't know if they heard him – they barely even slowed down.

"Oh, go fuck yourselves in the sphincter with a dead donkey," I hollered dismissively at their backs, and grabbed Howie. "Come on, let's dance."

Howie completely and utterly surprised me by knowing how to dance. Like, real dancing, not just swaying back and forth trying to hide an erection like most teenage guys do. I guess back in the fifties or whenever he was young, they actually knew dance steps. It was unfortunate in a way, because I didn't know anything, but he taught me, and since he was all fired up on brains, he did it really frigging well.

Kate cut in to dance with me, and then he cajoled her into a dance with him, and she was impressed by the fact that he could really dance. Then he claimed me back and held me like a prize.

I felt so… normal.

I was dressed up at the school dance like any girl, and I had a cute and worshipful boyfriend, which made me luckier than most of the girls in my school, who were either single or (worse), dating dickwads who called them fat and then cheated on them.

So mine was a zombie in an ancient tuxedo. I didn't care.

After a while I got too hot, so we slipped outside to cool off. It was nice out, even in my skimpy dress. March in Vancouver was still cool but felt like spring. Back home everyone was still walking through slush, and here we had cherry blossoms and daffodils. I'd had a lot of fun posting pictures of flowers for my friends in the snow to see. They were seething with envy.

Howie and I sat leaning against each other for a while, listening to the sounds of the night.

"Howie?"

"Mmm?"

"Do you still sometimes want to eat my brains?"

"All the time."

"Really? How do you focus on anything?"

"You get used to it. It's just part of what I am."

"You don't worry you'll just, like, bust out and eat someone?" I teased.

He snorted. "There's no excuse for that, any more than there is for a guy 'busting out' and raping a girl. We all have desires. We don't have to act on them."

I nodded.

"Thank you," he said, twining his fingers in mine. His touch still made me a little giddy.

"For what?" I could feel the rise and fall of his chest as he breathed in his stilted, irregular way.

"A wonderful evening."

"Howie, *you* bought the tickets, and *you* had to teach me how to dance, so why are you thanking *me*?"

"Because I'm just grateful you're with me."

"That's pathetic. Like, seriously, what's with the pathos?"

"One of these days you'll look at me and see a kid. You'll outgrow me."

"Howie… I love you."

He squeezed my hand tightly. "I know you do. But people grow and change. I am unchanging. My love for you is unchanging. I want you to know that I'll love you forever. Even when you get tired of me. Just... if you ever need anything..."

"Howie, stop. I'm not going anywhere. Besides, you'll age... a bit. I'll be an old lady dating a twenty-year-old and we'll end up in the newspapers as the grossest story of the year. Why not? You're legal age so I won't get arrested, and we already get made fun of all the time. Why should that ever change?"

He chuckled, even though we both knew that I was lying. I wanted to believe it, though.

"That works for me," he said. "I'll love you even when you're so old that you have hair on your lip and your breasts sag to your knees."

"That's... sweet, Howard."

"And who knows? Maybe my Dad will find the cure, and I'll be able to eat cheeseburgers and drive kids to soccer in a minivan and then have a mid-life crisis and buy a sports car."

"Or I could just become a zombie and live forever."

He became very still. "You don't mean that, do you?"

I thought about it. "I don't think so. I don't want to live off of brains. I want to graduate and have a career, and maybe have kids... I don't want to be seventeen forever. Quite frankly, seventeen sucks."

"Smart and sexy. No wonder I find you so irresistible."

"Besides, in a world where the zombie apocalypse is an ever-looming threat, there's no point speculating on the future, is there?"

Howie pulled me close and kissed me hungrily. He tasted like chemistry.

BONUS CONTENT!

Turn the page for a sneak peek at *History*, the sequel to *Chemistry*. Now available in digital and paperback in your favourite bookstore.

1
HOWIE

I never know when I'm dreaming, which is what makes my dreams so terrifying.

I thought it was a regular day – a happy one. I was just at school, waiting for Stella to get off her bus like I did back before I won her over. I remember watching her step down from the bus looking so sexy, and so pissed off. Nowadays, I picked her up at her house, but today, for some reason, I was waiting for her bus.

Yes, she was getting closer. I could feel her mind coming clearer and clearer among the buzz of all the other brainwaves around me. She stood out, like a diamond in a coal mine, like birdsong in the morning, like a beacon in the dark – like a gourmet meal at a hot dog stand.

But she wasn't on the last bus that pulled in. She was coming from another direction. I turned to follow her because everything in me points to her now. My soul is a compass that always leads to Stella. I turned toward her mind, and I saw her. She was driving a minivan. The back door of the van opened and a boy my age stepped out. He called, "Bye, Mom!" and took off toward the school without a glance back at her.

I went to the door of her van and knocked on the window. She rolled it down. She had changed. Breathtaking as ever, but my heart clenched when I saw fine lines around her eyes, a heaviness to her cheeks, a streak of grey in her hair.

"Howie," she said, "You need to stop this. I'm too old for you. I've got a life to live."

"No… Stella…" How could I explain to her? Her mind - oh, her mind – it was like light, like air, like something electric inside me. She was still beautiful to me. What did some crows-feet matter? Some grey? Her curves were curvier than ever, her brown eyes as warm, her lips as luscious.

And I began to beg; I couldn't bear to live a second longer without tasting her skin, grabbing her tight, burying myself in her flesh. The next thing I knew I was yanking open the door, snatching her. I meant to kiss her, but I bit down, and her flesh was warm and delicious in my mouth. I couldn't stop.

I could hear the screams from the people around me, but Stella wasn't screaming, Stella couldn't scream, she barely had a face, and it only took a quick smash of her skull on the windshield to crack it open, and her brains were in my hands, red as raspberries, and I couldn't get enough. My mind was swirling but my body knew what to do, following its instincts and thrilling to the taste, finally, the taste of what I never let myself even think of longing for.

I slurped and exulted in the sheer liberty of finally doing what my body longed to do - and oh, God forgive me. It was so good, so good.

I woke up slowly – at first with reluctance, because I kept thinking, *one more bite, just one more...* and then my consciousness kicked in and I pulled myself awake with horror and disgust.

I writhed in my bed, trying to rid myself of the terrible, terrible dream and I ended up sobbing into my pillow until morning.

I wouldn't sleep if I didn't have to, but sleep is vital. Sleep helps restore brain function, and when you're like me, you need all the brain function you can get.

Especially if you're dating Stella. Her brain is like a knife. When I'm not at my best, I feel unworthy of her, no more able to enter her sphere than my dog can enter mine. She tries to be understanding, but she gets impatient, and I can't blame her.

So, I try to sleep, because sleep helps. So do brains, but brains are hard to get, and my family has to ration them. The first week after I met Stella, I was eating three meals a day, sometimes four, just to impress her. My family put a stop to that. We just can't store enough pig heads in the house to keep up with that kind of demand.

Instead, I started digging into the dog food. We order it from the States and stack it in the pantry – canned brains in milk. I have no idea why normal humans would produce and consume such a thing. It works for the dog, who would eat anything if we let him, but we find it pretty unappetizing (and that's saying something). My family doesn't care if I dig into the dog's share. Canned brains are a little hard to get, but they're cheap and easy to store.

I gave up trying to sleep after my nightmare, and I went to go force down some canned brains. Maybe I should have two cans today since I didn't get as much sleep.

Otherwise, I might not be able to keep up with Stella, and I loved keeping up with Stella. When I was on, when I was *sharp*, I felt like we could take over the world together. Our banter was on fire.

Stella doesn't believe in soul mates, but I do, and she is mine. On good days, I thought that maybe this is why everything has happened to me. Maybe *she* is why I lived after watching my parents die, forced to live as a teenager for decades, slurping cold pig brains through a straw: It was all so I could wait for her.

On bad days, I knew that this was just a bright spot in an otherwise barren existence: that one day she would realize that I was too young for her, that I could never get a degree, give her children, earn a pension – could never be the sort of person that she can build a life with. And then she would leave.

She'd find someone else, someone who could grow old with her, someone who didn't start to drool unless he slurps a can of brains in milk every morning. Someone who wasn't carrying the most feared disease in the world, something considered to be fictional because people think that nothing so truly nightmarish could ever actually exist.

Every morning, I woke up determined to make today as perfect for her as possible. Because when that day happened, when Stella outgrew me, I didn't want to have any regrets. But sometimes, before I eat, I'm too stupid for my own good, because I was halfway through my second can of brains before I remembered: Today was Stella's birthday. And I was running late.

Stella's parents weren't surprised anymore when I call on her in the mornings. Usually I just took her to school.

Sometimes I cooked breakfast. Today I had something a little more elaborate in mind.

I arrived on their doorstep loaded down with bags. Stella was still asleep. I could usually count on Stella staying asleep until some sort of cataclysmic event woke her up. Even her phone, which played *Mars, Bringer of War* at seven every morning, couldn't make her budge (on an incidental note, I can't believe I just wrote that sentence. Twenty years ago, it would have made absolutely no sense. How do you set a phone to play a concert piece on a timer?).

Mr. Blunt didn't even bother saying hello or making pleasantries when I knocked lightly on the door. "Just come in, Howie, did you think we weren't expecting you? I suppose you've bought Stella a pony or something."

"Well, I wouldn't settle for anything less than a unicorn, and they were fresh out," I said. "How do you think she'll feel about cheesecake?"

"For breakfast?" said Mrs. Blunt.

"And bacon," I said, holding up a bag. "I'm making bacon."

"I don't see how you could go wrong."

Half an hour later I went upstairs with a plate of bacon and eggs, and a glass of chilled orange juice, no pulp. Mr. Blunt opened the door for me. "I'll just stand here and watch. You know. To protect her chastity."

I don't think Stella's father actually cared that much about Stella's chastity. He joked about it a lot, but he and Mrs. Blunt certainly gave us our privacy when we wanted it. He just loved making me uncomfortable, and I was acutely aware of two things as I stepped into her room that morning.

First, that Stella, beneath her thin cotton nightshirt, was basically naked, and second, that her father was standing there watching me.

So, I tried to shove all of my awkward adolescent lust into the back corner of my mind with the part of me that wants to eat people and focused on giving Stella a happy birthday.

I sat on the edge of her bed and put the plate on her bedside table. She barely budged. I ran my fingers through her long, thick brown hair and then stroked her face gently.

"Gorgeous… wake up… it's your birthday."

She opened her brown eyes and looked into mine. My God. I still got butterflies.

"Fuck off," she said and rolled over. Her brain waves went from a drowsy, pleasant buzz to a cacophony of irritation.

Oh, the things I wanted to do, to wake her up. But I just stroked her hair again.

"Happy birthday," I said, wishing I could put some cheer into the phrase. When the virus started eating my brain, it went for my processing and language centres first. Dad says that the centre that translates emotion into speech is one of the first to go. He doesn't know why. So, I could never convey my feelings for her the way I want to. I'm effectively brain damaged. The voice on Stella's phone (phones also have helpful robots in them now – it's wild) has more accurate emotional inflection. I'm the worst person to wish someone a happy birthday.

I tried again. "Happy birthday." I really tried to put the exclamation mark in.

Stella turned and squinted at me. "Aw. You're trying to sound excited. That's adorable. And pathetic." She buried her face in her pillow.

"Let me show you how it's done," said Mr. Blunt, coming into the room. He grabbed Stella's shoulders and shook her. "Stella! It's your BIRTHDAY! It's been EIGHTEEN YEARS SINCE YOUR FACE SQUEEZED THROUGH YOUR MOTHER'S VAGINA!"

"Don't you bring my vagina into this, Tim!" shouted Stella's mother from downstairs. "Every year you have to mention my vagina!"

"Let me go back to my dream," said Stella. "It didn't involve my mother's vagina. It was a happier place."

"What did you dream?" I asked. She just looked at me and raised her eyebrows slightly and gave a tiny smile. I felt a tightening in my groin. Why couldn't I have had *that* dream?

"Okay, then, consider this," said Stella's father. "As of today, you are legally entitled to vote…"

"… Goody…" said Stella into her pillow.

"And look up porn," said her Dad. "Just think, Stella, there's a whole world of porn out there, waiting for you, and you don't have to lie when they ask you to check the little box that says you are eighteen."

I hadn't ventured into the world of online pornography yet. If I did, I was afraid I'd never emerge.

"Also, there's bacon and eggs. And cheesecake," I said.

"Okay, I'm up. Jeez. You know what would be a nice birthday present? Sleeping."

"Sorry, honey, school trumps birthdays. Just look up porn during lunch."

Stella rolled her eyes at him and started to eat.

Mr. Blunt left us alone for a while, and we sat in silence while Stella scraped at her plate.

"So, are we going to talk about yesterday?" she said eventually, with a great air of casualness.

No, I thought. "If you really want to," I said. "It's your birthday." The one good thing about my expressionless voice is that my emotions rarely betray me. Stella was getting pretty good at picking up nuances, but when I wanted to hide my feelings, I usually could.

I didn't even want to think about yesterday. I had almost forgotten. I'm good at forgetting. The virus is my friend, sometimes.

"I want today to be a wonderful day," I said. "You only turn eighteen once."

"Yeah, *I* do. Not you."

"Technically, I turned eighteen a long time ago."

"Or you just turned twelve a whole lot of times. You have no idea how old you are, Howie! How do you quantify the age of someone who has lived for nearly seventy years, but looks seventeen?" her voice started to rise. Then she took a breath. "No. You're right. It's my birthday, and I say that we pretend nothing is wrong. Can you do that?"

"Easily," I said.

That was all I did every day. That was all I wanted out of life, forever. To pretend that nothing is wrong. Because when I remembered everything that *was* wrong, I felt overwhelmed by despair.

Can't get enough of Howie and Stella? To get fan-exclusive bonus novellas featuring your favourite characters from Chemistry, visit:

www.cllynch.com/bonus

ABOUT THE AUTHOR

C. L. Lynch is a thirty-something socially awkward introvert. She lives in Vancouver, British Columbia with her husband, two kids, various pets, and far too many unwashed dishes. She enjoys smashing tropes and hiding from adult responsibilities.

Visit her website:

www.cllynch.com

Or follow her on social media:

Twitter: @lynchauthor
Facebook: www.facebook.com/cllynchauthor
Instagram: @c.l.lynch

If you enjoyed reading *Chemistry,* please consider leaving a review at your favourite online store.

ACKNOWLEDGEMENTS

Thank you to my beta readers, who took the time to read and give me feedback on the deeply flawed early drafts of *Chemistry:* Skylah Van Wagoner, Kerry Purcell Harris, Jeannie Chiasson, Corinne Weagle, Nora Sargent, Karyn Wills, Ted Dewolf, Jodie Shackleford, Jessica Green, Amelia Kellum, Suman Gupta, my long-suffering husband, and my poor mother.

Without your encouragement, I would have consigned this book to the draft heap. Without your honest criticism, this book would have been even worse than it currently is.

Special thanks to Christian Dewolf, for being a combination of surrogate brother, idea-machine, story editor, and humorist of a calibre that I can only dream of emulating (seriously, look up his books and then buy them).

Finally, heartfelt thanks go to Rebecca DeVoe, for being Howie's Number One Fan.

Made in the USA
San Bernardino, CA
13 February 2019